VIRTUALLY MINE

The Lindstroms #5

New York Times Bestselling Author

Katy Regnery

writing as

Katy Paige

Cover Designer: Marianne Nowicki

Editing: Ellie McLove

Formatting: CookieLynn Publishing Services

First Edition: July 2020

Virtually Mine: a novel / by Katy Paige—1st Ed.

ISBN 978-1-944810-71-9

For Callie, who makes every day magical.
This one is yours.
I love you.
xoxoxo

CHAPTER 1

Once upon a time, there was a boy named Paul Johansson.

Paul had big dreams about falling in love.

He had big hopes for his own personal "happily ever after."

He just didn't have the best luck.

And he blamed this—in part—on the movie *The Princess Bride*, which his mother encouraged him to watch at the tender, impressionable age of ten. He was captivated with the angelic beauty of the heroine, Buttercup, his first genuine crush, but even more, he was desperate to be Westley, her handsome, quick-witted hero. What young boy, on the cusp of adolescence with pre-hormones raging, wouldn't want to be the hero to the perfect heroine (*who had long blonde hair and mouth-watering ta-tas in a low-cut dress*)? Who wouldn't want to be the swashbuckling pirate who saved the princess (*and got to kiss her…with tongue!*) before riding off *a deux* into a lavender sunset?

He'd walked into his fourth-grade classroom the next day on the hunt for *his* Buttercup. And while Paul's mission found no joy in elementary school, by seventh grade, he was fairly sure he'd found his princess.

Dana Durant, a transfer student from Florida, was everything Paul had been searching for. Tall, blonde, and ridiculously tan for January in Maine, Dana had a bright white smile and the most gorgeous set of ta-tas any boy at Kennebunkport Junior High School had ever seen. After watching her in the cafeteria for weeks and learning of her great love of chocolate pudding, he'd convinced his mother to buy some from the store and brought a cup in to school.

One cup of pudding.

Two spoons.

Her face had brightened when he sat down beside her and asked if she wanted to share, but his luck quickly soured when Bradford Kennedy Spearman sat down on Dana's other side. Bradford slipped Dana a note (*in flagrant disregard of their pudding date*), which she opened, checking the "yes" box with a proffered pen and flashing that perfect white smile at Paul's rival.

Sliding the untouched container of pudding back to Paul, she stood up, taking Bradford's hand and agreeing to be his date for the Winter Formal before Paul could tear the top off the pudding cup, let alone muster the courage to ask her.

By high school, Paul had developed into a handsome, fit young man who regularly whipped Bradford Spearman's ass on the tennis courts, thereby attracting the attention of one Sybil Wentworth.

Paul, who'd known Sybbie all his life, had recently noticed her Buttercup potential: she was a perky blonde, who also happened to be the high school Homecoming Princess and Kennebunkport Country Club tennis champion.

Won over by Paul's earnest eyes and wandering hands, they spent two summers hand in hand, winning at doubles, swimming in the club's pool and making out in the back seat of his dad's Jaguar convertible.

However, it turned out that Sybbie wasn't loyal to Jaguars—or Paul, for that matter—and finding her in the back of Bradford's BMW after the club Golf Championship had ended things between them.

Paul didn't mourn Sybil for long. Docile and appropriate with a perfect pageboy, she was basically a younger version of Paul's mother which—once Paul had the perspective to realize it—grossed him out sufficiently that he never looked at the back seat of a Jaguar the same way again.

With an available, though more guarded, heart, he packed his bags for Brown University and headed south to Rhode Island, putting dreams of Buttercup, Dana and Sybil firmly from his mind. Determined to put his studies first and ta-tas second, his good intentions lasted for about an hour, which is about the same time he met Gia Fortuna.

Gia, an international student from Italy and Paul's freshman hall RA, was everything that Sybil was not. Witty and irreverent, sophisticated, exotic and bright, Gia kept their conversations hopping during the day and introduced Paul to acrobatic sex and talking dirty at night. Within weeks he was ready to ask her to marry him and rode the wave of assumed true love, enjoying the bounty of Gia's physical offerings for the ensuing two years.

Sadly, upon graduating, his *princessa Italiana* had patted him on the head with a friendly smile, thanked him for the good times and departed for Milan without leaving him so much as a forwarding address. This efficiently broke his heart in half then torched it.

As Paul sorted through the ashes of his charred heart, he realized that Gia hadn't been "the one" either. She was beautiful, spirited, adventurous and sharp-minded, like Buttercup, but she was also fickle and unfaithful.

With a bird's-eye view at the lost loves of his life, Paul had to admit that while Sybil lacked some originality, Gia had been a little *too* edgy for him.

Somewhere inside of Paul was the ten-year-old who still wanted the fairy tale—Westley and Buttercup, a hero and a heroine. He wanted to be everything to the woman he loved, and he'd never meant everything to Dana, Sybil or Gia.

And then he met Jenny Lindstrom.

She had it all.

If any woman was Buttercup incarnate, it was her.

Beautiful, blonde, spirited, principled Jenny, whom he'd met when she was grieving the loss of her mother, was the younger sister to his best friend, Lars. Even as he'd lent Jenny his shoulder to cry on, his feelings for her had grown exponentially. At the school where he was a principal and she was a science teacher, he was constantly looking for her, finding her, and falling for her.

He had tried to do everything right with Jenny: he gave her space to grieve, made himself available to her as a friend, and then he fell genuinely and thoroughly in love with her, convinced she would reciprocate his feelings as soon as she was able. But when he'd finally offered his heart to her, she'd gently refused him and married someone else instead.

So it turned out that, once again, appearances had been deceiving.

Jenny wasn't Paul's happily ever after, after all.

Paul's beaten heart was resilient, though, even in the wake of Dana and Sybil and Gia and Jenny. He still hoped for true love, albeit more quietly now, a little gun-shy after a good bit of heartbreak.

He woke up every morning and devoted himself to his job: principal of the little high school in Gardiner, Montana, which was the best in the state. Paul had created a good life, by and large. He loved his students and his friends, and both filled his life with equal measures of happiness and companionship.

But he lived his life with quiet longing, his heart full of love for the right girl, just wishing deep down that he could finally find her: his heroine, his princess, the Buttercup to his waiting Westley.

Somewhere in this great wide world, he knew—he still believed with every beat of his heart—there lived a girl who would be his happily ever after.

***

"Earth to Paul! Come in, Paul!"

His friend Maggie stood behind the coffee bar of his favorite café trying to get his attention.

A smile spread across his face and he wished—for the thousandth time—that he could fall in love with Maggie Campbell. Maggie, the proprietor of the Prairie Dawn Café & Bookstore, was, along with Lars Lindstrom, one of his very best friends.

"Can't a guy daydream, Mags?"

"*Day*dream? It's almost ten o'clock, dreamer. We close at ten o'clock on Sundays."

He smiled at her soft Scottish burr, more pronounced after a long day. She nudged his elbows with the dishtowel she was using to wipe down the copper bar where he'd been sitting for the past two hours. Pivoting on the bar stool, he turned to look at the empty café. It had been hopping earlier, full of folks anxious to spend an evening in the air-conditioned café where they could read books, magazines and newspapers, listen to soft music and enjoy Maggie's many baked and caffeinated creations.

How had it emptied out so fast? He'd been lost in thought again. Feeling lonely. Thinking about Jenny Lindstrom.

When he turned back to Maggie, she was staring at him with her hands on her hips, lips pursed, dishtowel gone.

"Paul."

"Mags."

She wrinkled her nose. "I have a confession to make."

Paul sat up a little straighter, narrowing his eyes.

Oh, no. He *knew* that look.

Maggie was known to take more than a cursory interest in Paul's love life. The last three confessions she'd made to him had to do with setting him up on the most incredibly awkward blind dates known to man, in an effort to help him get over Jenny. Really and truly, he was mostly over Jenny at this point. She was married and had moved away to Great

Falls. He didn't need or want Maggie's unsolicited advice and help. Sure, there were some days when Jenny's loss still hurt. Let's face it: if any woman in the world could have been his Buttercup, Jenny was—

"Earth to Paul. *Again.* Do you want my confession or no?"

"Who've you set me up with this time?"

Her face broke into a bright, satisfied grin. "No one."

"Well, that's a relief because after my date with Ms. Phillips, I believe I told you to stop meddling."

Mary Phillips, the forty-something secretary at Grace Church, was not only ten years older than thirty-year-old Paul, but she'd spent the majority of their evening together complaining about the greasiness of the food at the Grizzly Guzzle Grill, or describing—in considerable, stomach churning detail—her various attempts to get rid of a bad case of shingles. As if that wasn't gross enough, she'd grabbed Paul's shoulders at her doorstep and smashed her red lips against his. It took every ounce of strength in his body not to push her into next week and run screaming into the night. He still hadn't mustered the courage to return to church.

"I admit, that wasn't my finest matchmakin' hour. She seemed bonnie enough when she came in for coffee. I dinna realize she was *diseased.*" She tilted her head to the side, her smile fading just a little. "I care about you. Just hate to see you so lonesome, Paul."

Her words made Jenny's face flash before him for a moment and he looked away, anxious that Maggie not see the pain that lingered there. She reached out, covering his hand with hers.

"It's been two years," she said softly.

"Just because she got married doesn't mean—"

"Yes, Paul, it does. It's time to give up and move on."

Maggie took another deep breath, withdrawing her hand and propping her elbows up on the bar as she looked at Paul.

"The feelings don't just go away," he confessed softly. *Nor the hopes and yearnings.*

"Jen wasn't right for you, Paul."

"So she said."

"You have all this bonnie romantic energy," Maggie cajoled. "I hate to see it go to waste."

She smiled at him gently and he realized she was either stalling or buttering him up.

"Time for confessions, Maggie. What'd you do?"

"Right." Maggie pushed off from the counter, scratching at a hardened drop of cream with one fingernail. "Well…"

"Stop stalling."

"I signed you up for…" She mumbled the rest staring with rapt fascination at the counter.

"You signed me up for what?"

"Internet dating," she mumbled again, a little louder, peeking up at him, then quickly back down again at the little spot she was scratching.

"You did what?"

She cringed. "I just want you to be happy!"

"So you signed me up for *internet dating? INTERNET DATING?* Are you crazy?" He knew he was yelling, but there was no one left in the café to hear and goddamn it, Maggie had no right to meddle in his life like this! "Do you know the kind of women who go on the internet to find someone? Haven't you ever watched *Dateline?*" He slipped off the barstool, shaking a finger at her. "You, you stay away from me—you're certifiable!"

"You canna seem to get over Jenny and all the dates I set up for you are disasters and then I started thinkin' that's because there's no one for you to date here in Gardiner, so why not cast a wider net and maybe I could find you someone nice!" Her words tumbled out louder and in a nervous stream.

Paul was furious. Part of the reason he'd left Maine was to get away from meddling family, and now here he was, thousands of miles away, saddled with a surrogate sister who was making him crazy.

"I never asked you to find me *someone nice*! You had no right to do that, Maggie! No right." He leaned forward, picking up his wallet from the bar and jamming it into his back pocket. "You think *I* need to meet someone? How about *you?* Mooning over Nils Lindstrom for—what's it been now? Five *years?*"

Maggie's chin bobbed as she swallowed and her eyes suddenly glistened like he'd smacked her. Paul knew full and well that Maggie and Nils had had a recent falling out.

Paul looked down, shaking his head back and forth. Bringing up Nils was a low blow and he felt bad about hurting her, but damn…just *damn*. He took a deep breath and exhaled loudly, trying to calm down.

"I'm sorry, Paul," Maggie began in a small voice. "I just—"

As her voice broke off, his shoulders slumped and he sighed. For all Maggie's blundering, he knew she wanted to help, and he loved her like a sister.

"Aw, Mags. Your good intentions are killing me," he said gently. "It's—it's okay. Just cancel it, okay? Or whatever you have to do. Deactivate it."

She bit her lip and he saw hesitation in her face.

"*What?*" he demanded, a warning in his voice, hackles raising again.

"Well, I wanted to give you a wee head start, so I looked over a bunch of different profiles to find someone nice," she said, picking up the dishtowel again and worrying it between her fingers. "I did a good job. I—I sorted through the girls and I sort of exchanged a few emails with one and…"

"And what?" he prompted. "*Just undo it!*"

She put down the dishtowel and turned to the back shelf, unplugging her laptop and setting it gently on the counter before him. She looked up at him with a hopeful smile as she opened it up and tapped twice on the space bar. "I will. I promise you I will…but first, meet Miss Mystic."

***

Zoë Flannigan pulled on the collar of her black T-shirt and twisted her neck, trying to get a look at whatever was causing a painful throb on her left shoulder. She sat up in bed, taking off the shirt gingerly and wincing at the brightness of the morning sun streaming in through her bedroom windows.

Twisting her neck as far to the right as possible only increased the throb to a sharp, stabbing pain. Seeing her shoulder blade was going to require a mirror.

She swung her legs over the side of the bed and groaned as the room started spinning, making the remnants of last night's partying swirl a warning in her belly. Closing her eyes and holding on to the sheets with fists, she waited until the spins stopped and her stomach settled.

Only then did she open her eyes.

The bathroom, about five feet away, looked about a million miles away from where she sat on the side of her bed, aching, nauseous and deeply hungover.

With a groan, she hefted herself off the bed and walked haltingly to the bathroom, her gait less a result of last night's debauchery than the fact that her leg was covered in scarred, twisted flesh. The bathroom light buzzed to life and Zoë backed up against the sink to look at her back in the mirror.

Holy shit.

A piece of plastic wrap affixed with white surgical tape, covered with once-seepy, now-dried brown blood covered a small area of her lower left shoulder blade. A tattoo of a small black lamb with a date underneath sat in the middle of a patch of red, raw, angry skin.

Apparently, she'd gotten a tattoo last night. *Great.*

She winced, wishing she could remember the events that led up to the new acquisition, but last night was a blur. She'd left the house with Sandy and Rob around ten and had a vague recollection of the clock reading three when she finally fell into bed, but other than those two details, her memories were foggy at best.

Sliding her glance to her right shoulder, she found another tattoo: a small cross with a date underneath in a soft, elegant cursive. Running her fingers over the older tattoo, she felt tears gather and closed her eyes against the unwelcome sorrow that had been her constant companion for almost two years. She was so goddamn sick of feeling sorry and sad.

Her stomach gurgled uncomfortably and she took a shaky breath, turning to survey herself in the mirror. Her dyed, jet-black, bobbed hair spiked out in ten different directions, and her eyes had dark black rings from a night spent sleeping in mascara. She had dyed her hair black last year as it grew back in and she'd gotten used to the darkness, wryly believing that it matched her low spirits better than her natural blonde.

The twelve-inch scar that ran from her hairline over her right eyebrow down the side of her face was more pronounced than usual because her makeup had gotten stuck in the jagged, lavender crevasse in her sleep. It would take one more round of plastic surgery before it could heal completely into a thin line of translucent white. She had another scar, three times as long, on her right leg running from mid-thigh to ankle that, despite the doctors' best efforts, would never heal completely. The leg had been mangled too badly to repair, leaving her permanently disfigured and causing a mild limp they promised would improve over time with regular physical therapy.

She took out the dark brown contacts she'd started wearing last year and noted that her blue eyes, which used to be so bright and open, were flat and bloodshot, accusing her from their cerulean depths.

Her gaze dropped lower and she smirked, unable to keep from admiring her full breasts in a black, satin push-up bra, the black a harsh contrast against the white of her chest. Despite the twenty-five pounds she'd packed on her small frame over the past two years—or probably because of it— they had a real *va-va-voom* effect. She squinted, looking more closely in the mirror, and noted a fairly obnoxious hickey taking up a good bit of real estate over her left breast. She shook her head in disgust, unable to even conjure one detail of the face attached to the lips that had given it to her. *Great, Zoë. Real classy.*

The mirror cut off the lower half of her five-foot-four-inch figure but she knew what was there: a smallish waist and a biggish ass. With her white skin, short, voluptuous stature and black bob, she was a life-sized Betty Boop.

"Zoë Holly Flannigan! Show yourself!"

Her aunt Sandy, who was only ten years her senior, called from the top of the stairs. Zoë rented the apartment over Sandy's garage and pop-in visits from her aunt were often and welcome.

"In here," she grated out in a gravelly voice.

Sandy stuck her head into the bedroom just as Zoë peeked her head out of the bathroom door, leaning against the doorframe as the room spun for a moment.

"Hey, Sand," she moaned uneasily, steadying herself. She flicked off the light and limped to the bed, sitting down carefully with a soft groan. "Refresh my memory…"

"The tattoo or the hickey?" asked Sandy, gesturing to Zoë's chest with a derisive flick of her eyes.

"Let's start with the hickey."

"Some friend of Rob's. He was all over you at the bar and you seemed okay with it at first, but then he asked about your face and you pushed him away, yelling that your boyfriend in Montana would kick his ass if he asked you about it again. I don't know why you're so touchy. You can barely see it anymore, Zo. I mean it. It's really fading."

She'd just stared at it in the mirror. It was far from faded.

Zoë rolled her eyes at her aunt and Sandy continued. "After I finally convinced you that you didn't actually have a boyfriend in Montana to kick anyone's ass for you, you stormed out of O'Byrne's and informed me that you were getting a tattoo and screw me if I didn't like it."

"Sounds like I was pretty charming."

"You were something, all right. Rob and I followed you to Shenanigan's and you pushed your way in front of two people and insisted your turn was next. Rob talked Max *out* of calling the police and *into* taking care of you."

"Rob could talk a bee into buying honey."

Sandy's face softened at the mention of her husband. "Yeah. He's smooth, that guy."

"And then?" Zoë crossed her arms over her chest protectively, ignoring the way her boobs spilled over the barely-there cups of her black bra.

"Max did the little lambie on your shoulder while you lay facedown on the table telling me all about your make-believe Montana boyfriend, Paul. Then you started crying, threw up on my shoes, and Rob drove us home." Sandy's face soured and she wrinkled her nose. "Tossed the shoes in the trash. You owe me fifty bucks."

"Sorry, Sand."

Sandy, who'd been a surrogate parent to Zoë since her teenage years, sat down on the bed next to her niece. Zoë put her head on Sandy's shoulder.

"You're outta control, Zo."

"Yeah," murmured Zoë, fresh tears stinging her eyes as she swallowed back some latent nausea.

"I promised my sister I'd look out for you, but you're making it hard."

Zoë loved the way Sandy pronounced "hard," with a strong New England accent, dropping the "r," just as Zoë's mother had.

Zoë's mother had passed away when Zoë was only sixteen years old, leaving her under the guardianship of her—at the time—twenty-six-year-old aunt. Sandy had stepped up to the plate with love and sympathy and spirit, never resenting the grieving teenager.

"Don't give up on me, Sand."

"Zoë, you gotta move on. Brandon and the accident? That was almost two years ago."

Zoë lifted her head, clenching her eyes shut.

"I can't—"

"I know you don't want to talk about it," said Sandy gently. "But you can't keep doing this either. Hooking up with random guys? Blacking out? Getting tattoos when you're wasted? I barely recognize you anymore. You're losing yourself, Zoë. You're losing everything good about yourself."

Zoë looked at her hands. She still wore her mother's silver Claddagh ring on the fourth finger of her left hand with the heart out, which meant that her heart was available. What a joke. Something that was broken wasn't available. Not to her. Not to anyone. Which was just fine, because who would want some physically and emotionally damaged girl anyway?

"You didn't mean to hurt anyone that day, Zoë. It was an accident, hon. You're too hard on yourself. You're both still alive, right? That's all that matters. When are you going to stop punishing yourself?"

Sandy meant well, but she conveniently sidestepped important details pertaining to the accident, in her goal to help Zoë move past it. Details Zoë couldn't forget, not for one second or one moment every day. Zoë had done something wrong—so very, very wrong. And she would never, ever forgive herself for it. Not as long as she lived.

Zoë swallowed, rubbing her hands together, wishing Sandy would stop talking and leave her alone, but after what she'd put Sandy through last night she could hardly kick her aunt out of the apartment she rented from her.

"I'm sorry about making a scene. And your shoes." Zoë stood up and walked to her bureau to fish some bills out of the messy depths of her black leather purse. She had a sudden flashback to a bright, lovely, hot pink floral handbag, perfectly neat and tidy, right down to the matching grosgrain wallet and sunglasses case. It felt like a lifetime ago. She shook her head and turned around, offering the bills to Sandy. "Here's sixty."

"You have to get yourself together, Zoë Holly Flannigan. Enough is enough," said Sandy, taking the bills and folding them in her hands. "How about seeing that therapist again?"

Therapy wouldn't help. Nothing would help. Nothing would take her back in time to that day to make better decisions. Nothing would change her face back to the way it was. Nothing would bring her nephew, Brandon's, legs back, and her sister Thea would never forgive Zoë for their loss. That was the heartbreaking truth, the root of her guilt and shame.

Zoë shrugged, giving Sandy a sad smile. "I should take a shower. Got to get to work."

Sandy reached out to put a hand on Zoë's cheek, over the scar she so hated. "How about we lay low for the rest of the week? Häagen Dazs? Bad reality TV? No more benders?"

Zoë nodded, blinking back tears.

Sandy smiled gently and turned to leave, but stopped as she got to Zoë's bedroom door.

"By the way…what's this sudden obsession with guys from Montana?"

Zoë felt the heat in her cheeks and turned away from

her aunt, heading to the bathroom.

"Probably just the beer talking," she said over her shoulder, closing the bathroom door behind her as Sandy headed back downstairs.

***

The sun streaming in through Paul's bedroom window woke him up bright and early. He glanced at the clock on his bedside table. 6:35 a.m. His body didn't seem to realize that high school principals didn't need to be up at the crack of dawn in the middle of the summer. Whether it was the peak of the school year or the last week in July, he was up at the same time every day, but this morning he was extra tired. He'd ended up staying at the Prairie Dawn until almost midnight last night.

Luckily, he had nowhere to be for hours. He had promised to keep Lars company as he scouted out some Yellowstone locations for an upcoming fashion shoot, but otherwise his day was empty. He rolled over, bunching the pillow under his head, an unexpected feeling of anticipation—of excitement and promise—making his heart feel lighter than it had in ages.

As soon as Maggie had turned her laptop around, Paul's heart had skipped a beat and he'd been unable to pull himself away. Miss Mystic, aka Holly Morgan, was everything Paul Johansson was looking for.

In her picture, she was wearing a white sundress with a V-neck that managed to be innocently tasteful, while highlighting her full breasts and small waist. Her skin was very light, even with a subtle tan, and she was holding a hot pink flowered purse over her shoulder. She was petite, no more than five-foot-five, if that, with long, wavy, blonde hair and rosy lips that smiled into the camera. He'd have to take Maggie's word for it when she said those eyes were blue because Holly wore Jackie-O style sunglasses, which covered a good bit of her face but lent a little glamour to the simplicity of her outfit. Her legs were long and shapely for someone so small and she wore hot pink shoes on her feet. God's honest truth, she was the prettiest thing Paul had ever seen, and that included Jenny Lindstrom *and* Princess Buttercup.

He must have stared at her for twenty minutes as Maggie upended chairs on table tops and started sweeping the wooden floor of the café. She finally called to him, resting her chin on the broomstick.

"There's more to the lass than a bonnie photo, Paul!"

He turned around, looking at Maggie in a daze, straightening his tortoiseshell glasses. "Her profile won't come up."

"She took it down, along with a close-up of her pretty face. Said she was gettin' too...er, *fresh* emails. But, I managed to take a screen shot of her profile before she did. She's an art teacher. She's smart, and nice too." Maggie walked over to him with her broom trailing behind. "I felt bad after settin' you up with Ms. Phillips. I made sure that I screened Miss Mystic first. We've written back and forth a few times over email."

"Where—Where are the emails, Maggie?"

She chuckled at his impatience, shaking her head at him

as he hunched over Holly's picture. "Still mad at me?"

"I'm sorry I yelled at you and called you crazy. Will you please show me the emails?"

"No," said Maggie, saucily. "Waitin' makes the heart grow fonder, wee lamb."

"Maggie," Paul said, doing his best to keep his voice controlled and even. "I was a bastard for yelling at you. You and Nils are very complicated and I have no right to judge. I trust you implicitly and thank God every day for your sisterly pushiness in my quiet life. Now, please. Show. Me. The. Emails."

"Well, since you asked me so sweetly…" She closed the browser and clicked on an icon titled "Miss Mystic." A grouping of three emails suddenly opened and Maggie clicked on the first one.

Paul spent the next half hour reading the three emails, smiling and laughing, reading bits out loud to Maggie, who rolled her eyes more than once, even though Paul could tell she was pleased with his reaction.

Holly Morgan was a twenty-four-year-old middle school art teacher, never married, devoted to her sister and young nephew after losing their parents years before. She lived in the same town as her sister and aunt, who had stepped in as her guardian after the loss of their parents. In fact, the picture of Holly in her white sundress had been taken at her aunt's wedding. She liked Chinese food, painting with acrylics and Jason Mraz. She drank way too much coffee, like most of the teachers he knew, and had her favorite students, though she said she tried not to let it show.

Paul's breath caught when he read that her favorite vacation spot was Moosehead Lake in Maine, because it was the very place he had spent many summers as a child. What were the chances that a girl from Montana would have spent summers in Maine? But it was Holly's answer to Maggie's final question that had made Paul's heart stop for a second: Holly's favorite movie was *The Princess Bride*.

That was the moment Paul fell in love with Holly Morgan.

He ended up re-reading all three emails twice more before he finally figured out that Maggie was ready to say good night.

"So?" she asked, sidling up to the bar in the dim light of the café, her bag over her shoulder.

He smiled at her, his hopeful heart full of gratitude for his meddling friend. "Miss *Mystic* is right. She's magical, Maggie. Do you know where she is? I'm assuming somewhere up around Mystic Lake in Custer? That's not such a bad drive. I mean, we can definitely exchange a few more emails to be sure she's comfortable meeting face-to-face, but I'd be ready tomorrow. The sooner, the better. We're both teachers, so maybe we could even get in a few summer dates before the start of the school yea—"

Maggie fidgeted nervously with her keys as her face progressively turned as red as her hair.

"Maggie? What's wrong?"

"I'll forward the emails and log-in information tomorrow mornin'. You can take over from here."

She turned away, putting away the broom and shutting

off the last light.

"Maggie. Is there anything you're not telling me? Any more confessions?"

She shrugged sheepishly. "Distance is nothin' if you really like someone."

"What *exactly* does that mean?"

"Well, there might be one wee, tiny snag. It's um, it's just that I misread the question. Where, um, where you *live*. I clicked on where you're *from* instead."

"What are you talking about?"

She grimaced, backing away from him, toward the back door that led upstairs to her apartment, as though making an escape.

"I should have clicked on Montana, but I clicked on Maine. The website sorted the girls regionally so Holly's not from Montana. She's actually from…New England. Miss Mystic isn't about her bein' magical or livin' up near Custer. It's about her livin' in Mystic, Connecticut."

He watched as she slipped through the door, bolting it behind her, and he heard a muffled "Sorry!" through the door as her footsteps sprinted around the corner and up the stairs to the relative safety of her apartment.

"Connecticut!" he exclaimed to the empty café. "Aw, Maggie, COME ON!"

But his nemesis was long gone.

Paul headed out the front door, pulling it closed behind him and listening for the lock to catch, his head spinning on the short walk home. No wonder she vacationed in Maine. She was from Connecticut. His previous elation mixed with deep disappointment and later, at home, sleep certainly hadn't come easily or lasted very long.

Paul rolled over and glanced back at the clock. 6:47 a.m.

He flipped onto his back and stared at the ceiling. Unbidden, the picture of Holly Morgan flashed before his eyes and he growled, clenching his eyes shut. What was the point of pursuing a woman who lived in Connecticut, for heaven's sake? He lived in Montana and had no intention of returning east for anything but an occasional visit. From what he had learned about Holly, she was deeply attached to her aunt, devoted to her sister and adored her nephew. That sort of woman wasn't going to consider a move out to Montana!

The smart thing to do would be to forget he'd ever seen the photo of Holly Morgan, forget he'd ever read her smart, funny words, forget he'd ever found out that the prettiest woman in the world with the sweetest smile, most luscious body and most impeccable taste in movies actually existed somewhere on the earth. The smart thing to do would be to delete the emails and forget that Holly Morgan existed.

But the thing about principals in the summertime?

They don't have to set an example for anyone. And they don't have to be smart if they don't want to be.

CHAPTER 2

Zoë's phone buzzed and she glanced down at it on her desk, wishing she could keep the inevitable butterflies at bay. No luck. At the sight of his handle, *PrincipalPaul*, on the notification banner, her heart leaped, sending a wave of anticipation and excitement throughout her body and making goose bumps pop up all along her arms.

PrincipalPaul has sent you a message.

She took a deep breath, staring at the notification. Would this message be from his friend Maggie again or finally from him? It was only eleven o'clock but she couldn't wait to find out and she certainly didn't want to pore over every detail of the message with Stanley staring over her shoulders.

"Going on my lunch break, Stan," she said to her boss, who worked at the desk beside her.

"A little early for lunch," he said in the same dry tone he used for every boring, utilitarian website he created.

"Just means I'll be here working all afternoon without a break."

"I took a chance hiring a quirky kid, Zoë. Don't make me regret it. You were supposed to bring an artistic angle to the business, which is all well and good, but that doesn't mean we're flimsy with our deadlines. I need that website for

Patterson Masonry finished by the end of the day."

Zoë nodded. "And it'll be gorgeous. And artistic. Don't worry. I'll stay late if I need to."

His droopy, watery eyes regarded her sullenly. "Well? Go to lunch then. Be back in forty-five minutes."

Zoë grabbed her bag from the back of her chair, heading first to the lobby kiosk for a cup of iced coffee, then to the outdoor plaza to the left of her building that had a fountain and several bistro tables and chairs. It was already sweltering out even though it was only mid-morning, so she shrugged off the cardigan she'd been wearing in the air conditioning and took a deep breath of the slow, brackish breeze blowing in lazily off the Atlantic.

She settled herself at an empty table and took out her phone, keeping it face down as she sipped her coffee. It's not that she wanted to prolong the torture of reading the message, but it had been so long since she'd felt this sort of giddy anticipation, she wanted to savor it for a few minutes. The two years since the accident had been fairly void of happy times, so connecting with Paul, through Maggie, was a bit of unexpected—and, as it turned out, welcome— sunshine in an otherwise bleak life.

A quick bolt of shame launched itself through Zoë's body as she reviewed the deception she was perpetuating by letting Maggie—and now Paul—think that they were communicating with the girl in the picture, when Zoë felt like she was a million miles away from the sunny, hopeful girl she had once been.

Honestly, she hadn't meant to deceive anyone.

Drinking wine with a girlfriend one night, and commiserating over the lack of quality men in their lives, they'd dared each other to set up profiles on MeetTheOne.com. To maintain a bit of anonymity, Zoë had decided to use her middle name, Holly, and her mother's maiden name, Morgan, for her User ID.

But after setting up an account and posting a pic, she and her friend had continued drinking, and had promptly forgotten all about their profiles.

When Zoë received an email last week, almost two years later, about her account expiring, she decided to check out her long-lost MeetTheOne inbox before letting the account lapse entirely.

Big mistake. There had been a lot of really jerky, disgusting emails from guys asking totally inappropriate questions or offering her hot, anonymous sex. *As if!* The odd, drunken hickey notwithstanding, Zoë wasn't stupid, and she certainly didn't have sex with total strangers.

Not that it was really an issue since her once active, if unfulfilling, dating life was nonexistent at this point. After the accident left her face and leg disfigured, and her heart heavier than she could bear, Zoë had pretty much cut off contact with her old friends and eventually they stopped calling. And what man, exactly, wanted to date a girl with scars like Zoë's? Not that she was looking, but she'd basically given up on meeting someone anyway.

But just as Zoë was about to exit the website—and good riddance!—she'd noticed the subject line of the most recent email: *I can personally vouch for this amazing guy!* She was intrigued by the subject line that she suspected was written by a woman and didn't use any of the more disgusting euphemisms for genitals as a come-on. She tentatively clicked on the email.

Right away she could tell this email was different from the rest. The woman writing it introduced herself right away, explaining that one of her best friends, a high school principal, was a wonderful guy who just couldn't seem to catch a break with the right woman. He had the biggest heart in Montana and deserved true love more than anyone she'd ever known. Zoë had been captivated by Maggie's description of the handsome, young principal: six feet, two inches, with a toned body, dirty blond hair and blue eyes. She said he was in above-average shape and wore tortoiseshell glasses. Zoë loved that detail. Only another woman would have supplied such a specific description.

Maggie said she'd chosen to write to Zoë because, after checking out Zoë's erstwhile profile, Maggie thought she might be a good fit for her friend, Paul. They seemed to have interests in common and she wondered if Zoë was still interested in meeting a nice guy. If she was, could she please write back?

Without thinking, Zoë had written back right away, asking about Paul—his likes and dislikes, his dating history and what he was looking for in a woman. Maggie had responded, giving Zoë more details about Paul. He sounded…amazing. A caring educator, a good friend, a lover of the outdoors and wildlife, romantic, kind and perfect. Within two days the women had swapped six emails and

Maggie had promised that if there were any further emails, they'd be from Paul.

Zoë had checked her phone every twenty minutes or so on Sunday afternoon, hoping that she'd hear from him. By ten o'clock he hadn't written and Zoë was surprised by how disappointed she felt. When Sandy and Rob had stopped by asking if she wanted to join them at O'Byrne's for a cold one, Zoë kept her heavy-hearted feelings to herself, threw her phone on her bed and agreed to join them. Except a cold *one* had quickly turned into a cold *six*, followed by making out with one of Rob's friends and getting an impromptu tattoo.

So was this Maggie telling Zoë that Paul wasn't interested, or was this finally a message from Paul? Wishing it didn't matter so much, Zoë took a deep breath, turned over her phone and clicked on the notification, watching the screens change slowly as the phone sought out a better signal.

After a few long seconds, she was finally directed to the website. Her heart fluttered wildly as she touched the screen, leaning over the little table to read.

***

Dear Holly,

Until last night I was pretty sure that my friend Maggie was on a mission to destroy my life.

(You should have seen the dates she was setting me up on. I'm still shaking.)

When she told me she'd signed me up for MeetTheOne.com, I wasn't very happy, I'll admit. Then I saw your picture.

I can't tell you, Holly, how moved I was by your sunny smile at your aunt's wedding. You looked so open and pretty, I couldn't stop staring.

I read the emails that you and Maggie exchanged and just about fell over when I read that *The Princess Bride* is your favorite movie too. Somehow that felt like a sign.

When Maggie explained you lived in Connecticut, I really considered whether or not it made sense for us to correspond, but I couldn't get your picture out of my head. I have no idea if you want to get to know a guy in Montana. (Truth be told, I think the guys in Mystic should be knocking down your door!) Anyway, I guess I'll leave it up to you.

Meeting like this is really awkward. I don't even know what else to say, other than this… I'd really like to get to know you.

I'm off to Yellowstone today with my friend Lars. The weather's clear and

warm and the sun's high. Hope it's
shining on you, wherever you are,
pretty Holly.

—Paul

***

Zoë didn't realize she'd been holding her breath until it came
out in a rush. Her heart pounded in her chest as she turned
over the phone. How could something as impersonal as an
email be so affecting?

Her lips turned up in a slight smile as she savored the
warmth and sincerity of his words. She was not surprised—
Maggie had been so effusive, there was no way Paul was
going to be another jerk—but she was unprepared for the
impact of reading his email. She had assumed the physical
distance between them would make him feel far away.
Instead, it was like she'd just spent ten intimate minutes
inside his head.

She sat back in the chair and let her damaged face bathe
in the warmth of the sun for a moment as he had suggested,
even though she knew it wasn't a good idea. Until her final
surgery in early October, it wasn't smart to discolor the
puckered, violet skin any further.

Pretty Holly.

The girl in the photo that Paul saw last night didn't
have puckered, violet skin testifying to an accident that had
splintered her family. It had been taken three years ago at
Sandy and Rob's wedding.

Zoë sighed.

It would have been far more honest to tell Maggie she

wasn't thin, blonde and blue-eyed anymore—*hell, she wasn't a lot of things anymore*—and offer a more recent picture of herself. In fact, she'd considered it. But after combing her phone for a more recent photo, she could only find one that wasn't horrible: she wasn't smiling, but at least it was taken in profile and didn't show her bad side.

That said, when she'd held the newer photo up to her computer screen, staring at the two incredibly different pictures of *before-the-accident* and *after-the-accident* Zoë, she couldn't bear to offer it to Maggie. Swap out the photo of the trim, blonde, sunny girl who used to be Zoë? For the heavier, black-haired, dark-eyed, tattooed, scarred disaster she'd become? Right. She'd never hear from him again, and for whatever reason, it really mattered to Zoë that she hear from Paul again.

Feeling like a lying piece of crap, she stared at her phone and considered deleting Paul's message, disabling her account and leaving him alone. He was a nice guy looking for love and she had no right to lead him on even the littlest bit. Yet when she visualized deleting his sweet email and disabling her MeetTheOne account, a terrible heaviness threatened to edge in on the little bit of hope she'd been enjoying.

Was exchanging a few emails *really* leading him on? It was more like being pen pals, especially if she was upfront about her intention to be friends. She could tell him about her life in Connecticut and he could tell her about Montana and Yellowstone; they could get to know each other, just as he suggested. No more, no less. They couldn't very well get *romantic* from so far away, could they? No, of course not. His email only *felt* intimate because it had been so long since a man—a nice, decent man—had been so kind to her. It was impossible to *be* intimate from two thousand miles away. There was no reason to overthink it.

Halfway convinced that she wasn't a horrible person for writing back and ignoring the guilt that wouldn't quite leave her alone, Zoë picked up her phone and pressed reply.

> Dear Paul,
>
> Your email made me smile. I think Maggie's intentions are good, but it certainly sounds like you have been out on a few really bad dates.
>
> Thank you for your kind words about my photo. It was taken two summers ago, at my aunt Sandy's wedding. She got married in Newport, Rhode Island, which isn't far from where I live in Mystic, Connecticut. Maggie mentioned that you went to school in Rhode Island so perhaps you've had a chance to visit Newport. That day was especially beautiful— bright sun, blue sky—and while my aunt Sandy doesn't generally stand on convention, her wedding on the beach was very traditional.
>
> What is your favorite line from *The*

Princess Bride? Tell me yours and I'll tell you mine. While you're at it, tell me your favorite scene too! ☺

Right now, I'm on an early lunch break from work so the sun *is* shining on my face, although it's getting very warm so I should probably go back inside.

I'd like to get to know you too. We could be pen pals. I think that would be fun.

Enjoy your day in Yellowstone.

—Holly

***

Paul got out of the shower and toweled off.

He wrapped the towel around his waist and lathered up his face to shave, taking an extra look at himself in the mirror. After six years in Montana, he was disappointed to note that he still looked like a preppy Johansson from Kennebunkport. His cheekbones were high and chiseled, and his square chin jutted out in a confident, almost arrogant way, like his father's. Though he was tan from a summer spent outdoors, mostly in Yellowstone, and his body was fit, it was also spare, not jacked-up like his friend, Lars, who was naturally muscular.

Jenny's husband Sam had once confessed that at first glance he thought Paul should be a J. Crew model rather than a principal. Paul had grinned at his old rival, but inwardly, he'd grimaced at Sam's assessment. Part of the reason he'd left Maine was to get away from his wealthy, entrenched family and the iron hold they would have had on him and his life.

Ding! He was distracted by his phone alerting him to an incoming message. Probably just Lars reconfirming their time and meeting place. Paul used a towel to wipe the shaving foam from his face and picked up the phone charging on his bureau.

MissMystic has sent you a message.

He chuckled softly, looking at the words, feeling a smile spread across his face. He'd written to her less than an hour ago and here was a reply already!

Leaning against his bureau, he took his time reading her message. It wasn't fair that she should start by telling him that he made her smile, because all he could think about was the picture of Holly at her aunt's wedding, and he wished he could see her smiling like that for him.

He thought about the many summer days he'd spent in Newport and wondered if he'd ever bumped into her—maybe seen her walking with a girlfriend or buying herself a tube of lip gloss at one of the tourist shops, on the beach in a floppy hat or in a bikini playing volleyball. He could have seen her a million times and yet it took Maggie's meddling for him to *meet* her.

He loved her questions about *The Princess Bride* and felt sort of bad that she was stuck teaching summer school. Well, he assumed that's what she meant by work; the only other summer job for teachers was summer camp, but that wouldn't be an indoor job.

The only thing that bothered Paul about the email was

her use of the term "pen pal." He sat down at the foot of his bed, clasping the warm phone between his hands as if it were an actual link to Holly.

Pen pals.

Ugh.

It was the internet-dating equivalent of saying "Let's just be friends," and maybe it didn't make any sense at all, but Paul didn't want to be "just friends" with Holly. Looking at her picture made his blood heat up, made him feel longing, hope, excitement. He'd only known she existed for a handful of hours, but he didn't think of her as his "buddy," and that's not the road he wanted to walk down with her. He wanted to leave the door open to a good deal more than that. It was absurd and defied explanation, but he just had a feeling about her that he couldn't shake. Being pen pals didn't figure into it.

He plugged his phone back in and finished shaving his face, nicking himself twice in the process. His instinct was to write back something along the lines of "I'm not looking for a pen pal," but he cringed at how bald and pushy that sounded. He didn't want to push her away. He wanted to get to know her.

And then it occurred to him: maybe saying she wanted to be pen pals was just her way of saying she wanted to get to know him too. Maggie had found Holly on a dating website, right? Called "MeetTheOne," for heaven's sake. So certainly she wasn't just interested in making a faraway friend. If that were the case, she would have had an account on "Meet A Pen Pal." He decided to turn up the heat a little in his next message and see what happened. He'd try to make it clear that he was looking for a little more than friendship at this point in his life.

He pulled on a pair of jeans and a clean white T-shirt. His days of jeans and T-shirts were dwindling now, he thought. In a few weeks, he'd be back in suits and dress shirts with a different tie every day. He had amassed quite a necktie collection over the years as principal of Gardiner High & Middle School; it had become the go-to gift from most of the kids and he tried to wear all of the ties at least once a year.

Checking his phone, he realized he had just enough time to write one more message to Holly before Lars picked him up. He poured himself a cup of coffee and sat down at his kitchen table.

Dear Holly,

What an awesome surprise to get your message. I was just about to head out when my phone pinged to let me know you'd written. I think that's about to become one of my favorite sounds.

I know Rhode Island well. I went to Brown and spent many sunny afternoons in Newport sailing with friends. It's always been one of my favorite places in the world and I still try to get there every summer. I wonder if I ever bumped into you. Nah, couldn't be. I'd have remembered a girl as pretty as you and definitely would have tried to get your number.

My favorite line from *TPB* is "Death cannot stop true love. All it can do is delay it a while." I know it's ridiculous in theory, but I love the intention of the words—the hope, the absoluteness. (Now I'm getting poetic on you! Watch out!)

My favorite scene is—brace yourself since my brothers informed me a million times with their fists that boys weren't supposed to like the kissing scenes! —in the very beginning when Westley pulls down the jug for Buttercup, and he stares into her eyes, and they realize they're in love and kiss on that hill while the sun sets. I guess that means I'm a romantic.

Probably showing my cards a little too much here, but why not? Wouldn't it be amazing to start a relationship with someone based on truth? Based on how you really thought and really felt and not have to backtrack later? This is who I am, for better or worse.

I hope I hear from you again.

—Terrible at Poker, aka Paul

***

Zoë was just heading back into her building when her phone pinged again.

PrincipalPaul has sent you a message.

Those butterflies in her stomach returned tenfold and she took a deep breath, moving to the far side of the lobby near the coffee kiosk and leaning on the wall behind a large potted fern. She looked at the time: 11:52. Damn, she was already late getting back, but she couldn't resist taking a look.

She felt her face soften as she started reading his words. He went to Brown, which meant that he was smart, and he sailed, which was a pastime Zoë used to love. Her finger slid down the screen and her heart caught, reading his words about love.

The intention…the hope…the absoluteness…and they realize they're in love.

She clenched her eyes shut for a moment, the hammering of her heart loud in her ears. She'd heard of women swooning from romantic words, but she'd certainly never experienced it. Goose bumps spread from her hands up her arms and a shiver went down her spine. A smart, sporty, handsome man who believed in true love? Principal Paul just got better and better.

She took a deep breath, feeling dreamy, and then opened her eyes, all of that delicious warmth turning to Arctic cold as she read the last paragraph.

Wouldn't it be amazing to start a relationship with someone based on truth…not have to backtrack later?

Her stomach rolled over and her mouth watered the way it did before she threw up. She stared at the words, feeling exposed, feeling caught, then telling herself to calm down: Paul was thousands of miles away. He wasn't accusing her of anything. He didn't know she was deceiving him.

But *she* knew, and her already-heavy conscience dipped lower.

She was pretending to be the girl she was *before* the accident. She was, in fact, deceiving him, while he was, as he said, putting his cards on the table. He was being up front with her; he was looking for love—for *true* love and honesty—and since Zoë could offer neither, it was her responsibility to delete his message and not write back again. It was the right thing to do. The kind and decent thing to do.

Decision made, her finger hovered over the red delete button. She felt a bead of sweat run from her hairline, down the ragged seam of her scarred face to her neck, detouring between the tattoos on her shoulders.

Press it, she told herself.

She *meant* to press delete.

Really, she did.

A good person would press delete and cut Paul loose without looking back.

Instead she shoved the phone into her black leather purse and hustled back upstairs before Stan noticed how long she'd been gone.

CHAPTER 3

Dear Paul,

You have a way with words. A romantic, indeed. As it happens, you chose my favorite scene from *TPB*, but not my favorite line. My favorite line dovetails nicely with yours: "Move? You're alive. If you want, I can fly!" Don't you love that? I'm guessing that's how it feels.

As coincidence would have it, I also went to school in Rhode Island: at Salve Regina in Newport. I think I was sold the first time my mom ever took us to see the mansions on Bellevue Avenue when I was very little. I thought I'd do just about anything to live in the Breakers. As it turns out, the closest I could get was a dorm on the same road. LOL. Like you, I enjoyed many days of sunny sailing. I wonder if we did, as you suggest, rub elbows at the same bar, once upon a time, waiting for the bartender to slide a cold beer our way.

It suddenly occurs to me that you have me at a disadvantage. Because you answered my ad, you've seen my picture, but I don't have a picture of you. Can you send one so I know who I'm talking to?

I agree with you, in theory. It would be something to get to know someone's heart and mind before anything else.

—Holly

***

Dear Holly,

Sorry I didn't write back yesterday. We ended up camping in Yellowstone and my phone died at some point overnight. The signal's not great in the park anyway, but as we got closer to Gardiner, my phone dinged as it was charging, and I got your message. My friend Lars thought I was crazy, grinning at my phone like a fool.

He's a tour guide and his family business was just contracted by *Trend* magazine for a photo shoot with the super model Samara Amaya. Lars and I scouted out some pretty cool locations.

Lars is one of four Lindstrom siblings and I guess he's just about my best friend in the world, followed closely by his brothers, Erik and Nils. The Lindstroms have been really great to me ever since I moved out here. They welcomed me into their family for holidays and Sunday dinners. I'm lucky to have their friendship.

I try to get home to see my family at least twice a year, especially at Christmas, but it's an awfully long trip.

You know what I like about Wednesdays? You get to start thinking about the weekend. What will you be up to?

—Paul

PS – My Principal picture is predictably dorky. I'll see if I can find another one. And hey…what did you mean by "I'm guessing that's how it feels"?

***

Dear Paul,

SAMARA AMAYA!! Wow! She's possibly the most beautiful woman in the world. Are you going to meet her?

It must be hard to live so far away from your family. I am very close to my aunt Sandy. My father was never really in the picture and my mom passed away when I was in high school. Sandy stepped in to take care of me since my older sister Thea was already in college. Sandy's amazing, and way more than just an aunt to me. I'll always be grateful to her.

I noticed you didn't mention the fourth Lindstrom sibling. Any reason for that? Just wondering. It sounds like they've been very good to you, but more importantly, it sounds like you appreciate them.

I don't know what I'll do this weekend. I live in an apartment over my aunt's garage and it could use a fresh coat of paint, so maybe I'll do some painting. And there's a cute movie with Emma Stone and Ryan Gosling coming out. Maybe I'll try to catch that. ☺

You'll be back east for Christmas, huh?

—Holly

PS – "I'm guessing that's how it feels"...to get a second chance at love when you thought all hope was gone. Like flying.

***

Dear Holly,

You've redefined "flying" for me and I don't think any other definition will ever matter again. ;)

Let's see...Oh, you asked about whether or not I'll meet Samara Amaya. Well, I guess I could if I wanted to, but I'm pretty distracted by another beautiful woman lately, so meeting her isn't really a priority. ;)

I'm so sorry about your mom. It must have been very hard to lose her. I was a guidance counselor for two years before taking my present position and it broke my heart to watch a teenager lose a parent. Teenage years are tough enough without that added challenge. I am sure you're grateful to Sandy. I think I am too. Is that okay?

You're astute. The fourth Lindstrom sibling is Jenny, the youngest. She used to be a science teacher at my high school, and – full confession – I had some pretty strong feelings for her at one point. She's a great girl. But she got married a couple of years ago and moved north to Great Falls. Maybe it still stings a little, but honestly, Holly? For the first time in a long time I'm not thinking much about Jenny Lindstrom Kelley, and that feels really nice. ☺

So, I had an idea: I was thinking we

could go on a date this weekend. The closest theater to me is in Livingston, MT, which is about an hour north, and *Closer to You* (that's the Emma Stone movie you're talking about, right?) is playing at 4:30 p.m. on Saturday. I was thinking if you could find a theater playing it at 6:30 p.m. where you are, we could go at the same time. And if you're up for it, we could even exchange cell phone numbers and text during the movie.

Man, I hope that doesn't sound creepy. I'm not trying to be pushy. I just thought it might be fun.

Let me know.

—Unpushy Paul

PS – DEFINITELY coming back for Christmas this year. Were you born at Christmastime, Holly?

***

Dear Paul,

LOL! Well, you're a creative one, aren't you?

Sure, I'm game. I found a 6:15 p.m. show in Stonington, so let's just hope the previews go a little longer at my theater. Saturday, right? Tomorrow?

I sort of suspected that the fourth

Lindstrom had a story. I'm sorry she hurt you, Paul. I hope you two can eventually be friends, especially since you're so close to her brothers. Maybe it's a little selfish of me, but I'm sort of glad things worked out (or didn't!) the way they did, or I wouldn't have gotten the chance to meet you.

Thank you for your kind words about my mom. I've learned that there are lots of ways to lose someone you love and none of them are good. Life can change in the blink of an eye.

You're a really nice person. I'm glad you—or Maggie, I guess—found me. I like getting to know you.

—Holly

PS – Yes, I'm a Christmas baby. ☺

***

Dear Holly,

I like you too. This has been the best week I've had in a long time. I'm like Pavlov's dog every time my phone pings, grabbing it and grinning like an idiot. When you wrote that you're sort of glad things worked out the way they did with Jen, I swear to God my cheeks started aching from smiling so wide. I know we've only been writing for a week, but you're doing crazy things to my heart with these emails.

I finally had my friend Maggie take a photo of me. It's not bad. You'll have to tell me what you think.

Hey, would you consider talking on the phone sometime? I'm ready whenever you are.

I tell you what, here's my cell number: 406-555-2364. If you want to text back and forth during the movie tomorrow, send me one. I'll be waiting. (Hoping. Praying.)

—Paul

PS – Christmas is my very favorite time of year, baby. ;)

***

Zoë didn't hear Sandy's footsteps, so she jumped a foot when her aunt was suddenly standing at the top of the stairs in Zoë's little living room on Friday evening.

"Zoë Holly Flannigan! Didn't you hear me calling you?"

Zoë tapped the small screen of her phone and shoved it in her back pocket, giving Sandy a smile.

"I was just reading something."

"Something pretty good, I'm guessing," said Sandy, cocking her head to the side and smiling. "You know what? You look good, Zoë. Whatever you're reading, keep reading it."

Zoë shrugged, looking down, feeling her face warm up.

"What's up?"

"Barely seen you this week. We never did our bad TV and ice cream date, but we could do it later? Rob and I are going out for supper first."

"Okay. Sounds good. Come find me when you get back."

"Great. Um, we're, um…we're going to see Thea and Brandon. Have a little pizza."

Zoë's heart dropped and she bit her lower lip, tasting blood almost immediately. "Oh."

"You should come."

"No. No, I can't. They don't want to see me, Sandy."

"Thea is your only sister; your only sibling. You should come with us, Zo. Start talking to each other again."

Tears glistened in Zoë's eyes. "You don't think I *want* to talk to Thea? You don't think I want that every moment, every single second, every day?"

"Hiding here isn't going to make it happen."

"She doesn't want to see me. She made that clear."

"It was almost two years ago, Zo. She was terrified out of her mind that her kid was dying. A few days before she was afraid that her little sister was dying too. She was there every day, Zo, while you were in the coma. She didn't leave the hospital without kissing you on the forehead and telling you she loved you, hoping like hell that you'd make it."

Useless tears tumbled out of Zoë's eyes. Sandy had told her this before, but Zoë always suspected she was trying to mend fences by embellishing the truth. Did Zoë believe that Thea stopped in to see her before she left the hospital every day? Probably. But she was probably hoping that Zoë *didn't* make it after what she'd done to Brandon.

"Hey, uh—not this t-time, okay?"

Sandy opened her arms and Zoë walked into them, savoring the familiar warmth offered by her aunt. "Think about it, Zoë. You've got to work this out with Thea at some point."

Zoë sniffled against Sandy's shoulder, wondering for the thousandth time what she would do without her aunt.

Sandy backed up, cocked her head to the side and smiled. "Want me to bring you back a slice?"

Zoë nodded. "Sausage?"

"You got it." Sandy turned and headed back down the stairs.

"Wait! Sand?"

Sandy turned back.

"Can you make it a tossed salad with grilled chicken instead?"

Sandy raised her eyebrows but had the good sense to nod, not grin, and head back down the stairs.

***

Zoë's unfamiliar descent into giddiness started around five o'clock on Saturday.

She'd been checking her phone pathologically all day, and by four, she started to wonder if the absence of an email meant that Paul might not be following through with their plan to go to the movies "together." Shouldn't he have at least written to her once? Just to reconfirm?

No, her conscience had needled her, *he shouldn't. And*

furthermore, he shouldn't be writing to you in the first place, since he's faithfully writing to someone that doesn't actually exist.

She kept telling herself that the situation wasn't too far gone yet; she still had space to pull back from him and no one would get hurt. But part of her knew she was lying to herself. A line had already been crossed. Having Paul in her life simply felt too good to let go right now.

She had scrubbed her kitchen and bathroom twice, checking her Wi-Fi connection obsessively and logging into MeetTheOne twenty-odd times to see if a message from Paul was waiting that just hadn't sent a notification to her phone. No messages. Nothing. Zip.

She did a face masque and put softener on her scar, then grimaced at her omnipresent black finger- and toenail polish, deciding it was time for a change. She spent a good half hour rooting around under her bathroom cabinet for the cotton-candy pink color she hadn't worn in almost two years. She turned on an MTV marathon of *The Real World* and was halfway through her manicure when she heard it.

Ding!

Her heart thumped like mad as she eyed the bright, buzzing screen across the room on the kitchen counter. She took a deep breath and turned her attention back to her fingers, relief seeping through her body. Sure, it could be Sandy checking on her from work or Stan asking for her to email a file. But it wasn't. She knew it was Paul.

Waving her tacky nails to dry them, she screwed the top back onto her nail polish and awkwardly made her way to the counter, shuffling along on the backs of her heels, trying to keep her bubblegum-colored toes off the plush carpet.

She swiped her finger across the screen and her lips tilted up in a smile as she saw the heavenly words:

PrincipalPaul has sent you a message.

> Dear Holly,
>
> I'm leaving for Livingston now. I hope you're still planning to "meet" me. Looking forward to our first "date."
>
> —Paul

Catching her reflection in the glass of her phone, she almost didn't recognize herself for a second.

The sun was shining through the window on her left cheek and her black hair wasn't visible in the small frame. But for the dark-colored contacts, she could have been old Zoë looking back. For just a moment she looked young and hopeful. She smiled a touch more broadly and had an idea. If she was going out on a date with Paul as Holly? Well, she should dress the part. Why not? Placing her phone gingerly on the countertop, she headed to her room to get ready.

***

Paul must have checked his phone thirty times on the ride from Gardiner to Livingston, glancing at it surreptitiously as he drove along, wondering if Holly would text him or not, unable to control the leaping of his heart at the prospect.

He couldn't figure out how and why she'd gotten so far under his skin so quickly. It wasn't like he could see her at school, watching her out of the corner of his eye as she walked down the hall to the craft closet or dressed up for Greet the Parents night. If she *was* a teacher at his school—

as Jenny had been—he'd be able to observe her around others: what made her smile, what made her frustrated. He'd know so much about her based on his extrapolations, without ever needing to say more than a word to her. In fact, if he made a project of observing her carefully, he would have eventually made educated assumptions about who she was, whether that was fair and accurate or not.

Instead, she existed in a totally different plane of reality, allowing him direct access to her head and her heart. It was almost impossible to make assumptions about her, and more and more, Paul was enchanted by the concept of getting to know someone—really *know* them—without the confusion of body language, tone, physical attraction, and assumptions.

One thing was for certain: the more he got to know Holly, the more he liked her.

He found street parking about a block away from the Empire Twin theater and made his way up the block, one hand in his pocket, palming his phone just in case it vibrated. He opened the theater door and stepped into the stale-smelling, air-conditioned half-light. There was a ticket window to his right.

"One, please. For the, uh, four-thirty show."

The girl behind the glass looked about the same age as his high school seniors and wore electric-blue eye shadow with silvery pink lip gloss. She snapped her gum loudly, looked meaningfully over his shoulder, then, convinced Paul had arrived alone, asked, "You mean the four forty-five show?"

Paul flicked his glance up to the marquis behind her.

Closer to You, which featured a glossy poster with Emma Stone kissing Ryan Gosling in a meadow by sunset, was playing at four-thirty while *The Last Firestorm* which featured fighter jets doing midair acrobatics over a burning city, was playing at four forty-five.

He tilted his head to the side. "I said four-thirty."

"It's a romance."

"Yep. I know."

"Just, uh, *one*?" she asked, raising her eyebrows and trying to look over his shoulder.

Paul put a ten-dollar bill on the countertop under the glass. "Yep. Just me."

With that slightly mocking smile still on her face, she let her eyes trail lazily down his body, resting briefly on his hips before slowly sweeping back up.

"I get off at five," she said.

"Good for you," Paul muttered without smiling.

The girl smirked, straightening her back so her small breasts jutted out toward him. "Want company? I'll come find you in the dark once it starts. You say yes, I'll let you watch for free."

"I tell you what," said Paul, placing a finger on his ten-dollar bill and sliding it closer to her. "You go ahead and give me my change for one ticket at four-thirty and I won't tell the theater manager that you're making passes at the patrons. Deal?"

She huffed, taking his money and slapping his change on the counter. "Weird for a *man* to see a rom-com all by hisself."

"*Him*self."

"Huh?"

"*Him*self. It's weird for a man to see a rom-com all by *him*self."

She curled her lip and narrowed her eyes. "That's what I said."

School wasn't in session and he wasn't her teacher, but Paul was compulsive about correcting children and he was about to try to explain it to her again when his phone blessedly buzzed, interrupting them. He knew it was Holly. He just felt it.

"*Him*self," he said again, which elicited another disgusted look from the girl. He rolled his eyes. "Aw, just forget it."

He fished his phone out of his pocket, but kept himself from looking at the screen, wanting to choose a good seat and get settled before he read Holly's text and wrote back. The theater was dark and mostly empty, except for a few ladies in the front. Not wanting to appear like a creepy old man sitting by himself in the back row of the theater, Paul chose an aisle seat three rows from the back, sat down and then raised his phone.

It's me. Are you there?

He smiled at his phone, running his thumb over her words, looking at the 860 area code of her previously unknown phone number and loving that she was suddenly only a phone number away now.

I'm here, he responded. Has yours started yet?

Not yet. Still previews. And hi. ☺

Heya Holly. I'm smiling so wide right now, it's ridiculous. Thanks for doing this.

Thanks for asking me.

How was your drive? he typed.

Fine. The theater's only 15 min from my apt. You?

Good. Sunny. The Yellowstone River snakes along by the hwy. Lots of mountains. Makes for a nice ride.

It's raining here. Perfect day for the movies. My drive wasn't pretty, though. Just highway I-95. I really don't like highway driving, but I was running late. I prefer back roads.

Back roads. I haven't heard that expression in a long time.

You don't use back roads in Montana?

Not like you do in New England. In NE there are a million ancient back roads you can use to take the scenic route or avoid traffic.

Exactly.

In MT, every route's the scenic route and there is no traffic.

You really love it there? You don't miss NE?

I do sometimes. At Thanksgiving and Christmas, mostly. Nobody does Christmas like Maine. That's why I go home.

And to see your family?

He paused before answering, briefly considering how much he wanted to say.

Finally, he typed "It's complicated," but frowned at the words before erasing them. He didn't want to send up a warning flag about him not liking his family or having problems with them. But the truth is: it *was* complicated.

Paul was a sixth-generation Johansson and his father's expectations had always been very clear: Brown undergrad, Harvard Law, then partner in the family law business like his older brothers, Ted and Bennett.

But going into the family law business in Boston wasn't what Paul wanted. He didn't want to make that ninety-minute commute every Monday morning, only returning north to Maine on Friday afternoons. Keeping an apartment in the city. The endless hours of work. The cocktails and work dinners that went way too late. The women. He bit the side of his cheek as his father's face came into focus, swiftly followed by his mother's. They were still together after forty years, but it wasn't a happy marriage. Hadn't ever been a happy marriage.

How in the world could he explain all of that in a text? Why would he even want to? *Hey, Holly, here's a look into my incredibly wealthy, incredibly privileged, incredibly dysfunctional, unhappy family. Want to get to know me better?* Yeah, right. What girl wanted that? Especially a girl who had lost her own parents but managed to hold on to strong relationships with her sister and aunt. No. Better that he gloss over it. He'd tell her all about it in nitty-gritty detail some other time.

Of course. To see them too.

Two brothers, right? Local?

Boston.

More local to me than to you, I guess.

His eyes narrowed, thinking of Ted or Bennett finding out about Holly and making a move on her just to spite him.

They're in Shanghai as far as you're concerned. And they smell. And have rotten teeth.

LOL! ☺

I love making you smile, Holly. ☺

Ooo! Movie's starting here. Yours?

Not yet. No spoilers, now, Miss Morgan.

Just then the lights dimmed in Paul's theater and he slunk back into his seat as the previews started.

Previews just starting, he typed. Then, Hey Holly?

I'm here.

That's the thing...I wish you really were.

He stared at the screen, but she didn't text back in the same rhythm they'd established a minute ago. Shoot. Had he gone too far? He waited a good thirty seconds and still no response, but he decided not to take it back or play if off as a joke. *A card laid is a card played*...and, anyway, he meant every word.

CHAPTER 4

Zoë stared at the little screen.

I wish you really were.

Goose bumps raised on her arm as her heart kicked into a gallop, but she only had a moment to enjoy the rush before guilt took over.

Yeah, right. If you only knew, she thought acidly, self-consciousness broadsiding her. She swore she could *feel* her scars throbbing.

She knew he was waiting for her to write back—she could *sense* it—but she didn't know what to say. Her fingers gripped her phone tightly as she glanced up at the screen where Emma Stone, wearing a white sundress and bare feet, was sitting on an old-fashioned country swing hanging from the branch of an ancient elm tree with her face bathed in sunshine and her light red hair back in a ponytail.

That's the sort of girl Paul wanted to be sitting next to, not Zoë.

She hadn't been truthful about highway driving either. It didn't *bother* her. It scared the holy hell out of her since the accident. Getting on the highway today for a grand total of eight minutes had made her hands sweat so badly, she'd had to pull over when she got off the exit, breathing deeply and drying off her dripping steering wheel with the hem of her skirt. She should have tried to be more honest, but she'd glossed over it, deciding to give him the lowdown another time.

Ugh, Zoë, she thought. *You're just a big liar, all the way around.*

She stared at the words hard: *I wish you really were.*

Zoë's heart and head agreed wholeheartedly.

She'd love to be sitting beside him. Unless Paul was grossly misrepresenting himself, he was a catch. Good looking, quietly successful, satisfied with his life, with deep friendships. Returning home a few times a year on a principal's salary meant that he probably had a strong relationship with his family too.

What girl wouldn't want that man sitting next to her?

On the flip side, why would a man—an amazing man with everything to recommend himself—be interested in someone with ugly, twisted scars on her face and body? Someone who'd unintentionally, but carelessly, allowed grave injury to befall someone she loved? Someone who had lied about her looks and important details of her life since the moment they'd met?

Zoë shouldn't be looking for Paul. She should be looking for someone as damaged as she was.

She looked up at the screen and watched Emma, dressed in '40s-style clothes, fry up eggs and bacon in an old-fashioned kitchen, chatting cheerfully to a basset hound at her feet while a radio played "The Very Thought Of You."

Her phone vibrated.

Holly? It's starting.

She stared at the phone screen, thinking for the hundredth time that she should cut bait and let Paul find someone as wonderful as he was.

I didn't mean to freak you out, Holly. Write back? Please?

Zoë winced at the words. She couldn't bear for him to think he'd done anything wrong by being honest with her and by speaking from his heart to hers. Still, she couldn't encourage a train of conversation that veered toward meeting in person either.

No problem! Doesn't that swing look like heaven? she asked.

Emma reminds me of someone in that white dress. ☺

My hair's not red.

Yours is like sunshine.

It was. Once. She smiled at her phone, feeling a sudden warmth ignite and establish itself as a low burn in her belly. She took a deep breath and sighed.

You're sweet, Paul.

You think so?

I do.

☺

She turned her glance back up to the screen where Emma was swing dancing with a redheaded actor wearing a khaki-colored WWII uniform, before kissing him on the cheek and making him sit down for breakfast.

Do you like music from the 1940s? Big band music? she typed.

I do. You?

Very much, she confessed. I used to be a pretty good dancer too.

Used to be? Are your dancing days over? Or are you just looking for a good partner?

She bit her lip at the *Glossing Ahead* sign on the road in front of her. Again, details for another time.

You volunteering? she demurred.

I'm not a bad dancer. My mother insisted every gentleman should know how to dance. I was forced to take ballroom dancing.

Forced, huh? Sounds like you absolutely loved it! LOL

I didn't mind. I got to hold hands with Evelyn Berry.

It was absolutely ridiculous that a strong slice of jealousy cut through Zoë, but it was an uncontrolled, visceral reaction. She hated the idea of him holding hands with some other woman. Any other woman. Of any age. At any time. Possessiveness hissed and spat, making her eyes narrow at the little screen in front of her. Her fingers moved like lightning.

Evelyn Berry? Where is she now?

Still somewhere in Maine, I guess. Why?

She better STAY in Maine.

Had she, now?

She had. (If she knows what's good for her.)

And if she doesn't?

Oh, Paul. A Maine girl versus a Mystic girl? It's simply not a fair fight.

Holly!! ☺

Zoë bit her lip and giggled aloud at her boldness. It felt

so unusual, sounded so foreign and fine to hear her own voice laughing, it made her breath catch and tears sprang into her eyes. Sitting in a dark movie theater two thousand miles away from the man who meant more to her every day, she wanted to weep. He'd made her giggle. Giggle. It had been months since she giggled spontaneously just because she was happy. It felt so good that her eyes glistened with gratitude she wished she could share with him. Instead she glossed. Again.

Now stop distracting me. I have to figure out what's going on here. I feel a love triangle brewing. She smiled as she pressed send.

You and me and Evelyn? he asked a moment later.

Bite your tongue.

How about you bite it?

She felt the burning in her stomach catch like fire on kindling and erupt upward past her chest to her shoulders, down her arms to her fingertips, which curled around her phone. Her heart pounded furiously at the suggestive question, feeling she was at a crossroads. Did she engage in a little sexy talk with him or shut it down? She couldn't very well call them pen pals anymore if she bantered back, but damn it if she couldn't help herself.

How about I do?

Oh, man, Holly. I REALLY wish you were here.

She shook her head, smiling sadly at the phone before turning it over on her lap and thinking, *Me too, Paul. Me too.*

***

Paul had absolutely no idea what was going on in the movie.

What's more, he was in total shock about what was going on in his body. His heart was thumping like crazy and all the blood in his head had rushed south as he read her words. He glanced down at the bulge in his lap, wishing it away. *She's a couple thousand miles away, buddy. Stand down.*

How had that just happened? How had they gone from chitchat to sizzle? Evelyn Berry. *Thank God for Evelyn Berry*, about whom he hadn't given a single thought in at least a decade. Holly had a little playful-jealous streak that was not only adorable, but a complete and total turn-on.

How about I do? Paul groaned softly and shifted in his seat, trying to find a more comfortable position to accommodate his aroused body.

He looked at his phone but she hadn't written back again. Settling back in his chair to try to catch up with the movie plot, he knew one thing for certain:

He wasn't going to be able to wait until Christmas to meet his Holly.

***

It turned out to be a pretty good movie, thought Zoë, wiping her eyes with the back of her hand.

The red-haired man in the beginning was Emma's brother who went off to fight in WWII. He met another man, played by Ryan Gosling, who became his best friend, but who accidentally killed him during a particularly confusing battle scene. Ryan returns to the states after the war and looks up Emma to explain what happened, but she immediately knows him as her dead brother's war friend and welcomes him into her life with warm, open arms. He falls so hard for her, he can't bear to tell her the truth so they fall in love with this huge, terrible secret hanging over his head. And when the truth comes out—

Zoë's phone buzzed as she made her way out of the theater.

So, what'd you think?

Texting while walking wasn't Zoë's forte, so she crossed the wet street quickly and ducked into Starbucks. She considered having a salted caramel latte, her favorite, but decided to have a less-fattening cup of regular coffee instead. She sat down at a small bistro table by the windows, which ran with rivulets of rain and made her feel very warm and cozy inside.

Stopped in at Starbucks. Raining cats and dogs here. I liked it. You?

It was good. Thank God the colonel confessed it was his gunshot that killed the brother. I was really squirming over his deception.

Reading this, Zoë flinched. Another reminder that she was lying to Paul. She shoved the feeling aside. It had been such a wonderful night; she wasn't going to ruin it with self-recrimination. She could beat herself up later.

I know. I was worried too…like, That's IT? You two BELONG together!

Sucker for a happy ending, Miss Morgan?

Absolutely. No question. No apologies.

Speaking of questions, can I ask one?

Sure. Anything.

I know it's about 8:30 there and it'll be almost 10:00 by

the time I get home, but…

What?

Could I call you? When I get home?

Her breath caught and she took a careful sip of her steaming hot coffee then stared at the screen until her eyes started to burn.

She should write back no. She had already crossed a line by letting their conversation this afternoon hurtle over flirty into sexy. If she intended to let this go, now was the moment. This was the time to say *No, Paul. No. You're terrific, but you deserve someone better than me. I'm not who you think I am.*

Wasn't that the right thing to do? Wasn't it?

It might have been the right thing to do at some point, she suddenly realized. But that point had passed.

Zoë wanted Paul.

She wanted him more than she'd wanted anything for two long, cold, sad years. She wanted Paul *more* than she needed to be a good person. She had no idea how to make sense of her and Paul, but she was very sure of one thing: saying no at this point was simply impossible, so she needed to make her peace with it.

I'll be waiting, she typed, tucking her phone back in her bag and trying to ignore the confusing feelings in her heart.

***

Paul was lucky he didn't get into an accident, driving like a maniac, well over the speed limit, to get home and call Holly. He parked his car in his gravel driveway and hustled up the stairs of his front porch, unlocking the door of the four-bedroom stone and clapboard house he had purchased when he moved to Gardiner. It was easily one of the most expensive houses in town—in fact, prior to Paul's purchase, it had functioned as the Yellowstone View bed-and-breakfast—but it was within means for Paul, whose trust fund tidily covered the expense. He knew he didn't need the extra three bedrooms, but when he moved to Gardiner, he intended to stay there, and he still hoped to one day have little bodies populating those other three bedrooms. Someday.

The thing about it, though, was that even though he liked his house, it had never felt like a real home. The truth is that Paul had always lived in houses—large, proper, professionally-decorated houses with beautiful furnishings, devoid of warmth, focused on status and wealth and the importance of *things*. Even now, in the house he'd bought for himself, he didn't feel like he was home. He felt like he owned a house that covered his head and offered a place to bathe and sleep. He'd done precious little to personalize the house after buying it, and any warmth that it had was a remnant of the previous owners who left just about all of the furniture…and hokey, western-themed decorations…and Cleo.

Cleo, a Yorkshire terrier deeply attached to the old B&B, was a contingency of the original sale: *You buy the house, Cleo comes with it.*

On cue, she trotted into the room, putting her little paws on his front leg and panting in excitement. She had been four years old when he purchased the house and the owners had stipulated that Cleo came with the house. No

Cleo? No sale. They were moving to a retirement home in Florida that wouldn't accept pets.

While Paul wasn't real fond of tiny, yappy dogs, he had wanted the house, which had a strange New England feel to it, so he'd agreed to let Cleo stay on. She was a gentle, affectionate little thing and had worked herself into his heart, keeping him company on cold nights, curled up by his feet.

Running into the house, he settled down on the couch in the front room, catching his breath. Glancing at his watch, he found it was 7:35 p.m.; 9:35 her time. He could call whenever he wanted to.

"Whaddaya think? Should I call Holly? Huh?" he asked the little dog who looked up at him adoringly, wagging her tail.

Practically humming with excitement and nervous energy, he headed into the kitchen and poured himself a glass of iced tea. Then he opened the sliding door to a back deck that had a good view of Electric Peak in the distance.

Electric. Yeah, that's about right.

The entire drive home, he tried to tell himself to calm down and step back. Although he and Holly had exchanged a week's worth of emails and an afternoon's worth of texts, he really didn't know her well enough yet to be *falling* for her. And yet, he thought about her more and more. All the time, even. He wondered what she was up to as his brain worked efficiently in two time zones. Who was she talking to, and were her students giving her a hard time? Did she miss her mother terribly some days and was there some gym teacher making goo-goo eyes at her from across the faculty cafeteria?

He had so many questions; there was so much he wanted to know about her—anything, everything.

He sat down on the porch swing, placing his tea on the table to his left as Cleo jumped up to sit beside him.

"Only one way to get some answers, huh, Cleo?"

He leaned forward to take his phone out of his back pocket and dialed Holly's number.

***

After Starbucks, Zoë stopped in at the grocery store, so it was late when she got home. She was surprised to find Sandy coming down the stairs of her apartment. Since Saturday nights were the busiest nights at the pizzeria her aunt owned and managed, Zoë wondered why her aunt wasn't working.

"Look at you," said Sandy, a curious smile lighting up her face. "Were you out on a date or something?"

Zoë glanced down at the ankle-length white, cotton skirt and aqua blue, short-sleeve polo shirt she was wearing with a turquoise bracelet. They were clothes and jewelry she hadn't worn in a long time, and while the elastic of the skirt's waistband had been kind to her fuller figure, she was busting out of the shirt a little. Putting them on had been a silly concession to Paul going out on a date with "Holly." That, and Zoë just wanted to amplify the "Holly" feeling.

"Nah," she shrugged, trying to look nonchalant. "Just felt like a change."

Sandy bounced down the remaining three steps and pulled Zoë in for a big hug.

"You're starting to look a little like yourself again," she said softly, then pulled back. "Where you been?"

"Just to the movies. Saw *Closer to You*. It was good."

"Yeah? I guess so. You don't look all mopey. You should go to the movies more often, Zo."

Zoë shifted her keys back and forth in her hands.

"You could start dating again, you know," said Sandy.

"Yeah, they're really knockin' down my door, Sand." Zoë jutted her index finger toward the scar on her face with a sardonic pucker.

"Hey, don't blame that! It's not that bad anymore. At all. *You* put out a vibe."

"Oh, I do?"

"Uh-huh."

"What vibe is that?"

"The stay-away-from-me-or-else vibe."

"Or else *what*? My giant five-foot-four frame makes them run in fear?"

"No one wants to get shut down when they ask out a pretty girl. You *act* closed, you *are* closed," said Sandy. She paused for a second, gesturing to Zoë's shirt and skirt. "But I like this. It's not as…angry."

Zoë took a deep breath and considered her aunt's words. Sandy was right. In the past few days, Zoë didn't *feel* as angry. Or as sad or sorry. Guilty? Yes, of course. But all around, she felt lighter since meeting Paul. In fact, she'd go so far as to say she felt more hopeful too.

"Maybe I don't need that therapist, after all," said Zoë, giving Sandy a small, unsure smile. *Maybe I just need more of Paul.* "Hey, why aren't you at the restaurant?"

"Didn't feel well," said Sandy, looking down.

A shudder went through Zoë and she heard her keys hit the ground. This was how it had started with her mother. Not feeling well. Little did they know cancer had already ravaged one breast, leeched into her lymph nodes and started an assault that couldn't be beaten.

"S-Sandy!" she murmured, her hands cold as ice, fear thick in her voice.

Sandy's face snapped up, eyes wide and surprised. She blinked twice, then—understanding Zoë's expression—shook her head back and forth. "No! Oh, no! No, Zo! Nothing like that!! I'm pregnant! I'm just pregnant."

Zoë's breath came out in a rush and her whole body relaxed to the point of feeling dizzy and limp. "Oh! Oh, God. Oh, geez, you had me scared for a minute."

Sandy took Zoë's hand and rubbed it between hers. "I could see Carly pass over your face like a ghost, Zo. I'm so sorry I told you like that. It didn't even occur to me."

Zoë looked at her aunt's face, realizing for the first time what she had said. She was pregnant! As Zoë caught her breath she started giggling and the giggle turned into all-out laughter as she clasped Sandy's hands, smiling at her aunt.

"Oh, my God! You're having a BABY! That's such great news, Sand!"

Sandy beamed. "You know we been trying, and suddenly my boobs felt really painful last week, and I tell you, Zo, I got scared, thinking of Carly, of what had happened to my sister. So, I went to my doc expecting some really bad news, but my boobs are fine! It's just one of the first symptoms of pregnancy!"

"When?" asked Zoë, glancing at Sandy's still-flat stomach.

"Spring," said Sandy. "And how's this for magic? I'm due on your mom's birthday. April eleventh. How do you like that?"

"I love it," Zoë sighed, smiling with real happiness for her aunt.

"If it's a girl, she'll be Carly. If he's a boy, Charley. Either way, I know this baby's connected to your mom, Zo. I know it."

Zoë felt pretty sure her aunt was right. She felt so happy, she didn't think before she said, "Did you tell Thea last night?"

"I did." Sandy nodded. "She asked about you, you know. Just like always."

Zoë stiffened then leaned down to pick up her keys. "What'd she ask?"

"How you're doing."

"How was..." Zoë gulped, and then raised her eyes to Sandy's. "Brandon?"

"He's good, Zoë. He walks like a normal kid. The prosthetics are amazing."

Zoë highly doubted he walked like a normal kid. Normal kids had legs made out of flesh and bone. Brandon had legs made from carbon fiber.

Sandy placed a gentle hand on her niece's shoulder. "When he's eighteen he can be fitted for a new kind of leg that attaches right into the bone above his knee. You don't have to take it on and off—it's permanent. Isn't that amazing? He's excited for that."

Zoë's heart sank. Most six-year-olds were excited for soccer, carnivals and swimming pools. Her nephew was excited about permanent legs to replace the ones he lost? Zoë shut her eyes, wincing. When she opened them, Sandy was staring at her, that concerned look back on her face.

"You okay, Zo?"

"I love you, Sand. Congratulations on the baby. I'm really, really happy for you and Rob."

She stepped away, heading up the stairs, wishing she could escape her life. Wishing the light moments she spent with Paul as Holly were enough to balance out the deep regret she felt as Zoë.

***

When Holly didn't pick up the second time, Paul put his phone down, furrowing his brows. It was the right number. It was the same number he'd used to text her earlier today. He opened a text box.

Hey Holly. Tried calling, but you're not picking up. Maybe you changed your mind?

He debated whether or not to send the message, and then he quickly pressed send and put his phone down on the cushion next to him. Cleo looked up at him with her big brown eyes.

Why wasn't she picking up? He picked up his phone and scrolled back through their messages. *I'll be waiting.* That was her last message. It wasn't an ambiguous answer. What had happened? She didn't like highway driving. Could she have gotten into an accident? Could something have happened to her?

His hands began to sweat. How would he even know? Maybe he'd just never hear from her again.

That possibility was like a punch in the gut. Sure he'd only known her for a week, and no, he'd never met her in person, but damn it, he liked her. He *really* liked her, and he didn't want for their fledgling relationship to be over. What he wanted—

Cleo yelped and Paul realized that his phone was buzzing and vibrating beside her. He grabbed it, almost dropping it from his slippery hands as he pressed answer and held it up to his ear. "Hello?"

"Paul?"

"Holly?"

"It's me."

It's me. He loved it that she said that. He smiled, relaxing into the swing cushion as he exhaled.

"I thought maybe you'd decided against talking."

"No," she said, and he closed his eyes, listening to her voice. It was soft and gentle, like a summer breeze on your cheek, a brush, a caress. "Not at all. I bumped into my aunt on the way home and she had some good news to share. She's having a baby."

"A baby! Wow! Congratulations, Holly. That's great. A cousin for you."

Holly chuckled lightly. "Yeah, I guess. That hadn't occurred to me yet. A cousin twenty-four years younger than me. Huh. Weird, right?"

"Not at all. Lucky little thing to have an older, wiser

cousin."

"Ha! Older, yes. Wiser…?"He smiled as her voice trailed off. He liked it that she could laugh at herself. "Anyway, sorry if I worried you."

"You did. I admit it," he said. "I was worried some guy saw you sitting alone at Starbucks and made a move on you."

Damn! Damn, damn, damn. Why did he *say* that? It sounded too possessive! They were just getting to know each other. He bit his bottom lip, grimacing, waiting for her response.

"Nope." She chuckled that soft, breathy little laugh again. "I guess I just wasn't putting out the 'I'm available' vibe."

It was on the tip of his tongue to ask *Any reason for that?* but he stopped himself. She was nice enough to let him off the hook, no need to push her.

"Phew!" he said. "Keep that up, Holly."

"We'll see…" she said. "So, Principal Paul, when do you go back to school full time?"

"I have another two weeks of summer break. Then a week of admin work before the kids come back. Although I should probably check in tomorrow; make sure the custodial staff has started their first day of school cleanup. Takes a month or so."

"Hallways buffed to a high shine?"

"Hey, Miss Morgan! Are you a teacher or something?"

"Flannigan."

"What?"

She paused for a second and he wondered if she was

drinking something hot because he could have sworn he heard her hiss and curse softly like she would if she burned her mouth.

"Are you okay?"

"Yeah, I'm fine. It's just—Flannigan is my last name. Morgan was my mother's maiden name. I used it for anonymity. You know…over the internet."

"Ohhhh." It had never occurred to Paul—not for one moment—that Holly was anything but what she'd represented herself to be, her name included. Flannigan was a perfectly nice name, but for a moment Paul felt gypped out of something. Who was Holly Flannigan? He was falling for Holly Morgan, not Holly Flannigan.

Then he shrugged, shaking his head. He was being stupid. She had every right to conceal her identity from internet creeps. It was smart. Not to mention, it didn't matter what her last name was. A rose by any other name would smell as sweet. Holly was still Holly.

"Miss Flannigan."

"The very one."

"It is really, really nice to meet you."

"I bet you say that to all the girls you pick up online."

This time, he was the one who chuckled softly, pulling Cleo on his lap and settling back into the swing, Holly's playful sweetness overtaking him as their conversation hit a steady rhythm.

***

Zoë got up and padded to the kitchen, the phone still attached to her aching, tender ear after two solid hours of talking to Paul. The clock on her microwave read 12:05 a.m. She opened the fridge and took out a bottle of white wine, pouring herself a small glass.

"It's after midnight here," she said. "I'm having a glass of wine."

"You pour yourself a glass. I've drunk a whole pitcher of tea in the past two hours, so I'll be back in a few minutes, okay?"

"Yeah, of course," she said smiling.

She felt her cheeks flush as her thoughts swiftly moved…there. He was going to the bathroom. He was going to open his pants and pull out his—

Zoë swallowed a big gulp of wine, wishing she could divert her thoughts. Instead her mind insisted on its present course, subtly changing the dynamics of the fantasy to include her, sitting on the edge of his bed as he unbuttoned, then unzipped his pants, pulling them down and off his bare feet until he was just wearing boxers in front of her. She'd lean forward and hook her thumbs into the waistband of the shorts, pulling them down slowly so she could—

"Holly?"

"Huh? Yes! I—I mean, yeah, um, I'm here."

"You okay?"

"Mm-hm."

"Tired?"

Turned on.

"A little," she sighed, placing her half-finished wine glass on the coffee table and lying back on her couch, switching ears. "I lit candles in my living room an hour ago so the light's soft and warm in here…and I don't have air conditioning, but I opened the windows and there's a breeze tonight. The air's still misty from the rain earlier and it makes the smell of the sea even stronger. You know that brackish, tangy, saltwater smell?"

"Mmm," he murmured. "I know it well."

"It's heavy tonight. Thick," she whispered.

"Holly." He said her name softly.

"Mmm?"

"I like you a lot."

"I like you too," she whispered, without missing a beat.

"When can you talk again?"

She groaned inside. She knew it was time to hang up. They'd been talking for hours and he thought she was tired. But she wished they didn't have to say goodbye.

"Maybe…later in the week?" she asked, cringing, hating herself for making him wait, but not wanting to seem desperate.

He didn't say anything, but she could hear him breathing and she was pretty sure he didn't like her answer. She almost retracted her words—telling him to call her tomorrow morning, tomorrow afternoon, tomorrow night, whenever he wanted to!—when he responded.

"Tuesday?"

She smiled. "I promise I'll pick up next time."

"Tuesday at ten your time?"

"It's a date," she said softly. "'Night, Principal Paul."

"Sleep tight, Holly Flannigan."

She drew the phone away from her ear and pressed the

red end button quickly, before she was tempted to try to revive their conversation again. Then she sighed, staring at the dancing light of the candles on her ceiling.

It shouldn't be possible to feel like this after a week.

It shouldn't be possible to feel like this about someone you've never met in person.

It shouldn't be possible to feel like this about someone two thousand miles away.

All of these concerns were quietly irrelevant as she let her eyes flutter closed, curling up onto her side, deeply certain of one thing:

It *was* possible, because Zoë was falling for Paul.

CHAPTER 5

As hot August winded its way into chillier September, Paul looked forward to the first day of school with anticipation, excited for fall and the school year ahead.

This time of year was galvanizing for Paul as he reviewed class lists and curriculums, communicated with his teachers about new policies passed down from the Gardiner Board of Education, and took a special interest in finding community volunteers to help with the rich roster of extracurricular activities that had helped to make Gardiner High the most highly rated high school in the state.

But he couldn't deny that his year was different.

He still reviewed the policies, class lists and curriculums, however, his head wasn't as "in the game" as it had been in years past; it was thousands of miles away in the salty-smelling air of late summer Mystic, CT, which captured his attention at all hours of the day.

Without realizing it, Paul had re-structured his life around the moments he "spent" with Holly.

He would wake up in the morning, shower, shave, get dressed, make himself a cup of coffee and take his laptop out to the porch swing where they'd had their first phone conversation. He kept a fleece jacket by the back door and threw it on every morning lately, settling into the swing with

Cleo, and starting his day writing a "Good morning" message to Holly.

They had settled into a routine of sorts: there was a message waiting for him every morning from Holly. Just a short note about what she'd be up to that day or what she was looking forward to tomorrow. She told him about the book she was reading and somehow convinced him to read it too. They talked about how they both went to college in Rhode Island, and she'd tell him about Mystic while he gave her a good education on Yellowstone.

Sometimes, though not often, her spirits dipped. She'd write less than usual or complain about the dog days of late summer. Once or twice she's made a general observation about life not turning out like she expected. Though it sometimes felt out of character—he thought of Holly, by and large, as cheerful and grounded—he liked her all the more for these complicated glimpses into her personality. He liked getting to know the woman behind the beautiful girl. He wanted to know *everything* about her, and he marveled at how open and real she was in their communications.

And, he thought smiling, she always ended on a positive note, making him laugh with a well-written observation or gently poking fun at herself.

Paul would sip his coffee, picturing Mystic as best as he could remember it from the one or two times he'd visited: the cobblestoned streets of the seaside village with an ancient harbor and tall ships. He'd picture her taking walks around the harbor in her white sundress, mentally wishing away the men who'd stop and smile at *his* Holly. Then he'd write back to her, sharing his plans to take a hike in Yellowstone or head up to the Target in Bozeman for start-of-year supplies.

And though he knew that much of their fledgling relationship was based on a certain amount of fantasy, he couldn't deny or explain the growing longing for her, to have her closer, to touch her face and hold her hand and watch the sun turn her blonde hair gold. He'd known Holly for exactly a month, but in that time they'd exchanged almost a hundred emails and texts back and forth and talked on the phone twice a week. Somehow, from ten states away, she'd managed to brush her fingers tenderly across his heart again and again. He felt an emotional intimacy with her that he couldn't, heretofore, recall experiencing with a woman.

But being away from her was starting to distract and frustrate him, the initial excitement of meeting her now tempering itself against the yearning he felt to have her physically close.

Juxtaposed against his feelings were hers, as he perceived them.

The time or two that he'd mentioned a visit before Christmas, Holly had changed the subject or put him off with reminders about how busy the beginning of the school year was for principals and teachers. She was right, of course. There was no way Paul could pick up and leave Gardiner now. But his mind turned often to the Columbus Day break. A weekend plus a Monday and Tuesday, the four days would be enough time to make it to Connecticut and back. While he generally used that weekend to prepare for homecoming activities, surely he could leave those preparations to his excellent faculty, along with a group of student and parent volunteers.

Last night, sitting at the coffee bar of the Prairie Dawn with Maggie, a tourist had taken the seat beside him. The thing about living in Gardiner? You knew everyone who lived there, so a new face stuck out like a sore thumb.

Turned out she was from New York, her name was Jane and she was working on the photo shoot for *Trend* magazine that Lars was handling. After talking about the visiting supermodel, Samara Amaya—who also happened to be Jane's cousin—the conversation had shifted back to what Maggie and Paul had been discussing prior to Jane's arrival: "Miss Mystic," and whether or not Paul should go for a visit.

After Maggie and Paul shared the whole story with a rapt Jane, she turned to Paul with a smile. "You must have liked her a lot out of the gate, to get to know her from so far away, once you realized the distance."

He thought of the picture of Holly, so fresh and lovely at her cousin's wedding. "You could say that."

"*I* could say that?" asked Jane in her deep, Eastern-accented voice. "Look at you. You're a goner."

"I like her," he had confessed softly. "I look forward to her emails and texts. I love talking to her on the phone. We talk about our lives, work, whatever, you know? I tell her everything lately. She's a teacher and I'm a principal so we talk about our students, our families, what we like to do on the weekends. Yeah, I like her."

"You like her *a lot*. Sounds like you're ready for the next step," said Jane. "When're you going to meet her? *In person?*"

"Heck, I'd love to meet her. But, I can't just pick up and go to Connecticut. The school year's just starting. I have commitments here."

Jane took another sip of her warm cinnamon milk then looked up at Paul again.

"You *really* like her?"

Paul nodded.

"Time to visit Connecticut," said Jane definitively.

"You think?"

Jane shrugged. "Don't you have a break coming up? A few days off when you could make a quick trip?"

"Columbus Day's a four-day weekend."

"There you go." She had smiled then wrinkled her brow as if remembering something unpleasant. Her low, throaty voice had a hint of sadness in it when she continued, "Probably best not to invest anymore of yourself until you meet her, you know? Anyway, that's what *I* think."

"Aye, the lass has some good advice, I think." Maggie had winked at Jane.

"May as well put your cards on the table, Paul."

Paul had walked home slowly, mulling over Jane's advice.

He appreciated having fresh eyes on the situation, and he couldn't help but feel Jane had a point. And once he really started thinking about meeting Holly in person, he couldn't get it out of his head. Leave it to a virtual stranger to show Paul something right under his nose: it was time to book a trip to Mystic. It was time to meet Holly in person.

When he got home, he'd logged in to an airline website only to discover that there were available flights that would have him in Hartford by Saturday afternoon of Columbus Day weekend, and home by Tuesday night. He wouldn't miss a minute of school and he had plenty of time to delegate the homecoming preparations. It just felt…right. Right to buy a ticket. Right to go see Holly.

So, he did it. Just like that.

He just hoped she'd be as excited to see him as he was to see her. Settling into his favorite seat, he dialed her number, loving that she picked up right away.

"Paul?"

"Holly."

"It's me."

He smiled, as he always did, at the sound of her voice, at the simple "It's me" that she said every time they reconnected over the phone again.

"How was your day?"

"Summer Sundays are long, aren't they?" she asked. "But the heat's supposed to break on Tuesday. That's not bad. Hey! Tuesday's your first day of school, isn't it? Good tidings all around!"

"It is!" he answered, sort of delighted she was keeping track of his schedule.

"You ready?"

"I was born ready, sugar."

"Sugar?" she exclaimed, giggling for him. It was a more and more familiar sound that he loved even more than the pinging of his phone when he had a message from her.

"Sure. You're sweet. You come from far away. And I bet you taste delicious."

He heard her gaspy intake of breath and his eyes flew open, realizing what he'd said. He wasn't thinking as he spoke, wasn't measuring out the appropriateness of his analogy. But the words were true, and he didn't retract them.

"Paul…" she breathed in a small, unsure voice, stepping back from him emotionally, as she always seemed to when he mentioned wanting to be with her, see her in person, visit her. He knew she was nervous—heck, he was too—but at some point, they had to take the plunge, didn't they? They had to meet in person.

Damn the torpedoes, full speed ahead.

"Christmas is too far away," he blurted out. "I bought a ticket, Holly. I'm coming to Connecticut in October."

***

Panic.

There was no other word for the way Zoë's heart leaped in her chest, doubling speed, while her hand holding the phone turned cold and the other one bunched itself up in a fist. All the safe, familiar warmth of the structure they'd created virtually—daily emails and texts, and a phone call every few days—was upended by his announcement, and despite the sweltering hot evening, she felt a chill go down her spine.

She didn't say anything, getting off the couch and walking to her bathroom where she flicked on the light and looked in the mirror. Taped to the left corner of the mirror was the picture of the "Holly" that Paul loved so much. Her eyes flicked to it and she grimaced.

"Holly? You still there?"

"Um, yeah. Give me a minute, huh?"

Zoë put the phone down beside the sink and stared at herself in the mirror. She'd tried to put in an order for clear contacts to replace her dark brown ones, but her ophthalmologist had insisted she needed two medical evaluations a week apart before a new prescription could be written, advising her it would be better to wait until after her October surgery. Her vision had changed drastically after the accident because of the head wound, and he wasn't comfortable prescribing interim lenses. If she insisted on new ones, they wouldn't be covered under her mediocre health plan, which meant that she was essentially stuck with brown, or wearing her old glasses, until after her October surgery.

She hadn't re-dyed her hair black, and the roots—a good two inches of new growth—were growing out a medium blonde. Zoë knew she needed to do something about it, but to go from black to her natural blonde was going to take several professional salon appointments and she needed to put a little money aside for such an extravagance.

The scar on her face wasn't pretty. And after the surgery in mid-October, it would be raw and seepy for a week or so before starting to heal. By Christmas, her face might start looking as it had pre-accident—with the exception of a thin, white scar she'd have forever— but for now, it still bothered her.

And while eschewing pizza for salads had helped her take off about ten pounds over the past few weeks, she wanted to take off the last fifteen before meeting Paul in person. She'd like to fit back into her old clothes nicely, while right now she was still pretty voluptuous.

Eyes. Hair. Face. Body.

She winced.

There was no way she could pass for Holly right now, which meant there was absolutely no way she could see him so soon. She'd be lucky if she looked like Holly-in-the-picture by Christmas. Christmas was her goal. They had—tacitly, if not out loud—agreed to see each other for Christmas! It wasn't fair of him to suddenly change the rules!

She picked up the phone.

"When are you coming?" she asked directly, her voice grim.

His voice was guarded and uncertain when he answered. "Columbus Day weekend."

Oh, the irony. Her surgery was scheduled for the Wednesday *after* Columbus Day.

"I wish you'd talked to me first," she said softly, unable to keep the chilliness out of her tone.

"I thought—I mean, I *hoped* you'd be happy."

Her heart clenched at the quiet hurt in his voice.

"Look Paul—"

"No, Holly. I need to explain first, okay? Why I did it. Where I'm coming from."

Zoë turned off the light in her bathroom and crossed her dimly lit bedroom to open the window next to a lavender suede bean bag chair. She took a bracing breath of the sea air before plopping onto the pile of mush, wrapping her free arm around her bent knees and holding them against her chest.

"Go ahead."

"Okay." He cleared his throat. "You ready?"

"I don't know," she answered honestly, her voice thready.

She wanted to hear what he had to say. She wanted to hear the words that were coming; the sweet words about what she meant to him and why he wanted to see her. Even though later—after he'd found out the full scope of her deception and never contacted her again—the memory of them would hurt like hell.

"Holly, listen. This last month has been..." he paused before continuing, "well, the best of my life. Getting to know you this way...I mean, I was really skeptical at first, but I feel like I have this direct line into your head, into your heart, without all the subterfuge and mixed messages that come from body language and making assumptions about someone. And you're...I mean, you're the most amazing woman I've ever met, Holly. The way you care about your students, your strength after losing your mom, your loving relationships with your aunt and sister. I love how you look on the sunny side, and you know? I even love it when you don't. I love how you say 'It's me' whenever I call you or you call me. Because, seriously, who else could it be anyway? It *is* you. Lately, it's *always* you. I'm not good at this, but what I'm trying to say—I'm trying to say that even though I've never laid eyes on you in person, I want to, I *need* to, because I'm falling for—"

"Stop!" Zoë gasped, her face flaming hot, her body trembling. "Stop," she whispered again, reaching up to rub her furrowed brow with her free hand.

Zoë had never wanted a human being to finish a sentence so much in her entire life, but she couldn't bear to actually hear him say the words only to retract them later. Which he would when he found out the truth. Of that she was sure.

"This is going too fast," she murmured, realizing he hadn't said another word since she'd interrupted him. "I don't—I don't know if I'm ready, Paul."

"Sweetheart," he said gently, and she felt—actually *felt*—a piece of her heart die at the simple beauty of the single, breathed word. "It's not for five weeks still. And really, you've already met me. Can't you get used to the idea of seeing me? In person?"

Sweetheart. There had never been a sweeter sound, a more welcome, more heartbreaking sound in the entire space of her life. When she died, the last thing she wanted to hear in her head was Paul Johansson's voice breathing *Sweetheart* in her ear once again.

She hitched her shoulder to the side, resting the phone between her ear and shoulder, rubbing her tired, glistening eyes with her fingers. A bead of sweat rolled down her face, plopping onto the swelling top of her breasts like a tear.

"Paul, I love where your heart is, but I don't feel like I deserve all of the wonderful things you just said about me.

I'm a little…overwhelmed. Can you maybe give me a day or two? To think about everything?"

"Holly, please don't hang up yet. Let's talk about it. Let's—"

"I just need to think about it, okay? I'm going to hang up now. You hang up too so I'm not hanging up on you, okay?" She was saying "okay" every other word.

"Okay. But, I meant every word, Holly. I won't take any of them back."

Yes, you will. Someday.

"Good night, Paul," she whispered

She hung up, letting the phone drop to her lap as she hung her head and sobbed.

***

Paul had braced himself for Holly to push back, but he'd never anticipated that she'd stonewall their whole conversation and hang up. He stared at his phone, at Holly's disappearing picture, vanishing as the phone faded to black.

He stood up quickly, scooping up Cleo as the swing pushed back in his wake, whooshing forward a second later to nail him on the backs of his legs. It hurt, which he welcomed; though it hurt a lot less than the fact that Holly hadn't welcomed his visit with open arms. He locked Cleo in the kitchen, put his phone in his back pocket, made his way down the porch steps and around his house, headed into town. He was halfway to the Prairie Dawn before he realized that was his destination.

You have all of this bonnie romantic energy, Maggie had told him.

Maybe *too* much.

Maybe he was pushing Holly too hard, asking for too much too soon.

But, no. No, that couldn't be. She wrote to him every morning and again every afternoon. She texted him when something funny happened in her day or just to tell him that she was thinking of him. They talked for hours and hours on the phone every week, and she never seemed anxious to hang up. He couldn't have misread the signs. She liked him every bit as much as he liked her. He could feel it. He'd place any bet on it.

So, what had he missed?

He hadn't missed her reticence to talk about meeting in person. He'd acknowledged it in his head, but decided to push her anyway, assuming it was just nerves and that she'd have to, eventually, overcome her fears. Apparently, she wasn't ready yet. At all. She couldn't even talk about a visit, let alone welcome it.

"Heya, Principal Paul. Beautiful evening, eh?"

He nodded to a couple taking an evening stroll.

"Principal Paul! Only two more days, sir!"

He high-fived a passing senior who played tight end on the football team.

"Hiiii, Principal Paaaaaaaul," sang a group of four sophomore girls, giggling as he smiled at them.

By the time he reached the Prairie Dawn, he'd run into at least a dozen students and almost as many parents. It was something he loved about Gardiner, knowing his families well enough to greet every parent and student by name, ask about their lives and interests, feel solidly a part of the community around him. A part. Not *apart*, as he had in Kennebunkport, where he couldn't stand the deference shown to his father and family. He didn't want to be a Johansson with the expectations that accompanied his family name. All he'd ever longed for was to be his own person blending in with those around him, without the heavy weight of his family's influence and money asserting itself when he simply said his name. He wanted to choose his own destiny, be his own person, make his own way.

He opened the door of the Prairie Dawn, marveling at the cool breezes circulating around the bookstore and café by the cheerfully-painted overhead fans. Maggie wouldn't need to turn on the A/C until next summer.

The screen door slammed behind him—a sound he recognized from the summer camps of his youth and the Prairie Dawn of his now—and he chose a stool at the copper coffee bar, waiting for Maggie to notice him.

When she turned around, her face brightened. "You're early!"

"Early?"

"For Euchre. With Nils and Jane." She flicked her wrist and looked at her watch. "About forty-five minutes."

Wow. His mind was so occupied with thoughts of Holly, he'd completely forgotten his promise to play cards with Maggie, Nils and their new friend, Jane. The same Jane whose advice last night had propelled Paul toward buying the airline tickets that had been such a disaster on the phone with Holly tonight.

"I totally forgot."

Maggie's eyebrows furrowed. "What's goin' on with you?"

"I bought the plane tickets. For Columbus Day. But..."

"But what?"

"Didn't go over too well. Holly got upset. Just about hung up on me."

Maggie's eyes went wide. "Hung up?"

"She wasn't comfortable," he sighed.

"But you've been talkin' and textin' for weeks."

"I know. I—I tell you, Mags, I'm a little confused. I thought she'd be okay with it. Or at least *open* to it."

"Tell me what she said."

"She told me to stop talking. That things were going too fast and she wasn't ready to meet yet. She asked for a few days to get her head around my visiting. Hung up."

"Well, maybe that's all it is? She needs a wee bit of time? To feel comfortable? You met online. Truly, Paul, you could be...anybody."

"What does that mean?"

Maggie picked up a dishtowel from behind the bar and swiped it across the counter. She pulled out a coffee cup, poured a cup for Paul and slid it over to him.

"I mean, you could say you're Paul Johansson, high school principal, upstandin' member of a small town in Montana. But, in reality you could be anyone. A murderer. An *ax* murderer."

"What? No! No way. We've talked on the phone. I've sent a picture. She *knows* who I am."

"She knows what you want her to know. What you've said. What you've told her. Maybe she just needs a little more time...to be sure she believes you are who you say you are."

"That doesn't make any sense. Why wouldn't I be honest? Why would I lie to her? What would be the point?"

"Not everyone's as good a person as you are, Paul." She smiled at him gently. "Many men aren't as up front, aren't as kind and honest. Give her a day or two as she asks. Let her adjust. She'll think about who you are, who she's come to know, and she'll come around to trustin'. Don't you have enough on your plate anyway with school startin' on Tuesday? For heaven's sake, maybe it's a good time to take a wee break from Holly and give her a little space to figure things out."

She patted his hand and tucked the dishtowel behind the counter, nodding to a table across the room asking for their check. "Summer and Bethany will be here in thirty minutes to take over. We'll talk more then?"

"Sure." He nodded, smiling at her weakly as he mulled over her advice.

Could Maggie be right? Maybe Holly just didn't trust him yet?

He hated the idea, but he had to admit it had merit. Paul wasn't a suspicious person – almost to a fault – and he probably missed a good bit of nuance around him because he was such a straight shooter. If someone said that they were born in such and such a year, in such and such a place, he'd believe them. He'd believe them until they gave him cause not to. It was sort of like: "Guilty until proven innocent." Only with him, it was: "Believed until proven untrustworthy."

He'd stay the course. As up front as they'd been with one another, Holly had no reason not to trust him. She'd come to trust him as completely as he already trusted her. Anyway, they still had five weeks before Columbus Day weekend. He took a bracing sip of coffee, feeling much better. Maggie was right. He'd let her adjust. Trust would come. He was sure of it.

CHAPTER 6

Thank God the next day was Labor Day, otherwise Zoë would have called in sick, because she felt awful. She barely slept more than ten minutes all night long, tossing and turning, trying to figure out what to do about Paul and his impending visit, alternately worried then depressed, but always desperate.

For the first time since meeting Paul, she didn't start her morning by sending him a "Good morning" message.

She simply didn't know what to say.

The bright sun made it impossible to go back to sleep, so she listened to the sounds of morning in suburbia: a sprinkler starting, cars pulling out of driveways, neighbors greeting one another. It all sounded so normal, when the space in Zoë's head felt anything but normal. It felt chaotic. It felt despairing. She wished it was raining and gray to match her mood.

Her plan had been to be "Holly-in-the-picture" again by Christmas, and then tell him all about the crazy way she'd embraced the dark side for a while...the accident, the way she grieved it by drinking too much and getting her two tattoos—one with the date of the accident and the other for Brandon—how she'd changed her appearance and quit her job...only to have him pull her out of the darkness and into his arms, into the light again. She would credit him with helping her find her way back to the part of her that was Holly, he would kiss her passionately, and they'd never be apart again.

That had been her plan, but it wouldn't work now. He had bought an airline ticket to come and see her. And seeing her was the problem—a big problem.

She stared at the bright sun bouncing off the ceiling and frowned as she reviewed her options.

She could tell him she wasn't ready for a visit and put a hitch in the lovely momentum they'd managed to build despite the distance between them.

She could break things off clean, beating him to the punch. It would break his heart, but at least he wouldn't have to suffer through her deception.

She could tell him the truth as she should have long ago. Of course, she'd never hear from him again, which would break *her* heart, but at least she'd have the satisfaction of knowing she'd done the right thing.

The thought of stalling, of putting him off, felt awful. It would kill the excitement between them. And why would he want to invest himself in her anymore if she refused to see him? It would change everything between them, and frankly, what they had was too new and too unique to survive.

But breaking things off clean with him was so upsetting it made her want to throw up.

I won't do it. I won't lose him. I won't push him away and turn my back on him when I lo—

She sucked in a breath, truncating the direction of her

thoughts, blinking her eyes furiously.

You do not love him, Zoë. You've never even seen him in person. More importantly, he's never seen you. Don't bring love into this.

Knocking out her first two ideas only left the last as viable: telling the truth.

She groaned, turning over on her side, tears falling sideways down her face to soak into the pillow, making a wet splotch beneath her cheek.

"I miss you, Mom," she sobbed, feeling sorry for herself.

As much as Sandy had tried to be both aunt *and* mother to Zoë, it just wasn't the same…especially since losing Thea. Her older sister. Her *only* sister.

Oh, God. If Zoë could go back and change one thing in her life, it would be that day. That terrible, terrible day.

She tried to keep the memories away, but they rushed at her, taking advantage of her sad mood, the events of that day unfolding before her like a horror movie.

The strap on her nephew Brandon's car seat was broken.

She'd noticed it right away. She should have called Thea to leave work, go home for the backup car seat and come meet her.

If only she'd made that decision.

If only she could go back in time and make that call.

But she hadn't. Instead, she'd used the regular seatbelt, buckling her small, four-year-old nephew across the lap.

Why? Well, partially because Zoë was in a hurry, but partially because she resented single mom Thea for using her as a taxi service and free babysitting.

It wasn't fair that Thea had had a child, but Zoë, whose work hours more closely matched Brandon's pre-school schedule, was responsible for him after school every day. It was a Friday, and Zoë had been invited to join some of the other young teachers for margaritas down by the harbor. If she could drop her nephew off at the pizzeria with Sandy, she might be able to still meet the girls for the second half of happy hour.

While Zoë usually drove Brandon through neighborhood back roads from his pre-school to Sandy's restaurant or his house, that day she had taken the highway to save time; moreover, she was distracted and annoyed, speeding so she could get to her friends. She didn't realize the driver to her left was in her blind spot. By the time his pickup truck had blared the horn, it was too late. Her much smaller car careened into and bounced off of his. She lost control, spinning across two lanes, into two other cars, before smashing into the guardrail to the far right of the highway. She didn't actually remember hitting the rail.

The last thing she felt was an almost weightless feeling of flying, her entire body lifted away from her seat.

The last thing she heard was Brandon's scream, swallowed up by the high-pitched screech of colliding metal.

"Stop!" she sobbed, clenching her eyes shut tight as she hugged her arms around her body, pushing the memories away with all her might. She pulled her knees up to her chest and ran her fingers down the two-foot scar on her leg—felt the twisted, mangled skin that would never look normal again. For a moment she imagined it throbbed with the memory of hot, jagged steel slicing into her skin.

Almost unbelievably, Zoë and Brandon had survived. But not without lifelong injuries and a cache of nightmarish memories.

She had lost her mother to cancer.

Then, she had lost her sister and her nephew.

She wasn't losing Paul too, damn it.

No. It's not fair!

"Zo? Zoë? You here? Me and Rob are going to a barbecue at the Tapley's later and I was wondering..." Zoë sat up in her bed just as Sandy walked into her bedroom. Her aunt's brows furrowed in concern. "...if you wanted to come with."

Zoë took a ragged breath. "N-No, thanks."

Sandy stepped to the side of Zoë's bed, reaching out to hold her niece's chin in a firm grip. "What's going on?"

"Don't feel well."

"That's obvious. You look like hell. You sick? Your stomach?"

Zoë wrenched her chin away and looked down, shaking her head back and forth slowly, feeling miserable.

Sandy sat down beside her. "Zoë, you're scaring me. Don't scare me in my condition."

Zoë raised her head, and then totally lost it when she saw the compassion and love in Sandy's eyes. She hurtled her body toward her aunt, sobbing against her shoulder like the world was about to end.

"What? Oh, Zoë, honey, what is it?"

"I m-met a g-guy!" she wailed.

"You met—"

She felt Sandy's strong hands on her shoulders, and she was suddenly jerked away from the comforting warmth of her aunt's body.

"*This* is about a guy?" Sandy's eyes were wide, and her lips were pursed. "You're scaring me to death over *a guy*?"

Zoë nodded.

"A really great guy," she protested through sniffles.

Sandy took a deep breath and shook her head. "I'm going to go make a pot of coffee and you're going to get cleaned up. Then you're going to come sit on my back porch in the sunshine and tell me all about it. You hear?"

Zoë managed a small smile and nodded, taking a deep sobbing breath. "Okay."

***

An hour later, Sandy sat across from Zoë, alternately staring at her and shaking her head back and forth. She took a long sip of coffee then set her mug back down on the picnic table, crossing her arms over her chest and facing Zoë again.

"It's a mess. You're right about that."

"I've totally deceived him, Sand. You remember how I looked at your wedding? Wearing that white sundress? Blonde hair. Blue eyes. Twenty-five pounds thinner. No facial and body scars. Art teacher at SB Butler Elementary. I was a totally different person. That's who he's expecting to see when he gets here. Not..." she looked down at her body then back up at her aunt. "...*this*."

Sandy pursed her lips. "If he only fell in love with a

picture, he deserves a letdown. People aren't pictures."

Zoë loved her aunt for defending her, but she knew Paul wouldn't forgive her for deceiving him. If she tried to tell him, he'd hang up on her and no matter how many times she tried calling and texting him, he'd move on. She shuddered to think of his reaction if he actually traveled all the way to Connecticut only to learn the truth.

"He won't see it that way," Zoë said softly. "He'll see that I lied to him."

"But, if you explained…setting up the account so long ago…meeting his friend Maggie…how you kept meaning to tell him, but …but the right moment never came along? He might understand."

Zoë snorted lightly. "Maybe. If I had him tied to a chair and he couldn't leave and was forced to listen to me. But, even then—"

"What did you say?" Sandy uncrossed her arms, sitting forward, at attention.

"Even then, he wouldn't—"

"No. The other part. About him not being able to leave."

"If I had him tied to a chair and he couldn't leave and was forced to listen to me?"

"Yeah. That part." Sandy nodded. "That's your answer."

"Kidnapping him?"

"Not exactly…"

"Then what?"

"You have to go to him."

"Go to him? Let him see me like *this*? Um...is the sun too bright for you? Do you have heatstroke?"

"Listen to me, Miss Smartmouth: if you're face-to-face with him *here*, he can just leave and go home. You have to be face-to-face with him on *his turf* when you tell him the truth. He'll have nowhere to go. You keep saying that if you tell him the truth he'll shut you down, hang up, never write back, right? Or if you tell him in person, he'll just go home. Well, you can't run home if you're already there."

"Sandy! Have you missed *everything* I've said? I don't *look* like Holly. I don't have Holly's job. Holly doesn't have tattoos. Holly isn't *emo*. She doesn't have black hair and dark brown eyes. Holly doesn't have a foot-long scar on her face and a two-foot-long scar on her leg. Holly's a *whole human toddler* thinner."

"First of all, stop talking about Holly and Zoë like you're two separate people. You're freaking me out. You *are* Holly. Last I checked, you're Zoë Holly Flannigan." Sandy shrugged. "Second of all, that stuff doesn't matter."

She could feel her eyes bulging out of her head. "Doesn't matt—Look, Sand. You love me and I appreciate it when you say that you can't see my scars anymore, but that's only because you look at me with love. You compare now to two years ago, and yes, it's better. But I still get looks. I still get questions. I still get assholes like that guy last month at O'Byrne's who make comments under their breath."

"But Paul's not that guy," said Sandy, quietly but firmly, taking another sip of coffee. "You gotta go to Montana, Zo. It's the advice Carly would've given you. I know it."

Zoë smiled sadly and her shoulders drooped in defeat when Sandy said "Cah-ly" because it sounded so much like her mom, it was like she was there with them.

Sandy folded her hands on the table, training her eyes on her niece. "Carly told me to go for Rob. Did you know that? I didn't like him. I thought he was too straight and narrow. Too buttoned up. He'd come to the pizzeria every other week and do the books for Grammy and Pop. An accountant. Woo-hoo! What's more boring than that? Carly said it was the way he looked at me. Always asked me out and always said 'I'll try again next time, Sandy' when I said, 'No way.' Carly said, 'Rob loves you. Rob's always gonna love you, even when you're gray and your boobs sag to your knees and you got three kids giving you wrinkles. Rob's still gonna come home on time and say thanks when you put a hunk of meatloaf in front of him.'

"You know, I didn't even say yes to a date with Rob until after Carly was gone and I was so lonesome for her. I remembered what she said about Rob the next time he came in with white flowers for me and Grammy. I was so sad and he was so nice…I gave him a chance, almost more out of respect for my dead sister than any other reason. And you know what? She was right. She sure was right. Rob's not a rock star, but I'm puking three, four times a day and Rob's telling me I'm beautiful. Now, you listen to me, Zo, 'cause it sounds like my voice, but it's your mom talking here. You gotta go to Montana."

Zoë swallowed uncomfortably, hating the fact that there was a teeny, tiny part of her that loved Sandy's suggestion, that embraced it, that had already decided then and there—without asking Stan for a week off, or buying a ticket, or figuring out how the heck to tell Paul what she needed to say—that she was headed to Montana.

"But the way I look…"

"Just be yourself," said Sandy, reaching over to hold Zoë's hand. "From what it sounds like, he's already in love with you."

"You're a better aunt than I ever was," Zoë whispered, tears springing into her eyes.

"That's not true. You love Brandon. You and Thea and Brandon will find your way back to each other again one day. I know it. And little Carly here knows it too." Sandy rubbed her stomach lovingly then stood up, her palms braced on the table. "Speaking of little Carly, I'm gonna go throw up. Then you're gonna buy a ticket to Montana. And then we're heading to the mall to get you a few new things for your trip before I go in to work."

***

Holly never wrote her good morning email and by noon Paul's heart ached from missing it.

He started to wonder if he'd made a massive mistake in telling Holly he was coming to visit. But he kept circling back to the same thought: he was ready to meet her and his feelings weren't just going to go away. He'd been straight with her from the beginning about not wanting to be pen pals. About wanting to know her on a special level. She hadn't shut things down and had always seemed as into him as he was into her. He was taking Maggie's advice and giving

Holly a little time and he just hoped that she would come around, see things as he did, and trust him to come and visit her.

But what if he had pushed her too far? He suddenly thought, panic sluicing through him like cold water. She lived in Connecticut. It wasn't like he could stop by her house after school and put things right. If she chose, she never had to write to him again. She could change her cell phone number and never look back. And he'd have all his life to regret pushing her when she wasn't ready to see him yet.

He hated feeling regret. He hated feeling helpless. Today was not getting better.

He could smell barbecue grills heating up all over town as he sat on his back swing next to Cleo, forcing himself not to text her or email her or call her. Some Labor Day for him. He'd been invited to many barbecues, but he didn't have the heart to go. Later, he'd check out the fireworks in the park, but mostly just to be sure no high school kids were hiding out behind the school getting drunk or pregnant. The afternoon stretched before him open and endless, his thoughts besieging him no matter how hard he tried to keep them at bay.

"What do you think?" he asked Cleo, who looked up at him and wagged her tail expectantly. "You think I should go to one of those barbecues?"

She stared at him then cocked her little head to the side, as though trying to understand.

"Nah. I'm no good today."

"Just today, huh?"

Paul looked up, surprised to hear Lars's voice, and watched his best friend make his way around the porch and up the stairs.

"Hey, Lars."

"Heya, Paul. Cleo."

Lars pulled up a chair and put his booted feet up on the white porch railing.

"Don't you have about a hundred parents who want to make you a hot dog today?" Lars asked with an easy grin.

Paul shrugged. "Not in the mood."

"Since when?"

"Huh?"

"Man, you're acting weird lately. Going to the movies on a perfectly sunny afternoon, and missing barbecues on purpose. Since when are you not in the mood to go hang out with your students and their families?"

"I'm just not. Can you leave it alone?"

"Sure." Lars looked away from Paul in the direction of Yellowstone. "Want to come to the park? I'm tracking some grizzlies. Mama and cub getting closer and closer to the road."

At the mention of the word "park" Cleo jumped off the swing and put her front paws excitedly on Lars's leg, her tail wagging hopefully.

"Nah," said Paul. "Sorry, Cleo. Not up for it."

"Come on," said Lars, scratching under the little dog's chin and glancing over at Paul. "Cleo's up for it. I could use the company…and some advice."

Paul straightened up a little, distracted by something

other than Holly for the first time all day. Lars Lindstrom didn't ask for advice. He was about the most relaxed, happy-go-lucky person Paul knew. Paul and Lars could spend four hours huddled in their ice-fishing shack on Upper Slide waiting for a bite and never say anything of real importance to one another over the course of a whole afternoon. But Paul loved Lars like a brother, and whatever Lars needed, Paul was only too happy to help.

"What's up?"

"There's this girl…"

"Park girl?"

In the Lindstrom family vernacular, "park girls" were young women who came to Gardiner to hike in the park, looking for adventure and a little romance on the side. Lars—and his brother Erik, before Erik got married and moved away—regularly hooked up with park girls throughout the summer. He never got serious with any of them, of course; they were harmless flings. For years, however, Paul had warned Lars for years that some girl was going to get her heart broken and create a mess. He wondered if that's what had happened.

"No! Well, I mean, she's *here* for the park, but she's not a *park girl*. She's with the, uh—the photo shoot I'm helping with." Lars looked away from Paul, took off his cowboy hat and rubbed the back of his neck with his hand. It was a tell that Paul recognized, cluing him into the somewhat surprising fact that Lars *liked* this girl. "She's a real smart-ass. From New York. She's not the prettiest girl I've ever seen, but I'm—I can't stop thinking about her. There's something about her and I can't get her out of my head. She's all fun and funny and nice one minute, then she gets all cool and professional the next. Hot and cold. I can't tell if she likes me or not. And the voice on this girl, Paul? Shoot. It's like honey. It's like hot…drizzled…honey."

He's talking about Jane, Paul realized, remembering Jane's distinctive throaty voice. *Lars is falling for Jane.*

But he kept this information to himself. He wanted Lars to feel comfortable talking and Lars might clam up if he knew that Paul and Jane had already met.

"You think I understand women?" Paul asked.

Fat chance. I had one hang up on me twelve hours ago.

Lars chuckled. "She's coming out with me tonight. To the fireworks."

"That's good, right? What's the problem?"

"I think I like her," said Lars, staring at Electric Peak, his voice soft but firm. "*Like* like her."

Paul stayed quiet. He felt the gravitas of this admission—when the Lindstroms fell, they fell hard—and Paul sensed there was more to come. Sure enough, he was right.

"I kissed her yesterday," Lars confessed, still looking straight ahead. Paul sensed this wasn't some kiss Lars bestowed on a park girl without thinking. He sensed it meant much more. "I shouldn't have done that."

"Why not?"

"She's a job. She's from New York. She's leaving. I don't want to get attached to her. Hell, I don't know what I'm doing. She's got me all turned around. She's complicated. I don't like complicated."

Paul thought of what he'd give to have Holly in Gardiner tonight, to be able to take her to the fireworks.

Anything. He'd give just about anything. He'd certainly put up with a little complication.

"Don't worry about it," said Paul lightly. "See what happens tonight. Have fun with her. Don't overthink it."

"Yeah?"

Paul shrugged, and just then, he felt his phone vibrate in his pocket. He reached for it, almost afraid to look at the screen.

Are you there? It's me.

"Yeah," he said, looking up at his friend and smiling. Five words. Just five words and all of the burdens of the morning fell from his shoulders, leaving him hopeful that he and Holly would work things out, after all. "You like her. Just have fun."

Lars stood up and put his hat back on his head, looking mollified.

"Sure you don't want to come track some grizzlies?"

"Nah. But, I'll look for you later at the fireworks."

"Don't look too hard. I might not want to be interrupted, if you know what I mean."

"All the more reason to interrupt you then," he said, teasing his friend. "With Erik gone, someone's got to give you some hell."

"Asshole," Lars muttered, giving Paul the finger as he made his way off the porch, back around Paul's house to his truck. "Seeya later."

"Seeya!"

As Lars pulled away, Paul looked back down at the message, anxious to talk to Holly.

I'm here, he typed.

I'm sorry about last night. I'm sorry I hung up.

Can I call you? Can we talk now?

Okay.

He pressed her number and it rang once before she picked up.

"It's me."

"Hey," he said, relieved to hear her voice.

"I'm so sorry—"

"No, don't—it's okay, Holly."

"I was just really surprised."

"Yeah, I sort of got that."

"I thought about it, and you're right. I need to meet you too."

Of all the things Paul had expected her to say, this wasn't one of them. Disbelief, excitement and relief fought for his attention at once. "You do?"

"I do," she said softly. "I just need to get used to the idea, okay?"

"Anything you need, sweetheart."

She paused for a second and he imagined her smiling as wide as he was.

"Paul?"

"Yeah?"

"What you said last night. Before I interrupted you—"

"Yeah."

"I just wanted to say…Me too. I'm falling for you, too."

"Aw, Holly," he murmured, surprised by how hard her words hit him. The most beautiful girl in the world was falling for him. Life just didn't get any sweeter than this.

She hurried on, her voice nervous and a little urgent. "It's important to me that you know that. Really *know* it. Remember I said it and meant it. Don't forget."

"Forget? Sweetheart, I'm going to live on it until I see you in person."

His heart felt so full he thought it would burst right out of his chest. And that'd be okay. Because Holly was falling in love with him, and there was nothing—nothing—better than that in the whole, wide world.

"Holly, I'm…I wish you were here. I don't know what else to say."

"Say you'll call me tomorrow. Tell me all about the first day of school."

"You can't talk any more now?" He wished he could spend all afternoon on the phone with her. Five minutes just wasn't enough.

"I'm actually at a barbecue. Well, in the bathroom talking to you at a barbecue because I was being so quiet and looking so sad, people were asking me if I was okay. I couldn't think about anything else…I—I had to make things right with you. I hated the way we left things."

"I just passed up the chance to go to Yellowstone with Lars because I was in such a bad mood. Knew I'd be terrible company because I couldn't stop thinking about you either," he said and he could hear the laughter in his own voice, taking some small pleasure in knowing that they'd been miserable together.

"Not anymore?"

"Nope. One-eighty. I'm on top of the world, Holly."

She did that light chuckle that he loved so much.

"Stay there," she said, "on top of the world. I'll see you there soon."

"Soon, sweetheart."

"Bye, for now," she whispered.

The line went dead, and he pressed end.

Soon. He counted quickly in his head. Thirty-seven days. Thirty-seven days! It sounded like an eternity, and yet he knew he should be grateful. When he'd woken up this morning, he'd come close to losing hope that they'd be able to work things out. Now here he was *seeing* her in a little over a month!

He smiled, shaking his head and laughing, and Cleo looked up at him like he was losing his mind.

"Cleo, I can't stay here all day with you! I have barbecues to go to, and there's going to be fireworks tonight and tomorrow's the first day of school…and you know Holly, right? She's going to want a full report!"

Cleo barked her support, and Paul jumped off the swing feeling ten feet tall. There wasn't a thing in the world that could rattle his good mood for the rest of today. Holly was falling in love with him and he'd see her sweet face in a mere five weeks.

Westley had finally found his Buttercup and just as he'd

always known: nothing—not a little distance or a very unconventional meeting—could stop the course of true love.

CHAPTER 7

Twelve days and two hours later, Zoë buckled her seatbelt in preparation for landing, tucking her iPad back into her carry-on bag and taking a deep, shaky breath.

She'd be on the ground in Bozeman in about fifteen minutes.

Stan was surprisingly easygoing about Zoë taking a week of vacation, perhaps because she'd promised to work her butt off in the days preceding her trip, and she was as good as her word, pouring all of her nervous energy into finishing all of her outstanding projects.

She'd lost another five pounds—partly because her stomach flip-flopped so much in anticipation of her trip, she could barely eat anything! Sandy had taken her shopping at the mall twice, which had made Zoë uncomfortable at first, but she had to admit that Sandy had a good eye for choosing flattering clothes.

Shifting in her seat as they broke through the clouds, Zoë gasped at the beauty below from her bird's-eye view. She could see a small city and a scattering of suburbs, but the landscape was dominated by mountains and her fingers itched with a longing to try to capture the stunning view on canvas, reminding her of her "cover story."

Until she figured out how to meet and speak to Paul, she'd decided to embrace her creative side and tell anyone who asked that she was an artist from back east visiting Gardiner to do some paintings of the park. She'd even packed a small bag of acrylics, pastels, charcoal and pencils, quality paper with a good nubby texture and her collapsible easel. As long as she was going to be in one of the most beautiful places on earth, she may as well try to capture it.

In all honesty, though, she shouldn't need her "cover story." She wasn't planning to use it for long. She had booked a room at a bed-and-breakfast on Paul's street, and she fully intended to stop by his house tonight to meet him in person and tell him the truth about everything. Sandy had let her practice her speech about fifty times and Zoë was well prepared for her confession.

She was also terrified.

She knew he would be angry.

What worried her the most, though, was rejection.

Over the past two weeks, since Labor Day weekend, her feelings had only deepened. Paul had easily slipped into calling her "Sweetheart," and in Zoë's mind, they were an "official" couple, so much so that when Stan's somewhat eligible son had stopped by the office last week to see his dad and ended up asking Zoë out for coffee, she'd said no. Two months ago, she'd have been delighted that Bruce had noticed her, but now, Zoë's heart was firmly taken by a man she'd never touched, never seen, never even met in person.

A man who very well might turn his back on her in a matter of hours.

He had every right to turn his back on her. Although Zoë tried to force that painful reality from her mind, she'd had to prepare herself, in some small part, for the possibility that Paul wouldn't listen, wouldn't be able to hear her—that he wouldn't want to know her anymore once he understood the breadth of her deception.

It made her stomach flip over with despair when she thought of losing him. After a month of wonderful she could barely stand the thought of returning home to nothing.

"Flight attendants, prepare for arrival."

The landing gear fell into place and her hands gripped the sides of her seat as her heart fluttered. No matter what happened, there was no turning back now.

She had been surprised to learn that there were only two ways to get to Gardiner. There were no buses, trains or other manner of public transportation, so Zoë had been left with the choice of renting a car and driving herself the ninety minutes south on unfamiliar highways, or hiring a car service. While driving on local highways at home was bad enough, Zoë briefly tried to convince herself to drive when she learned that the only Gardiner tour operator that offered round trip airport service was called *Lindstrom & Sons*.

How ironic that her first point of contact in Montana would be one of Paul's best friends.

She'd spoken with an older-sounding man who'd identified himself as Carl Lindstrom, and told her that his son, Nils, would be waiting for her at baggage claim.

Zoë knew who Nils Lindstrom was, of course. Paul had told her all about the Lindstroms in their many phone and email conversations. Nils was the oldest of the four Lindstrom siblings; the older brother of Paul's best friend,

Lars, and Paul's one-time crush, Jenny. Zoë was going to have to be very careful on the drive to Gardiner; she didn't want Nils to sense anything odd in their conversation. She didn't want anyone else to figure out who she was before she had a chance to talk to Paul.

As the plane taxied to the gate, Zoë's heart thumped in her chest, but she pushed her nerves and misgivings to the side, reminding herself of what she knew for certain:

Zoë Holly Flannigan was in love with Paul Johansson.

This was the only way.

***

Paul loved taking a run on Saturday afternoons in the fall. Starting from his house on Stone Street, he would jog south past the high school, around the community park to the Roosevelt Arch, all the way down Park Street to the Yellowstone River, then loop south on Reamer Road into the park a ways before heading north on 89 back home. It didn't take more than forty minutes. Just enough to work up a sweat and do a little thinking.

Invariably his thoughts turned to Holly.

Twenty-five days. Twenty-five more days until he'd board a plane for Hartford, rent a car and drive north to Mystic. Mostly it felt like eternity. He could hardly wait.

As they swapped stories about the first weeks of school, he'd been filled with a sense of emotional completeness, only challenged by his physical longing for her. If he was honest, he'd admit that there were days when the sound of her voice—the sound alone—aroused him. The physical ache was so profound that at least twice he'd taken a cold shower after hanging up, which hadn't really helped anything. His body wouldn't be satisfied until it was holding hers, touching hers, his lips capturing hers for kisses, his hands cupping the soft flesh of her breasts in his hands, flicking his thumb over her nipples until she moaned in pleasure and her eyes rolled back in her head as he thrust into—

A truck honked loudly at Paul and he realized he'd veered off the jogging path into the street. He waved sheepishly, righting his course.

This happened more and more often lately—getting distracted by an intense sexual daydream involving Holly.

And heck, it was uncomfortable to live in such a prolonged, heightened state of unfulfilled longing. Most days he felt like a teenager again, his head creating mind-blowing fantasies that kept him in a perpetual state of arousal. Even when he took care of his urges in the shower, it wasn't long before he was practically aching for her again. Aside from the fact that Paul hadn't had sex in several months—the last interlude being a one-night stand with a "park girl" that Lars had set him up with in June—constantly talking to Holly and thinking about her had become an extended sort of torturous foreplay.

He stopped for a moment at the arch, catching his breath, leaning up against the cool stone in the sunshine.

He had to stop thinking like this.

Realistically, he knew that as much as he hungered for her, they would probably need a little while to get used to each other before he could make a move on her, and October might not afford enough time for that to happen.

Oh, sure, he *fantasized* that they'd rip off each other's clothes at first sight, stumbling through her apartment and falling onto her bed where they'd stay without eating or drinking for four days having epic, nonstop sex until he *had* to drive back up to Hartford to catch his flight home.

He leaned over, putting his hands on his knees and taking a few deep breaths before restarting his run.

You're going to have to control yourself, Paul. You're going to have to take it slow.

He didn't want to scare her. He wanted to do everything right.

It had only occurred to him once that they may not have the physical chemistry in person that matched the emotional chemistry they had over the phone, but Paul had quickly pushed the thought from his mind, convincing himself that their first kiss would be so electric, they wouldn't be able to keep their hands off each other after that. He was already so crazy about Holly—certainly with the idea of her—there was no way that chemistry wouldn't follow.

***

Zoë recognized Nils Lindstrom immediately.

Besides the fact that he held a sign with the name "Zoë F." printed neatly, Paul had recently sent her a photo of himself with the two older Lindstrom brothers posing near the Roosevelt Arch. She forced herself to note him, then look away, as if scanning the arrivals area for her name, then circling back to him, and catching his eyes.

"Zoë?" he asked as she approached him, his eyes

lingering momentarily on her facial scar before holding eye contact.

"Yes."

She smiled at him tentatively, pushing her freshly-dyed black hair behind her ears. She'd started wearing it in a pageboy recently, curled under at the ends and held back with a simple headband. The style was, as Sandy noted: *More preppy, less angry.*

He reached for her bag. "Let me take that for you. Got any more coming?"

She nodded and he led her over to the baggage claim area.

"I have a suitcase and my art kit."

"You an artist?"

Nils's voice was gruff, as Zoë had expected from what she knew of him. She glanced to her left and realized how massive his body was—tall, and almost overwhelmingly muscular. His blond hair was cut short in a military-style buzz cut and he kept his eyes down.

"Mm-hm. I've come to Montana to paint."

"Yellowstone?"

"Hopefully," she said, pointing out her black rolling suitcase. Nils hefted it off the belt like it was made of air, pulling up the handle so it was ready to roll.

"Did you book a tour with us?"

"N-no," she answered. Honestly, she hadn't given much thought to what she'd do during her week in Gardiner. It all depended on how Paul took the news of her identity. There was every chance she'd be back at the airport by tomorrow, flying home in tears. She tried not to think about that. *Stay positive. Stay positive.*

"Well, I got a group going out overnight on Tuesday. Bunch of older ladies. There's space if you want to go."

"Wouldn't I be horning in?"

"It's not a *private* group," he clarified. "If it was, I wouldn't have offered."

He sighed loudly, and for a moment she thought he was annoyed with her until he gestured to the slowing belt.

"Damn it! Not again. You said you had one more bag, right?"

"My art kit," she said forlornly, looking at the empty belt as it grinded to a stop.

"Give me your claim ticket." She fished it out of her purse and without another word he pivoted, pulling her suitcase behind him, headed for the baggage claim help desk.

Zoë plopped down in a nearby chair, trying to steady her racing heart. This was Nils. Nils, Paul's friend. One degree of separation from the man she loved. She had to get a hold of herself. Did she want to go on a tour? Her answer should have been "Of course!" Saying no made no sense when, as far as he was concerned, she was *here* to paint.

Nils returned a moment later.

"It's still in Providence. Didn't even make it to Minneapolis."

"Oh…" Zoë furrowed her eyebrows. "Is there a nearby art store?"

"There's a Target here in Bozeman. Want me to take you there? To buy a few things?"

It was unlikely that Target would have what she needed. She had packed an additional blank sketching notebook in her suitcase. She could surely buy a piece of charcoal or some pencils in Gardiner. As much as she would miss her paints, there was no reason to go out of their way; traveling to Gardiner as an "artist" was mostly just her way of heading off questions about the purpose of her trip, anyway.

"It's okay." She smiled up at his blue eyes, relieved to see warmth behind their icy color. "I can sketch instead."

He nodded, gesturing to the door and she followed him. He sure wasn't a man of many words. Silent as they walked over to a small passenger car that read *Lindstrom & Sons* on the side, he popped the trunk and put her suitcase inside. "Keeping your bag with you?"

She nodded.

"Front or back?"

"Excuse me?"

"You want to sit in the front seat or back seat?"

Wouldn't it be awkward to sit in the back being driven around like Miss Daisy? Anyway, she needed to use the time to get him talking, answer a few questions for her about Gardiner, and, if she was lucky, Paul.

"Front, I guess."

He opened her door, handing her a bottle of water and pouch of trail mix before shutting it.

They rode in silence for a few minutes as he navigated the airport exit. Zoë unscrewed the cap of her water bottle, looking out the window at the mountains as they made their way onto the highway.

"Hey," he said, the way someone does when they have an idea. "I just thought of something. My friend Paul is the principal at the local middle-high, and I bet his art department has a bunch of supplies he could let you borrow. I'll give him a call as soon as we reach Gardiner, okay?"

As soon as Nils said Paul's name, Zoë gasped, and her big gulp of water went down the wrong pipe. She sputtered, trying to keep water from leaking out of her nose.

"Are you all right?" He turned his head away from the road twice, quickly, looking over at her.

"Water went down wrong." She coughed, clearing her throat. "I—uh, well, thank you. You don't think, um, this principal will mind?"

"Paul? Nah. He'll be happy to lend a hand."

"You sure? I don't want to inconvenience anyone." She paused, realizing the opportunity to try to get Nils talking about Paul. "He must be very…kind."

"Oh, sure. It's a small town. Everyone knows everyone. Everyone's willing to give a hand. He's not from here. Paul. He's from back east, like you. You *from* Rhode Island?"

Shoot. She hadn't thought this through—he learned about her city of origin by tracking down her lost bag.

"Near there," she hedged. "Where's he from?"

"Paul? Paul's from Maine." Nils looked over at her briefly. "You ever been to Maine?"

"Many times," she said softly, turning to look out the window.

Paul's from Maine. They weren't remarkable words at all, but hearing someone speak about him so casually, so matter-

124

of-factly, made her heart almost burst with tenderness. Nils had spoken to Paul countless times, touched his arm or shoulder inadvertently, maybe even hugged him at Christmas. Paul—the actual, flesh and blood of him—had never seemed so real. So close and yet so uncertain.

She suddenly felt like crying, whether from relief or fear, she didn't know. Relief because he was so real now, and in a manner of moments, she would see him, maybe touch him, watch his blue eyes flash with understanding...or fury. Her eyes burned with tears and she clenched them shut, hoping Nils wouldn't notice.

"You must be good and tired," he said gently. "We'll be there in about an hour. You just relax now."

"Thank you, Nils," she said, keeping her eyes trained on the river that snaked beside the highway out her window, white water rushing south toward Gardiner where her fate awaited in Paul Johansson's unaware hands.

***

The Mountain View Inn was nothing to write home about, but Zoë reminded herself she wasn't in Gardiner for a vacation. She smiled at the innkeeper who told her that breakfast ended promptly at nine o'clock, then handed Zoë an old-fashioned metal key, pulling the door to her bedroom shut and leaving her in peace.

Zoë looked around her room, her Gardiner home away from home.

The bed was covered in a patchwork quilt and looked plush, if lumpy. A wingback chair sat on an area rug beside a window and a simple bureau had a silk flower arrangement in a vase on top of a crocheted doily. The room smelled faintly musty, but not entirely unpleasant, and while there was no TV or telephone in the room, she'd been told she could use the house phone downstairs. She'd paid a little extra to have a bathroom in her room and was grateful for the privacy. She left her suitcase by the bureau, dropped her carry-on bag on the bed and sat down in the chair by the window.

As they had approached the inn, Nils had pointed to a stone and white clapboard house, saying, "Remember Paul, who I mentioned before? That's his place, there. Used to be a B&B but now it's his. Lives there alone in that big house."

Except for Cleo, Zoë thought, staring at the house until it was out of sight.

She was here. She was actually here and there was nothing left to do but freshen up, go downstairs, walk down the porch steps, and cover the half-block distance to Paul's front door. Her heart beat mercilessly and her hands were icy cold. She leaned her head back against the chair and closed her eyes, feeling miserable. She'd come a long way to tell Paul the truth, but it was almost unbearable to imagine his reaction now that she was here.

He'd been so up front with her—so clear that he was building their relationship based on honesty and trust. There was no way he would be able to hear her words and still have space for her in his life. This entire plan suddenly seemed like a very, very bad idea.

She heard a soft buzzing sound and realized it was coming from her bag. She got up, unzipped the outside pocket to take out the phone then lay back on the bed.

Two texts: one from Sandy, one from Paul.

She clicked on Sandy's first.

Hey, Zo. Let me know you got there safe. And don't get scared. You have to trust what you've built. If he really loves you, he'll recognize Holly in Zoë's face. Whether you call yourself Holly or Zoë, you're still you, and that's who he loves. Good luck.

She took a deep breath, eternally grateful for Sandy's excellent timing and encouraging words. But at the same time, she grimaced.

Trust what you've built.

She shook her head. *I've built a relationship based on lies. That's the problem.*

Looking back down at the phone, her face softened as she touched Paul's name with her fingertip to read his text.

Hey, sweetheart. I guess you're leaving for that conference tonight and I know you won't be able to talk much this week. These state recertification seminars stink. Maybe we could chat tonight? Travel safely and remember how much I care for you. –P

She put the phone down by her side, reviewing the latest in her long list of lies to him. She didn't know how much she'd be able to text him once in Gardiner, so she'd told him she was spending Sunday through Thursday in New Haven, attending a mandatory statewide recertification seminar.

She sat up and hit reply.

I wish I could, but I have dinner with colleagues at

eight. I'll try to text here and there when I can, but let's plan to talk on the phone next week. Until then... –H xoxo

She stared at the screen, waiting for a minute then heard the ping of a new message.

Got it. Text me when you get home. I'll miss you, Holly. But only 25 more days until our visit. Not long now. –P

She stared at the words *Not long now*.

That's for sure, she thought, putting her phone on the bedside table and opening her suitcase to take out some new jeans and a pretty black peasant top that showed just enough skin to make things interesting. She got changed quickly then headed into the bathroom to apply her makeup and brush her hair.

When she was done, she considered her reflection for a moment. Her black bangs dusted the white skin of her forehead and the rest of her hair curled lightly behind a simple black and white plaid hair band. Her scar was pretty well concealed, her eyes were lightly made up and she chose a simple gloss for her naturally rosy lips.

She wore a silver necklace with a single heart charm dangling—a gift from Sandy—that drew her eyes down to her breasts, which swelled appealingly against the curve of the blouse. She put silver bangles on her arm and tucked the shirt into her jeans, which fit like a glove, showing off her curves without making her look fat. She slid her feet into black leather flip-flops that had a simple silver buckle on the thong of each sandal.

Assessing her appearance, she had to admit that while

she wasn't as pretty as Holly-in-the-picture, she didn't look bad either. She looked nothing like the Holly he was expecting to meet in October. Not even a little bit. She just hoped that was okay.

"Time to go," she whispered to herself. "Be brave."

She exited her room, heading off—a bundle of nerves wrapped around a nerve-wracked, heavy heart—to make her confession.

CHAPTER 8

No Holly for a week.

He couldn't help it.

Paul felt disappointed.

He had become accustomed to talking to her several times a day via text and email and on the phone at least once a week. Thursday felt like a long time.

He thought about writing back one more time, but he needed to respect her work schedule and he didn't want to be some clingy, cloying virtual boyfriend who wouldn't give her an inch of space.

He opened the fridge and took out a bottle of cold water, rolling it across his sweaty forehead before taking a long gulp. It was so cold it almost gave him a brain freeze, but tasted so good after his run, he quickly finished the bottle.

Twenty-five days, Paul. That's not much, he thought. *Not even a month. Not even—*

His thoughts were interrupted by the high-pitched squeal of braking tires followed by the sound of frantic yelling. He raced into the living room, looking out the picture window at the road, where he saw a car stopped on an angle, the driver standing beside his car, talking to a disheveled, dark-haired young woman who was holding something brown and shaggy against her chest.

"Oh, my God!" he whispered. *Cleo!* She was holding Cleo.

He sprinted out the door to meet Maurice Evans walking the young woman across the street toward Paul's front porch, his arm around her trembling shoulders.

"Heya, Principal Paul!" Maurice said, worry etched on his wrinkled face as he shepherded the girl up the porch steps. "Cleo came bounding from your front porch into the street. I would a hit her if'n this young gal hadn't jumped in the way and grabbed her!"

Paul's eyes shifted to the "young gal" in question. Her dark head was down, grasping the dazed bundle of shivering dog in her arms. Paul reached out to touch her gently on the arm.

"Hey," he said gently. "You okay?"

She raised her head slowly, keeping her eyes down, staring at his throat until the last possible second when she raised her eyes to his. He heard her breath catch as she gazed at him, no doubt a vestige of the adrenaline rush that had accompanied her rescue of Cleo. Her deep, dark brown eyes riveted on his face, and he wondered for a moment if she was in shock because she stared at him with such a steady, bewildered gaze, fraught with emotion.

"Um…"

"Did you hit your head?" he asked softly, reaching out and touching her black hair. He took the liberty of running his hands over her head, feeling her scalp under his fingers. No warm, sticky blood, no bumps, just the silky softness of her shoulder-length black hair.

"N-no," she murmured, her voice breathy and deep. She finally dropped her eyes back to Cleo, scratching behind the quivering dog's ears.

"Aw, hell, I'm sorry, Paul, but I gotta pick up Mary Beth at the choir rehearsal. She'll raise hell if'n I'm not there on time. You take care of this little gal, now, huh?"

"Of course," he said, staring at her dark, bowed head. "I'll take care of her."

"Sorry for almost runnin' you down, Miss—?"

The young woman looked up at Maurice, blinking at him for a second before blurting out: "Oh. Zoë. I'm Zoë."

"*Miss* Zoë?"

"No. Miss F—" she stopped for a moment, then cleared her throat. "Zoë's, um…fine."

"Well, Miss Fine," said Maurice, "you've got some courage in that there heart of yours. You take care o' her now, Principal."

Maurice tilted his baseball cap at Zoë and made his way back down Paul's porch steps to his car, pulling away a second later.

Paul looked down at Zoë, who was watching Maurice drive away. Looking at her profile, he had a better view of the scar on her face. He'd noticed it when she first looked up at him. It was a long crevice on the right side of her face, maybe eight or ten inches long and slightly discolored. Not fresh, but not too old either. He wondered what had happened to her.

She bent her neck back down, cooing to Cleo who looked happy as hay pressed up against Zoë. Her little tail wagged enthusiastically under Zoë's elbow…which drew his eyes to her chest. It was totally wrong of him to notice her breasts, but her loose, low-cut blouse made it hard to look away. His mouth watered. He forced himself to say something appropriate.

"Were you hurt at all?"

She looked up at him, nodding her head slowly. "I tripped when I caught her and skinned my knee."

He realized how close he was standing to her, literally *in* her space, her elbow brushing against his chest. Why was he standing so close to her? What was the matter with him, crowding her like that? It must have been when he felt her head for blood and bumps. He'd never moved away. He stepped back self-consciously, gesturing to Cleo.

"She looks fine. Want me to take her? And if you want to come in, I can see to your knee."

"Are you okay now, little one?" She asked Cleo, handing the little Yorkie back to Paul.

Paul took her from Zoë and tucked her under his arm where she wiggled in protest, apparently wanting to return to Zoë's soft warmth.

"Thanks for saving her," he said. "She came with the inn."

Geez, what a stupid, nonsensical thing to say.

But Zoë didn't seem confused or curious at all. She just looked up at him, those deep brown pools alert and thoughtful and…familiar.

Wait. Familiar? No. He didn't know any brown-eyed brunettes her age, and yet…

"Have we met?" he asked her, tilting his head to the side.

"Not yet," she answered in that dazed, breathy voice that, frankly, he found a little bit distracting.

"I'm Paul." He held out his hand. "Paul Johansson. Thanks for saving my dog."

"I'm Zoë," she said, taking his hand in hers, "and it was my pleasure."

***

Zoë swallowed uncomfortably, waiting for him to let go of her hand, but he held on to it, staring at her, and she almost started to panic.

Was it possible that with dark hair, dark eyes, a scar and a little extra weight that—somehow, someway—he could still recognize her?

Look away, Zoë.

She knew she should, but she couldn't help staring up at him, drinking him in. He was so beautiful, so dear to her, his hand so strong and warm in hers...she couldn't bear to look away.

He must have been out for one of his late-afternoon weekend runs because his dirty blond hair was wet and spiky from sweat, as though he'd drawn a hand through it, and his face had the rosy flush of exercise under an even tan. His blue eyes, which were greener than she'd anticipated, sparkled with intelligence and compassion, and his angular, chiseled face was so handsome, it just about made her heart stop.

Maggie wasn't entirely accurate in describing his body.

Fit was an understatement. *Cut* was more like it.

"You just, um—you look familiar to me," he said, furrowing his brows together.

"I never—" She cleared her throat. "I've never been to Montana before."

"Tourist, huh?" he asked, withdrawing his hand slowly as he stared down at her.

"Um…" *Tell him who you are!*

But before she could say anything else, he'd pulled away from her, opening the front door for her to follow him inside. She took a deep breath, giving herself a little pep talk about composure, and preceded him into his house.

She chuckled lightly in wonder, standing in his living room—everything was just as he had described it: stairs directly in front of her headed upstairs to the four bedrooms, and to her right was the front parlor with a potbelly stove, a couple of couches, a desk, a fireplace and an open-plan dining area with a table for ten. Just beyond the table she could see the kitchen in the back and the sliding doors that led to the back porch beyond. She knew if she walked out there, she'd find his favorite swing with a view of Electric Peak. It's where he always sat when he wrote to her. He called it "their place."

"Make yourself at home," he said, putting Cleo on the floor. He started up the stairs, calling over his shoulder: "I'll be right back with the first-aid kit."

She tilted her head, watching as he took the stairs two at a time, and listened at the bottom of the stairs as he moved around upstairs, the floorboards creaking pleasantly.

I'm here, she thought to herself. *I'm really here.*

Now that you're here…tell him, said the voice in her head, brooking no argument.

I will, she fired back. *Just let me catch my breath.*

She ran her fingers lightly along the back of the couch as she made her way into the cozy living room, sitting down gingerly on the edge of a rocking chair in front of the stove. Cleo scampered toward her, putting her little paws up on the un-scraped knee of Zoë's scarred leg.

"You wanna come up?" she asked, scooping Cleo into her arms and sitting back as she settled the little dog on her lap. She rocked back and closed her eyes for a second, scratching idly behind Cleo's ears, and inhaling deeply.

His house smelled like wood fires and pine and fresh air. Bacon was fried not too long ago and clean laundry had been recently folded. It was homey and comfortable, a combination of smells she could get used to. Fast.

Her hand was still warm from his touch and she brushed her fingers over her lips lightly until Cleo demanded another ear scratch. Zoë sat up straighter, opened her eyes and grimaced.

He is unbelievably handsome.

He was *much* more handsome in person—his blue eyes quick and concerned, focused and warm up close as they couldn't be in a photo.

He towered over her, his tall, hard-looking body still somehow elegant and she longed to see him with his glasses on. She had worried, at some points during their correspondence, that she wouldn't be attracted to him once she met him, that he would somehow fail to live up to the expectations she'd placed on a couple of photos. She'd had no cause for worry. Her entire body was tingling and pulsing just from being around him, which was making it hard for her to focus, hard to remember the reason she was here in the first place.

You should have told him before coming in the house! You should have gotten it over with, because now——

"I see Cleo's made herself at home! I hope you don't mind?"

She looked up. He'd changed from his workout clothes to worn jeans and a clean white T-shirt. And—*oh, crap!*—he had his glasses on now, which made him not only sexier, but more familiar to her.

Keep your panting tongue in your mouth, Zoë!

"No, she's...fine," she managed, looking down quickly, hoping he didn't see the naked lust on her face.

Holding up a small red pouch bearing a white cross, he gestured to her knee. "Mind if I take a look?"

Without waiting for an answer, he knelt down in front of her, his waved, dirty-blond head bowed over her knee. She rocked forward in her chair, achingly aware of him so close to her, forcing herself not to reach out and run her hands through his hair as he had run his hands through hers on the front porch.

He looked up with a grim face. "I don't think your jeans are salvageable. Mind if I rip them open a little more?"

He had brushed his teeth while upstairs. She could smell the mintiness of it, feel the warmth of his breath on her hand, which still idly patted Cleo. If he leaned forward just a touch his lips would touch her hand. The idea made her moan softly.

"Painful, huh?" he asked, mistaking the small sound for pain.

"Mmm." *Painful, all right.* "You can rip them."

He leaned forward slightly, hooking his index fingers into the frayed, dirty hole over her knee. The pads of his fingers touched her skin as he yanked the fabric roughly, the sound and gesture making her whimper with longing.

"You okay?" he asked, flicking his blue eyes to hers.

"Mm-hm," she murmured, barely able to make a coherent sound with his fingers on her skin. She couldn't ever remember feeling this turned on. Not in her entire life.

"Be brave." He gave her a half smile. "Just another minute, okay? I'll clean it up and bandage it and you'll be all set. Why don't you tell me something about yourself…to get your mind off it."

She cleared her throat, looking up and away from where he had his head bent over her leg so intimately.

"I, um…I'm here to—oh!"

He had dabbed the scrape with alcohol, which burned a little, but she wouldn't have gasped from that. Zoë had withstood far worse pain in her life. No, she gasped because after applying the alcohol, he blew lightly on the cut, his breath cool and hot at once, making goose bumps pop up all over her body.

"Sorry!" he said, leaning back to look at her again with a small, encouraging smile. "Had to disinfect it. I know it stings."

She smiled at him weakly, held captive by his blue eyes that crinkled at the corners.

Why did he have to be this gorgeous? Why couldn't he have misrepresented himself too?

"It's okay."

"So, you're here to…" He blew lightly on her knee again.

"…to paint a little, except—"

"Hey wait!" His head snapped up and he cocked it to the side smiling at her in recognition.

He knows me! Oh, my God, he knows who I am and he's…he's smiling!

They spoke at the same exact time.

She lurched forward in the seat, blurting out her practiced speech: "Just let me say that I never meant to—"

At the same time., Paul said: "You're the artist Nils picked up at the airport!"

"Wait! What?" she asked, taken aback. She was literally a breath away from saying: *Just let me say that I never meant to deceive you*…Instead she stared at him, confused.

"Nils Lindstrom? The guy who picked you up at the airport? He's my friend. He told me you were staying at the Mountain View, just down the street. He sent me a text telling me the airline lost your painting supplies. He asked if I could help you out."

"Oh," she murmured, her shoulders drooping in frustration…and relief. She was grateful for the reprieve, even though it had been the perfect opening. "Yes. They never made it on the plane. They're still in Providence."

"Rhode Island?"

"Uh-huh."

"Hey! How about that! I went to school in Rhode Island! Brown University!"

"Small world," she said, looking back down at Cleo and distracting herself by scratching behind the small dog's ears. The voice in her head insisted it was time to confess. She told the voice in her head to shut the hell up.

"For the record, you're welcome to any art supplies you want," he said with a warm smile. "I will gladly fling open the doors of the art department, and I hope you'll pilfer to your heart's content."

"Oh, I couldn't—"

"I insist," he said, taking the strips off the adhesive of an oversized Band-Aid and smoothing it over her wound.

"As you wish," she said softly.

His head jerked up and he blinked at her, making her think about what she'd just said. *Oh, no!* It was *the* catchphrase from *The Princess Bride*—the movie they'd bonded over. It must have bubbled up from her subconscious.

She chuckled nervously, and after a moment, he grinned back, but it didn't reach his eyes. He was distracted, still smoothing his fingers over the bandage, back and forth across her knee, touching her skin at the edges.

"I—um…I love that movie. *The Princess Bride*," he said softly, looking down at his fingers and jerking them away from her knee. Clumsily gathering the medical kit together, he took a deep breath and sighed. "It's, um…it's my girlfriend's favorite movie too."

He stepped away from her, placing the first-aid kit on the stairs before turning back around. When he did, he looked sheepish, his hands jammed in his pockets like they were being punished.

Oh, my God, Zoë realized, looking at him. *He feels guilty.*

She'd have to dissect that later. For now, she couldn't bear the uncertainty on his face, knowing she was the duel cause.

"Everyone loves *The Princess Bride*," she said, forcing a lightness into the low, breathy voice she'd been using since rescuing Cleo. "It's a great movie."

He nodded solemnly, but kept his distance, standing next to the newel post on the staircase.

Zoë looked down at her knee. "Thanks for bandaging me up."

Her words seemed to break the tension between them, and he ran a hand through his hair. Holding the back of his neck with his palm, he looked at her. Whatever internal struggle he was battling, he decided to overrule it with a warm smile.

"Least I could do. After all, you saved my dog. I mean, I inherited her, but I'd miss her a lot if she was gone."

Zoë placed Cleo on the floor and stood up. She needed to get out of his house. She obviously wasn't ready to tell him the truth yet, which meant she needed to figure out what the heck she was doing.

"Well, I guess I'll…" She gestured to the door, moving

toward it to leave.

"Hey!" he called from behind her. "Do you drink coffee?"

She met his eyes over her shoulder. "Sure."

"Then, let me take you out for a friendly cup of coffee tonight. Just to say thanks. And I'll get you those art supplies tomorrow."

His use of the word "friendly" wasn't lost on her, and she couldn't help but wonder if its use was in reaction to Zoë or out of respect for Holly. She'd think about that later too. On the up side, however, it meant she didn't have to tell him the truth *right* now. With a confirmed date for coffee later, she'd have ample time to regroup and tell him tonight instead.

"I'd like that."

He took his phone out of his back pocket. "It's six now. I'll come by at eight?"

"Eight's great," she said, grinning awkwardly at the rhyme. "I'm at the—"

"Mountain View."

She looked at him quizzically and then remembered. "Nils told you. Right. Very *friendly* town you have here."

If he caught her use of his word, he didn't let on. Instead he grinned back at her. "Wait till you get to the Prairie Dawn."

"The Prairie Dawn?" she asked, even though she knew exactly what it was. Heck, she knew Gardiner so well from his descriptions, she could probably walk there from Paul's house blindfolded.

"My friend Maggie's café. We'll head there for coffee."

She nodded, turning around to face him. She couldn't bear to leave without touching him one more time. *One more time when he doesn't know yet. When he doesn't hate you.* She stuck out her hand.

He glanced down at her hand, then back at her eyes, and for a brief, terrible moment she thought he'd refuse to shake. Then he took a breath and raised his hand, engulfing hers in its strong warmth. She resisted the urge to sink into the contact. How she wanted to close her eyes and step forward against his body, to feel her breasts pressed against his chest, his arms wrapping around her. After a month and a half of virtual foreplay, shaking his hand simply wasn't enough.

"Thanks again, Zoë."

It was the first time she'd ever heard her name—her real name—pass his lips, and her body practically hummed in pleasure. She had to drop her eyes before he saw, before she gave herself away, but couldn't resist squeezing his hand lightly before letting go.

"See you at eight," she said, stepping back and closing his front door behind her.

***

Paul stared at the door, bewildered.

Damn it! Damn, damn, damn it!

He clenched his jaw, turning away from the door, reflexively pulling his phone out of his back pocket to check it, as though Holly—from thousands of miles away—had somehow caught him in the act of being attracted to another woman and written him an email to confront him. Part of him felt relieved to see that there were no messages from her.

What the hell is wrong with you, Paul? What the hell?

She's not even your type. Not even close.

Just in case you'd forgotten? Holly's your type. Sweet, sunny, smiling Holly with blonde hair, blue eyes, a trim body and a tan. Not this girl. Not this black-haired, dark-eyed, ghostly pale girl with a massive scar on her face and tattoos on her back!

She's edgy, he thought, his eyes softening as he thought about her dark eyes under that fringe of black hair.

Wait. He didn't *like* edgy, did he?

No, his brain insisted swapping Holly's face for Zoë's. *No, you do not like edgy. You like sunny. Sunny like Buttercup. Sunny like Jenny. Sunny like Holly.*

He rubbed his forehead, exhaling in an exasperated puff. He didn't realize he'd been holding his breath. He'd probably been holding it since Zoë closed the door behind her. Heading through the kitchen, he grabbed another bottle of water before settling on the back-porch swing. He felt another wave of guilt sitting in his special *Holly* place.

Damn it. Why did you have to invite Zoë out for coffee?

He knew why. He wasn't thinking with his head. When she'd breathed the words "As you wish" in her low voice it was possibly the sexiest thing he'd ever heard in his entire life. His whole body had reacted to the whispered words, blood rushing to places that had no business being excited by Zoë when he was seeing Holly in twenty-five days.

But, it was more than the catchphrase from his favorite

movie. Her voice was so deep and soft and breathy and light; there was something about it that felt familiar, but he couldn't quite place it. Not only that, he'd been shaken up both times he'd touched her hand. A million times he'd shaken the hands of parents and students, other teachers and single women too, and never held on that extra beat—never staring into their eyes like he was attracted, like he was interested. What was it about clasping Zoë's small hand that had felt so right? He shook his head, disgusted with himself. Nothing. That's what. Because he couldn't be interested. He was already taken.

Maybe it was his pent-up lust for Holly that he was projecting onto Zoë. He was so aroused all the time lately, maybe all it took was one unexpected girl on his doorstep and he was transformed into an overeager teenager lusting after a veritable stranger.

This thought comforted him a little bit because it meant that his reaction to Zoë was arbitrary and he placed distance between them in his mind. It had nothing to do with Zoë personally, per se, it was just that Paul was so hot and bothered by the thought of Holly, touching another woman was somehow affecting him. He took a deep breath and sighed in relief.

Hey, it could even be a sort of reverse Florence Nightingale syndrome too…when he'd promised Maurice to look after her, it had felt good. Saying those words had felt good and cleaning up her knee had felt good—helping her, taking care of her. They were the sort of words Westley would say about Buttercup. Speaking of Buttercup, Zoë was *nothing* like his ethereal blonde princess, which definitely meant he *wasn't* attracted to her, right?

Except she had saved Cleo, injuring herself in the process, but never crying or complaining. She had courage, that was for sure. She was *brave* like Buttercup. And she was tender with his little dog, cradling Cleo gently against her amazing breasts.

Amazing. Breasts.

He grinned to himself, remembering Westley's comment as Buttercup held a knife to her own chest, believing he was dead and about to kill herself in sorrow. "There's a shortage of perfect breasts in this world. It would be a pity to damage yours."

Zoë's were perfect too. *What any man wouldn't give to—*

Wait! Stop! He clenched his eyes shut, fisting his hands. *Stop thinking about her breasts! Think about Holly. Sweet Holly.*

He fumbled, grabbing his phone out of his back pocket and clicked on Holly's phone number, then quickly hung up before the call connected. She was out to dinner. *You don't want to be a clingy, cloying boyfriend, remember?* Anyway, he shouldn't need to track down Holly just to convince himself he wasn't interested in Zoë. He was falling hard for Holly, planning to tell her exactly how he felt when he finally saw her in person in a little more than three short weeks.

He stared at Holly's picture on his phone for a moment, wishing for the first time that he had a close-up of her face. She stood at a bit of a distance from the photographer, under a weeping willow tree beside a bush with small white blossoms and suddenly he wondered what she smelled like. Zoë smelled like honeysuckle. He'd smelled it on her skin as he bent over her knee, and recognized it from his childhood—the thick, sweet, heavy scent of summer, of—

Stop thinking about how she smells!

Feeling frantic, he opened a text box.

Sweetheart. I miss you. I can't wait to see you. Twenty-five days. –P

He pressed send then studied the words, feeling better. He scrolled back to the picture of Holly, taking in her hair and her pretty white dress, the pink shoes on her little feet. She was the person he was falling in love with, with whom he wanted to build something real and enduring. Holly. Not Zoë, who he barely knew at all.

He smiled at her sweet picture, feeling centered, and put the phone back in his pocket. Zoë seemed like a really nice person and he was grateful to her for saving his dog. But Paul was already taken by the prettiest, most amazing girl in the world, and no one, including edgy Zoë from Rhode Island with perfect ta-tas, was going to change that.

CHAPTER 9

As Zoë stepped out of the shower her phone buzzed on the bedside table:

Sweetheart. I miss you. I can't wait to see you. Twenty-five days. —P

Envy colored the words green and she actually considered throwing the phone across the room before stopping herself. That would be crazy. That would mean she was jealous of…herself.

Rolling her eyes at the absurdity of the situation, she took a deep breath, backing away from the big pile of crazy in her head, and placed her phone gently back down on the bedside table.

She never, ever should have let things get this far. She should have been up front with him from the beginning. She should have handed him Cleo, put out her hand and said, "My full name's Zoë Holly Flannigan and you've been writing to me for over a month now. I know I don't look like the blonde girl in the white dress, but I promise you that's who I am, and if you'll give me a chance, I'll explain everything and hopefully you'll understand how all of this happened."

Right.

He would have looked her up and down with horrified

realization, called her a liar and slammed the door in her face.

She saw the way he'd backed away from her when he said, "It's my girlfriend's favorite movie too," and she understood his true meaning: he *wasn't* available to her.

Then again, she thought, letting the towel drop provocatively to her waist and staring at her naked breasts in the mirror, he hadn't looked at her like she was a leper either. Her breasts were full and firm, almost perfectly round with deep pink areolas and pink rosebud nipples. Several times she'd caught his eyes flicking to her chest with interest, and he'd certainly held onto her hand longer than he'd needed to, *both* times.

Zoë let the rest of the towel drop, inspecting the rest of her body in the mirror. Her eyes were drawn to the scar on her leg first, but she didn't focus on it. She could see the extra pounds holding on to her frame, especially in the swell of her hips, but she didn't really mind them. They gave her womanly curves that weren't unattractive. She turned slightly, looking at her backside and decided that she'd lost enough weight. She didn't need or want to be skinny Holly anymore.

What would he think of her body? she wondered, tilting her head to the side, as he'd done. Would he ever have a chance to see it?

She certainly hoped so.

Their chemistry had been, in a word, *electric*, and she knew he felt it too or he wouldn't have looked so guilty about Holly.

For Zoë's part, she could never remember being so acutely aware of a man in her entire life. While it was possible her senses were primed from their intense correspondence, the physical attraction could have gone either way in person. There was no mistaking the way it had gone for her. She shivered remembering his smell, his voice, the warmth of his skin, his breath as he blew lightly on her knee.

While she pulled on black panties and a matching black lace bra, a single thought appeared and planted itself in her brain:

Why do you have *to tell him?*

Zoë looked closely at her face, into her own blue eyes, before covering them with contacts, as she let the question bounce around in her head.

Because it's the right thing to do.

She knew it was the right thing to do. Hell, she'd bought a ticket and come all the way to Montana to tell him, to do the right thing. But now that she was here…now that she'd seen him and spoken to him, touched him…the stakes were higher. Infinitely higher. She couldn't bear to lose him now.

But you will. You'll lose him if you tell him.

She put her hands on her hips, taking a deep breath. It was probably true. Paul had always been so honest with her, so forthright. If she told him she'd been lying to him about important parts of her life, he wouldn't hear her. No matter what her reasons. No matter what she said.

What if you gave him a day to get to know you? Just a day, no more. You're off to such a good start. Wouldn't the truth go over better if you weren't some anonymous stranger when you finally told him who you were?

Zoë was in love with Paul.

She'd been intimately connected to his head and heart for weeks now; the only wild card had been whether or not they'd have chemistry. Now that she knew they did, or the real potential for it, at least, her feelings were growing exponentially. She couldn't lose him. She couldn't risk telling him too soon and having him walk away from her.

He cares for you as Holly…if you gave him a chance to get to know Zoë too, and if he liked her, wouldn't he be more likely to give Zoë Holly a chance? Wouldn't it be harder for him to turn his back on you if he liked you both?

It made sense. It would be easy for him to turn his back on Zoë if he didn't know her. But if he got to know her a little and liked her, well…maybe he'd be more apt to give her a chance.

Just don't tell him tonight. Don't rush to tell him the truth only to lose him entirely.

Zoë took another deep breath, the idea gaining traction.

I have every intention of telling him. Just tomorrow, instead of today.

A few hours difference wouldn't matter, would it? And she was sure that those few hours letting him get to know Zoë would soften the blow when she finally admitted she was Holly too.

Tomorrow, she promised herself. *No question. I'll just enjoy him tonight and I'll definitely, definitely tell him tomorrow.*

She hoped she wasn't making a massive mistake, but couldn't help but feel that letting him get to know her a little bit couldn't make matters worse at this point, and maybe, as she had reasoned, it would even help her cause. Plus, truth be told, she just wanted to enjoy him for a few hours. She just wanted to see him hanging out with his friends, sit next to him, walk beside him, get to know him in person without the complication of her real identity.

You mean the betrayal *of your real identity*, one small part of her heart whispered, not letting her entirely off the hook.

"Just one night," she whispered back out loud. "Please. Can't I just have that? Then I'll tell him. I promise."

She smiled at herself in the mirror, tentatively at first, then broader as she thought of his kindness to her, how gently and tenderly he'd cleaned her wound, blowing on it, bandaging it. A shiver of pleasure went down her spine and her eyes softened as she bit her lip lightly with longing.

"Just one night," she whispered again.

She pulled on an ankle-length black column skirt, a plunging light blue tank top and a black cardigan sweater which she pushed up to her elbows. She ran some mousse through her hair until it was slick and sleek, then curled up the ends in a kicky flip and added a pair of black sunglasses as a hair band. She put a silver bangle bracelet around her wrist and the silver heart back around her neck. Slipping her feet back into black flip-flops, she surveyed herself in the mirror. Not bad. Not bad at all. She adjusted the top of the tank top a little, until the swell of her cleavage showed off her assets without being slutty. If she was going to keep deceiving him for one more night, she may as well make the most of it.

"One night. Make it count," she whispered to herself, thinking of how much was at stake. She placed a cool hand over the warm skin atop her thumping heart, feeling the strength of the beat, trying to convince herself that she could navigate this unchartered territory.

You must, she thought. *You can't lose him.*

Nodding to her reflection with finality, she set about doing her makeup as carefully as possible, then grabbed her old-fashioned metal key and headed downstairs to wait for Paul.

***

He groaned softly when he saw her on the porch swing.

It's not like he could have asked her to wear a poncho for their coffee date, but she wasn't making things easy on him. She was wearing some form-fitting blue top that outlined her perfect chest, creating a tempting swell of soft, creamy skin that made his fingers twitch.

Did she have to look so good? So edgy and urban and put together? She looked like a Bostonian or New Yorker, and something inside of Paul responded to her look after years of seeing women in cowboy hats and western boots. She looked like she was ready for a late summer stroll in downtown Cambridge or Greenwich Village, and Paul sort of loved the familiarity of this strange, intriguing visitor.

He had promised himself not to look at her body at all, only her face, but this plan wasn't exactly helping him to feel less attracted to her. Looking at her deep dark brown eyes was just as captivating as looking at her perfect chest. Those eyes seemed to beckon him as she stood up from the front porch swing at the Mountain View Inn, wide and vulnerable eyes, drawing him in, her lips turning up slightly in a tentative smile.

"Hey, Zoë," he called from the foot of the stairs, determined to keep their outing light and friendly, despite the effect she had on him. "Ready for coffee?"

When she took a step toward him, he realized that she favored her left leg pretty significantly. Had she hurt herself today? More than a skinned knee?

"How's the leg?" he asked, feeling worried about her, looking up to meet her eyes.

He saw something troubled, but vague, pass over her face as she shrugged. "It's fine. Just a little skinned."

Had he imagined the instability in her balance as she stood up? He barely noticed it as she approached him, but it didn't stop him from instinctively offering her his hand as she reached the top of the stairs. She seemed surprised, but pleased, and slipped her hand into his, letting him help her down the stairs.

"I love the weather here," she said in her low, sexy voice once she was standing before him. "So nice and cool."

He felt it again, that feeling of recognition, of knowing her, of familiarity. She was so much smaller than he—maybe five-foot-four inches to his six-two. Not much bigger than Holly, he thought, although Zoë was a good bit sturdier than his slim, willowy girlfriend.

His attention was drawn to the scar that ran from the

bangs over her right eyebrow down the side of her face, luckily skirting her eye. What had happened to her?

He looked up at a passing gray cloud. "Could get a shower."

"This is my favorite weather," she said. "It must be my Irish blood. Give me rainy and cool any day. I hate the heat."

"It's getting cooler and cooler now. I bet we get a freeze soon." He could smell that honeysuckle scent she wore, and imagined her rubbing oil on her skin that diffused as it warmed with her body heat. God, it was distracting.

"A freeze! We're still a month or so away from a freeze at home. Come Halloween, maybe."

When had they started walking? Suddenly they'd walked a quarter of a block and Paul realized he was still holding her hand. He glanced down at her dark head. Did she notice it too?

A sharp twinge of guilt assaulted him as he thought of Holly and he loosened his fingers gently, dropping her hand to adjust his glasses, then shoving his hands in his pockets. He had no business holding her hand, no matter how unintentional it was or natural it felt.

"Halloween's pretty cold here," he offered. "Won't get much above forty degrees by then."

She had her hands clasped behind her back and her skirt undulated as she walked, as black as her hair.

She reminded him of the girl in the old Kurt Vonnegut story "Miss Temptation," in which a bit actress, Susanna from New York, rents an apartment in a small New England town for a summer stock play. Vonnegut described her as having black hair, midnight eyes, creamy skin, and noted that she was always barefooted. She wears low-cut tops and undulating skirts and anklets with little bells that tingle with every step she takes, announcing her arrival. The villagers in the story can't get used to her exotic presence in their quiet, humdrum midst. They can't assimilate her strange, unconventional beauty to the ordinariness of their everyday lives.

Finally one of the men in town—a young man, bitter and overcome with longing for her—confronts her.

"There ought to be a law about girls acting and dressing the way you do," he says. "It makes more people unhappy than it does happy. You know what I want to say to you, for going around making everyone want to kiss you?"

"No," the girl in the story answers, and Paul always imagined her face would look shattered and shocked by the unkind assault.

"I say to you what you'd say to me if I was to try and kiss you: The hell with you!"

Paul had always sympathized with Susanna when he read the story, the unwitting victim of an unfair attack. What right did anyone have to make her feel bad because she was so beguiling?

For the first time, however, Paul related better to the young man, and it bothered him quite a bit.

"Are you always so quiet?" asked Zoë, interrupting his thoughts. He looked up as they passed Third Street, headed toward the Yellowstone River.

"No," he said. "I'm not. Sorry. I was just thinking about

a short story I read a long time ago."

"Which one?" she asked, glancing up at him. "I love short stories. Maybe I know it."

"An old Kurt Vonnegut story."

"Hmm. From *Welcome to the Monkey House*?"

"Yeah! In fact, it is," he said, surprised she'd guessed the collection of stories so easily.

"My copy's so dog-eared now, I finally bought it on my Kindle. I read it cover to cover at least once a year."

"Which one's your favorite?"

"Oh, no," she mumbled in her distracting, breathy voice. When he looked down at her, she was biting back a smile. "You go first."

"I won't tell you mine until you tell me yours."

She chuckled. "Hard ball. Okay. My favorite's 'The Long Walk to Forever.'"

The thing is? Paul loved "Miss Temptation" but "The Long Walk to Forever" was—hands down—his favorite story too.

He sucked in a deep breath. He barely knew this woman. Why did it feel so intense, so complicated, just to walk along next to her?

"Mine too," he admitted.

"No! Really?"

He nodded. "Vonnegut called it a 'sickeningly slick love story.'"

"I know. It's in the preface. But it was a true story. He actually spent that afternoon with his wife."

"Hey! You really did read it cover to cover."

"Sure. Why would I lie?" Instead of letting him answer her question, she quickly asked another. "So that's the story you were thinking about? As we're walking? Should I read into that?"

He knew she was teasing, but he couldn't help the way his heart skipped a beat at her question.

"No!" he exclaimed, guilt and surprise making him answer too quickly and too harshly. "No way! Not at all! No. I have a girlfriend. I wasn't even thinking about *that* story. I was thinking about a different one."

"I was just...teasing," she said quietly, crossing her arms over her chest.

Her voice was small and hurt and he felt like a spaz, like an ass, like he'd just said: *"To hell with you!"* like the bitter young man, full of painful longing, in *Miss Temptation*.

"Sorry," said Paul, nudging her gently with his elbow. "Me and Holly? It's a weird situation. I guess I'm a little...I don't know...out of sorts over it."

"Would it help to talk about it?"

Paul shrugged. "Maybe."

She pointed ahead to a wooden gazebo situated adjacent to a restaurant across the street. "You think they'd mind if we sat there for a bit?"

"Nah. But, I mean...you're here to paint or be on vacation and so far, you've rescued my dog, almost been hit by a car, skinned your knee and been roped into coffee with a grouchy local. Doesn't sound like a very fair deal to you."

"I guess it's up to me what a fair deal looks like, huh?"

He stared at her upturned face, that feeling of knowing

her infusing his whole body. Could he have met her while he was at school in Rhode Island? Did she summer in Newport? Have a job there at some point? Why did he feel like he *knew* her?

"Who are you?" he breathed, the words falling out of his mouth before he had a moment to review them.

She held his eyes, standing beside him on the corner of the street as they waited to cross. Her whole body seemed to tense up for a moment before relaxing.

"I'm Zoë," she said.

"Just Zoë?"

"Zoë's fine," she muttered softly.

"Fine. That's right. Zoë Fine."

"Hey," she continued, anxious to steer him away from the subject of her name, "you never told me. What story you were thinking about? When you were so quiet before?"

Before he could stop himself, his gaze dropped from her eyes to her lips, to her breasts, where they lingered before he forced his eyes to slide back up her face. He felt the flush of heat on his cheeks as he stared at her, noticed a blush of color on hers too.

"'Miss Temptation,'" he whispered.

***

Zoë stared up at him, feeling her eyes widen in surprise.

"Oh!" she gasped, looking down quickly, her cheeks aflame with awareness, with arousal.

"Miss Temptation." Wow.

Zoë knew the story well.

It was the ultimate *turned-on/can't-have* fantasy, especially because it ended with an ambiguous fate. The young man apologizes to Susanna, who, after some honesty about her hurt feelings, forgives him and allows him to take her out on a date.

Zoë's pulse sped up as she realized that Paul had thought of the story while walking with her, wondering if she reminded him of Susanna, the dark-haired temptress. She furrowed her brows. *No. It couldn't be.* He had just made a show of telling her he had a girlfriend.

When she glanced up at him, she caught the flexing of his jaw, something she might do if she were frustrated or angry with herself.

Suddenly, she heard the crack of thunder. The light changed suddenly from dusky lavender to yellow.

He took her hand as the sky split open with rain, pulling her across the street to the wooden gazebo that sat at the edge of a restaurant parking lot, overlooking the Yellowstone River.

Safely under cover, she looked down at their joined hands in the half-light of the small gazebo. There were blond hairs peppering the masculine contours of his; she could feel them under her fingertips. She longed to bring his hand to her lips, to press them against those wiry blond hairs, to lay her cheek upon them and tell him everything.

Instead, she wiggled her hand away and sat down on the bench that followed the curve of the small, round, open-air shelter. The rain intensified, pattering on the roof over their heads, making the river below them rush a little louder.

Paul ran his hands through his wet hair, wiped them on

his jeans and sat down a respectable distance from her.

"They take a walk at the end of that story, too," she observed, flicking a glance at him. "The girl and the man who yelled at her."

He'd been looking at the floor, but he raised his head, his blue eyes piercing and troubled. "What's your story?"

"What do you mean?" she asked.

"Why are you here? In Gardiner?"

"Vacation. To paint." She looked down at her lap. She owed him something more. A little bit of the truth. "To see someone."

"A friend?"

She shrugged.

"A man?" he pressed.

"Mm-hm."

"Who?" His eyes narrowed just a fraction.

"It's complicated," she said, a note of warning in her voice as she turned away. "Tell me about this girl who's got you in knots."

He clenched his jaw again, then relaxed, settling against the gazebo railing and looking straight ahead, away from Zoë.

"Holly," he whispered reverently.

The acutely surreal nature of the moment wasn't lost on her. He was about to talk to her about...herself.

"Okay. So, what's the story with Holly?"

The sky thundered another warning and the rain switched from steady pattering to loud pouring. Paul slid closer to Zoë on the seat, until he was only a few inches away. She knew it was probably for the sake of their conversation—so that he could hear her better under the rainfall—but she teased herself for a moment that he wanted to be closer to her too. His hand rested on the bench beside her thigh, distracting her.

"Let's see…Holly. She's beautiful. She has long blonde hair and blue eyes. She's petite and slim and stunning. The sunniest girl I've ever seen."

Zoë bit her lip and looked away from him, her heart dropping with a painful thud as he described the way Zoë *used* to look. She'd known that her looks were important to him, but hearing the reverence in his voice as he talked about her picture made her realize how very far she was from where she used to be. She propped her bent elbow on the railing behind her and supported her head with her hand, grateful for the rain, for the way it mirrored the deep sorrow that was taking over, the feeling of overwhelming defeat.

"I mean…I think."

"You think?" she asked.

"Yeah. I've only seen one picture of her."

"Oh?" Her voice, which she'd carefully modulated at a breathier version of itself, didn't need any help in sounding thin and thready.

"Mmm. I met her online."

"Huh."

"You don't think that's weird?"

"Lots of people meet online," she answered dismissively. "But it's the perfect place to catfish someone. How can you be sure she's been honest with you?"

"I just know. We agreed to build our, um, relationship on trust. I know her. I mean, I really, really *know* her. My heart knows her heart." He paused for a second, moving his elbows to the railing and leaning back a little bit, relaxing into the subject of his nonexistent dream girl. "Truth?"

"Yes, please."

He glanced askance, grinning at Zoë. "It's just gravy that she's so beautiful. It doesn't really matter to me. She's funny and smart. She teaches art to kids and she loves the same movies I do. We talk about books and our jobs and our families and what we want from life. She's kind and surprising and amazing, and she loves deeply."

"You?" Zoë asked. When he didn't answer, she clarified her question: "Does she love you?"

"God, I hope so," he murmured low and quick.

She winced at his words, at the intensity of them, the way he said them without having to think. And the irony of his hopes, which she could have confirmed beyond any shadow of doubt right then, right there.

Tears burned her eyes as her lids slowly lowered at the bitter sweetness of his words. She trembled and felt her lungs working to keep her breathing steady, not to give herself away. Here was the man she loved, telling her he hoped she loved him, and she was helpless to say anything in return.

"I still haven't met her in person yet. That worries me sometimes," he confessed. "She's on a pretty high pedestal in my head and I just hope—"

"What?"

"I just hope she's everything I—I mean, I hope we, um…*click*. On a, um, *personal* level. You know?"

Oh, she knew. She'd feared the same thing until she'd met him in person today, when those particular fears were assuaged tenfold. Just looking at him made her fingers long to touch him again. God, if they ever actually got the chance to *click*, they'd—

"You'll click," said Zoë quickly.

"Yeah? You think so?"

"You're crazy about each other. You'll click."

He turned to her, cocking his head to the side, and smiling gently. "Hey…how do you know she's crazy about me?"

"I just—I mean, how could she—" Zoë took a deep breath, looking from his bright blue eyes to the river below them. "Rain's stopping."

"Yeah. I guess it is."

He stood up. She brushed her eyes with the backs of her hands before looking up at him, but they still glistened, and he noticed when their gazes met. His eyes softened with gentle concern.

"You look sad. Are you okay?"

She sniffled once and gave him a small smile. "It's nice to see someone so happy."

"Are you…*un*happy?"

"I'm—I'm not…I'm just not as happy as you," she finished lamely.

"He's unkind to you? The guy you're here to see?"

"No! Not…not exactly," she said softly, looking down.

"Doesn't he see what he has in you?"

"I haven't been honest with him."

"Well, you can fix that, can't you? Tell him the truth about—whatever's bothering you?"

"I wish it were that simple," she said, standing up and crossing her arms over her chest.

"I'm a good judge of character, Zoë. You're a good person. You saved my dog, which means you're brave. You're kind and patient, listening to me yammer on. You're a good listener." He put his hand on her elbow, turning her slightly to face him. "And you're very pretty."

She couldn't help the smile that spread slowly across her face as he stared at her, his warm bluish-green eyes holding hers, the heat of his hand on her skin.

"He's an idiot if he doesn't figure it out soon."

She scoffed, shaking her head at the sheer absurdity of the moment then tilted her head to the side, searching his face. All she could think—*all* she could feel—was:

He loves me. He loves me as much as I love him.

She uncrossed her arms and reached one hand up to his cheek, letting her fingertips lightly, tentatively graze his skin before palming the side of his face, her skin resting flush against his.

"Thank you," she whispered.

He looked surprised at first, but then his smile faded as he glanced quickly from her eyes to her lips, where they lingered for a moment before returning to her eyes. She stepped forward, one small step, until her breasts brushed against his chest and she heard his breath catch. She stared at his lips, and then flicked her eyes back up to his. His chest rose and fell into hers with the force of his breathing. His brows furrowed in confusion, then realization. Suddenly he stepped back from her and turned, facing away.

"We could get that coffee now," he said tightly, under his breath.

Zoë dropped her hand from his face.

Oh, my God.

She'd been about to kiss him.

If he'd just dipped his head the smallest bit, his lips would have landed on hers. Her heart beat wildly as she stared at his back, her breathing as labored as his.

She couldn't do this anymore. She couldn't keep up this charade. She had to tell him, just tell him and whatever happened, happened.

"Paul, I need to—"

"No, listen." He turned around, one hand up, halting her words. "It's not your fault. It was just an intense moment. Talking about relationships and everything…and anyway nothing happened. Don't apologize."

"I wasn't going to apologize. There's something I need to say—"

"It's okay. Really. I mean it, Zoë. We're both just, you know, figuring out our way with the special people in our lives. Sharing matters of the heart and feelings and—well, like I said, nothing happened, okay? Let's forget about it."

Her shoulders sagged as her courage retreated.

"I promised you coffee, Miss Fine, and I aim to deliver."

He grinned at her, gesturing to the archway of the little gazebo, and she forced her feet to move, one in front of the other, back out onto the gleaming sidewalk.

CHAPTER 10

"So, you're going to meet my friend Maggie, who owns the Prairie Dawn, and probably Lars Lindstrom. He's a brother of Nils, who picked you up at the airport today, and his girlfriend Jane will probably be there too."

"Will Nils be there?" asked Zoë.

There was no earthly reason why her question should bother him, but he'd be lying if he said it didn't.

Damn it, he'd been close to *kissing* her a few minutes ago. When she'd touched his cheek and stepped toward him, it was all he could do not to pull her into his arms and slam his mouth down over hers. Anything to relieve the longing he felt.

It was only because they'd been talking about Holly and his feelings for her, right? Just for a moment, his feelings for Holly and the closeness of Zoë must have gotten mixed up in his head. Thank God he had stopped himself before he did something he really regretted. It had nothing to do with Zoë. Nothing. It couldn't.

Except. It *could*.

Because he couldn't deny that he'd been attracted to Zoë from the moment she'd raised her dark eyes to his, holding Cleo on his front porch. And the more time he spent with her, the more he felt drawn to her, like he knew her, like she already meant something to him, even though he barely knew her at all. Something was happening to him, and if he was honest, he'd admit that it wasn't just because of churning up all of his feelings for Holly. It was her. *Zoë.* Something about *her.* She was getting under his skin. When he'd seen the profound sadness in her eyes, it had been like a punch to the gut. He hated seeing it. And he wondered again—what in the world had happened to this girl?

Why was her face scarred? And why did they guy she was meeting not value her? Is that why she was so sad?

For years he'd watched the Lindstrom brothers, ready and willing to beat up anyone who dared to look at one of their women cross-eyed, and for the first time, he understood that protective feeling on a visceral level. Who was this guy? He deserved a beating and good. And Paul sure wouldn't mind being the one to give it to him.

Testosterone-fueled revenge fantasies aside, however, he knew it wasn't his fight. He needed to stay away from Zoë. He needed to give her the art supplies tomorrow and not see her again after that. He'd made a commitment to Holly, spoken or unspoken, and he was a man who honored his commitments; a man who didn't break a woman's heart.

He felt better as he resolved to stay away from Zoë. He'd have coffee with her tonight. A friendly cup of coffee, surrounded by his friends. Then he'd walk her home, get her the art supplies in the morning, and that would be an end to this little flirtation. He'd go see Holly in twenty-five days, as planned, with a clear conscience and an open heart.

"Paul?" she prompted.

What had she asked? Nils. She wanted to know if Nils would be there. Was she interested in Nils? Damn Nils, anyway.

"No," he said roughly. "Is that okay with you?"

"Um. Sure."

"Sorry for snapping."

"I thought you were friends."

"We *are* friends."

"Are you mad at him?"

"I'm not mad at him. He and Maggie have a *thing*. Just so you know. He's not available."

"I didn't *ask* if he was available."

"I know you didn't. I'm just saying—"

"Did you miss the part back there where I said I was in the middle of something complicated too? I assure you I'm not looking for—"

He put his hand on her arm, making her stop walking, and turning her to face him.

"I'm sorry," he said, looking at her face, feeling helpless. The next words came tumbling out roughly, troubled, a remnant of his stream of consciousness. "I like you."

Zoë looked surprised at first, and then he watched her face soften, her pink, glossy lips tilting up at the corners in pleasure. "I like you, too."

He knew he was sending her wildly mixed messages. Best to just clarify everything once and for all.

"But I'm *with* Holly."

"I understand." Her smile faded until her face was expressionless, and her glance darted to the hand that still held her arm. "Maybe you should let go of my arm."

"Sorry," he said again, jerking his hand back. "I'm a disaster. Bet you're wishing you'd said no to coffee, huh?"

"No. Not at all," she said, gently. "I don't know anyone in this town. It would have been a lonely first night. Instead I have someone to talk to, and take a walk with…and I even get to go for coffee and meet some of his friends. And he's getting me art supplies in the morning. It's not such a bad deal for me."

Her graciousness made him feel even worse, even as it made his heart continue to soften toward her, this strange, dark, sad girl. He took a deep breath and sighed.

***

With Paul's hand on the small of her back, Zoë stepped into the Prairie Dawn, her lips tilting up in a smile as the place of her dreams materialized before her in the space of one step.

It was a large open-plan room with rustic wooden columns at intervals and brightly colored throw rugs covering parts of the scuffed wooden floor. Bookcases and windows lined the walls from floor to ceiling to Zoë's right with brightly upholstered seat cushions under every window. Several overstuffed chairs and a few mismatched wingback chairs dotted the landscape of the room and several bistro tables tiled with small pieces of mosaic glass offered cheery places to share a cup of coffee with a friend. Finally, to her left she saw the small copper coffee bar where Paul had first seen her picture.

Zoë sighed in pleasure, glancing up at Paul, whose eyes were fixed on Zoë like he couldn't look away, like watching her reaction to the Prairie Dawn was the moment on which the fate of the world rested.

"Paul!"

He turned from her toward a voice in the back of the café, and Zoë followed his glance to a table populated with four people: a large blond man who pulled a wingback chair up to the table, held a curly-haired woman on his lap. Lars and Jane, check. Jane had her head resting on Lars's shoulder when they had arrived, but now she looked up, eyes warming as she waved at Paul.

Another woman, with strawberry-blonde hair in two braids, stood up and waved them over, putting her hand on the shoulder of another man—also redheaded—seated beside her. From Paul's description, she knew the woman was Maggie, and she was pretty sure the younger redhead was Maggie's visiting cousin, Graham.

Zoë knew full and well that Maggie had seen a close-up face shot of her before she had taken it off MeetTheOne, and she prayed that with her darker hair and dark eyes Maggie wouldn't know her. Her pulse leaped into a gallop as the moment of truth neared. Paul moved easily through the maze of tables and chairs and Zoë took a deep breath, following at a close distance behind him with her head down.

They stopped beside the table and Zoë raised her head, her dark eyes smacking into Maggie's green ones right away.

Maggie blinked twice, her face segueing from friendly openness to mild confusion in an instant. Zoë could see the question *Where do I know you from?* flit across Maggie's face as

Maggie tilted her head to the side, staring openly at Zoë.

"Who's this?" asked Jane in her smoky voice, shifting on Lars's lap to extend her hand to Zoë.

"This is Zoë," said Paul, looking over at Zoë and smiling. "She saved Cleo from the front wheel of Maurice Evan's Chevy this afternoon."

Zoë took Jane's hand, smiling uneasily, worried about Maggie.

"I'm Jane. This is Lars." Jane nodded to the blond god holding her around the waist.

"Heya, Zoë," he said, letting go of Jane only long enough to shake Zoë's hand.

"You look like your brother," said Zoë, smiling back at Lars with a little more confidence. Maggie hadn't said anything yet, but Zoë was still stalling on their formal introduction.

"Which one?" asked Lars, quirking a brow at her.

Jane slapped his chest lightly. "How would Zoë know Erik?" She turned back to Zoë. "Do you know Erik?"

"No. Not that I know of."

"See?" She winked at Zoë. "She means Nils."

"He picked me up at the—"

"You're the artist," said Lars, his eyes brightening with recognition.

"Wow." Zoë peeked up at Paul, smiling. "This *is* a small town."

"We're all in each other's business," said Maggie. "That's just what we do."

Zoë's smile faltered, but she took a deep breath and

reapplied it, turning to Maggie. "I think that's nice."

"Do you, now?" asked Maggie, putting out her hand, her face pleasantly neutral as she stared at Zoë without wavering. "I'm Maggie. I feel like I know you from somewhere."

"Unlikely," said Zoë, dropping her hand as Paul dragged over a chair and bumped it lightly against the back of her legs. "I've never been here before."

Maggie nodded slowly, her eyes narrowing on Zoë's facial scar before returning to her eyes. Zoë sat down and Paul dragged another chair over to sit beside her. The redheaded man across the table stared at her.

"Since nobody cares to do the honors, I'll introduce myself," he said in a thicker Scottish accent than Maggie's. "I'm Graham. Maggie's cousin."

"Hey, Graham," said Zoë with a chuckle, ignoring the way his eyes flicked to her breasts before licking his lips suggestively. He couldn't be more than twenty-one years old. *Cheeky.*

Paul cleared his throat loudly and Graham looked away from Zoë, smirking at Paul. "How's Miss Mystic?"

Wow, this is weird. They sit around and talk about me? Huh. All eyes turned to Paul, so Zoë twisted slightly in her seat to do the same.

Paul glanced at Zoë for a split second before speaking, and she could have sworn she saw some emotion cross his face—regret or guilt or...what? Was he reluctant to talk about Holly in front of her now that they'd almost kissed?

"She's...she's great. She's at a teacher's conference this

week."

"How many days now? Until your visit?" asked Jane. Lars tugged Jane closer and as she relaxed back into his arms, he landed a quick kiss on her neck.

"Twenty-five." Paul crossed and uncrossed his legs so that his shoe brushed Zoë's leg through her skirt.

"Paul's headed to Connecticut to meet his girlfriend, Holly," said Maggie to Zoë, sitting back in her chair, watching Zoë with slightly narrowed eyes. Zoë could see her mind working and her heart sank. It was only a matter of time until Maggie placed her face. Hopefully she'd at least have tonight to build some sort of rapport with Paul...*before* Maggie outed her.

"Paul was just telling me about Holly on our walk over," said Zoë neutrally.

"Paul's *virtual* girlfriend," said Graham, winking at Zoë.

"I assure you, she's real," said Paul softly, and Zoë's heart clenched from his words and his solid tone.

"So glad to hear it," said Graham, looking pointedly back and forth between Zoë and Paul. "When you two walked in together, I thought maybe you'd thrown over Holly for..."

"Zoë," she reminded him, raising an eyebrow at his teasing. "And no. We just met."

"Ohhh, So you're not a pair." Graham winked at Zoë, his gaze flicking briefly to her chest again before he picked off a piece of the muffin in front of him. As he popped a piece of muffin in his mouth, two dimples cratered his cheeks as he grinned at Zoë, chewing slowly. "Well, that's good."

Paul cleared his throat, crossing his arms over his chest and his elbow brushed the side of Zoë's breast. He didn't mean to do that, did he? Whether he did or not, it made her more aware of him, and nervous.

She turned her attention across the table and caught Graham's eyes frankly appraising her chest again. He was a good few years younger than Zoë, but cute in a self-assured, bad boy sort of way. His hair was more red than blond, almost the same color as Prince Harry's, with bright green eyes, and Zoë could see the end of a tattoo snaking out from the cuff of Graham's long-sleeve shirt, wrapping around his wrist. He reminded her of some of her more cocky fifth graders, full of piss and smart comments, brimming with hormones, just as ready to take a swing at someone as charm them.

Maggie placed a hand on Zoë's arm. "What can I get you to drink, Zoë? Cappuccino? Latte?"

Paul turned to Zoë, leaning forward and lowering his voice. "Whatever you want. It's on me."

"Black coffee's great," she answered, feeling her face flush from his attention.

"Two black coffees, Mag," confirmed Paul. "And thanks."

Maggie stared back and forth between Paul and Zoë for a moment before affixing a smile on her face and turning toward the coffee bar. But Zoë had seen the wariness in her gaze. Maggie sensed that something was off here. Damn woman's intuition, anyway!

"So, Zoë, what're you here for? Family? Holiday? On the lam?"

"Nothing so dastardly." Zoë chuckled, looking up at Jane's teasing emerald eyes. "I always wanted to see Yellowstone."

"And you're an artist, right? What's your medium?" asked Jane, her head nestled on Lars's shoulder.

"Oh, I love acrylics and oils. Pastels. But I can make do with charcoal and good paper if there's nothing else around."

"I heard you lost your supplies," said Lars, smiling at her raised brow. "Yes, Nils again."

"That's a shame," said Graham. "How'd it happen?"

"My art bag never made it on the plane," said Zoë shrugging.

"I've got her covered," said Paul, shifting in his chair until his hip lightly grazed Zoë's.

Zoë turned to him because his voice was low and a little bit terse, and totally directed at Maggie's cousin. There was definitely a little rivalry between the two men and Zoë realized that every time Graham spoke to her, Paul ended up brushing against her. Were the two things related?

"Paul said that I could borrow some supplies from the art department at his school," she explained.

"Your knight in shining armor," said Jane, kicking Paul lightly with a sneakered foot and winking at him. "Hey! I have an idea!" She turned to Lars and kissed his lips lightly. "How about we take Zoë to the park tomorrow with us?"

Zoë could have sworn she saw a twinge of disappointment on Lars's face before he composed himself, smiling warmly at Jane. "Whatever you want, Minx."

"It would be the nice thing to do…since she's new here…"

Lars turned to his best friend. "Paul, what do you think? Make it a foursome? The girls can do their artsy stuff and maybe we can finagle a trout or two."

"Where're you thinking?" asked Paul.

Lars shrugged. "Jane liked Gibbon Falls when we went, but her camera ran out of juice and she couldn't get any shots. I've been meaning to take her back."

Zoë watched him run his fingers lazily up and down Jane's arm and she had a sudden, desperate pang of jealousy watching their easy affection.

"It would be a great place for you to paint or draw, Zoë," said Jane, encouragingly.

"Might even catch a rainbow," said Lars to Paul, dropping another kiss on Jane's neck distractedly.

Paul turned to Zoë and she shifted her gaze from the adoring young couple to Paul's cerulean eyes. "What do you say, Zoë? You up for a day trip?"

She was, of course, desperate for a day trip with Paul, but it complicated things. She was supposed to tell him the truth first thing tomorrow. She bit her lip, knowing she should say no, but she couldn't make herself form the word.

One more day couldn't hurt, right?

She couldn't look away from him as she nodded her head.

"I'd love it."

***

She needed to stop biting her lip like that. It made it impossible for a man to think of anything but kissing her and he didn't want to think about kissing Zoë. Unfortunately, he was having trouble looking away and his heart lurched into a gallop as he imagined pressing his lips to hers, biting that lip with *his* teeth instead of hers. Blood rushed to his groin and he bit down on his tongue purposefully to distract himself.

Stop this now.

Control yourself!

Holly, Holly, Holly!

He forced himself to turn away from her, only to catch Graham's annoying smirk across the table.

"Sounds like fun," said Graham, who only had eyes for Zoë.

Paul didn't know Graham McAlpin very well. He'd kept mostly to himself for the week or so he'd been visiting, but Paul had heard stories from Maggie, and none of them were very good.

He'd been a wild child—a hellion, who'd gotten into a fair amount of trouble back home in secondary school. But apparently he was good with a hammer, so his mother, Maggie's aunt, had shipped him off to Gardiner for a few months to help his cousin with renovations on the Prairie Dawn. According to Maggie, the twenty-year-old could use a "wee break" from his "associates" in Glasgow. Paul hadn't pressed her for more information on these nefarious-sounding "associates," but looking at Graham's tattooed arms, facial scars, and cocky bad boy grins, Paul was reading Graham loud and clear.

Graham was trouble with a capital T and the way he was looking at Zoë made Paul want to smash his fist into Graham's face and give him a new scar for his collection. He tried to calm down, reminding himself that Graham wasn't much older than some of his more challenging seniors, but—Holly or no Holly—he couldn't help the wave of protectiveness he felt for Zoë. He was definitely not interested in Graham joining them for their trip to Gibbon Falls tomorrow.

"I'm sure Maggie needs you around here tomorrow, huh, Graham?"

The younger man rolled his eyes, glancing at Zoë and then back at Paul. His brogue was thick when he answered slowly, his tone laced with challenge. "Ooo, I wouldna dream of hornin' in on yer double date, laddie."

It was on the tip of Paul's tongue to argue that it wasn't a date, but Maggie returned with their drinks, setting the brightly colored ceramic mugs on the table in front of Paul and Zoë.

"Here's yer coffee. Is Gingy bein' a brat?"

"Gingy?" asked Zoë, picking up her mug and blowing lightly over the steam.

Paul couldn't tear his gaze away from her pursed lips. Damn, but he was weak.

"Gingy for his ginger-colored hair," she tousled it affectionately and Graham gave her a look, pulling away. "My wee cousin's come to spend the fall with me. He's goin' to build a deck off the back of the Prairie Dawn. Will be nice for next summer."

Lars stretched his arms over his head yawning, and Jane kissed his cheek before slipping off his lap and offering him her hand to pull him up.

"Lars is sleepy," she announced.

"Lars is often kept up all night long," Lars teased her and she drew her hand back, as if offended, putting it on her hip instead.

"Not that I'm complaining," he clarified, standing up and wrenching her hand away from her waist so he could lace his fingers through hers. "Take me home, Minx."

Jane smiled at the group still at the table. "Graham, glad you finally joined us. Mags, I'll catch you tomorrow or next week. And you two...we'll see you tomorrow. Pick you up at your place, Paul? Ten o'clock?"

Paul nodded at Jane. "Sounds good to me. Zoë?"

"Can we get into the school first? For the supplies?"

"Sure," said Paul, grinning into her deep brown eyes. "I'll pick you up at nine and we can go choose whatever you like."

Jane and Lars headed out and Zoë turned back to Paul.

"Sorry you got railroaded into going to the park tomorrow."

"Are you kidding? Miss an opportunity to best Lars in trout fishing? I live for that!"

She smiled at him and he had that feeling again. Like he knew her from somewhere. He wished he could figure it out and be done with it.

"If you say so. I'll be your cheering section."

"I'm counting on it. He has Jane, so it's only fair

181

that…" His voice trailed off as he realized he was about to say I *have you*.

"Zoë," said Maggie, breaking the rhythm of their conversation, "Come up to the baked goods case. I'd like to give you somethin' to take back to yer room."

"Oh, there's no need—"

"But I insist," said Maggie, brooking no refusal.

Zoë stared at Maggie for a moment before standing up hesitantly and following her across the café, leaving Paul alone with Graham. He watched Graham stare overtly at Zoë's ass as she walked away.

"She's hot," said Graham, grinning at Paul. "I wouldn't mind—"

"Save it." Paul put up his hand. "Whatever you're going to say, I don't want to hear it."

"Why not?" Graham leaned forward, resting his elbows on the table. "Oh! Oh, I get it. You don't want her, but you don't want anyone else havin' a taste neither."

Paul shook his head. "That's not it at all."

Graham swirled the coffee left in his cup, staring at Paul with a knowing smirk. "You can barely stop lookin' at her. Been starin' at her since the second you two walked in here, laddie."

Paul's nostrils flared with annoyance, but he didn't deny it. First of all, rising to bait wasn't Paul's style. But, secondly, the kid was right. In the absence of a response, Graham continued, upping the ante.

"Shite, man, I get it. She has the best tits I've seen in—"

"If another word comes out of your mouth, my fist's going in it, " Paul growled in warning.

Graham stopped talking but his eyes widened in pure enjoyment and his smirk grew into a smile. He didn't say anything else, just stared at Paul with that knowing, highly annoying grin.

Maggie and Zoë returned to the table, but Zoë didn't sit down. She looked pale as she clutched a small brown bag with white knuckles. Had she somehow heard Graham's insulting assessment of her?

"I have to go," she said softly, looking to be on the verge of tears.

Paul flicked his glance to Maggie, who looked down at her coffee cup, lips pursed.

"Are you okay, Mag? Is everything—?"

"All fine," said Maggie, giving him a half-smile.

"Zoë?"

"It's time to go," she murmured, taking a step away from the table.

What in the world had just happened between these two at the baked goods counter?

"Get home safe," said Maggie lightly.

"Thanks," Zoë whispered, then turned and rushed to the door without another word or second glance.

"Wait!" Paul blurted out, standing up swiftly. He shoved his chair back and started after her, but Maggie's hand on his wrist stopped him for a moment.

"Paul, we need to—"

"No, Mag. Not right now. She's obviously upset." He

wiggled his wrist away, feeling annoyed with his friend and giving her cousin a scathing look. "I have to go."

Maggie's eyes widened in surprise before nodding slowly. "Okay, then. I guess you do."

Without another word he hurried to catch up with Zoë.

CHAPTER 11

Zoë's heart hammered as she turned onto the sidewalk and her bad leg, stiff from sitting, shot darts of pain up to her waist, making her limp more pronounced as she forced herself to move faster.

Stupid girl! Stupid, stupid, stupid! You should have just told him like you planned! Now it's a total mess!

Frustrated tears coursed down both cheeks mixing with raindrops and she smacked them away angrily, the little paper bag with the scone hitting her nose. She didn't know the moment that Maggie realized who she was, but when she asked her to come and choose something to take back to her room, Zoë sensed the jig was up.

"I know who you are," Maggie said as soon as they walked away from the table. "It took me a few minutes to recognize you, but I had the benefit of that other photo. The close-up one that you took down before Paul checked out your profile."

Zoë had swallowed the ostrich-egg sized lump forming in her throat.

"Please don't tell—"

"That man is like a brother to me and he has had enough bad luck, Holly. I don't know what your game is, but—"

"No games! I would never hurt him."

"What's yer real name?"

"Zoë Holly Flannigan."

"I see." Maggie looked pointedly at Zoë's black hair. "Why d'ye look like this?"

"It's a long story," she breathed, her voice trembling.

"Most lies are intricate."

Zoë cringed, hot tears burning her eyes.

Maggie pointed at the scones. "You say you wouldn't hurt him, but he has no idea who you are. I can tell."

"No," Zoë whispered. "He doesn't know it's me."

"Then I predict him gettin' hurt. He deserves to know who you are," Maggie had said, taking a little paper sack from the countertop. "When exactly is that goin' to happen?"

"Soon. Tomorrow."

"This is *real* to him. Tell him tonight."

"I-I can't. Please."

"Tonight."

"I *can't* yet," whispered Zoë fiercely, holding her ground with strength she didn't know she had. "It's real to me too. I don't want to lose him."

Maggie's hard green eyes searched Zoë's face and seemed to soften slightly as she digested Zoë's whispered words. "He's been happier these last few weeks than I've ever seen him. Ever."

"Me too," whispered Zoë, feeling miserable as Maggie assessed her with a frank, worried face.

"I shouldn't believe you."

"*Please*," Zoë pleaded, her voice shaky with emotion.

"All right. But soon and no mistake, lass," said Maggie finally, picking up a scone with tongs and putting it into a small paper bag. She faced Zoë, her eyes slightly narrowed and lips pursed. "And if you don't, I will."

Zoë had nodded slightly then looked away, her face flaming with heat, the temporary reprieve making her shoulders sag with relief. Maggie handed her the paper bag then turned without another word, heading back to the table where Paul and Graham waited for them.

Whether it was the way her plan to spill the beans had been derailed by their first meeting over Cleo's mishap or the pure wonderfulness that was Paul or the way Maggie had just verbally bitch-slapped her, she wasn't sure. All she knew was that she needed to get out of the Prairie Dawn before she burst into tears and embarrassed herself. The lump in her throat was relentless and painful and she clenched her jaw trying to distract herself from the pooling tears. She needed to run back to her inn, hide under her covers and cry for an hour. Maybe call Sandy for a pep talk and then decide how she was going to tell Paul the truth tomorrow.

So, she'd said a hasty goodbye to Paul, then turned around and ran out of the homey little café.

Zoë was good at running away and hiding. In little and big ways, she'd been running away and hiding for a couple of years now—

"Zoë! ZOË! Wait up!"

Being chased, however, was something new.

***

Paul called to her, but she didn't slow down.

If anything, she seemed to move faster, making it to the bridge as he finally caught up with her.

"Zoë!" he panted. "Wait! Why'd you leave? Why are you running home? What's going on?"

She looked up at him and despite the rain, he could tell in an instant that she was crying. She turned away, taking a step toward the railing of the bridge and holding the slick metal in her hands as her chest heaved up and down.

He stepped toward her, putting his hand gently on her back. "Hey…"

Before he could get out another word, she spun into his arms, resting her cheek on his chest. He could feel the shudders shaking her back, the deep, heavy sobs of someone who felt intense sorrow. Instinct took over. He wrapped his arms around her, pulling her close to his body, instinctually offering her whatever comfort he could.

Her small body leaned into his, and it made him wonder again about this strange, vulnerable, injured girl. This brave girl who saved dogs and was a good listener and had scars on her face. He couldn't seem to help himself from wanting to protect her, take care of her, learn the secrets behind her sad eyes. Why did he feel such a strong, insistent pull to her? And what did it mean?

Determined not to overthink the act of comforting another human being in pain, he clasped her more closely, reaching up with one hand to gently brush the wet hair back from her temples in a soothing, monotonous motion. He didn't know how long they stood like that in the dim light of the evening while the rained soaked them and the

Yellowstone River rushed black below them, but he knew that if she had needed him to, he would have gladly stayed all night.

Finally she drew back, using her fingers and palms to swipe away the raindrops and tears under her eyes and on her cheeks. Paul looked down at her, at the dark, sad eyes that still glistened with tears.

He took a deep breath, knowing it was time to loosen his grip and let go of her, but he was distracted by the scent of honeysuckle…and just like that, the world melted away and he couldn't think of anything but the girl in his arms.

He closed his eyes, lowered his head and pressed his lips to hers.

***

One minute she'd been trying to get back to her inn as fast as possible, and the next moment she was in Paul's arms, sobbing against his chest, taking advantage of his solid warmth.

The crying had been about everything: losing her mother, the accident, Brandon's legs, her own injuries, falling out with Thea, pretending to be Holly, falling in love with Paul, knowing that he felt something real for Zoë, and the terrible inevitability of having to tell him the truth and how much it could potentially hurt him when she did.

Everything was a mess and she couldn't figure out how to unravel it all into order and sense and goodness. So, she cried. Her shoulders trembled as he ran his hands gently, soothingly up and down her back, before brushing her hair from her face. Eventually the slow, languorous movements made her tired, burning eyes heavy and she took a few deep breaths as her tears tapered off.

She stepped back from Paul, swiping away the tears under her eyes with her fingers, she'd raised her gaze to his. The soft glow of the street lamp in the rain caught the light blue of his eyes. The rain beat down harder and it felt like waking up inside of a dream—like whatever happened next, it wouldn't actually be real.

And in that moment, she forgot about Holly and Zoë and Zoë Holly, about the internet and lies and Maggie's sharp assessment of her willful deception. She forgot about Mystic and Montana and legs that limped and hair dyed black and heartbreaking tattoos of little lambs with all four legs intact. She couldn't see beyond the man holding her.

When he closed his eyes and lowered his lips to hers, it was all she could do to keep from fainting.

***

He caught her lower lip between his, just as he'd wanted to every time she'd bitten it that afternoon and evening. Shivers sluiced up his arms as he moved his hands from her damp back to her face, pressing his palms against her slick cheeks, the tips of his fingers threading through her wet black hair.

Zoë moaned into his mouth and the sound was like liquid heat in his veins, racing through his body until it reached his heart, setting it on fire, making it hammer as his feverish blood shot down past his waist. He pulled her closer, parting the pliant seam of her lips with his tongue, tilting his head to better fit his mouth flush over hers.

She flattened her hands on his chest as he explored her

liquid heat, swirling his tongue around hers and groaning as she stepped into him, pressing her belly into his hips.

He wanted to touch her—all of her—to slide his hands under her shirt and feel the softness of her skin. Drawing his fingers from her hair, one of them gently tracing the scar that ran from her hairline to—

"Paul, wait—" she murmured, her voice breathy and overwhelmed.

She pulled back from him, dropping her chin so that his lips grazed her forehead.

His chest moved up and down as he panted, acutely aware of her hands on his chest, of her fingers moving slightly with every shallow breath, gently molding over his muscles. He looked down at her little fingers and the reality of what he'd just done broadsided him like a sucker punch. His fingers, still on her face, trembled, and he dropped them silently, stepping back from her.

"Zoë. My God, I'm so—I don't know why I did that…I—I don't know what to say."

There was no doubt in his mind who had started that kiss. It was his fault and his alone. She had been vulnerable—crying and sad—and it had bothered him so much, he'd wanted to give her whatever comfort he could offer. But to take advantage of such a moment. He swallowed painfully, furrowing his brows in shame, daring to look at her.

"It's…it's okay." Her eyes looked stricken, but not in the same way they had a few minutes ago, and he realized, with some small consolation, that they didn't look hopeless anymore. "Don't say you're sorry."

He didn't know how to take her words. Was she just being kind to him by trying to smooth over the awkwardness of his actions? Or was she actually worried he regretted kissing her?

"I'm not," he answered softly without thinking.

The muscles in her face relaxed and she exhaled, taking a deep breath and putting out her hand. He took it, silently, lacing his fingers through hers as they walked the rest of the way across the bridge.

***

They didn't say another word to each other on the short walk back to Zoë's inn. He didn't ask her why she'd been crying and she didn't ask him why he had kissed her. They both seemed to understand that there wasn't room for such questions right now, nor space for the answers, which would further muddy the waters between them.

Zoë needed to clear her head and figure out what she should do next. And that couldn't happen while she was within touching distance of Paul.

As they neared the front porch of the Mountain View Inn, Paul spoke softly, his voice laced with regret. "Zoë, I—"

"I know you're with Holly," she said quickly. "I know that. But I'm only here for a few days and I'd like to spend time with you. We don't—I mean, we won't kiss again. We can just chalk that up to an emotional moment, okay? But, I just—I like being around you." They stopped under a streetlight and she shrugged, looking down at their hands, which were still clasped intimately together. Did he realize they were still holding hands? "Please don't cancel coming to the falls tomorrow."

His Adam's apple bobbed as he swallowed. Then he reached up and tucked a piece of damp black hair behind her ear, looking at her tenderly.

"We're *both* taken," he said softly. "Both with someone else."

She bit her lip and dropped her eyes, unable to speak, almost unable to bear the irony that they were, in fact, taken by each other.

"Come to the falls," she whispered.

He was staring at her lips with a fierceness that she could see, but couldn't necessarily explain. Finally, he sighed, long and hard, looking over her shoulder at the Mountain View Inn porch, then shaking his head back and forth as if in surrender. His lips—the lips she could still feel on hers— tilted up in a small smile.

"I'll come get you at nine," he said, dropping her hand. "'Night, Zoë."

Relief.

"Good night, Paul," she whispered, watching him turn and walk away.

Exhaling a ragged breath, she hurried up the porch stairs, opening the door of the inn and going directly to her room. She threw the key on the antique desk beside the door with a clatter, running her hands through her hair. She paced the room once, then twice, before peeling off her wet sweater and sitting down slowly, disbelievingly, on the edge of the bed.

"Oh, my," she whispered, laying back on the bed as tears pooled in her eyes.

Staring at the ceiling, she allowed herself, just for a moment, to relive their kiss.

His lips had been warm and soft on hers, stealing her breath as he moved them gently, then more insistently against hers. But truth be told, it was the way he'd touched her scar that had stolen her heart. He didn't avoid it, this ugly part of her. No. He went out of his way to connect with it. Tears spilled out of the corners of her eyes at the thought of such tenderness, but shame arrived quickly on its heels. Guilt and shame in equal shares.

"What a mess," she sighed.

Her original plan was to walk to his house, knock on his door and tell him the truth.

She was so derailed from that plan now, she didn't have a clue of how to get back on track.

Fix this, Zoë, before it's too late.

Walk to his house. Knock on the door. Tell him the truth.

It's just as good a plan now as it was five hours ago. Just do it.

The voice in her head was firm and reasonable, and she gravitated toward it. Maybe he'd even feel softer about everything since they'd already had a chance to connect a little bit. She sighed, sitting up and wiping the tears away. She was strong. She had the courage to do this.

She slipped her shoes back on and went into the bathroom to brush her damp hair into a ponytail, giving herself a quick pep talk before heading for the door.

Hearing the knock from outside was the last thing she expected. Her pulse raced and her heart leaped, imagining it was Paul. But when she opened the door, she was surprised to find Maggie standing on the other side.

"Can I come in?" she asked.

"I was just going to—um, sure." Zoë stepped back to let Maggie in the room.

Maggie walked over to the windows and peeked outside at the street below.

"Never been in here," she said lightly, giving Zoë a half smile before sitting in the wingback chair. "It's cozy."

Zoë closed the door and sat down on the bed across from Maggie, her nerves shot. Was Maggie here to tell her that she'd already gone to Paul?

"When you ran out," said Maggie, "it upset him."

Zoë swallowed, staring at Maggie, not knowing what to say.

"It occurred to me after you left that I didn't give you a chance to explain anythin'. Called you a liar. Threatened you. Tried to boss you around." She flinched, looking down at her hands before raising her gaze again. "I'm sorry. You have to understand. I love him. Like a brother or a cousin. I'm certainly closer to Paul than Graham. Can't see him hurt and know I did nothin' to stop it."

Zoë leaned forward. "I don't want to hurt him."

"If your name's Zoë Holly Flannigan, where'd the surname Morgan come from?"

"It was my mother's maiden name."

"Holly Morgan. I see." Maggie nodded. "What about

the hair? Your eyes? That scar on your face? You look very different, Zoë. Like a totally different person."

"I opened that account two years ago. About a week later, I was in a terrible accident, and everything changed. Someone I love very much was hurt. *I* was hurt."

Zoë took a deep breath, biting back her tears. Slowly, she pulled on the fabric of her skirt, bunching it up around her thighs until her right leg, with its twisted, purple, mangled flesh, was on full display.

Maggie gasped, covering her mouth with her hand.

"What happened to you?"

"My car was run off the road. My nephew was in the back. He was only four. He lost both of his legs. They were…crushed."

"I'm sorry," said Maggie, her eyes soft with sympathy.

Zoë was grateful for her kindness and hated it simultaneously. She pushed her skirt back down, smoothing her hands over her lap.

"Everything changed in the blink of an eye. I felt dark inside, and changed my looks to match. I don't work as a teacher anymore. I barely see my sister; she can't stand the sight of me. When you—" Zoë's voice broke and she bit her lip, composing herself before continuing. "When you wrote to me and told me about Paul, it was like—it was like the sun coming out after two years of darkness. And then I met him, and he was just so—so wonderful. I almost told him several times: *I'm not the girl in the picture anymore. But I couldn't do it.*

"Maybe I was living in a fantasy, but the plan was for him to come home for Christmas, and I knew I could look more like my old self by then. My hair would have grown out to shoulder-length and I could have dyed it back to my natural shade of blonde. I could take out these—" She extended her eye open between her thumb and forefinger and took out one of the brown contacts, balancing it on the pad of her forefinger. "—and be blue-eyed again. By then, I would have had my final facial surgery—it's scheduled for October—and the scars would have been mostly healed by December. I would've looked like the picture by Christmas when he came home to see his family."

She placed her contact lens in the case on the bedside table, followed by its mate, and then she clicked the container carefully shut.

"But he decided to visit you in October instead," said Maggie from her chair in the corner, putting the pieces of the puzzle together.

"Yes. And I knew..." Zoë took a deep breath before turning to face Maggie. "I knew if he came to Mystic and found Zoë instead of Holly, he'd turn around and go home. He wouldn't forgive me for lying to him, for deceiving him. But I thought if I came here and told him the truth to his face, he'd have no choice but to listen.

"I walked over to his house this afternoon, intending to tell him everything, but his dog almost got hit by a car, and I lost my nerve, and the whole—"

"I see," said Maggie.

"I never meant for it to get this far."

Maggie didn't say anything, just stared at Zoë, as though trying to decide if she believed her story or not.

"Every day I told myself to be honest with him. But he was so wonderful. My life had been so awful and then suddenly here's this man dropped into my lap." Zoë looked down, smiling at her hands on her lap. "And he's funny and kind and he's everything I ever wanted. He makes me *want* to be the girl from the picture again. He helped me to remember who she was—who *I* was before my life was torn apart. He's already made my life so much better and brighter and…" She looked up, meeting Maggie's softening eyes. "I fell in love with him, Maggie."

"I can see that," said Maggie. "The problem is, I think he's in love with Holly."

"I know. He told me."

"He *told* you?"

"Mmm. We talked about Holly tonight as we were walking to your café."

"That must have been…bizarre."

"It was."

"And…I wouldn't stake my life on it, but it appears that he has feelings for *you,* too. For *Zoë,*" said Maggie, deliberately, raising an eyebrow.

"I know," said Zoë, thinking about the kiss they'd just shared. "It's getting…messy."

"Och, lass," sighed Maggie, shaking her head. "It's way past messy. No *gettin'* about it."

"I'm going to tell him. Tonight. In fact, I was headed there when you knocked on my door."

Maggie held Zoë's eyes for a moment before wincing. "I don't know if you should. I just—"

"Wait. You *don't* think I should tell him?" Her words came out in a rush, eyes wide with confusion. "*You* said I should tell him tonight."

"I know I did, but…it's going to hurt him. He likes both of you."

"He can have both of us."

"He won't see it that way. Not…yet."

"What are you saying?"

"I'm sayin' he needs to *love* Zoë in order to hear her out."

"He's a good man," Zoë whispered. "If he thinks he's cheating on Holly with me, he'll feel terrible. No. I can't do that to him. I need to go over there and tell—"

Maggie reached out and took one of Zoë's hands in hers. "You love him?"

"I do," said Zoë, thinking that meeting him today was the final test and he'd passed with flying colors. Was she in love with him? "Completely."

"It's a proper mess and no mistake. But he loves Holly and he likes you. And you love him. Tellin' him the truth right away will ease your conscience, but you're right, you'll probably lose him. And worse, he'll lose you."

Zoë grimaced at the pain Maggie's words caused her heart. She swallowed painfully as Maggie squeezed her hand.

"Take a moment, lass. You need to think. You have to figure out a way to make this work. Find the right time to tell him. I wouldn't go over there, guns blazin', tonight. If I were you, I'd sleep on it a wee bit. Look at it again in the mornin' with fresh eyes. That's my advice, for whatever it's worth."

"It's worth a lot," Zoë told her.

Maggie stood up, walking toward the door.

"Thank you for coming over, Maggie. For giving me a chance."

Maggie opened the door then turned to look at Zoë.

"Figure it out fast, lass, because he cares for you so much and he's…well, he's special."

"I know."

"I believe you do."

Maggie gave her a small smile, but Zoë could see the worry behind it. Then Maggie turned and walked into the hallway, pulling the door shut behind her.

***

Cleo didn't like getting her paws wet, but Paul needed a walk, and Cleo was going with him whether she liked it or not. She walked daintily on her little feet, trying to minimize her contact with the cold, wet sidewalk as they started out for the arch.

Paul could barely get his head around everything that had happened in the past five hours, but of two things he was absolutely certain: first, he felt like crap for cheating on Holly and second, he had no business going anywhere near Zoë tomorrow.

He couldn't account for his actions. From the moment he'd seen her holding Cleo, he'd felt some strong, strange pull to her—to protect her and take care of her. Rescuing his dog showed amazing bravery, but then she showed another side of herself later, patiently listening to him talk about Holly in the gazebo next to the Cowboy Lodge. And still another side when she melted into him, crying against his chest, taking the comfort he offered her on the bridge. She looked sure-footed, but she walked with a limp; it had been more pronounced as she tried to run away from him. She looked tough, but everything about her was soft and vulnerable.

Oh, man. This is bad. This is trouble.

Come on, Paul. She's not your type at all!

And she wasn't…but he was attracted as hell to her—there was no point in denying it. His whole body had hummed with arousal as he kissed her. She had this sad-but-courageous thing going on and it was irresistible to him. He wanted to comfort her, just as much as he wanted to stand back and admire her, just as much as he wanted to see what she looked like naked. On her back. In his bed.

Try doing a little more standing back and admiring, Paul. That'd be a good idea.

Kissing her on the bridge had crossed a line. A major line. If he was a single guy, it would be a different story. He'd be thrilled that Zoë blew into town. He'd be all excited and dreamy tonight, full of anticipation for their day in the park tomorrow, and maybe even letting his imagination wander all the way to the possibility of love. Yeah. He'd certainly entertain it.

He thought of the way her dark eyes had glistened in the moonlight right before he'd dipped his head and kissed her. His lips could still feel the softness of hers under his. He could still taste her in his mouth, the slight, sweet bitterness of the coffee, the smell of honeysuckle, and that sexy moan that—

Enough!

You shouldn't be thinking of her like this! You're not *a single guy.*

He was a guy who'd already met a wonderful girl, and regardless of whether or not he'd met her in person yet, he felt a commitment to Holly. A commitment solidified by his intent to visit her in a few short weeks. Holly deserved his best—his whole heart. She deserved to be loved the way Westley loved Buttercup, unreservedly, without limits or boundaries.

He wasn't free to pursue Zoë, even if he wanted to.

Which begged the question...

"Do I *want* to pursue Zoë?"

Cleo answered him by looking up and whining lightly before trying to tug him back toward the house.

"Of course not!" he told the little dog, turning to follow as she led the way home.

He wanted Holly. Sweet, sunny Holly who probably smelled like vanilla.

She wouldn't cry on his chest or look up at him with dark, wounded eyes. She'd tease him playfully and make him laugh, her blue eyes twinkling and golden hair shining. She'd be his Christmas sweetheart; his sunny princess who came from a loving family, had a perfect job and didn't complicate his life with heroic gestures and vulnerable eyes.

Is that really what you want? Seems like something inside of you is pulled toward someone like Zoë too. Seems like maybe you like a little...complicated.

"No!" he said so loudly that Cleo jumped, putting her tail between her legs.

"Sorry, Cleo," he muttered, reaching down to scoop the quivering dog up and carry her the rest of the way home. She relaxed into the crook of his arm, resting her chin on his forearm contentedly.

No, he thought again, evenly, calmly. *I don't want complicated. I want Holly. I won't be pulled toward Zoë anymore. I won't allow it.*

I'll still go tomorrow, but we'll have a friendly, appropriate outing and then say goodbye. I'll go to school on Monday, she'll deal with the issues in her own life, and we'll part friends.

Holly deserves nothing less than my whole heart, and when I see her, I intend to give it to her.

So, that was it. He would see Zoë tomorrow, keep things friendly and then say goodbye. And there was no way he was touching her again, that was for sure. Kissing her once, which he blamed on an unexpectedly emotional afternoon and evening, was one thing. It was an accident, a mistake, a one-time error in judgment that he would not be duplicating. Absolutely not.

Because he knew in his heart if he did it again, it wouldn't be a mistake anymore. It would be a deliberate choice. It would mean that he wasn't worthy of someone as wonderful as Holly.

It would mean the unthinkable:

He'd have to let Holly go.

CHAPTER 12

The two-hour time difference meant that Zoë was up by six o'clock and dressed and ready for the day by seven. With an hour to kill before the inn offered breakfast, she peeked out the window and decided to walk to the Prairie Dawn for a hot cup of coffee and a scone. She'd somehow lost the one Maggie had given her last night. Not surprising, considering what had happened between her and Paul on the walk home.

Tucking her phone in her pocket, she headed down the stairs wearing a new pair of skinny jeans and a black, long-sleeved, scoop-neck T-shirt, ready to start her day…until she opened the front door and gasped.

"Gah! Cold!" she yelped, closing the door again with a slam.

She turned gingerly to be sure the innkeeper wasn't standing behind her with a stern and disapproving expression and was relieved to find herself still alone. Running upstairs, she grabbed the black cardigan she was wearing last night, grateful it had dried in its spot draped over the radiator. Seeing her earbuds lying on the bedside table, she picked them up too, popping them in her ears and choosing one of her favorite Colbie Callait songs for the short walk to the Prairie Dawn.

There's something about an empty sidewalk, early in the morning when you're wide awake that makes you feel like the only person in the world.

The sweet words of "I Do" made her shoulders rock back and forth and she moved her hips lightly as she walked merengue-style with little bouncy steps, occasionally snapping her fingers to the buoyant beat, forgetting the confusion of last night and the cold of the morning as the sunny song made her heart feel lighter.

"I do, I do, I do do do do do do do do do ..." she sang louder than usual, pushing through the slight pain of bending her knees with each step, leaning into the rhythm and the carefree happiness of the song. She pointed to her ring finger along with the lyrics then shrugged her shoulders with attitude, making her way merrily down empty Stone Street.

The thing is, if she hadn't needed the sweater, she would have already been halfway to the Prairie Dawn and she wouldn't be deaf from the music blaring in her ears. She wouldn't have walked by Paul's front porch just as he closed the door behind him, heading to the exact same place. And he definitely wouldn't have had the questionable pleasure of hearing her cheerful, if slightly off-key, rendition of Colbie's popcorn hit, complete with her spirited, if completely and utterly embarrassing, merengue-style dance-walk.

"You make me wanna say I do—Oh my God!" she gasped, feeling a tap on her shoulder and spinning around to slam into Paul's solid chest.

Her cheeks flamed with heat as she grappled for the earbuds, finally finding the cords and yanking them out of her ears. *That's right. He wakes up at 6:35 every morning, every day, whether school's in session or not.*

She peeked up at him.

Something she hadn't known until now? He woke up looking like a god. Like a freshly showered, devastatingly handsome god who was trying desperately not to grin at her, blue eyes sparkling with merriment. Lord only knows how long he was standing there watching her sing and dance down his street. She would have been completely mortified if she wasn't distracted by something else…

He had grabbed her around the waist as she fell into him, and she was acutely aware of the heat and pressure of his hands as they steadied her, finally sliding down to rest on the swell of her hips.

"I didn't mean to scare you," he said, losing his battle with composure and breaking into an ear to ear grin. "But…wow!"

Zoë cringed, forcing herself not to think about his hands, which lingered on her body. They felt so good and so right there, she didn't have the willpower to back away. She looked up and met his eyes, putting a little sass in her voice. "Wow, what? You never take a morning walk-dance to Colbie Callait? You're missing out."

At the mention of Colbie, he seemed to realize he was still holding her, and his hands flew off her waist like she was suddenly made of fire. It took Zoë a second to process his reaction before remembering that "Holly" had mentioned Colbie Callait on her MeetTheOne profile.

"Probably more fun to watch anyway," he muttered, his smile fading just a little bit, as if he'd done something wrong.

"If your idea of fun is a sloppy merengue and off-key singing."

"Didn't sound off-key to me...or look very sloppy, for that matter."

Zoë grinned at him, wondering if they could get over the awkward Holly moment. "I used to love to dance."

"Used to?" he asked in an echo of the text chat they'd had at the movies several weeks ago. "Why not anymore?"

She took a deep breath and said, "I had an accident a couple of years ago. It messed up my right leg."

He furrowed his brows and she had a feeling he was remembering her limp last night as she tried to run home. He nodded slowly, glancing down at her leg. "What happened?"

"Car accident," she said, and it surprised her that her eyes didn't tear up and that old lump in her throat didn't appear even as it had last night when she told Maggie. She was somehow able to say the words without them totally decimating her. "Bad one."

He was still nodding. His glance flicked to the scar on her face that he'd traced with his finger as he'd kissed her yesterday evening, and she wondered if he was thinking about that too.

"Yeah," she confirmed softly, touching the line with her own fingers. "That too."

He stared at her like he was seeing her for the first time, his blue eyes staring so hard, it was like they were looking into her. She wondered if he could see through the brown contacts to the blue eyes hidden underneath.

"Damn, you're brave," he murmured.

Zoë swallowed, shaking her head. "No. No, I'm not."

She turned away from him, shoving her earbuds in her pocket and pausing "I Do" as she resumed her walk toward town. He turned quickly and joined her, his arm brushing hers as he caught up.

"Where you headed?"

She was glad he didn't ask any more questions about the accident. While she was relieved she'd been able to talk about it without getting emotional, she wasn't anxious to share more details. Not now, anyway. Not yet.

"Prairie Dawn," she said, glancing up at him. He must have just shaved because his jaw was smooth. She was dying to touch the warm, soft skin, to run her fingers along the strong line. She shoved her hands in her back pockets instead, recalling the way he'd dropped his hands from her hips.

"You seemed pretty anxious to get out of there last night," he said mildly.

She stopped walking and looked up at him. He stopped at the same time she did, and gazed at her with worry and...tenderness? Oh, God, it was. *Does he even realize how he's looking at me?*

Her tongue darted out to lick her lips nervously and his eyes dropped to her mouth before he blinked them quickly and switched his gaze awkwardly to the mountains over her shoulder.

"Hey," she started, "I owe you an apology for crying all

over you. I was—I don't know. Tired and jet lagged, probably."

"Lot of tears for jet lag."

"Okay," she said softly. "The truth is, I don't know if things are going to work out with the guy I told you about."

"He lives here?"

"Around here," she said, resuming their walk.

"Have you seen him since you got to town?"

"He didn't know I was planning to come," she answered honestly. "He's not expecting me."

"Huh. Was he not home when you stopped by?"

"Things got complicated."

"Because of Cleo...and me," said Paul, and she heard the regret in his voice.

"No—" she started, but he cut her off.

"I'm complicating your life as much as I'm complicating mine. I had no business kissing you, Zoë."

Don't say you're sorry. Don't say you're sorry.

To her relief he didn't.

To her frustration, he said something worse:

"I promise never to do it again."

That's great. Just great.

They walked the rest of the way to the Prairie Dawn in awkward silence and Zoë revisited Maggie's words from last night:

You have to figure out a way to make this work.

Kisses or no kisses, that's exactly what she still intended to do.

***

"If it isn't the bonniest lass in Gardiner!" exclaimed Graham from behind the copper bar.

"Where's Maggie?" asked Paul, feeling irritable at the sight of her disrespectful, foul-mouthed cousin. The last person he was in the mood to see this morning was Graham.

"She's not feelin' so very well, laddie. Under t'weather."

"What's wrong with her?"

Graham pantomimed throwing up. "Case of the heaves. Bloody disgustin'."

Paul's nose inched up in distaste, wrinkling at Graham's colorful description. "Are you running things?"

"That I am," he said, looking away from Paul dismissively and winking at Zoë. "What can I get the lovely Zoë?"

Paul rolled his eyes. Zoë smiled back at Graham, and Paul was pretty sure he could see her molars. "Cappuccino?"

Graham put his hand over his heart as though wounded. "Challengin' me with special orders on my first day!"

"No! Black coffee's fine!" she blurted out, her cheeks rosy from Graham's stupid flirting.

"Nae, lass. Only the best for you. Cappuccino it is! Sit awhile and I'll bring it over when it's ready." Zoë grinned at him and turned away. Paul and Graham watched her sit down on the window seat, one leg curled under her body as she reached for a newspaper and perused the front page.

The two men faced each other, Graham's smile fading quickly to a mocking smirk. He leaned forward across the bar, toward Paul, speaking in a lower voice. "Just so as we're clear, I'm aimin' to hit that."

Damn, but he hated this kid's guts. He balled his fists in front of him and spoke in a low-toned, angry whisper.

"Just so as *we're* clear, *laddie,* try it and the only thing that'll get *hit* is your face."

"But you're not interested," Graham said sarcastically.

"I'm not interested in someone like her getting seduced by someone like you."

He stepped back, that idiotic smirk taunting Paul. "Oooo. *Seduced.* There's a fine and fancy word for it. If it makes you feel any better, I'm not goin' to seduce anyone. I was just plannin' to knock boots with her 'til I got bored."

"I swear to God——"

"You swear what? I thought you had a virtual girlfriend to worry about. It's none of yer business anyway." He sauntered away, pouring milk into a metal pitcher. He asked over his shoulder, "You want anythin'?"

"Cappuccino," said Paul tightly.

He hated to admit it, but the kid was right. It was none of his business if Graham wanted to pursue Zoë or if Zoë wanted to "knock boots" with Graham. But it sat like acid in his stomach, the idea of Zoë with this guy. She deserved a nice guy. She deserved much better than smart-ass Graham.

He turned his back to the bar, leaning against it as the familiar sound of steaming milk filled the otherwise quiet of the small, empty café. He couldn't help but watch Zoë, the way her black hair gleamed in the sunlight streaming into the window, the way she turned the pages of the newspaper softly.

She'd been in an accident that maimed her leg, but somehow, she still started her days dancing down the street, singing pop music, hips swaying appealingly, face bright and alert and cheerful. So many people would have retreated from the world—hidden or run away. She was probably the bravest person he'd ever met.

He felt a surge of guilt remembering her words. *It got complicated.*

Yeah, I'll say.

The reality was that despite his pep talk to himself last night about staying away from Zoë, he had felt the leap in his heart when he saw her dancing down the street, singing a touch too loud for a quiet Saturday morning.

She'd been singing the song "I Do," a song Paul had discovered after meeting Holly. It was a sweet song—a young woman who hadn't had much luck in love had finally met a man whom she wanted to marry, raise a family, and grow old with. He'd liked the sweetness of it right away and had listened to it a time or two thinking of Holly.

Now he'd never be able to hear it again without thinking of Zoë. And the way her body felt pressed against his, her hips held tightly by his fingers? Forget it. Complicated was just the tip of the iceberg.

She turned her head to look out the window and he could see the scar on her face, pink and shiny with the teeny, tiny dots on either side that would have been from the needle puncturing her skin, to pull it back together after it had been split open. He couldn't begin to imagine what she'd been through.

So why wasn't this guy treating her with tenderness and respect? She flew all the way out here to see him, right? What was the matter with that guy anyway?

For God's sake, if she were mine—

He turned away from her, opening his eyes wide at the direction of his thoughts, his breath catching in his throat as he realized what he was about to think. He ground his jaw, feeling suddenly stricken. He had thought the words *If she were mine*, almost as if he wished she was.

Stop thinking about her like that!

He turned back to Graham, frustration and annoyance making his voice low and bitter. "Need some *help*? Takes Maggie half the time to make twice as many."

Graham turned to Paul, holding two mugs of perfect cappuccino. He smirked at Paul's tone, glancing at Paul's crotch, then back up to his face.

"Sour mood, eh? I bet they're blue," he whispered. He raised his eyebrows at Paul in challenge then called out in a cheerful voice, "Cap's ready, Miss Zoë."

Paul took the mugs, giving Graham an ominous scowl. "I've got it."

Graham's tasteless comment wasn't too far off, though. Paul's body was having a hard time accepting his head's no for an answer. It was only going to get worse if his heart started caving in too.

***

An hour later, Paul unlocked the front door of the Gardiner Middle and High School, holding it open for Zoë, who followed him into the quiet building, openly gawking at his

213

tight ass as he turned back to relock the front doors.

They'd had a nice conversation over coffee about Gardiner and how Paul had ended up there after growing up in Maine. He mentioned that his family had once taken a summer vacation to a dude ranch in Wyoming and Paul had been overcome by the beauty of the park; he'd known then that Wyoming or Montana would have to figure into his future.

It was surprisingly easy to act as though everything he told her was new; she loved listening to him tell her about going to Brown, opting out of the family business and choosing to go into education instead. And being able to ask questions made the conversation so much less one-dimensional than their texting conversations had been. There was nothing quite like staring into someone's eyes, listening to the changes in their voice, watching them smile or shrug or grimace as the story demanded. Zoë loved that she'd gotten to know Paul over the internet and during a handful of phone conversations, but sitting next to him was infinitely more intimate, if distracting. As they sat together on the window seat, her knee had rested lightly on the edge of his thigh, but she had savored the contact, minimal though it was, and wondered if he had noticed it too.

"So," he said, rousing her from her thoughts as they stepped into the cool, dark front hallway of the squat, brick public building. "Here we are. Zoë, meet my school. School, this is Zoë."

She heard the note of pride in his voice, and peeked up at him, smiling at his handsome face as he looked right and left down the front corridor, as though making sure naught was amiss. And nothing was. The floors were buffed to a high shine, the display cases held several decades' worth of school trophies and a banner over the double doors to the cafeteria read "WELCOME BACK STUDENTS!"

Zoë took a deep breath, the old public-school smell making her miss her teaching days, even as she welcomed the familiarity of it.

"The smell, right?" Paul asked smiling. "How many years since you've been back to high school?"

"Oh, I used to—" She stopped herself just before blurting out that she used to be an art teacher. That would have been a little too close to Holly's story. She had to think fast, but she didn't want to lie. "—sub."

It was true. She had been a sub for six months out of college before finding a permanent position.

Paul's eyes widened and his mouth formed an O. "You were a teacher? I had no idea!"

"Well, how would you?"

"We have teaching in common," he said, staring at her, a slight smile on his face. Then he chuckled lightly, leaning toward her and flicking on the hallway light on the wall behind her shoulder. His arm brushed her shoulder and he smelled like fresh air and coffee and she fought against letting her eyes close in blissful awareness of him.

"How long ago?"

"W-what?" she asked, her voice even breathier than it had been since arriving in Gardiner.

"How long ago? The subbing?"

"Oh! Um, right out of college."

He gestured to the hallway and she fell into step beside him.

"Did you want to teach? Or were you just killing time as you found your way?"

"I love kids," she evaded. "I loved the days I spent teaching."

"So, why didn't you stick with it? You're patient and kind and easygoing. I bet more than one kid had a crush on his pretty sub."

"Oh." Her cheeks felt warm from his flattery. "I may go back to it at some point."

"What lured you away?" Her answer sat like a rock in her stomach, but she forced herself to tell the truth. "I'm a website designer."

He nodded with a "nothing wrong with that" look on his face. "Well, that sounds interesting."

She scoffed good-naturedly. "It's not, really. My boss hired me to bring a more creative edge to his company, but it's hard to be creative about pool cleaning and window treatment businesses, you know?"

"Sounds like you should go back to teaching," he said, stopping beside a door neatly labeled "Art Studio A," his hand on the doorknob.

"Maybe I will," she said honestly, crossing her arms over her chest. Maybe she would. No, not maybe. She would. Stan had been kind to her, giving her a good job with a decent salary when she'd needed one, but she was sick and tired of the mind-numbing days under the fluorescent lights of his office. She missed being in a school. She missed working with kids. She'd call her old principal when she got home—

When she got home.

It hurt to even think it.

Will Paul have rejected her by then? Will he have told her he could never be with a liar and tell her never to contact him again? How would she bear it? How could she possibly stand to lose him? To lose this sweetness, this attraction, the most amazing connection her heart and mind had ever known in all her life?

"Zoë? Zoë?"

She looked up and he was staring at her, head cocked to the side.

"I lost you there for a sec. You okay?"

"Huh? Oh, yeah. I'm good. I'm fine." She took a deep breath, offering him a tentative smile. "I was lost...um, in my thoughts."

"Too bad you're not still a sub," he said, opening the door and preceding her into the room to turn on the lights. "I'd hire you from New Year's to Memorial Day here in the art studio. Mrs. Kaye is leaving on a maternity absence. And while I totally respect the right for any woman to stay home with her kids, it sure does complicate staffing."

"What do you mean?" asked Zoë, trying to ignore the way her heart fluttered wildly at the thought of staying in Gardiner with Paul *and* having the opportunity to teach again.

"A lot of teachers don't come back. They take the three

months' leave, then extend to six, then break the news that they're going to stay home for a few years and not come back, after all. Again, I am all for women making their own decisions about staying home with their children. But I have to hire a three-month sub, then see if the sub can extend her placement with us, and then I have to hire a full-time replacement after all."

She nodded distractedly. She hadn't thought about her principal having to find a sub for her and a permanent replacement. Her idea of calling to get her old job back suddenly felt pretty unrealistic.

"Here we are," Paul said, gesturing to the left wall with one hand. "Do your worst."

Zoë lifted her eyes to the wall and felt her face break into a grin. Art supplies covered an entire wall of shelves.

"Wow," she sighed, moving toward the wall and finally being totally distracted by something other than Paul Johansson. "Wow. You've got everything."

Metal shelves were neatly labeled and the supplies on them arranged so that students would be able to find everything they needed to spark their creativity. Paints, acrylic and oil, pastels, watercolors, brushes in every possible shape and size. She looked lower and found chalk and charcoal in neat buckets, waiting for a student to claim them, and lower still markers in a variety of tip points and colors.

"We take specials and extracurricular activities really seriously," he answered, grinning at her, and she could tell he was pleased by her reaction.

"I guess you do!" she said, genuinely impressed. "No

wonder you're ranked first in the state."

"Hey," he said, touching her elbow so that she turned to him. His forehead creased as he stared at her. "How'd you know that?"

Oh, crap! That wasn't something she should know! He shared the news with her over the phone last week, but she knew it wasn't going to be announced publicly for another two weeks. She turned back to the art supplies, stalling.

She swallowed uncomfortably, having a wild impulse to tell him everything. Just start talking and tell him everything and not stop until he escorted her back to the front door of the school and locked her out.

Instead, she remembered something she'd read in the local paper this morning while waiting for her coffee.

"I-I mean, I'm *assuming* you will be. I read in the newspaper this morning that it's going to be announced soon and that Gardiner's in the running."

He stared at her for an extra beat before his face relaxed and he nodded. "Yes, we're a finalist this year. He hesitated. I shouldn't tell you this. They contacted me last week. ...we won. We're first."

"Wow!" She turned back to him, her face a beaming smile. "That's just—that's amazing, Paul! Congratulations! You must be so proud!"

He nodded modestly, but he looked delighted. And young. And beautiful.

She couldn't stop herself.

She opened her arms, stepping toward him, and without a moment's hesitation, he pulled her into his body for a hug, pressing her tightly up against his chest, his arms encompassing her whole body. Zoë closed her eyes, twisting her neck to rest her cheek on his shirt, relieved that she hadn't been found out, the adrenaline rush still making her feel a little dizzy. She wobbled on her feet a little and Paul leaned back to look at her, but he didn't let go.

"Did I hurt your leg pulling on you?" he asked softly.

She shook her head slowly, holding his eyes.

Something shifted in the air between them, and she was suddenly, achingly aware of his closeness.

"Zoë, I…" His low, deep-conflicted voice trailed off as his gaze flicked to her lips. "I promised I wouldn't…"

He wanted to kiss her again.

And she wanted him to.

But she saw the pain in his eyes, the terrible fight he was having with himself, and her love for him overrode her almost painful desire for him. She pushed back against his chest, turning quickly back to the art shelves. But longing for him pooled low in her tummy, throbbing and painful, and her eyes burned with tears. She wanted him. So much. So badly.

"Choose whatever you want, whatever you need," he said softly from behind her. "I'm going to stop in at the office. I'll meet you back at the front doors."

She nodded, not trusting her voice. She listened as he crossed back to the door that led back out to the corridor.

"Zoë?"

"Mmm?" she murmured with her back to him.

"Thank you," he whispered, before leaving the room

and closing the door behind him.

***

Paul was grateful to be sitting next to Lars in the front seat of his truck and not next to Zoë in the back. Although there's nothing he'd like better than to sit beside her, he was proving to have little to no self-control where she was concerned. Anyway, before they left Gardiner and lost the cell signal, he wanted to send a quick "Hello/I miss you" text to Holly.

Hey Holly. Hope all is well in CT and you're settling into your hotel. I really miss you. If you can talk before Fri, please call. –P

He pushed his phone in his back pocket then heard an almost immediate ding ring out in the car. He fished his phone back out quickly, but there were no new incoming messages. It must not have been his phone. Turning his head slightly, he saw Zoë looking at her phone-on-one side of the back seat and Jane looking at hers on the other—*must have been one of theirs*. While he had the phone back out, he scrolled through his texts with Holly for a moment, realizing that she'd never written back to the text he sent yesterday afternoon, and here he was sending another.

He blew out an annoyed breath, tucking his phone away again. *Talk about needy.*

He had promised himself not to act like a needy, cloying boyfriend while Holly was at her conference and now here he was, texting her repeatedly. Even worse than the action was the reason behind it. Guilt. He had sent both messages not because he'd seen something that reminded him of Holly or because he had something meaningful to share with her, but because he felt guilty about his attraction to Zoë.

You shouldn't need to hear Holly's voice to be assured that she's worth holding out for.

Then again, he couldn't deny his attraction to Zoë, or his growing admiration of her. She was a complex combination of contradictions and he could feel her getting under his skin; she was little and curvy, she was vulnerable and guarded, she was sad and hopeful.

He was interested in her.

There. You admitted it.

Did it make him any less committed to Holly just because he was interested in Zoë? Was there room for both situations in his life?

He mulled this over for a minute while Jane leaned forward to plug her iPhone into Lars's radio. A second later an older, bluesy-style rock and roll song came through the speakers. Paul didn't know the song but the lyrics in the first verse included the words "Now, baby, you're casting your spell on me..." and Paul looked out the window, smiling lightly. Wasn't it strange when that happened? When a song you'd never heard before nailed the way you were feeling?

Yes, he decided. *There's room for both, as long as you're just figuring it out. But you're going to have to make a choice. Soon.*

In the side mirror to his right, he saw Zoë's face peeking out of the window behind him. Her black hair was blowing back, and while her sunglasses kept her eyes hidden, she was smiling and occasionally looking back at Jane as they sang along to the song. He stared at her in the mirror until he realized she was staring back at him. She lowered the glasses and he watched, transfixed, as one eye winked, almost in slow motion, before she pushed the glasses back up on her nose.

Paul looked away from the mirror, sitting back in the seat, unable to keep the giddy grin from spreading out across his face.

Figure out what's between you and Zoë. But you're going to have to make up your mind who you want in your life. Sooner rather than later...before someone gets hurt.

CHAPTER 13

Zoë couldn't get over the wild beauty of the falls. It was like nothing she'd ever seen before, and even though she'd been trying to capture their rushing majesty with pastels and chalk for over two hours, she didn't feel that anything she had created was doing it justice.

"Hey, Zoë! You almost ready for lunch?" asked Jane with a sunny smile, walking over to Zoë from the other side of the viewing area where she'd been experimenting with different angles, lenses and filters. "Lars texted me. The guys are taking a break."

They'd left the car at a parking area near the road at the top of the falls and the girls had walked the short way to a viewing area where Zoë had helped Jane set up her tripod before finding a rock where she could spread out her art supplies. Before they'd parted, Lars had explained that Gibbon Falls was located roughly five miles upstream from the confluence of the Gibbon and Firehole Rivers and had a drop of approximately eighty-five feet. They'd made a plan to meet up in a few hours and then Lars and Paul had headed back to the car to suit up in waders and vests, grab their fly fishing poles and lure kits.

But first, Lars had pulled Jane into his arms for a kiss and Paul had turned to Zoë with soft, warm eyes. "You'll be okay up here?"

She nodded, smiling at him. "Sure. Jane'll be with me."

"You'll be able to see us down there. If you want to, you can—I mean, you can come down if you want to watch. Or—or draw, you know. Down there. Near me."

"I'd love it," she said, and felt a shiver as his face broke into a pleased smile.

"Just be careful on your descent. In fact, have Jane call me. I'll come up and get you, okay?" His eyes were filled with tenderness and concern and Zoë couldn't look away from him. She could barely speak. "I'll catch you something."

"Oh, yeah? A pet?" she asked softly.

"Well...no. We can't keep 'em but we could name one before we throw him back." His eyes twinkled with the silly sweetness of his suggestion.

"Name him?"

"Sure," he said, stepping closer to her. His eyes grew more serious suddenly, holding hers. "Zoë, I want—"

"You ready, man?" Lars slapped Paul on the shoulder.

Paul jerked his head over to face his friend then turned back to Zoë.

"Yeah. Let's go."

He gave her a half smile as he followed Lars over to the truck.

Zoë stared after him, her feet unable or unwilling to move. What was he about to say? What did he want? Frustration and excitement fought for her attention and she finally let excitement win for one important reason as something new dawned on her:

He didn't look guilty.

When he'd been flirting with her just now and even when he started to get serious before Lars interrupted them, he didn't look guilty. He looked easy and relaxed and playful without the pain she'd seen in his eyes when he'd almost kissed her in the art studio two hours ago.

What had changed on the drive to the falls? she wondered. Then, thinking about the warmth in his bright blue eyes she added: *And please can it stay that way?*

She wasn't surprised to get his text as they left Gardiner. She knew that he'd felt conflicted in the art studio and it was the second time he'd reached out to "Holly" when he felt a pull to Zoë. Something awkward had occurred to her, reading his short text in the truck.

Did she have a right to feel slighted that he was showing interest in Zoë? Did it mean that what she'd shared with him as Holly didn't matter? Did it make him somehow unfaithful to her as Holly that he seemed interested in her as Zoë?

No! she answered the ridiculous thoughts. *He doesn't know it, but he's responding to the same things about you in person that he responded to virtually. You're the same person. You don't lose anything if he likes both parts of you.*

But it didn't sit entirely well with her and she wondered, yet again, about telling him the truth. It's just that she'd hung out with him for almost twenty-four straight hours now, and with every passing moment, the stakes grew higher. Losing him was more and more unthinkable. Her only hope was that if he fell hard for her as Zoë, she'd have an easier time holding on to him when he found out she was Holly too.

"This is great!" exclaimed Jane, finally standing behind her. "You're really talented!"

Zoë looked up at Jane over her shoulder, envious that Jane's love life was so easy, so figured out, so solid.

"Thanks," she said. "Sure beats building websites."

Zoë stood up, wiping her palms on her jeans and placing the pastels carefully back in the box in rainbow order.

"Can I ask you a question?" she asked Jane, who was gathering Zoë's papers into a portfolio folder.

"Sure. Anything."

"About Paul…"

"What?" Zoë looked up at Jane's expectant face and suddenly didn't know what to say.

"Do you like him?"

Zoë smiled sheepishly, shrugging. "What's not to like?"

Jane's eyes brightened and she grinned. "You like him. I knew it!"

"But it doesn't sound like he's available. He's mentioned, um—"

"Miss Mystic. *Holly*," supplied Jane and Zoë felt a stab of guilt to be deceiving her new friend. "Yeah, he met her online. But…"

Jane handed Zoë the neatened portfolio and paused, looking into Zoë's eyes.

"They haven't met yet," Jane said quietly, looking away, as though she were betraying someone.

"So…"

"So, if I were you? I'd try to figure out kind of quick if you're really interested. Because she's stiff competition, but you're here and she's…"

"Not," said Zoë, quietly. "But is he the type of guy who could move on so quickly? From her to me?"

Jane started back to the truck to drop off their supplies and Zoë walked beside her.

"Here's the thing…I'm sure Holly's a great girl. I'm sure she is, or he wouldn't like her so much. The timing sort of sucks for him. If he'd met you several weeks ago, he wouldn't have known Holly yet." She touched Zoë's arm when they reached the truck and Zoë turned to Jane. "Know how Lars and I finally got together? It was because I decided not to regret anything. I was about to leave for the airport when someone very wise told me that the saddest word in the world was 'regret.' It really resonated with me. I mean, I'd only known Lars for a week, but I knew if I left him, I'd regret it more than anything in my life.

"Don't get me wrong…I sort of hate it that I'm telling you to go for him when Holly's in the picture. But I like you. And *he* likes you—I can tell. And more than anything, I just want him to be happy, because he's a good man. He deserves to be happy."

"I agree."

Jane unlocked the truck door with Lars's keys and placed her camera bag and tripod gently on the front seat. She turned to Zoë and Zoë gave her the caddy of art supplies and portfolio which Jane placed on the floor before closing and relocking the door.

"No regrets, Zoë," said Jane, smiling.

"Good advice."

"Oh!" Jane reached into her back pocket, pulled out her phone and then looked up at Zoë, grinning. "Lars says to stay put. Paul's coming up for you."

Zoë grinned back at her friend. "No regrets, Jane."

***

"You're making me look bad," griped Lars. "Should I go up and get Jane too?"

"Don't be an asshole. Did Jane massively mangle her leg in a car accident a couple of years ago? Oh, she didn't? Then I guess she's okay making her own way down."

"Touchy." Lars went to work spreading out the red-and-white-checked blanket on a bank beside the water and unpacking the picnic basket. "Tell Jane to call out if she needs me."

"Think of it this way: you'll get a few minutes alone. I'll take my time getting back down here with Zoë. Just have all your clothes back on by the time we get here."

Lars's grin was wolfish. "I like the way you think, my friend."

When Paul got to the base of the rocky hill that led to the parking area, he encountered Jane. "You seen my man?"

"Thataway," said Paul, gesturing with his head as she passed him.

"Wait. Paul."

He turned back to find her facing him, hands on her hips.

"Zoë," she said.

"What?"

"I like her."

"Me too."

Jane looked uncomfortable then added. "She likes you."

"She told you that?"

Jane nodded, biting her lower lip, and before processing her words, he had a fleeting thought that Jane biting her lower lip did nothing for him.

"She likes me?"

Jane nodded. "Yeah."

"Thanks, Jane," he said, turning away from her, excited to see Zoë again, even though they'd only been apart for a couple of hours.

"Hey! Lover boy!"

When he looked over his shoulder, Jane was still standing there in the same place. "What about Holly?"

Paul cringed, sighing, all that feel-good euphoria leeching out of his body.

"I don't know, Jane." He scratched his chin, could smell the fish on his hands and wished he'd been able to wash off before collecting Zoë. "I'm in a bad place."

"Did you make promises to Holly?"

"She's amazing, Jane. She's sunshine and happiness. She's gorgeous. Funny. Super happy with her life. Close to her family. The perfect girl."

"I don't care about that. Did you make *promises*?"

"Not in so many words. But we've talked about our feelings."

"How do you feel about her?"

"I feel like…" He threw up his hands in frustration. "She's this amazing…*possibility*. This beautiful idea. But, right now, she doesn't feel *real*. She feels like a fairy tale."

"And Zoë feels real?"

"Zoë *is* real. She's a real person and she's here. Right here, right now. She's not gorgeous, but I want to touch her all the time. And she's not sunny, but she's strong and brave. And she's not super happy with her life, but I get the feeling she wants to change that. And she's not perfect, but I can't get her out of my head. I haven't stopped thinking about her since I met her. She's no fairy tale, but…"

"But," said Jane gently, reaching out to touch Paul's arm. "Real girls aren't fairy tales. Don't you know that?"

"I kinda want the fairy tale, Jane." He smiled at her, shrugging lightly. "*You* got it."

She seemed to consider this for a moment, and then she nodded. "I guess I kinda did. But hey," she said, walking backward in the direction of their picnic. "If you haven't made a commitment to Holly, keep your mind open. I'd hate for you to miss out on something *real* saving yourself for something…*hypothetical*. What you *really* want might be right in front of you."

"The thought has occurred to me." Paul nodded. "I don't want to hurt anyone."

"I think someone always gets hurt when it comes to love. I think those tough choices are part of what gives it a foundation. Someone will get hurt. You can take that to the bank. Just do your best." As she walked away, she yelled over her shoulder: "And take your time getting down here!"

Paul grinned, starting up the rocky uneven hill before him. It was a good ten-minute climb. When he finally got to the top he found Zoë leaning on Lars's truck.

"Hey," she said, smiling at him like she'd never seen anything as good as him walking toward her. It was all Paul could do not to grab her and kiss her.

"Heya," he said.

"I could have come down with Jane."

"I didn't want you to."

"Oh."

"I didn't want you to get hurt. I wanted to help you." He glanced at her leg, then back at her face.

She swallowed, looking down for a moment, and he wondered if he'd somehow overstepped his bounds. Happily, when she looked up again, her expression was amused.

"Cute," she said, gesturing to his waders.

He glanced down then shrugged, looking back up at her laughing brown eyes. "What? This doesn't do it for you?"

"I didn't say that."

"So these *do* do it for you?"

"I didn't say that either," she giggled, and the sound was like déjà vu. He'd heard that giggle before. Definitely. Somewhere. Was there an actress that giggled the same way Zoë did? Emma Stone, maybe, with her low, breathy voice like Zoë's? That must be it, because he could swear he'd heard it before.

"You look good," he said softly, tucking a strand of her

glossy black hair behind her ear. "You got some color today."

"A little," she confirmed, feeling her cheeks flush deeper under his gaze.

"How'd you get so pretty?" he breathed, stepping closer to her.

"Oh, I'm—"

"Don't say you're not. I'm big on telling the truth."

Her face fell, her forehead knitting in distress. He put his knuckles gently under her chin and tilted her face back up to him, surprised to see tears in her eyes.

"Did I say something wrong?"

"Nothing," she said in a whisper. "You're just so lovely."

He heard the soft strain in her voice and pulled her into his arms, closing his eyes as he felt her relax against his chest. He wondered if she was thinking about the guy she'd come to Gardiner to see. He wondered if that's who made her feel like crying. That must be it. Anger bubbled up inside of him that anyone would dare to treat Zoë as less than the amazing woman she was.

"This guy is not good for you, Zoë." He drew back and she lifted her eyes to look at him. To his relief, she wasn't crying, although her eyes were still a little glassy, capturing his with their uncertain, hopeful, heartbreaking depths. "If you were mine…"

Her eyes dropped to his mouth and he watched, transfixed, as she murmured, "If I was yours…"

He could tell her, or he could show her.

Simple choice.

He kissed her.

***

Zoë closed her eyes as he leaned over her, claiming her lips with his. He tightened his arms around her, pulling her body flush against his, and she slid her flattened hands up his chest until they rested lightly on the throbbing pulse of his throat.

She was terribly in love with him.

And it *was* terrible.

It was terrible that she had lied to him. It was terrible that she would eventually have to tell him the truth. It was terrible that she didn't know how to make it all okay. It was terrible to love so hard. It was terrible to want this much. It was terrible to know that she would never, ever love someone as she loved Paul Johansson.

His tongue slipped through her lips and all thoughts slipped from her head. She arched her back to fit better against him, and he held on tightly to her, pressing her up against the hardness between his thighs and pillaging her mouth with his tongue. He stroked the satin muscle then nipped at the soft skin of her lips, blowing her mind with the savage heat that they generated simply by touching.

She ran her hands through his thick blond hair as his hands moved from her back to her hips, his fingers slipping under her T-shirt to touch the soft skin underneath. Her fingers tensed in his hair from the sharp sweetness of the sensation and she moaned into his mouth, wanting more, wanting his hands all over her body. With increasing passion, she dug her hands into his—

"Excuse me! This is a public park! Oh, really. This is disgraceful!"

Paul pulled back from her abruptly and her eyes flew open. She caught his startled expression, staring at someone behind her with a mixture of surprise and chagrin sweeping across his flushed face. She dropped her hands to his shoulders and felt them lightly shaking under her fingers; with one look at his face, she realized he was chuckling inside and trying very hard not to break into gales of laughter on the outside. She held on to him, feeling herself dissolve into quiet giggles, finally resting her forehead on his chest as her shoulders shook.

"S-Sorry, ma'am," she heard Paul say, his voice just keeping it together as his chest still trembled lightly, rippling against her with silent laughter.

"Well, I should say so! There are *children* milling around!"

"Yes, ma'am," said Paul, his voice merry under contrition, another round of trembles making Zoë giggle harder. "Poor judgment."

"Indeed. Get a room. Or keep it clean."

Zoë snorted lightly against his chest, unable to keep the giggles under control.

"Yes. A clean room. Thank you."

Paul stepped back then, taking her hand and pulling her away from the sour-faced, grumbling grandmother behind them.

"Thanks for letting me take the fall," he said, grinning

at her when they finally got to the trail at the top of the cliff.

"No problem!" She giggled, pushing a flyaway hair out of her face.

Paul caught it and tucked it behind her ear, leaning down to give her a short kiss on the nose before sighing heavily.

"Don't say you're sorry," she said, loving the way the sunshine made his hair sparkle like gold.

"I'm not," he said, searching her eyes, his smile fading. "How come you couldn't have come to Gardiner a month ago, Zoë?"

She shrugged.

"The guy…" he started.

"Don't think about him," she answered, biting her lip and loving the way it attracted his eyes like a magnet when she did. "Things have changed."

"What? How? You came here for him—"

"And found you."

He put his hands on her hips, pulling her to him, resting his chin on her head.

"Zoë," he breathed, and she heard the deep emotion in his voice. "I want—"

"I know there's a lot going on in your head, but…could we just be in the moment?" she asked softly. "Just for today? Just pretend we're both free to do whatever we want. Can we do that? Couldn't we do that?"

He leaned back, smiling down at her and nodding.

"We could do that."

Then he took her hand and led her carefully back down

the trail to join Jane and Lars for lunch.

***

The ride home found Jane in the front seat with Lars, with whom she chose music and traded whip-fast banter, while Zoë sat in the back, tucked up against Paul, her weary head on his shoulder, his arm around her.

Jane and Lars had been thoroughly composed by the time he and Zoë had reached them for lunch, although the careful observer might have noticed the twigs in Jane's hair and Lars's heavy, slightly frustrated-looking bedroom eyes.

Yup, remembered Paul, turning to look out the window. *There had definitely been shenanigans.*

Lunch had been high-spirited, with plenty of teasing, and he'd loved watching Zoë. She took it all in stride, giggling and rolling her eyes at turns, giving as good as she got, clever with a turn of phrase, her brown eyes warm and sparkling.

Lars had taken Jane's hand and led her away on the excuse of checking out some rock formations on the other side of the falls, and Paul had turned to Zoë, happy to finally have her all to himself. He lay back on the blanket and she lay down beside him, her shoulder barely brushing his, but insanely distracting all the same.

"Hey," she said after several moments of staring up at the bright blue sky.

"What?"

"Remember earlier today? You started to say something, and you didn't finish. Something about wanting…"

He had pressed his arm up against hers, finding her hand and lacing his fingers through hers. "I wanted to ask you over for dinner tonight."

"Really?"

"Yeah. What do you think?"

She'd brought his hand to her lips and kissed it softly before murmuring, "I think yes," forming the words against the back of his hand, which made her lips touch lightly against his stimulated skin. Then she lowered their hands without letting go, resting them in the small space of blanket between them.

That's the first time Paul felt it.

In his heart. In his gut.

Inconvenient, and yet indisputable.

Not only was he falling for Zoë, he was letting it happen.

The scenery flew by as they neared the Roosevelt Arch and Jane peeked back to look at them. Paul caught her mossy green eyes and gave her a lazy grin.

"She's asleep," Jane whispered.

"I thought so," he murmured back.

Her breathing had been deep and even for a good fifteen minutes now. The un-air-conditioned truck was warm from sitting in the sun all day and the breeze from Jane's window was cool, creating the perfect conditions for sleep. Plus, he imagined that going up and down that hill had been challenging for Zoë. He'd noticed a more pronounced limp once they'd made it back up to the top.

Jane turned back around, her left arm reaching out to

massage Lars on the back of the neck and he turned to his girlfriend, stepping on the gas a little harder before returning his eyes to the road. It wasn't long before they pulled up in front of Paul's house.

Paul shook Zoë's shoulders lightly.

"Zoë," he whispered in her ear. "We're home."

"I'm so tired," she murmured, looking up at him with heavy-lidded eyes in the dim light of the truck. The sun was almost down.

"I'll walk you to your inn," he said. "We can do dinner another time."

Lars opened her door, and helped her out as Paul came quickly around the truck to take over.

"Night, guys," he whispered to Lars and Jane, whose elbow rested on the windowsill. "Thanks for today."

"Thanks so much," said Zoë, her voice raspy and low from sleep.

"Come find me at the Prairie Dawn tomorrow if you want, Zoë. I'll be around."

Zoë smiled at Jane and nodded. "Will do."

Paul saluted Lars, then took Zoë's hand, leading her onto the sidewalk as Lars pulled away.

"I'm awake. I can do dinner," Zoë said, looking up at him with glassy, tired eyes.

"Rain check," said Paul, pulling her toward her inn. "How about tomorrow?"

"Tonight," she whispered as they reached the front porch at the Mountain View, stopping to face each other at the bottom of the steps, their hands still laced together.

"Tomorrow," he insisted, landing a light kiss on her head before dropping her hand.

"Okay," she sighed, her smile loose and dreamy as she stepped up three steps and found herself finally eye level with him. "Tomorrow."

"Okay," he said.

He stared at her in the twilight, the hum of the streetlights and smell of BBQ enveloping them as night inched forward.

He made no move to leave her.

So far, he had kissed her twice.

Zoë decided to even the score.

***

She licked her lips as she dropped her eyes to his mouth, leaning forward slightly and trusting him to catch her from falling. as though on cue, his hands spanned her waist at the same moment her lips landed on his. Her breasts pressed against his chest as he pulled her closer to him, and she stepped down once, closing the rest of the distance between them.

She poured everything she felt for him into that kiss, blurring the lines of Holly and Zoë for herself until they united as one person in her mind, utterly swept away by the man who stood before her.

It was the gentlest kiss they'd shared yet, soft and full of tenderness; the sort of tenderness people share when they're realizing, for the first time, that they have feelings for each other.

"Zoë," he breathed, releasing her lips. "Zoë… Zoë…"

She bent her head to the side as he dropped soft, slow kisses to her jaw, her throat, the soft skin behind her ear, relentlessly brushing his lips against her sensitive skin. She pressed closer to him as she imagined his lips continuing their journey down her neck to the soft hollow of her collarbone, grazing it lightly with his teeth before using his tongue to—

"Come up," she murmured, her heart clutching with want.

He drew back and swallowed, his eyes shuddering closed as he shook his head lightly.

"No," he whispered.

"Come up," she asked again.

"No, love," he repeated, dropping his hands from her waist.

Zoë drew back from him, confusion cooling her blood and bringing a tingly, embarrassed flush to her cheeks.

"Okay."

But it wasn't okay. She didn't understand. He wanted her as much as she wanted him. She couldn't have misunderstood that.

Tears burned the very backs of her eyes as she turned away from him, running up the stairs and into the inn. She shut the front door without glancing back at him and leaned against it as the first tear of disappointment and embarrassment coursed down her cheek.

A faint rapping directly behind her head made her quickly wipe the tear away with the back of her hand. She took a deep breath and composed herself before opening the door.

His face. Oh, God, his face.

He flexed his jaw twice, holding her eyes unmercifully.

"Do you have any idea how hard that was?"

"To say no?"

"To say no."

"Good," she whispered, unable to keep the touch of bitterness out of her voice, even as his eyes were beseeching her to understand, breaking her heart with the strength of his longing.

"I just needed to be sure you knew that," he whispered.

Then he turned and walked away.

CHAPTER 14

"Zoë! I'm dyin' here! Why haven't you called?"

Zoë rubbed her eyes and looked at the clock on the bedside table. 5:47 a.m.

"It's early here, Sand."

"Well, it's almost eight here and I gotta go open the shop soon. How's it going? How'd he take the news?" Zoë rolled over on her side, propping herself up on one elbow.

"Well, I, um…"

"What? He's mad? He's happy? You're killin' me…what happened, Zo?"

Zoë cringed, stalling for time.

"Oh, crap. You didn't tell him yet."

She could hear the flat disapproval in Sandy's voice and she groaned, falling onto her back, staring at the ceiling.

"It's complicated."

"No, Zo, it's not. We practiced. The whole reason you went out there was to tell him the truth. Did you forget that?"

"Forget it? It's torturing me every second that I'm with him."

"*With* him?"

"Yeah, I mean, I'm spending time with him."

"As Zoë."

"Of course as Zoë."

"But he still thinks he's cyberdating Holly?"

"Yeah," Zoë said quietly, guilt infusing the single word.

There was a long pause on the other end of the line before Sandy spoke again. "You're messin' with his head, Zo. It's not right."

"He likes me for me. He likes *Zoë*. We're hanging out. We've kissed—"

"Kissed? Oh, no…"

"No, it's not like that. It's not a hookup. I love—I love him, Sand. I *love* him. I can't lose him and all I think while I'm around him is that he's such a stickler for the truth. He's such a good man, and when I tell him I've been lying to him, he's going to walk away. I just want it to be really, really hard for him to walk away."

"Zoë. It's not going to be hard for him to walk away from a pile of lies."

Zoë's eyes filled with tears, spilling from the corners of her eyes.

"Why can't I have a little happiness?" She sobbed. "I don't deserve something good in my life, do I?"

"Oh, honey, of course you do. But good things don't usually grow from bad foundations. You're making a mess of this." Sandy paused and Zoë heard her take a deep breath and sigh. "Maybe you need to get some space from him and remind yourself why you went out there and what you need to do. Before it's too late."

"I don't have a car, Sand. It's a small town and my inn

is on the same block as his house. Where am I supposed to go?"

"Go on a tour. Isn't there a big park right there?" The way Sandy said "park" like "pahk" made Zoë sniffle and grin. She sounded like home.

"Yeah. There's a big park."

"So? Go on a tour for a day or two. Clear your head. When you get back, you go right to his house, knock on his door and tell him the truth. Lay your cards on the table. Be brave. And you know what? Maybe he won't walk away, Zo."

"He'd never trust me again," she whispered, more to herself than to Sandy.

"You'll never know unless you give him the chance to decide."

Zoë took a deep sobbing breath and wiped her eyes, asking how Sandy was feeling and reminding her to take good care of herself. She thought about asking about Thea and Brandon, but she didn't want to further muddle her already precarious composure and break down into more tears.

When they said goodbye, Sandy reminded her, "You got so much good in you, Zo. So much. I bet he sees it. I know he does. I was wrong before…it's going to be hard for him to walk away."

"Thanks, Sand," she said in a shaky voice, pressing end on her phone and placing it back on the bedside table.

Sandy was right. She needed to tell Paul the truth and perhaps placing a day or two of space between them would make it easier for her to steel herself. She got out of bed and got dressed quickly. It was almost seven o'clock when she started into town, hoping to catch one of the Lindstroms open for business. She'd noticed their office yesterday, a stone's throw away from the Prairie Dawn.

It had rained overnight, and the sidewalks were wet, and the misty air was heavy and cold on her walk into town. As she passed Paul's house, she noticed two upstairs lights were on, but she kept moving, quietly and quickly. She wasn't going to be distracted from her plan.

Walking over the bridge, she glanced down at the river below, thick and wild from so much rain last night, then continued across, looking fondly at the gazebo in the parking lot of the Cowboy Lodge where she and Paul had talked on Saturday night during that intense rain shower. She passed the Prairie Dawn, where she saw Maggie behind the counter, working at a laptop, and Graham taking chairs down from tabletops, getting ready to open in the next few minutes.

A few storefronts later, she stood in front of Lindstrom & Sons, which was open for business early, as Zoë had predicted. She was fairly sure some tours must have to leave in the early morning.

When she opened the front door, an overhead bell jingled cheerfully, and three sets of bright blue eyes looked up at her in surprise.

"Zoë!" said Nils, standing up from behind his desk and coming to the door to extend his hand. "It's good to see you again."

"You too," she said, smiling up at the hulking blond

man.

"This is my dad, Carl." He gestured to an older, white-haired man sitting at the adjacent desk. Mr. Lindstrom rose, putting out his hand.

"Good to know you, Zoë."

"You too, Mr. Lindstrom."

His eyes were light blue like a husky pup's, so icy blue they'd almost be disconcerting if they hadn't been accompanied by a tan, weathered face that crinkled with a warm smile.

"You're an early bird!"

"Still on Connecticut time, I guess."

"You from Connecticut?" asked Nils, crossing his arms over his chest as he leaned against his father's desk. "I thought Rhode Island."

Zoë swallowed. *Caught in a lie.* "I flew out of Rhode Island. I actually live in Connecticut."

Nils's eyes narrowed just a fraction before he gave her a small smile.

Zoë turned her eyes quickly to a strikingly pretty blonde, blue-eyed teenager sitting at a desk beside Mr. Lindstrom.

"'Morning," said Zoë.

Carl gestured to the young woman. "This is Julie Sørensen. My niece. My sister's girl."

Zoë offered her a warm grin, which Julie returned. She might be as old as eighteen but not much older than that. "Hey, Julie."

"Hi," she answered, Lindstrom-blue eyes trained on

Zoë.

"Julie's come to help out for a while. With Lars leading so many of his own tours lately, we needed someone here to answer phones and whatnot. Just got here yesterday, but she's already settling in."

"How're you liking Gardiner, Julie?"

She offered Zoë a tight smile that didn't quite reach her eyes. "It's just fine."

Zoë had lots of experience with quiet teenagers who had much more going on in their heads than showed on their faces. She'd lay any bet that Julie's still waters ran pretty deep. She watched as the younger woman settled back into her work, reaching for her mouse and concentrating on the computer screen in front of her.

"Well, what can we do you for, Zoë?" Mr. Lindstrom looked at her from over his wire-rimmed reading glasses, setting a pile of papers to the side of his desk and picking up another. "Nils can help you with whatever you need."

Nils gestured to the small loveseat that sat in front of a coffee table in the windowed front area of the small office. Zoë sat down on the edge of the loveseat. Nils settled across from her in one of two wingback chairs.

"I thought I'd take a tour," she said. "At the airport, you mentioned a group on Tuesday? Tomorrow?"

Nils nodded. "Yup. Still on. But one change. We're out for two nights now. Not one."

"Oh." Zoë hadn't planned on being away for two nights. Frankly, wasting one night away from Paul felt like a big enough sacrifice. Two felt like eternity.

All the better to steel yourself for returning to tell the truth.

"Okay," she said. "Two it is."

"We're back on Thursday afternoon. Gardiner Harvest Dance is Thursday night which is sort of the way we wrap up that tour."

The Harvest Dance. It sounded like something out of the 1940s. She wondered if it was held in an old barn with folk dancing, fiddle music and fruit punch. She grinned at Nils.

"Harvest Dance?"

Nils grinned back sheepishly. "Old Gardiner tradition. It's held out in an open-air pavilion about fifteen minutes north of here near Bald Mountain. Bald Mountain Resort puts it on every year. They decorate it all up for the fall and there's dancing and the like. Folks like it."

"Folks'll have their traditions, *Største*," said Mr. Lindstrom from behind them, licking his forefinger to separate papers.

"*Ja*, Pappa," answered Nils gently, shrugging at Zoë with a sheepish grin.

She raised her eyebrows in question at his nickname. "*Schtor—*"

"Means biggest or largest. In Norwegian," he explained in a soft, warm voice.

"Oh."

"My mother was Norwegian. I'm the oldest of four. So... *Største*," he said, his cheeks flushing pink.

"I like it," she said, wanting to put him at ease.

She couldn't help but notice Julie's blue eyes peeking at

them from behind her computer, and decided to include the teen in their conversation. "You're Norwegian too, aren't you, Julie?"

She nodded. "*Ja.*"

"Do you have a Norwegian nickname?"

"I—I mean, I don't—I—" Her mouth sort of hovered open like a fish gasping for air.

Nils twisted his neck to wink at his much younger cousin before turning back to Zoë. "She has one, but no way she's telling."

Julie's eyebrows knitted together briefly in consternation before she buried herself in her work with unflinching attention. Zoë was curious, but Julie's nickname would have to be a story for another day. A day when her uncle and cousin weren't there to tease her.

"So," Nils said, his gruff, business voice returning, "do you want to go? For the two nights?"

"Yup. Sign me up."

He stood up and went to his desk, returning with some forms. "Just fill these out."

"Oh, um. I forgot to ask…how much walking's involved?"

"Usually a fair amount. But this tour is special, so not as much."

As relieved as Zoë was to hear that, her curiosity was piqued. "Why's this tour so special?"

Nils took a deep breath and cleared his throat. "You ever hear of the Blazin' Grannies?"

She shook her head slowly, eyes widening.

"Well, you're about to."

***

With her tour organized and paid for, Zoë headed back toward the Prairie Dawn to get a cup of coffee. On the short walk, she considered the decision she'd just made, hoping it wasn't a massive mistake.

Apparently, The Blazin' Grannies was a group of older ladies who had decided "not to wait for death lyin' down." The group of forty-five ladies between the ages of seventy-five and ninety lived year-round in Tampa, Florida. They planned three annual trips with their retirement money, always to adventurous places, always with a flair for danger. The tagline of their peculiar club was: "I'd rather die living!"

This fall's trip had twelve grannies visiting Yellowstone Park under the protection and direction of Carl and Nils Lindstrom, although Zoë couldn't help wondering if the Lindstroms maybe needed a little protection of their own. These ladies sounded feisty!

For his part, Nils seemed pleased—and perhaps a little relieved—to have one other young person joining the excursion, and Zoë couldn't deny that she was sort of looking forward to the adventure. Or would have been, if it didn't mean leaving Paul.

She opened the door to the Prairie Dawn and it swung back fast on its spring, that familiar summer camp sound reverberating in her ears as she made her way to the coffee counter where Maggie stood, elbows on the counter, laptop in front of her.

"Heya, Zoë," she said, pushing the laptop away and

gesturing to a bar stool. "Sit and rest."

"Morning, Maggie," she answered. "Think I could get a cappuccino?"

"Extra foam?"

"Sure," Zoë said, pulling up a seat.

Maggie turned to the counter behind her, then glanced back at the three or four patrons scattered around the café before catching Zoë's eyes.

"I'm glad you stopped by. Been wonderin' about you."

"I haven't told him yet," Zoë whispered.

"Didn't think so. He'd have come in here ragin' if you had." Maggie turned to her as the coffee brewed. "What're you goin' to do?"

"Actually? I'm going out of town for two nights. Put a little, um, distance between us. Get my courage up. Then I'll come back and tell him first thing."

Maggie blinked at her. "Where are you goin'?"

"Tour. With the Lindstroms. With, um, Nils and Mr. Lindstrom. And a bunch of old ladies."

"A bunch of old ladies? Heaven help Carl Lindstrom," Maggie grinned. She slid the hot mug over to Zoë then headed to a table in the corner who had gestured for service.

Graham sauntered up beside Zoë, hands on his hips, which held a leather utility belt slung low and manly. His eyes dipped meaningfully to her cleavage and lingered there before he looked up with a lazy grin.

"Mornin', Zoë," he drawled in his heavy brogue. "You're lookin'…fine."

She shook her head lightly at his flirting. "You are a

very bad boy."

"You dinna know the half of it, lassie."

"But I'm betting you'd love to show me."

"You name the time and the place. I'm easy."

"You don't say."

"Hey, now. You're the hottest thing Gardiner has to offer." He straddled the stool beside her, legs wide open, facing her, one knee lightly brushing her hip.

"You think so?"

His eyes slipped to her breasts again briefly and his mouth turned up into a teasing grin. "Yeah, I'm pretty certain."

"What if I said I'm taken?"

"Do you have a virtual someone too?" he asked mockingly, making air quotes with his fingers when he said "virtual someone."

"What if I did?"

He scoffed. "I'd say 'screw virtual.' The real thing's right in front of you."

"A very, *very* bad boy," she amended, sipping her coffee and grinning playfully at Graham.

***

Paul loved Monday mornings.

He loved the way every Monday felt like a fresh start, a chance to touch kids' lives and make their teenage years the best they could possibly be.

But tossing and turning until two o'clock in the morning didn't make for a very bright-eyed and bushy-tailed principal this particular Monday. His body clock still woke him up at six-thirty, but he was hurting from a lack of sleep. There was only one answer for it: a double espresso from the Prairie Dawn. Paul had just enough time to get there and still make it to school.

Giving himself permission to explore his attraction to Zoë hadn't helped diminish his guilt over Holly. Paul still had serious feelings for Holly, despite his pull to Zoë. He was in deep, dark water with these two women and he knew it. One of them was going to be rejected. One of them was going to be hurt in the long run.

And yet, he couldn't bring himself to text Holly the truth—not that she'd been answering his texts anyway while she was at her conference—and tell her that he'd met someone who was distracting him. He knew he should; he prided himself on being truthful, practicing integrity, living his life aboveboard. But the honest reason was that he was sure Holly would break things off with him, and after weeks of the most amazing correspondence of his life, he wasn't prepared to lose her.

Nor, however, was he interested in staying away from Zoë, even going so far as to show her a respect borne of true affection last night when he refused to join her in her bedroom. He saw her eyes. He knew that if they'd ended up on her bed, there was every likelihood they would have slept together. But he didn't want that for them. He liked her too much to rush things, no matter how much he wanted her.

Not to mention, if he slept with Zoë, his hands would be tied, and he'd need to break off things with Holly immediately.

It hadn't been easy to say no to Zoë, especially once he realized how much it had hurt and embarrassed her, which was never his intention. There was nothing, literally *nothing*, he wanted more than to feel his skin pressed up against hers, his lips against hers, pushing into the softness between her hips as she raked her nails down his—

He forced his thoughts to safer waters, but Zoë's face emerged in his head again quickly. What was it about Zoë that was so irresistible to him?

He sighed. He didn't need to enumerate her virtues. The list was long and grew with every moment he spent with her. Something about her called out to something in him. He couldn't stay away.

Which is why seeing Graham pressed up against her at the coffee bar made him want to strangle the kid. He flinched, watching through the window as Zoë giggled and flirted with the randy twenty-year-old. Something inside of him clenched with jealousy and anger at the sight of them together.

He pulled open the café door and strode to the bar, pushing the seat beside Zoë out of the way so that he could stand directly behind her, facing Graham.

"Paul! I never get to see you before school!" Maggie smiled warmly as Zoë shifted in her seat, turning to face him, her knee and elbow touching him, her brown eyes warm and surprised as a smile spread out across her pretty face.

"'Morning," she said, in that sexy, breathy voice of hers.

He couldn't help smiling back, despite the close proximity of Graham. "'Morning."

Was she thinking about how they parted last night? Of his confession of how much it hurt to say no to her? Why the hell had he said no? What an idiot!

"How'd you sleep?" she asked.

"Not great," he answered honestly. "I was...distracted. You?"

"What're you drinkin'?" Maggie interrupted, her hands braced on the counter before him.

"Double espresso, Mags. To go."

He glanced down at Zoë to find she was still staring up at him. Graham peeked around her shoulder.

"Och! Don't you look smart today, Mr. Principal. Sharp as a bloody tack, you are!"

It took Paul a moment to realize that Graham was referring to his ridiculous tie. It was a drab tan color, covered in moose antlers, interspersed with the words "Moose on the Loose" in bright right intervals.

Given to him at Christmas by one of his Special Education students, Paul made a concerted effort to put it in the rotation more frequently than others. Whenever Ida saw him wearing it, she gasped, running down the hall to hug him, and chanting "Moose on the loose...moose on the loose!" in her high-pitched, childlike voice.

Okay. So, it wasn't the sharpest tie ever, but seeing Ida's blue eyes so pleased and excited made it one of his favorites, hands down. Not that Graham would understand or respect such a story anyway.

Paul turned to Zoë, ignoring his young nemesis.

"You still coming for dinner?"

"Planning on it," she said, but her smile faded a little from happy to tentative. "Should I bring anything?"

"Do you have a specialty?" he asked, hoping to cajole that big smile back.

"I do, actually," she said, grinning. "Don't plan dessert. I'll bring what I need."

"A dinner party!" exclaimed Graham. "Why, I'd love to come! Thanks so much for the—"

"Thanks, Maggie," said Paul, interrupting Graham and taking his coffee from Maggie. "Does seven work?"

"Works fine for me," said Graham.

"You're *not* invited." Paul finally acknowledged him with a curt glance, before looking back down at Zoë.

"See you then," she said, biting her lip.

He shouldn't have.

He knew it even as he bent his head toward her.

He had no business kissing her in a public place in front of his friends and maybe even on display for one or two of his student's parents.

He had no business staking that sort of claim on her; the sort of claim that says: *She's mine.* But between Graham flirting with her and knowing he had to make it all day before seeing her again, plus that damn blood heating lip-biting thing she kept doing, he just couldn't help it.

He brushed her lips with his, sighing as he felt her hand move to rest on his cheek, cupping it gently. When he drew back, she looked dreamy, drunk, and definitely wanting more.

Good. Remember that when I leave, and Graham is all over you.

"Seven," he said again, gazing into her dazed eyes.

He didn't dare look back at Maggie as he turned and headed out the door.

***

It had been a long day not thinking about Zoë.

He reminded himself not to think about her when he made the morning announcements and he forced himself not to think about her when the president of the school board stopped by with new budget guidelines. He pushed her out of his mind when he got between two fighting seniors in the lunch line and he made sure she didn't cross his mind when he visited the music room to check on the freshman play rehearsal.

By the time he walked home that evening, it was all he could do not to stop by her inn, take the stairs two at a time, knock on her bedroom door and bury his tongue in her mouth, his hands in her hair, his—

Instead he tried not to look over at the temptation that was the Mountain View Inn as he passed and hurried to his own house where he had a shower to take, a salad to make, potatoes to bake and steaks to marinate before grilling. He was no gourmand, but any man worth his salt could grill a steak.

By the time the doorbell rang at seven, everything was ready. The table was set with matching plates and he had lit candles, feeling a little silly, but unable to remember the last time he'd invited a woman to dinner. He was dressed casually in jeans and a long-sleeved gray T-shirt and ran his hand through his drying hair once before opening the door.

She was wearing the long black skirt she'd worn for coffee on Saturday night, but she'd paired it with a white button-down shirt left open at the neck and tied in a knot at her waist. He didn't know how she'd gotten her hair mostly into a stubby, little ponytail, but she had, and wisps of black hair framed her face. She had silver bracelets on her wrists that clinked together and a silver anklet that jingled as she walked past him. Blood rushed from his head, racing south with gasping speed. *Miss Temptation. In the flesh.*

She smiled and sidled past him into his house, slipping off her shiny black flip-flops by the door and turning to hand him a brown paper bag of groceries.

"I promised I'd make dessert," she said, cocking her head to the side.

He was staring at her. He'd barely moved since opening the door, but he raised his hands to take the bag.

Damn! Get it together!

"You look…" he started, letting his eyes start at her pert ponytail, trail down her neck to the swell of her breasts, to her small waist, down the column of her skirt to the sparkling silver anklet. "…like Susanna."

She chuckled lightly, holding his eyes, pleased. "She's fictional."

"Not anymore."

"I'm not that exotic," she demurred.

"You are to me."

Her cheeks flushed pink, but she didn't look away. "Why?"

"Because you look like you look, and you show up here

259

suddenly out of nowhere and make me feel…"

"Feel what?"

His lungs filled and emptied painfully as he searched her eyes. *Helpless.*

"Oh," she breathed. "I see."

But instead of letting him kiss her, she turned away from him, stepping into the kitchen.

Paul glanced down at the bag in his arms, trying to compose himself, which was difficult since he wanted to drop the groceries on the floor, grab her arm and carry her up the stairs to his bedroom like a Neanderthal.

"Some of that needs to be refrigerated," she called from his kitchen, bending down to pick up Cleo and cradle the little dog in her arms.

Was it crazy that he felt jealous of his dog?

Paul took a deep breath. "Sure."

He followed her to the kitchen, shaking his head briefly, trying to clear it. He placed the bag on the kitchen counter.

"Would you like a drink?" he asked.

"Yes!" she said, chuckling lightly.

Thankfully, it broke the tension between them.

"What do you want? Wine? Beer?"

"Wine."

"White or red?"

"Red."

"Merlot or Cab?"

"Cab."

"Californian or Australian?"

"You know wine!" she said, smiling up at him.

"My parents insisted."

"Like dancing lessons," she said.

"Yeah." He chuckled, then cocked his head to the side. "Did I tell you that?"

"You must have mentioned it," she said quickly. After putting Cleo on the floor, she took a few groceries out of the bag, placing them in the refrigerator.

Paul took two bottles down from a wine rack that took up most of the space between the top of his kitchen cabinets and the ceiling. "Margaret River or Napa Valley?"

"Margaret River," she said, closing the fridge door and folding the brown paper bag against her chest before tucking it neatly between his coffee maker and microwave.

"Over Napa?"

"Sure. Why not give an underdog a chance? The Aussie wines are some of my favorites."

"*You* know your wine."

"Maybe I dated a sommelier," she said, leaning against the kitchen counter across from him, eyes sparkling.

He didn't want to think about her dating anyone. In fact, the swift and furious desire to obliterate the memory of any other guy who had ever smiled at her—touched her, made love to her—suddenly overwhelmed him. He swallowed uncomfortably, staring at her teasing face, his pulse racing with irrational need and desperate want.

Taking a step toward her, he set the bottle down to her left before placing his hands on the countertop on either side of her. He felt his breath hitch to be so close to her again as her chest rose and fell, brushing against his every time she inhaled. She was beautiful as hell and she was no princess, but he wanted her more than he'd ever wanted another woman. Ever.

"I couldn't stop thinking about you today," he murmured, lowering his mouth to hers.

She shifted up on her tiptoes, which made her anklet jingle, and he pulled her into his arms roughly, groaning into her mouth as she stroked his tongue with hers. He lowered his hands to her hips and lifted her easily onto the counter in front of him, slanting his head to deepen their kiss. She raised her legs, her skirt riding up as she locked her ankles around his back, the anklet tinkling again as she drew him closer.

"I thought about you too," she whispered as his lips skimmed the column of her throat, resting briefly on her pounding pulse. "I couldn't wait for seven."

"Me either," he confessed, capturing her lips again, as his fingers curled into fists on her lower back.

He had never felt this kind of raw, visceral connection to a woman. Their chemistry far surpassed anything Paul had ever experienced, and he had to wonder if that made his attraction to her a once-in-a-lifetime sort of occurrence. Because it felt that way. It felt charged and fierce and unequaled.

She moaned into his mouth, arching her back, and his hands unfisted, his fingers sliding under her shirt to touch the hot, soft skin underneath. His body hardened in anticipation and he wondered if she could feel him, thick and throbbing, at the apex of her thighs where she held him. He hoped so. He wanted her to know.

Buzzzzz!

Through a haze of lust, Paul heard the oven timer sound, letting him know that the potatoes were ready.

Breaking off their kiss, he skimmed his lips across Zoë's forehead tenderly before turning off the stove, then reached over her head to take down two wine glasses. Still perched on the counter, Zoë grinned at him before smoothing her skirt, which made her anklet jingle again.

"*That* is driving me crazy," said Paul.

"Too bad," she said, winking at him.

"Every time you move, it jingles, and it does something to me. Makes it so I want to touch you. So I *have* to touch you."

He dipped his head and planted his lips on her neck for a fleeting moment, then pulled out the drawer beside her and rifled through it for a corkscrew.

"Miss Temptation," she said. "When I saw it in a store window today, I couldn't resist."

"When I opened the door, it was like a fantasy come to life. I swear I wanted to…"

"What?" she murmured with wide, dark eyes trained on his. "What did you want to do?"

His breath hitched and he forced himself to look away from her, twisting, then pulling until the cork dislodged with a pleasing pop. He glanced back up at her.

"Take you upstairs," he answered honestly.

"Without dinner?"

"*For* dinner."

"You're naughty," she said, but she was pleased. He could tell.

"Not usually. Usually I'm just Principal Paul."

"I like Principal Paul," she said softly.

Her simple words made him beam like an idiot as he handed her a glass of wine, the red liquid swirling round and round the wide bowl.

"What're we drinking to?" she asked, slipping off the counter.

"To you, Zoë," he answered, holding her dark eyes, as he lifted his glass to touch it against hers. "I'm drinking to you."

CHAPTER 15

Paul insisted Zoë put on his navy-blue fleece jacket and they reset the table on the back porch.

She'd imagined him on this very porch so many times and smiled at the swing to the left, then took in the rest of the covered space; room for a table with four seats, a barbeque grill and a small serving table. Looking out at the view, she found Electric Peak in the distance based on his descriptions alone. This was where he'd written to her, gotten to know her, and fallen for her. Zoë felt an immediate comfort in her surroundings.

Being wrapped up in his jacket, surrounded by his scent, was the warmest, happiest place Zoë had ever visited. She sat at the table and sipped her wine as he stood at the grill, telling her about his family.

As she listened, it surprised her to learn that he hadn't been completely forthcoming about his relationship with them during their correspondence; he wasn't close to his family. He had more or less left Maine purposely to place distance between himself and his family and start his own life in Montana.

"Do you go home?" she asked, lightly swirling her wine glass, which sparkled in the candlelight.

"Honestly? It's awkward. I go for Christmas, or like, if

there's a wedding or something back east, I try to go. My brother Bennett is a total asshole. Sorry. But he is. And my other brother Ted is a puppet. He's the youngest and he does whatever Bennett and my father tell him to do."

"Which is?"

"Yale undergrad. Harvard Law. Family firm in Boston."

"You don't think he's happy?"

"I don't think he ever looked around long enough to decide if it was what he wanted. And Bennett..." he swore lightly under his breath.

"What?" she asked, longing to know everything about him. "What about Bennett?"

"He's like a sociopath. Super charming. Really good-looking. Insanely successful. But he's void of feelings. He'd step on your face if it helped his purposes. He's cold."

"No," breathed Zoë. "It's not possible if he's your brother. Something must have happened to him."

"If it did, I don't know what."

"How much older is he? Than you?"

"Eight years."

"And he's close to your dad?"

"Sort of. I think he kind of hates my father, but he smiles through it. It's creepy."

"And your mom?"

"She and Bennett are like oil and water. She gets on better with Ted."

"You don't include yourself at all."

"I guess I don't feel like a part of them," he confessed, shutting the lid of the grill and taking a seat at the table

266

across from her. "But in a nutshell? My father's disappointed in me. My brothers think teaching's a joke. And my mother…"

"What about your mom?"

He smiled lightly, joining her at a seat across the table. "She's okay. She can be pretty great one-on-one…when she's not being a super-snotty society wife."

It sounded complicated and Zoë thought about never knowing her father, her mother's death, her broken relationship with Thea. Listening to Paul's brokenness with his family made her want to fix the problems in her own, made her wonder if she had the strength to reach out to Thea and Brandon once she got home again.

"You love your mom," Zoë said quietly.

He looked up at her, looking unsure of what to say. Or maybe he just didn't want to talk about his family anymore.

"What about you?" he asked, taking a sip of his wine and stretching his legs out under the table until his bare feet found hers.

"My dad left when I was too little to remember. My mom passed away when I was in high school." She knew that she was sharing facts she had shared as Holly, so she didn't mention Sandy. "I have an older sister."

"And nephew," said Paul quietly, his eyes darting to her scar before returning to her eyes.

She nodded, relieved that he didn't appear to be correlating Holly's history to hers.

"I don't speak to my sister," she blurted out. "She hates me, pretty much."

"Because of the accident."

Zoë nodded, biting her lower lip and willing the tears away. She didn't want to cry. She wanted to be able to talk about it without the crushing sorrow. So far, she was doing a better-than-usual job at keeping it at bay.

"His car seat wasn't working right. I knew it. I should have figured out another way to get him home, but I was in a rush. We were sideswiped on the highway and he…he just…" Her voice trailed off as she shook her head back and forth slowly, unable to say any more, losing the battle for composure.

She didn't notice him get up, but suddenly he was squatting beside her, taking her hand in his. With his other hand he brushed away the tear that had escaped.

"Zoë."

She looked up.

"You didn't mean to hurt anyone."

"But I d-did."

"It was an accident."

She twisted toward him, dropping her head to his shoulder and letting him pull her onto his lap on the floor of the porch. Curling into him, she closed her eyes, sobbing softly against his chest as he held her tightly.

"The s-steaks are burning," she finally sighed, taking a deep breath that smelled like Paul and burned barbeque.

"I don't care."

"I keep d-doing this to you. C-crying all over you like a l-lunatic."

"Do you hear me complaining?"

"No," she conceded, wiping the last of her tears with the back of her hand.

"You know, I used to be a guidance counselor?" He nodded. "Yup. For two years outside of Boston before taking the job as principal out here. So, here's my therapist question for you. Can you make space for this in your life? Can you figure out how to live with it?"

"He lost his legs! I can't. Ever."

"Kids are so resilient. He'll be okay. Don't get me wrong; it's terrible it happened. But I bet he lives with it better than you do because it's what he knows. He manages. You're still grieving what he lost, but my guess is that he's not. Not like you are. Zoë, you can't live like this. You have to find room for it in your life so it doesn't break your heart every day." He paused, pulling back to look at her. "And I think you should talk to your sister because it sounds like you really miss her."

Zoë swallowed the lump in her throat, nodding her head. "I know. I will."

Paul took a deep breath and sighed glancing at the grill. "You okay now? Can I go look at the damage?"

She nodded, easing up off his lap and offering him a hand.

He took her hand and stood up nimbly. He stared at her for a moment then lifted one finger, tracing the jagged scar on her face gently from her hairline to her neck, finally resting two fingers over her thumping pulse.

"You're amazing," he murmured, and Zoë forced herself to meet his eyes, not to look away as though she were unworthy of his praise.

A slow smile spread across his face and he dropped a quick kiss to her lips before turning away and opening the grill.

"Uh-oh. Do you like your steak super crispy?"

Zoë wrinkled her nose.

Paul winked at her. "How about an omelet?"

***

After a dinner of omelets and salad, Zoë was feeling pretty relaxed.

It had been, hands down, one of the best evenings she had ever spent with anyone, anytime, anywhere. The only thorn in her side was the underlying fear about telling him the truth on Thursday.

In her mind it looked like this: It was as though they were holding hands as they walked together, but Paul didn't know a massive, rolling, raging river was coming up and it was going to block their path. And maybe—just maybe—if they could somehow find a way to hold on to each other and jump together, they might make it to the other side. With a heavy heart she couldn't shake the feeling that he'd drop her hand and walk away, leaving her alone on a raging riverbank with the full weight of her deception for company.

Paul smiled at her across the table, oblivious to her inner struggle.

"What are you thinking about?" he asked, rubbing her toes with his. "So intense."

"I have something to tell you."

"Me first." He took a sip of his wine and leaned

forward, folding his hands in front of him on the table, raising his beloved blue eyes to her face. "I'm going to break things off with Holly. I'm falling for y—"

As much as she longed to hear his voice say the words, she didn't want to hear them until after she'd told him the truth. Only then would she know he truly meant it.

"I'm leaving," Zoë blurted out.

"W-what? You're what?" Paul's face contorted with confusion, changing from soft and loving to troubled and upset in the space of a second. It made her hate herself.

"Just for a couple of days," she added, pulling her feet back from his and drawing them up to the edge of her chair so she could wrap her arms around her bent legs.

"What the hell? Where are you going?"

"The park. With Nils."

She watched as Paul's face transformed again—this time from confused to thunderous. He sat back in his chair, staring at her with hurt eyes.

"And his father!" she amended quickly. "And, like, a dozen old ladies."

His jaw relaxed, but he didn't say anything. He took a sip of his wine and stared at her, his expression closed and upset.

"You're going on a tour." He put his glass down and took her plate, piling it on top of his roughly, their lovely easiness all gone. "For how long?"

"Three days," she whispered.

His eyes widened as he stared at the plates. His lips were a thin line as he looked up at her, taking her silverware and letting it clank angrily onto the empty plates.

"Two nights in the park with Nils Lindstrom, huh?" He stood up and gathered the plates and utensils in his hands. "Have a great time."

He turned and made his way back into the house, leaving her alone. She heard the dishes clatter in the sink and got up quietly to follow him. It was like his jealousy was doing something to her insides, making her hot, making her want him more than ever. And since it was likely this was the last night they'd have together before he learned her true identity, she couldn't bear it if they wasted it arguing.

"Can I help you clean up?" she asked him, standing in the kitchen doorway.

"Why did you come here?"

"To Gardiner?"

"To dinner!" He stood against the sink with his hands on his hips, his chest moving up and down with the force of his breathing, his eyes narrowed with anger. "What was the point?!"

A small smile spread out across her face as she approached him.

"You're jealous."

"Of course I'm jealous."

"You don't need to be jealous," she said gently, sliding her hands through his bent arms and flattening them on his back.

"No?" he asked. He still didn't touch her, but his voice softened.

"No. from what I hear, Nils doesn't have eyes for

anyone except for Maggie..." She pressed her chest to his and felt his breath catch as he looked down at her, working his jaw, eyes still hurt and uncertain. She shook her head at him, smiling tenderly. "...and I only have them for you."

His breath caught, but he didn't say anything.

"I came to dinner because I've never met anyone like you, Paul. From the first moment I looked into your eyes I knew who you were. Meeting you...KNOWING you is like finding something that I thought was lost. I came to dinner because I've been falling for you since the second I met you. And it feels like a lot longer than it's actually been. I came to dinner   because—"

"Wait. Back up. What was that part? About falling?"

Smiling into his eyes with all the love in her heart, she said softly, "I've been falling for you since the second I met you."

"Yeah. That part."

***

He caught her under the knees and lifted her off the ground, his lips finding hers swiftly as he cradled her in his arms, holding on to her tightly and kissing her like the world was ending. He strode from the kitchen, passing briefly through the living room and taking the stairs two at a time, even with her extra weight in his arms. Kicking his bedroom door open with his foot, he lowered her onto the bed, pressing his body on top of hers, bracing his weight on his elbows as he held her face tenderly between his hands. He sucked on her lower lip before slipping his tongue between her lips.

This wasn't just about passion or heat or chemistry—

although he felt those things with Zoë—this was about that earth-shattering moment when you realize that you're giving your heart to someone and you're plunging headlong into love and it feels so good and so terrifying and so necessary to the very survival of your soul that you have no choice but to surrender.

He leaned back, panting, and moved his fingers to the buttons of her shirt, working slowly and placing a kiss on her warm skin as each button revealed a little more of her. Finally he got to the knot at the bottom and untied it, spreading her shirt open. She sat up and he quickly pulled it away from her body, dropping it on the floor beside the bed.

She held his eyes in the dim light offered by the moon through his windows and reached around slowly to unfasten her bra, using her arms to keep it in place even as the clasps drooped at her side and the straps fell from her shoulders. He reached forward slowly, gently, tugging at the tiny white bow in the middle of the sheer fabric until she relaxed her arms, letting him pull her bra away.

"Zoë," he breathed. "You're so beautiful."

She didn't say anything, but her lips tilted up as she lay back on his pillows, offering herself to him.

"Kiss me," she whispered, her voice thick with passion.

He braced himself over her, looking at her face, the blackness of her hair against the white of his pillow. He wove his fingers into her hair behind her ears, pulling it from her ponytail, tilting her face up to crush his lips to hers.

She reached up behind his neck and pulled his body completely down on top of hers, and the sudden heat of the skin-to-skin contact made him groan into her mouth. He kissed her as her fingers clutched his back, until her nails dug into his skin, until soft whimpering noises rose up from the back of her throat.

***

Zoë knew they had to stop soon, but my God, the feeling of his hot, muscular chest pressing down on hers felt so unbelievably good; it was like she was a teenager again, making out with someone for the first time. She couldn't remember a feeling this amazing, this intimate, as an adult. It even scared her a little.

She bent her knees and drew her legs up to cradle him between her legs, and he groaned into her mouth, pushing against her, simulating the act of sex.

Zoë wanted him. She wanted him more than she'd ever wanted anyone in her entire life. But having sex with him before telling him the truth could cost her everything and she knew it. She needed to push him away. Before things got too far.

She turned her head to the side, breaking off contact with his hot, gorgeous mouth. Without missing a beat, he brushed his lips on the soft skin behind her ear, taking the lobe between his teeth gently while his hands kneaded her hips.

"Paul," she sighed.

"Mmm?"

"We have to stop."

"No," he groaned, his lips lingering on the skin beneath her ear.

"Yes."

He lifted his head to look at her face. Searching her eyes and finding no reprieve, he rolled off her, lying beside her. She glanced to her right and saw his chest rising and falling with the effort of his breathing as he tossed an arm over his eyes. She looked away, forcing her fingers not to wander to his body.

"Zoë."

"Paul."

"I, uh, I need to take a quick shower."

"Are you serious?"

"Um, yeah. I'm serious. I'm dying here."

She turned onto her side, facing him.

"Do you wish we had—"

"No," he answered simply, but his voice wasn't convincing, and he didn't turn toward her.

"Are you mad at me?"

"No, love." He turned away from her. "I just wish we didn't have to stop but now that we have, I just—I just wish that I didn't feel so guilty about…"

She crossed her arms over her chest, hating the way his words made her feel, hating how much she had complicated things between them.

He looked back at her over his shoulder, giving her a weak smile.

"Give me a minute?"

She nodded, offering him a small, sad smile in return.

A minute later she heard the shower running and she leaned over the bed, feeling around for her bra and shirt. She

276

slipped the bra over her shoulders and fastened it, then pulled the shirt on, rolling up the sleeves but leaving it open. She sat back against the headboard of his bed and turned on the bedside light, noticing a picture frame facedown on the small nightstand.

She turned it over gingerly and it made her heart clench to see that it was the photo that Thea had taken of her at Sandy's wedding a little over two years ago. She held the frame in her hands, staring at herself. Her smile was bright and big, and she suddenly remembered that when she smiled, her cheeks had brushed the bottom edge of the Jackie O.-style sunglasses. Thea told her she looked like a movie star from the 1940s in those glasses and Zoë had giggled just before Thea snapped the picture. It was the last candid photo Zoë had of herself before the accident—the "before picture" to trump all "before pictures."

"That's her," said Paul softly. "Holly."

Zoë looked up to see Paul standing in the bathroom doorway with a towel wrapped around his waist. She could practically *feel* her eyes dilating at the sight of him freshly showered, his hair and chest dripping with droplets of water. She could have sat there gawking at him forever. Except…

Holly. Holly. He's talking about Holly.

"Yeah," she said. "I figured."

He crossed the room and sat down on the edge of the bed beside her, taking the frame out of her hands and looking at it for a moment before turning it over, opening the drawer beside his leg and pushing it inside.

"This isn't who I am," he muttered, shaking his head. "I

don't lead women on. I don't date two women at once. I don't do this."

Her heart twisted to see him suffering; he was an honorable man in what he thought was a dishonorable situation and it killed her that she had put him there. She had to tell him. She had to tell him the truth so that he'd know he wasn't doing anything wrong.

"Paul, what if Holly were here?"

"Like if she was standing here and I had to choose between you two?"

She shook her head. "N-no. I mean—"

"It doesn't matter. I told you earlier..." He turned to her, pain on his face, but not uncertainty. "...I choose you. I'm breaking up with Holly tomorrow."

"But you care for her."

He swallowed and nodded, turning away from Zoë. "I do. She's great. She deserves a lot more than a guy who falls for someone else over the course of three days."

It wasn't lost on Zoë that he said he had fallen for her—for *her*, as Zoë—but she couldn't let herself get sidetracked. She wanted to try to tell him the truth. She cleared her throat.

"What if...I mean, what if you could have both of us?"

His head whipped to face her, eyes wide, brows knit together. He blushed as he answered her. "Like at the same time? Like a...a...oh, well, no. Not that it doesn't sound...I mean—I mean, I guess I'm just not that kind of guy. Call me old-fashioned but—"

"No, you're not getting what I'm—what if you *didn't*

have to choose?"

"You're not making sense. Of course I have to choose."

Her breathing had progressively gotten so heavy and fast that she felt light-headed. Her blood was rushing from her head, making her heart race. She was panicking. She recognized the symptoms—she'd had dozens of panic attacks the year after the accident. She needed fresh air; she needed to get back to her hotel room.

"Damn it," she muttered, pressing her cool hands to her cheeks and trying to take a deep breath. She could feel them trembling against the increasing heat of her skin.

"Zoë, what's going on? Are you okay?"

"I have to go," she said, scrambling off the bed as her eyes welled up with tears.

"Let me get dressed. Let me walk you—"

"No. You don't have to." She hastily tied her shirt at her waist, buttoning two buttons with shaking fingers as she rushed out of the bedroom, heading for the stairs.

"Zoë!" he yelled from his bedroom. "Stop!"

She scurried down the stairs, pausing at the landing to try to get a deep breath into her lungs before reaching for the doorknob. His hand shot out, flattening against the door, holding it closed.

"Please let me go," she murmured, unable to face him.

"Not until I know you're okay."

He took another step closer to her and she could feel the heat of his body behind her. The corded muscles of his forearm brushed against her hair and she stared at his wrist, at the veins running down to his wrist from his elbow. Out of the corner of her eye she could tell that he was only wearing jeans and his chest still glistened from his shower.

"I'm okay," she whispered.

"I shouldn't have had that picture out," Paul said softly, his hand falling away from the door and slipping around her, under her breasts. "I'm sorry. None of this is your fault. It's my problem and it's not fair to burden you with it."

Her eyes shuttered closed and her nose flared with the intensity of her breathing. He was *apologizing* to her. The guilt she felt was so overwhelming, she felt faint. She let her body go slack against him. His other arm came around her, but he didn't force her to turn around, he just held her tightly, her back against his chest.

"I wasn't pushing you away up there," he said softly, bending his head to move his lips closer to her ear. "I don't know how this happened between us so fast, but it did. I'm sorry I'm going to hurt Holly, but I'm not sorry for wanting you, Zoë. I'm not sorry you came here for vacation. I'm not sorry you saved my dog. I'm not sorry I kissed you that first time or the second time or any other time after. I can't stop myself. When I'm around you, I just…just, I don't know. I've never felt chemistry like this with anyone else in my whole life, and I don't know how it's possible to feel like I do so quickly, but I do. And if you do too, I just want to give it a chance."

She leaned her head back against him, her chest rising and falling swiftly under his hands. A tear snaked down her face, following the crevasse of her scar.

"This is crazy," she whispered, personal agony wrenching her heart.

"Then give me a chance to get to know you better. Come to the Harvest Dance with me on Thursday night."

"The Harvest Dance?"

"Yeah. Be my date. We'll go out to dinner first and you can tell me all about Nils and the old ladies. And we can just dance to slow dances if you—"

She spun in his arms, lifting her hands to his face and pulling his lips down to hers without warning. His arms tightened around her and he thrust his tongue into her mouth without preamble, urgent and demanding as he tasted her. The pressure of his fingers intensified in her lower back until his knuckles curled and he pushed her more tightly up against him. Her fingers played with the short hair over his ears and her thumbs stroked the stubble of his jaw gently, memorizing the textures of him, the way he felt, the way he made her feel.

She pulled away from him, breathless and overwhelmed by his goodness, by how much she never wanted to spend another day of her life without him. His surprised lips tilted up in a smile and she felt him chuckle.

"I guess that's a yes? For the dance?"

She nodded, unable to keep the grin from her face, despite the sheer screwed-upness of the entire situation. He was just too adorable, and she loved him too much.

"Let me walk you home?" he asked.

She shook her head, blinking back tears, backing out of his arms and finding the doorknob.

"No," she said, swiping at her eyes. "This is a good ending."

His forehead creased. "Ending? I don't like that."

"For tonight. A good ending for tonight."

His worried expression softened, and he tucked a piece of black hair behind her ear, rubbing the earlobe between his thumb and forefinger gently as he smiled at her again.

"Can I watch you walk away?" he asked, his eyes dropping to her backside before sweeping back up to her face.

"You mean limp away? Does that get you hot?"

"*You* get me hot, whatever you're doing."

She glanced down at his bare chest, muscular and toned, the contours highlighted by the dim light of his front hallway.

"I guess I know what that feels like," she said, low and silky, letting her eyes sweep slowly back up to his.

He started to reach for her, but she sidestepped him, opening the door and slipping outside into the cool of the evening.

"Thursday?" he asked, looking hotter than fire leaning up against the doorway in nothing but a pair of unbuttoned jeans and a grin.

"Thursday," she said, turning to walk down the porch steps and heading toward her inn. When she glanced back, he was still there, watching her walk away, listening to her anklet tingle softly all the way home.

CHAPTER 16

The next morning *something* was not sitting right with Paul.

He just couldn't figure out what.

It was a lump in his stomach, an ache in his heart, a buzzing in his brain. But without a name, without a form or story or hint. Something wasn't right.

It had nagged at him last night as he finished the dishes, and later he had tried to figure it out as he stared at the ceiling in bed, wishing he could go to sleep, distracted by the faint scent of honeysuckle on his sheets.

As he sorted through his thoughts in the growing morning light of his kitchen, some obvious issues sprang to mind—most notably, the fact that he was going to have to call Holly and break up with her today, and if he couldn't get a hold of her, he at least needed to text her that they needed to talk. Thinking about that talk made him wince. Was he making the right decision? To push away a girl like Holly? He shook his head as he tapped the on button of his coffee maker. The decision was already made, he thought wryly, remembering Zoë's head buried in his pillow.

He could still feel her trembling in his arms, still taste her in his mouth. He breathed deeper and grinned, putting his favorite mug under the coffee maker and pushing the bright blue button. Oh, man, she was hot.

He shook his head, heading out to the swing, Cleo at his heels. The cold air was like a slap in the face and made him refocus on the call he had to make to Holly. It made him feel like total crap, what he was about to do to her. She didn't do anything wrong. She didn't deserve to get a phone call from him breaking things off before they'd even had a chance to meet. It made him feel like the worst player who ever lived. Paul had never aspired to being a heartbreaker...he wanted to be like Westley. One woman. One man. True love. Instead here he was about to break Buttercup's heart.

It also bothered him that he appeared so fickle—that his feelings for Holly had been so easy to dismantle. It was as though they hadn't been as real or powerful as he'd thought as he got to know her. He'd been so sure at the time that what they were building between texts and phone calls was real and lasting, but it wasn't anywhere near as strong as Zoë's presence in his life after a mere four days. He sighed, shaking his head at his weakness, disappointed with himself.

Cleo shivered beside him and he reached for the blanket on the back of the swing and wrapped it around her.

Yeah, the situation with Holly definitely wasn't sitting well with him, and it probably wouldn't feel better until she'd had a chance to really lay into him and tell him what a weak, shallow, jerk-off he was and how much better off she was without him.

He'd listen to every single word without complaint. He deserved all of it. He should have had the self-control to break off things with Holly before starting anything with

Zoë. It's just everything with Zoë had happened so fast, had felt so…inevitable.

He picked up his phone. It was time to bite the bullet.

He opened a text box and started typing.

Holly, I need to talk to you today. I know you're busy but it's important. Please text back or call

He stopped typing, staring at the message. God, he was a selfish bastard. Was it fair to break up with her while she was at a conference? Was it okay for him to interrupt her time there just because he couldn't handle the guilt for a few more days?

His thumb moved slowly, and his phone clicked softly as he pressed the back button repeatedly, erasing the characters one by one. He needed to wait until Friday. That was the least he could do.

He sighed, checking the time. He had about thirty minutes before he needed to leave for school, and as he erased the text to Holly, his thoughts turned to Zoë once again, to how much he wished she wasn't going away.

His face softened thinking about her, even as whatever was nagging at him seemed to intensify with thoughts of her. He had known her for such a short amount of time, but she had wiggled her way into his heart with unerring accuracy, and there was nothing he could do about it. And yeah, he hated that she was headed out of town for two nights, but with him in Zoë's life and Maggie in Nils's life, he didn't see anything happening between them.

So, what was it? What was needling at him so insistently? What was the *something*?

What if you could have both of us? What if you didn't have to choose?

He heard her words from last night in his head and realized, with blinding certainty, that the something wasn't his own laughable self-control or the looming doom of having to explain everything to Holly and break up with her.

It was all that business about not having to choose.

He hadn't known Zoë for very long, but despite her edgy looks, she didn't seem so free-spirited that she'd be up for an "open" relationship. So what did she mean when she said that?

He rolled the empty coffee mug back and forth in his hands, brows knitted together in confusion. He tried looking at her words from a few different angles, but he couldn't make sense of them. Did she mean she'd somehow tolerate another woman in his heart? No, that couldn't be it. *No* woman would go for that.

He looked at his phone again. He probably had about five minutes before the Lindstroms picked her up; he could easily run over there to talk to her.

Just like you keep bothering Holly. Needy.

Okay. No need to go over there, but a quick phone call just for reassurance couldn't hurt, could it? He looked up the number of the Mountain View Inn and dialed the number.

The number rang as he walked into the kitchen, putting his coffee cup in the sink.

"Mountain View."

"Hey Ann Marie, it's Paul Johansson. How're you doing today, ma'am?"

"I'm very well, neighbor. What can I do you for?"

"You have a guest staying with you...her name is Zoë Fine..."

"You mean Flannigan. She's right outside waiting for the Lindstroms. Hold on."

Flannigan! Zoë Flannigan?

His head jerked back like he'd been slapped, and the rest of her words faded out of earshot as his mind reeled.

Zoë and Holly have the same last name?

"W-wait...did you say..."

Flannigan. His heart started thumping uncomfortably and he heard the innkeeper speaking softly, as if holding her hand over the mouthpiece of the phone.

Finally someone spoke.

"Paul? It's me."

It's me. In Holly's voice. He'd heard it dozens of times.

"H-Holly?"

He started breathing faster, his mind working wildly to try to figure out what was going on.

He pulled the phone away from his ear to look at the caller ID, which read MtnViewInn. His brain muddled with confusion.

"No. It's, um, it's Zoë."

"Zoë?" he asked, trying to take a deep breath, but unable. Zoë had answered the phone *It's me*, in Holly's voice. He'd bet his life on it.

"Yeah. Zoë," she said firmly, her voice lower and breathier than it had been a moment ago. "Is everything okay?"

"Y-yeah," he mumbled.

There was a long silence between them before she offered in a nervous voice, "Thanks for last night. It was great."

He tried to concentrate on what she was saying, but he couldn't figure out what the hell was going on. The call was definitely coming from the Mountain View Inn, the voice he'd originally heard pick up the phone was Holly's, but now it sounded like Zoë. Was this his mind playing tricks on him? Was he going crazy from a mixture of lust and guilt?

"Zoë."

"It's me. I'm here…"

"I just wanted to say…I mean, I wanted to ask you—"

"Listen, Nils just pulled up. I have to go. Can we talk when I get back?"

"Do you have a cell number?"

There was a long pause. Too long.

"I don't, um…my cell isn't working here."

"Okay." He grimaced and his chest tightened as unfamiliar tears of confusion popped into his eyes, surprising him, burning painfully. Her phone had been working fine three days ago as they drove into Yellowstone with Lars and Jane.

"Paul…I'm…I'm crazy about you. I need you to know that. It's important to me that you know it. Really know it. Don't forget, okay?"

His eyes clenched shut painfully and he braced his hands on the kitchen counter. They were the exact same words Holly had used two weeks ago when she told him she was falling for him.

"Hol—Zoë…"

"I have to go," she said, and it came out a little bit like a sob. "I'll see you Thursday."

The line went dead.

He held the phone up to his ear long after the call had disconnected. He absently placed the phone on the counter, his mind reeling. The uneasiness in his stomach made him feel nauseous and he grimaced, swallowing back the cereal and coffee that threatened a reappearance.

Staring out the window, he tried frantically to make sense of what had just happened. Zoë's last name was Flannigan, and her voice sounded identical to Holly's over the phone. Could Zoë be a cousin of Holly's? No. Holly didn't have a cousin yet. Her only aunt was pregnant with her first child.

Was there any chance his guilt about breaking up with Holly was overriding rational thought? Was his mind playing tricks on him? He might be able to believe that if it was just the familiarity of Holly's voice when he picked up the phone, but her last name? It was too much of a coincidence. That was Holly on the phone. He was sure of it.

He picked up the phone and hit the caller ID button again to be sure of the number he'd just called. MtnViewInn. There's no doubt that he called the Mountain View Inn. The voice was definitely Holly's, even though she *said* she was Zoë.

What the fuck is going on?

Hearing the roar of a van engine outside, he realized

she wasn't gone yet and he sprinted out of his house just in time to see the Lindstrom & Sons van turn right off his road, headed toward the Roosevelt Arch. He stood under his porch watching as the van kicked up dust, headed for the park.

"Shit!"

Zoë or Holly, or whoever the hell she was, was gone.

Suddenly he heard her words in his head again:

What if Holly was here? What if you could have both of us? What if you didn't have to choose?

His eyes fluttered closed and he lowered his body raggedly to sit down on the top step of his porch as her words came rushing back to him—puzzle pieces, jagged and anonymous on their own, fitting together with heartbreaking precision. It was all there. All of it. He'd just been too much of a blind idiot to put it all together.

Oh, my God.

There was only one explanation and it smacked like a hit to the chest, shattering the bones of his ribs into shards that staked his gasping heart.

Oh, my God.

Zoë is Holly. Holly is Zoë.

Zoë was an artist and Holly was an art teacher.

Zoë's bags were left in Rhode Island and Holly lived in Connecticut.

And Zoë was here in Gardiner…to see a man, a man shrouded in confusion and uncertainty every time Zoë mentioned him. Paul had held her, reassuring her, telling her that the guy was an idiot if he didn't see how great she was.

But she had answered that she didn't know if it would work out, *He's my whole world, but I haven't been honest with him.*

Well, that was a fucking understatement. The whole thing had been a lie.

It suddenly occurred to him that Holly probably didn't even exist. The blue-eyed blonde schoolteacher with a sunny smile was really an edgy, brown-eyed, dark-haired woman who built websites and had endless amounts of sorrow etched—literally—into her face. Had she just used the persona "Holly" to lure him into her world? That picture had probably been scanned from a magazine or copied off the internet. Holly and Zoë looked *nothing* alike.

He stood up and sprinted up the stairs, throwing open the front door and not stopping until he sat on the edge of his bed. He took out the framed picture that Zoë had been looking at last night and stared at it. Hard. The woman in the picture had long, blonde wavy hair, but it was impossible to tell her eye color behind the sunglasses. The skin of her face was tan and flawless and her body was much trimmer than Zoë's, with long, perfect legs. They didn't look a thing alike. Except for the smile. He stared at it hard, thinking about Zoë smiling at him in the candlelight from across the table last night, and realized in horror that it was the same smile.

He threw the frame across the room angrily and didn't look up as the glass shattered against his wall, small pieces bouncing from the wall to the carpet below.

A terrible thought suddenly occurred to him, and his face contorted.

Had it all been a game to her? Was this something she

did? Meet men over the internet and pretend to be one person only to show up later to reveal herself as someone totally different?

His eyes burned and he covered them with his hands, bowing his head in frustration and anger and confusion and a growing, aching sadness.

He needed answers and he needed them now. Even if Holly's phone number worked on Zoë's phone, she wouldn't have a signal by now, and anyway, she was a big liar. It would take a face-to-face conversation to try to unravel Zoë/Holly's thick and tawdry web of lies. No. Screw the liar. He'd get his answers somewhere else.

From someone he actually trusted.

Something had happened between Zoë and Maggie when they met for the first time on Saturday night, he was sure of it. There was only one other person in Gardiner who might have some answers, and he wasn't going to work until he got some.

***

"Maggie! I need to talk to you!" he strode into the café with purpose, his heart racing from the exertion of the fast walk. His eyes narrowed with challenge, and, more and more, with despair and deep embarrassment…and fury.

Maggie's green eyes widened into saucers and she leaned back from the bar where she was chatting with Miss Phillips, of shingles fame. Paul didn't even nod to the older woman. He stood by the bar, hands on his hips, fuming, eyes locked with Maggie's.

Maggie took a deep breath, staring at his eyes, then

looking away uncomfortably. She swallowed as she took a step toward him.

Oh, she knew something, all right.

"She told you," she said softly.

"*She told me what?*" he bellowed, gaining the attention of every newspaper-reading, coffee-drinking patron in the Prairie Dawn, who stared at the generally good-natured high school principal with eyes wide and mouths dropped open.

His yelling seemed to spur Maggie into action and her brow furrowed as she walked out from behind the bar, took hold of his sleeve and pulled him back out the front door. He had no choice but to follow behind her. She held onto his arm as they walked around behind the café toward the river, not stopping until they reached a picnic table by the water that had seen a few too many winters. She maneuvered herself to sit down on the beat-up bench, folded her hands in front of her on the weathered table and looked up at Paul.

He was too angry to sit. "What the *fuck*, Maggie?"

"You're *not* goin' to be usin' that language with me, Paul Johansson. No matter how angry you are, you'll be tonin' it down." She held his eyes until he looked away. "Now start over or we're done here."

"Am I losing my goddamned mind or is Holly actually Zoë?"

Maggie took a long, deep breath through her nose then nodded. "Holly and Zoë are the same person."

He placed a palm on his chest as his heart galloped painfully and his breathing hitched uncomfortably, making him ache.

"How—when did you find out?" she asked.

"I called her inn this morning and found out her last name is Flannigan. She forgot to disguise her voice and I recognized it. She must have forgotten to be Zoë for a minute. Little. Fucking. Liar."

"I'm warnin' you about the language."

He wished he could calm the fierce thumping of his heart, which reverberated in his ears, making his head pound. He nodded once in acknowledgment of her words before continuing.

"We had dinner last night. Me and Zoë. It was amazing. I told her I was breaking up with Holly and she said—she said… *What if Holly was here? What if you didn't have to choose? What if you could have both of us?'* It wasn't sitting right with me, so I wanted to call her before she left for the park this morning, and…and…and I called her and…"

His voice was practically a whisper as he sank down on the edge of the table beside Maggie, his anger losing momentum as he felt his heart breaking. He was the stupidest, blindest man who ever walked the earth. How could he not have seen it? How could he have been such an idiot?

"…figured out that Zoë's Holly," Maggie murmured. "She came here to tell you."

Maggie's words poured heat and anger back into his blood and he almost sighed with relief, grateful for a distraction from the crushing sorrow.

"Tell me *what?* That everything between us is a big, fat fucking lie? I mean, do I even know who the *fuck* she is?"

"That's it." Maggie slapped her hands on the picnic table and got up like she was leaving. Paul grabbed her wrist.

"Wait. Stop. Please." He looked up at his friend and knew she had to see it in his eyes by the way hers softened. She had to see that the ground was shifting madly under his feet and the world he'd been living in was crumbling around him. She could see. She knew. She sat back down slowly, giving him a warning look.

"No more f-bombs, Paul. I mean it, now."

"Sorry. I won't curse like that, Maggie. I'm sorry. I'm a mess. I'm trying to understand what the f—hell is going on here."

"She's just—"

"She's just a goddamned liar. Jesus, Maggie, I don't even know what's real and what's not real!"

"I don't think that's true at all. You're upset and you're overreacti—"

"Oh, am I *overreacting*? Am I? Because it seems like the woman I have fallen in love with—*twice* now—has been lying to me since day one."

"Paul, you need to *listen* to what you're sayin—"

"How did *you* know? How did *you* know, and I didn't know? Am I that much of an idiot? That blind? Was she laughing at me the whole time?"

"No," said Maggie gently. "I saw the original picture on the website before she took it down. She looks very different now, but I figured it out. And no, Paul. She wasn't laughin' at you. Never once. Not at all. She's been a wreck since she arrived, tryin' to figure out how to tell you, how to make it right."

"Are you sure? 'Cause this is a pretty good joke on me. She poses as a hot, put-together blonde and then shows up later as an edgy, tattooed—"

"Be careful what you say. I can't unhear your words."

"I mean, is this how she gets her kicks? Duping guys into thinking she's one thing, then—"

"*Enough.*" Maggie's tone was harsh and final. "Enough. I don't even know who *you* are right now. She made some mistakes. She liked you too much to come clean. For God's sake, she didn't *kill* anyone."

Paul's eyes widened at Maggie's tone and he swallowed, clenching his jaw painfully.

"She killed my heart," he whispered, staring, crestfallen, at his friend. "I don't understand."

"Will you let me talk? Let me *help* you understand." Her voice softened and she cocked her head to the side, her eyes compassionate and gentle. "Take a deep breath…good. Now another. I need you to calm down and then we'll talk about it all."

Paul swallowed the gigantic lump in his throat, taking two deep breaths. He glanced at his watch. "I have to call school and tell them I'm running late."

He took his phone out of his back pocket and moved away from Maggie, dialing the number of the school secretary. In seven years, he'd never missed a day of school and now he was deliberately going in late to sort out his train wreck of a love life. He took another deep breath, explained to the secretary that he'd be about an hour late and then hung up. Turning to Maggie, he came and sat across from her at the table.

"Okay. I'll shut up. Please tell me what's going on?"

Maggie held his eyes for a moment before nodding.

"The picture? The girl in the white sundress? That's her. The same girl that's here in Gardiner now. Zoë. Zoë Holly Flannigan. It was taken two years ago at her aunt's weddin' by her sister. Two years ago—when she was sunny and bright, when she was an art teacher with her whole life ahead of her—she placed an ad on MeettheOne.com one night with a girlfriend. A week or two later, she was in a car accident and it changed her life.

"When I first found Zoë on the datin' website, there'd been another picture up of her smilin' face, but I only saw it once before she took it down. You never saw it at all. When she walked into the Prairie Dawn with you on Saturday, I recognized her right away, but couldn't place her immediately. I knew her, I just didn't know from where. And then I watched her face as you talked about Miss Mystic. She squirmed in her seat and—I don't know. I knew. I just knew it was her. I mean, she looks worlds different. The dark hair, dark eyes, the scar—"

"Her eyes are brown now. Did the accident change her eye color too?" he asked acidly. "This is insane, Maggie."

"They're contacts," Maggie told him. "She showed them to me."

Paul's jaw dropped, staring at Maggie, trying to process all of this information.

"She *showed* you her contacts? What the hell are you

talking about?"

"I confronted her at the Prairie Dawn on Saturday night. Right before she left...I told her that I knew who she was. I was angry and suspicious of her, just like you are now. You knew somethin' was up between us because after I upset her, you chased after her. I thought about tellin' you the truth then, but I just—" She shrugged, looking like she might cry. "You already liked her. *Zoë.* I couldn't tell you who she was because I was afraid you wouldn't give her a chance."

"And why should I?" he muttered.

Maggie ignored him. "I needed to be sure she wasn't playin' games with you or settin' you up for a fall, so that night, I went to her room at the Mountain View."

"Wow," he deadpanned. "Good thing I didn't take a fall."

Maggie shook her head, glancing up at him with sad eyes.

"I did what I thought was best," she whispered. "There's no guidebook for this situation."

"You don't say." He clenched his jaw. "Keep going."

"I asked her the same questions you're askin' me now...why her hair and eyes were dark. The scar on her face. I wanted to know why she was here and if she was goin' to hurt my friend. She told me about the accident. Told me she'd filled out that web profile a week before the accident and forgot to take it down. She said that when I wrote to her...Oh, Paul." Maggie shook her head, looking away from him. Finally she composed herself and looked him right in the eyes when she continued. "She said it was like the sun comin' out after two years of darkness. That you were just so wonderful. She said she tried to tell you several times that she wasn't the same girl she'd been in the picture, but she couldn't do it. She said she couldn't risk losin' you."

He winced, exhaling, not even realizing he'd been holding his breath as Maggie was speaking. Her words felt like hope to him, like possibility and hope, but he pushed them away. He needed his anger right now. He needed to protect himself.

"It made her *happy*. *You* made her happy. So, she just pretended to be the girl in the picture. The girl she was before the accident. But when you told her you were comin' for a visit, she panicked. She decided she should come out here and try to tell you the truth. But then she met you and she couldn't do it. She couldn't bear to hurt you or have you…reject her."

Paul tented his hands in front of him and bent his head, resting his forehead on his hands.

"She's in love with you," Maggie said softly, and Paul's eyes whipped up to lock onto hers. "She loves you. I asked her three times and she said yes every time. She was tellin' the truth."

He'd be lying if he said the words didn't matter. They mattered. They were everything to him. But he only had a moment to enjoy them before his wary disappointment returned with crushing force. He scoffed bitterly.

"Telling the *truth*, Maggie? That's a laugh. She wouldn't know the truth if it walked up and punched her in the nose."

"Paul," Maggie started, shaking her head. "Look in your heart. She's the same person. Holly. Zoë. It's just a name. Who she is, the woman who loves you, the woman you fell for…is *her*."

He felt his anger slip away again until he was defenseless, emotionally naked, laid out and flayed open. Hopeful. Hurt. Longing. Oozing.

Hurt won. It didn't matter that she told Maggie that she loved him because whatever she felt for him couldn't be real if it was built on lies and deception. Not to mention, she'd told Maggie, not him. She hadn't even trusted him enough to tell him the truth after meeting him. And it hurt so badly, he felt like his heart might stop beating and he'd just die. Right there on a beat-up picnic table.

"My mind is…blown. I just feel so…" *Sad. So fucking sad.*

Maggie reached out and touched his arm. "I'm sorry."

"For not telling me? For finding her in the first place? For knowing who she was three days before I did? For what, Maggie?"

"For all of it."

"It's not your fault," he said, covering her hand with his gently. "She deceived you too."

"I don't think that was her intention. I think it just…happened."

"Lies don't just happen. She knew what she was doing." He shook his head back and forth, biting on his lower lip. "You know the weird thing? I was so worried that I was going to hurt one of them. Holly or Zoë. It never occurred to me I'd be the one in pain."

"I think you're lookin' at it all wrong," said Maggie gently.

"How's that? What other way is there?"

"We all lie. In little ways. Sometimes in big ways. Sometimes outright. Sometimes," she shrugged, moving her hands to her stomach, where they lay still, one over the other, "by omission. Think of what she's been through. Think of why she did it. Maybe she felt you wouldn't want her if she told you the truth. If you knew, she'd hurt you emotionally the way the accident had hurt her nephew physically. If you knew she lied about her life. If you knew she wasn't sunny and perfect anymore. If you found out she wasn't a teacher. You set the bar so high. She thought she'd lose you."

"So, this is my fault?"

"No. Of course not. But give her a chance. Try to see it through her eyes."

"Her *brown* eyes?"

"Her blue eyes. Her *real* eyes," said Maggie. "They're still there. They're just hidin'."

"That's the problem, though, isn't it? We had the same amount to lose, but we weren't on a level playing field. *She* was hiding. *She* got to know *me*, but *I* never got to know *her*. I have no idea who she is. She lied to me from the beginning. There's nothing else to say."

"She's not perfect. Sometimes you have to hold things back. To protect yourself. To protect someone else," Maggie said softly, intensely, more to herself than Paul.

"Well, *I* certainly wasn't the one she protected," said Paul, standing up and pulling his legs out from under the table.

"Are you so sure about that?"

"Yeah, I am. Because I've never hurt this badly in my life."

Maggie's face was unspeakably sad as she looked up at her friend. "She loves you, Paul. I'm sure of it."

Paul winced. "*Who* loves me? I don't even know who *she* is."

Then he turned, walking away, leaving Maggie alone at the weather-beaten picnic table overlooking the rushing river.

CHAPTER 17

Zoë opted to sit shotgun beside Nils in the van, but the beauty of Yellowstone blurred into a watercolor of blues, browns and greens as she stared out the window, biting on her nails, worry making her stomach roll around until she felt sick.

She had awakened a little later this morning and had been rushing around packing her bag, finally making it down to the front porch swing to wait for Nils at 7:25 a.m. when the innkeeper peeked out the front door, telling her Paul was on the phone. Without thinking, without modulating her voice, she picked up the phone and answered "Paul? It's me." just as she always did when he called her at home.

She cringed as soon as the words left her mouth, balling her free hand into a fist when he stuttered the name "H-Holly?" into the phone. He had recognized her voice right away, and even though she asserted that she was Zoë in a lower voice, she couldn't be sure if she'd covered the blunder or not. Her face flamed as she'd tried to smooth over things, but her heart was beating like crazy and she'd been so anxious to get off the phone she'd almost hung up on him when Nils pulled up.

As the van pulled off Stone Street, she glanced in the side-view mirror and saw him race out of his front door like he wanted to catch her before she left. She didn't know if that was a good sign or a bad sign, but something told her it was probably…bad.

A sick feeling poured over her and her fingers trembled as she unscrewed the bottle of water wedged between her thighs. *Oh, my God. What if he knows?*

After last night's *What if you didn't have to choose?* conversation, he could easily put it all together, and she wouldn't be there to explain or try to make him see things her way. He'd have two full days to stew about it until she returned to Gardiner. By then, he'd probably hate her guts permanently and never want to speak to her again.

Panicking, she picked up her cell and turned it back on, hoping for a signal so she could text him, so she could at least tell him she loved him. No signal. Not a single bar. Short of walking back to Gardiner and speaking to him face-to-face, she was out of luck.

Her eyes burned with tears, and she curled up into a tighter ball on the seat, grateful that Nils was so quiet and the ladies in the back of the van were so loud. No one seemed to notice the girl sitting in the front seat, in silent agony, staring blankly out the window.

***

Nils pulled the fifteen-passenger van into an assigned parking space at the Grant Village Campground after telling Zoë and the other twelve ladies that he and Mr. Lindstrom would be setting up the tents before starting a campfire and cooking their dinner—franks and beans, a typical trail meal—over an open fire.

"There's bathrooms that way and the camp store back

over there," said Nils looking over his shoulder at the ladies populating the van. "Would be a good idea for all of you to find a green stick to roast your hotdogs. Feel free to take some pictures, but you don't want to wander off too far into the woods. Remember what we told you all earlier today. There's plenty of wildlife here, even in the campground, and we'd hate to have to save you from an angry bison or bear."

"Wouldn't mind if your father had to save me!" tittered one of the old ladies.

Zoë grinned.

They'd been hell on the older Mr. Lindstrom at every tourist stop, hanging on his every word, batting their eyelashes, holding on to his arm, asking him to be in their photos. Zoë wondered the last time the quiet, older gentleman had received so much feminine attention and whether or not it was actually welcome, despite his polite response to it.

At the moment, he was driving the supply and luggage van, and Zoë was fairly sure he was taking the long way to the campsite, hoping the dozen horny old ladies had dispersed by the time he arrived.

"Very funny," said Nils, humoring the giggling ladies. "Now, please heed my warning. We want you all back in one piece for franks and beans."

"I'd like to sample your father's frank and beans," said one older woman in the back row , and they all exploded into varying degrees of cackles and giggles.

Nils glanced at Zoë, his face sour, shaking his head in disbelief and disgust.

"Well, you'll have to take that up with him, ma'am."

"Don't you worry, sonny! I plan to!"

"Yes, ma'am."

Zoë snorted indelicately beside Nils, hurrying to cover her mouth with her hand as her quiet laughter got the better of her. If someone had told her at eight this morning that she'd be laughing by five this evening, she'd have said it was impossible.

What had started as a doomed, terrible day in her head had—almost impossibly—improved. The ladies heckling Carl Lindstrom had distracted her from her phone call with Paul and the wonders of Yellowstone were harder to ignore than she would have believed. Every time they stopped, there was something else to behold and admire, her artist's mind wishing she had more time to stay and paint, to draw, to try to capture the stark, complex beauty of the hot springs, the bubbling jets of geyser steam, the lush beauty of Hayden Valley.

"Your bags will be moved into your tents as my father and I finish setting them up and we'd like to ask that you're all back to the campsite for dinner at six-thirty."

"If we're not, will your father give out spankings?"

Nils's face whipped to Zoë's, mouth open, eyes wide, as the ladies chortled behind them. Zoë shrugged, trying not to laugh. Nils blew out an exasperated breath and shook his head, opening his door and leaving the van without a word. He opened the main doors on the side of the van and Zoë waited as the ladies filed out, chirping and chatting among themselves and dispersing toward the bathrooms, camp store and other communal buildings afforded by the large campsite.

Finally he opened her door too. She shifted in her seat to face him.

"You don't need to open my door."

"Thought you could help me."

"Put up tents?" she asked, raising her eyebrows. "I don't know the first thing—"

"Just hold the stakes for me," he said easily, offering her his hand. "And if you feel like it, maybe tell me why you been so quiet today."

This surprised her. Maybe he could listen to her and she could listen to him.

She put her hand in Nils's tan, weathered mitt of a hand gratefully and let him help her down. Her leg was stiff after so many hours riding between stops.

Mr. Lindstrom pulled up in his van and rolled down the window. "They mostly gone?"

Zoë's lips tilted up in a smile. "Coast is clear."

Mr. Lindstrom parked his van next to the passenger van and joined Nils and Zoë.

"I'm not one to say a bad word about ladies...but they are a rowdy bunch, I tell you."

"Pop, me and Zoë'll handle the tents if you want to get started on the fire."

Zoë was pretty sure he hadn't heard Nils. Mr. Lindstrom looked a little stunned...and maybe a little nervous too. "I mean, one of them grabbed my...my backside. Pinched the dang thing."

"We're home on Thursday, Pop. Gotta hang in there for another day or two. Fire?"

"Yeah. Yeah, I'll tend to the fire. Zoë, you're helping out with the tents? Don't you want to go to the store or look around a bit? Can't be fun for you to help Nils put up the tents. Did you say you were an artist? Why don't you do some art or something?"

Zoë smiled at the white-haired man. He was good-looking for his age and in good shape. No wonder the older ladies were in such a tizzy over him! He looked weathered and strong like a cowboy who'd seen and done it all, his light blue eyes holding Zoë's with warmth and kindness.

"No, sir," she said, smiling at him. "I don't mind helping a little."

"Well, get to it then, Nils." He shivered, looking toward the store with wide eyes. "I think I'll go get lost in the woods and find some wood. Don't tell 'em where I went, now."

Zoë pretended to lock her lips and throw away the key.

Nils, who'd started unpacking his father's van as Zoë chatted with Mr. Lindstrom, handed her an armful of stakes and she followed behind him as he spread out a clear plastic tarp and then opened up a royal blue nylon bag and shook out a tent over the groundcover.

"So?" he asked, busy putting poles together, not looking at her. "You want to talk?"

She stood off to the side, awkwardly holding a couple dozen dirty plastic stakes in her arms.

"I didn't—I mean, I wouldn't have figured you for the sort who offers to let a woman spill her guts. No offense."

She bit her lip, hoping she hadn't hurt his feelings.

"None taken. Stake."

She handed him one and the hammer made a pleasing pinging noise as he pounded it into the ground.

"You don't have to talk, but I know that sometimes you gals get things stuck in your heads and it's just better for everyone if they just come on out already," he said, then added softly, "I had a mother and I have a sister and…"

He was a little bit old-fashioned and she found it didn't bother her at all.

"A Maggie," she blurted out. "You have a Maggie, too."

Nils looked up at her, one eyebrow cocked up. "Stake."

She handed him one and he hit it into the ground again, only harder and louder than the one before.

"We're talking about you, not me," he finally answered, looking up at her.

"You and Maggie are together, right?" Paul had kept Zoë updated on Nils and Maggie's on-again-off-again romance which currently was "on," as far as she knew, though Nils didn't look very happy when Zoë mentioned Maggie, which she found odd.

He sighed. "Stake. Let's just worry about you."

She watched him silently as he wove the poles into the slit on either side of the tent and in a matter of minutes, a tight, taut, bright blue tent had been erected.

She followed him to the next patch of waiting grass, watched as he took a bright orange nylon tent out of its bag, spreading it out on the ground over a clear plastic tarp like the other one.

She wondered how in the world to begin.

Well, Zoë. At the beginning.

"I met a man. On the internet."

"Okay. Stake."

She handed him one.

"About a month ago. And he's…amazing. He's the most wonderful person I've ever met. In my whole life. I didn't mean to find him…really, he found me. Or his friend did. She answered an ad I forgot that I'd ever placed. She told me all about him and he sounded so…"

"Stake."

"…well, wonderful that I started writing to him. But, the picture I had posted with the ad? It was how I looked two years ago. I was blonde and thin and I didn't have any tattoos. And my life doesn't match the profile anymore either. At that time, I was a middle school teacher. I had a different life. In a lot of ways, I was a different person."

She sighed, getting lost in her thoughts for a second, thinking about the framed picture sitting in Paul's bedside table. How many nights had he fallen asleep looking at that old picture of her? How important was it to him that she look like the picture?

"Stake," Nils said, drawing her back to their conversation.

She handed one over.

"He liked the picture so much…well, I didn't have the heart to tell him how much I'd changed in the two years since that photo was taken. And I sort of liked being that girl again. That girl was so young and hopeful."

"And you're so old and washed up," he muttered sarcastically. "Stake."

She shrugged as he took it out of her outstretched hand.

"I don't *feel* young and hopeful."

"Neither do I," he grunted, grabbing another clear tarp from the back of the van and shouldering a bright yellow nylon bag.

"Should I keep—?"

"Yeah, go on." He shook out the bright yellow material, lining it up over the clear groundcover.

"Anyway, I made a mistake. A big one. I lied about who I was. I lied about what I looked like. I just pretended that's what I still looked like. Worse, I pretended that's what my *life* still looked like."

"Stake. What does your life *really* look like?" He looked up at her, his face void of judgment.

She tossed him a stake and he caught it in one hand, the other hand swinging the hammer by his side as he looked into her eyes.

"Messy." She swallowed down the lump in her throat. "I was in a bad accident. I hurt myself—my face and my leg. I hurt my nephew; he *lost* his legs. I quit my job and took a job as a web developer. I hide in a little office all day. I got dark brown contacts, cut my hair and dyed it black because that's how I thought I should look. That's how I *felt*. Dark. Bad. See this?" She turned her back to him and pointed to her left shoulder under the spaghetti strap of her tank top. "That's the date of the accident. And this one?" She tapped on her right shoulder. "In honor of my nephew Brandon, my little lamb, who will never be the same."

She turned to look at Nils. His blue eyes seared into hers for a moment before he threw the hammer on the ground and tugged at the corner of his T-shirt. He raised it, showing off a set of abs that should make any woman weep, but did little for Zoë but pique her curiosity. He pointed to a small tattoo on his left pec, over his heart. She stepped toward him and looked at it more closely.

Two small crosses sat over his heart, side by side, with the year written underneath in Roman numerals. Ten years ago.

She looked up at his serious, troubled eyes as he lowered his shirt slowly.

"Stake," he said quietly, deep sadness and profound sympathy etched into his features. She handed him one and he turned his back to her, picking up the hammer and whacking the stake into the ground with a merciless force.

"What does yours mean?" she whispered, knowing it was bad, knowing it was heartbreaking, wondering if it had anything to do with his on again/off again relationship with Maggie.

"So, here you are two years later. You meet a man from Montana over the internet."

He wasn't going to tell her anything. Okay.

"Well, he told me he was coming for Christmas and I came up with a plan. I would grow out my hair, dye it back to blonde, lose some weight, get my old job back, get clear contacts, finish my last facial surgery and by the time—"

"Paul got back east, you'd be Holly again, right?" He stared at her, eyebrows raised.

"Right," she murmured. "You knew? When did you know?"

"I knew when you filled out the forms in our office yesterday. Zoë Flannigan. Everyone who knows Paul knows the name Holly Flannigan because he won't shut the hell up about you. I put two and two together and…"

He leaned down and hammered in the last stake, the bright yellow tent joining the neat line beside the royal blue and sunset orange.

"I'm a terrible person."

"Nah. But, you're making a mistake."

Nils headed back to the van and returned with another tarp and a bright green nylon bag. Zoë counted the stakes in her arms. They were halfway done.

"What do you mean?" she asked, watching as the wind picked up the thick nylon for a moment. She placed her foot on a corner to keep it in place.

"You can't go back. Not when something like that happens. Your accident. Oh, sure, you could color your hair and get your old job back. But you're a different person. You say you were pretending to be someone else all the while you were getting to know him, but that's impossible. An accident like that? It changes you. Forever. You can't go back. You are who you are."

Tears pricked and burned her eyes as they welled.

"Then it's over. There's no point. He's lost to me. He wants the girl in the picture."

"Stake."

She threw him one.

"Don't kill me now," he grumbled.

"Sorry," she sobbed, letting the stakes fall to the ground, her shoulders shaking.

Nils stood up, but he didn't approach her or touch her or otherwise move to comfort her.

"Hey, now," he said gently. "I think you're looking at this all wrong."

"What do you mean?"

"Paul fell in love with *you*. With whomever you are now. That's who he talked to and emailed with. That's who he got to know. You think you were pretending to be someone else, but it's impossible. Who you are still shines through. And he's in love with you. Not with a picture. Not with your job. Not with your blonde hair. Not with your blue eyes, which, by the way, you still have. It doesn't matter what name you used. It doesn't matter you have two little tattoos on your shoulders. The terrible thing that happened to you is part of who you are. You. The girl Paul loves is standing right here." Nils pointed a thick, tan finger at her. "And he'll get good and mad at you because you lied to him. But the reason he can't stay away from you now that you're here? Because you're the girl he loves. Packaging don't matter. His heart knows yours."

Tears coursed down Zoë's face as she stared at Nils, and her heart, which had been so heavy—so terribly, unbearably heavy for weeks—felt something it hadn't felt in a very long time:

Hope.

She launched herself toward him and he caught her in his arms, patting her back awkwardly. "There, there. You remind me of my *lillesøster*, Jenny. Trying so hard to be brave on the outside when you're just a mess of crazy feelings on the inside."

When she leaned back to look up at him, he gave her a sour look. "You cried all over my shirt."

A small giggle burst up from her throat and she snuffled with an unladylike snort. She'd cried all over two or three of Paul's shirts and he'd never said a word. *Do you hear me complaining?* It made her smile, remembering.

"Go back and tell him the truth. Let him get mad and yell and stomp around a little. Then he'll come to his senses. He'll know it's you he loved all the while. Paul's sturdy like that." He gave her a grim smile then turned back to his work. "I'm just about done. Why don't you go explore the campground a little?"

"I'll be back for franks and beans," she said, giving him a small smile as she brushed her hands on her jeans, turning toward the camp store where she saw several of the ladies making their return to camp.

"Zoë!" he called to her.

She turned and faced him, cocking her head to the side.

"You can't go back to the person you were before, but just remember something important: Paul never met her. *You're* the only girl he knows. *You're* the girl he loves. *You.*"

Then he leaned back down, unfurling a red tent, and she smiled at his back through the tears that brightened her

315

eyes.

***

Paul woke up on Wednesday morning with a scorching hangover after spending most of Tuesday night drinking a bottle of Coonawarra cab in addition to the bottle from Napa Valley that Zoë had rejected. After drinking both bottles on an empty stomach while re-reading every email and text he'd ever received from Holly, he'd finally thrown his cell phone into the porch wall and stumbled up to his bedroom.

Unfortunately, he'd forgotten about the glass from the shattered picture frame on his bedroom floor and proceeded to get three shards in the pad of his foot, which had bled all over his sheets. He spent the first thirty minutes of his day picking them out and cleaning the wounds, dumping bottle after bottle of water down his throat, chased by several Advil. He still felt like total and utter crap.

His head hurt. And his foot. And his heart.

And yet, what he had discovered—with increasingly confused feelings last night—was that the emails and texts written by "Holly" could have just as easily been written by "Zoë." It's true that she had lied about her job, the status of her family relationships and the way she looked. But her words and feelings? As he re-read them, he realized that they sounded like the Zoë with whom he'd just spent four days.

He'd finally thrown his phone across the porch not because of something she'd written to him, but because of a theme that was practically redundant in every email and text he had written to her; repeatedly he talked about how she looked—her blonde hair and blue eyes, her pretty smile. How the hell had she been able to stand it? All of his gushing about a pretty girl who hadn't existed in years.

Had he—initially, at least—just fallen in love with a picture? He had to face the reality that he probably had. Because he'd wanted Holly, partially, for how she looked in her picture. Sunny, pretty and bright. A princess. A buttercup. And he'd wanted her perfect body and shiny smile in his life.

In spite of his feelings for Holly, however, Zoë had knocked the wind out of him pretty much from the first moment he'd met her. He couldn't deny his feelings for Zoë, or how much he wanted her—dark, complex, brooding, sad Zoë, with her high emotions and broken past and broken body that set his on fire. He'd wanted her—oh hell, he *still* wanted her—with a fury, a fierce longing such that he had never, ever known. Not for Alice. Not for Gia. Not for Jenny. And not for Holly.

Still, in a quiet, strange way, he missed Holly. He missed her, even though he was two years too late to meet her. He missed the *idea* of her.

And yes, he missed Zoë, who'd already spent one night in Nils Lindstrom's blond, buff, blue-eyed company.

But more than anything, Paul felt unlucky in love again, because he didn't know what to do next.

The idea of Holly was gone, but Holly's words and thoughts and feelings were now owned by Zoë's face. And Zoë, for whom he'd felt such an instant and binding connection, had lied to him, deceived him, let him fall in love with her, even as he struggled over his guilt for betraying Holly. His longing for her and anger toward her were locked in a brutal battle, and overshadowing everything was the notion that no matter how he felt about Zoë, he simply didn't know if he could ever trust her again.

And still. In spite of his hurt pride and betrayed trust, there was one thing he knew absolutely, as sure as his heart beat in his chest: the thought of losing her completely was so painful, so leveling, so discouraging and unacceptable, he'd taken it out of the equation. There had to be a way for him and Zoë to be together. He would just have to figure it out.

By the time his school day was over, all he wanted to do was straighten up his house from last night's debauchery, clean up the glass on his bedroom floor, take a hot shower and do something—anything—to take his mind off of Zoë for a few hours. There had to be some mindless television show or game on the tube tonight. He breathed deeply as he walked home, relieved to have a plan.

He'd order a pizza, stick with Coke and STOP. THINKING. ABOUT. ZOË.

Which is why arriving at home to find Maggie and Jane waiting for him on the steps of his front porch wasn't exactly a welcome surprise.

"Heya," said Jane as he approached.

"Heya, Paul," said Maggie, standing up.

He stopped at the top of the steps and Jane stood up, leaning toward him gingerly and wrinkling her nose. "It's seeping out of your pours. What'd'ya do? Drink a distillery last night?"

He shrugged out of his jacket, took a deep breath and sighed. Seriously? Two women nagging at him was the last thing he needed.

"Ladies, I'm fine. I'm going to clean up my house, order a pizza and watch the game."

"What game?" asked Maggie.

"Any game that you two *don't* want to watch."

"We already cleaned up," said Jane, gesturing to the key over the doorframe.

"Pizza's coming in half an hour," added Maggie with a sheepish smile.

"What is this, an intervention?" he asked.

"Pretty much," the women answered simultaneously.

Paul blew out an exasperated breath, stepping between them to unlock the front door and just get it over with already.

An hour later, most of the pizza was gone.

He'd built a fire in the back-parlor fireplace and Paul sat facing it, sandwiched between Maggie and Jane, who was the only one of the three of them enjoying a glass of wine. It had turned Paul's stomach when he considered having a glass with her, and Maggie had turned one down, too.

The kindling caught and the dry wood snapped and crackled hungrily, instantly warming up the little room whose picture windows had the same view of Electric Peak as his back porch.

"So. Are we going to talk about her?" asked Jane with her usual directness.

Paul gave her an annoyed look.

"Well, at least you're not so very mad as you were yesterday."

Paul turned to Maggie. "Sorry again for the language."

Maggie shrugged. "I get it."

"Okay, can I say something?" asked Jane, and it briefly occurred to Paul that it wasn't a question worth answering. "You remember that night a few weeks ago? At the Prairie Dawn? When I was so sure that Lars and Sara were going to get it on, and you said to me: '*Her hope is treacherous only whose love dies with beauty, which is varying every hour.*' *You* said that Paul. You! I mean, are you just in love with a pretty girl in a photo? Do you not want her now that she looks so different?"

"You think that's what's going on? Zoë's not *pretty enough* for me?" He paused, feeling anger bubble up inside of him. He turned to Jane, eyes narrowed. "God, you must think I'm an asshole to even say that, Jane."

Jane squirmed beside him, taking a sip of her wine and shrugging. He turned back to the fire, wondering if Zoë'd had the same question in her head and hating him if she never felt like she wasn't enough for him.

"For the record? I'm more attracted to Zoë than I've ever been to any woman, any time, so you can just forget that line of reason, oaky?"

"Duly noted," muttered Jane. "And for the record, I didn't think it was true. I just had to make sure."

"Paul, the way you've been with her? I mean, it's like you had an instant connection to her. Like some part of you knew exactly who she was. And I think somethin' in your heart recognized her. Recognized *her* heart."

He winced, clenching his jaw once, Maggie's words hitting their mark with impressive precision.

"Listen, even before you two came here tonight, I already knew I couldn't give her up. I just don't know how to trust her again. From now on, anytime she talks to me about her past or her family or her life, I'll wonder—for a moment—if she's telling the truth. I don't want to live like that. I want her, but I need to be able to trust her." He reached for his glass of Coke on the table and took a long sip.

"Phew!" said Jane, her voice full of relief. "Why didn't you tell us sooner? So, we *don't* have to talk you into giving her a chance?"

"It's more complicated than that. I *want* to be with her. I just don't know what that looks like. And I'm hurt. And still a *wee bit* mad," he said in Maggie's accent, giving her a look.

Jane sighed. "Sara tried to seduce Lars. You guys know that, right? They *came this close* to kissing." She gagged for effect then took another sip of wine. "But, when he told me about it, he said he didn't want her. He said: "All I ever wanted, from the beginning, was you.""

Her voice sort of ran out and ended in a dreamy whisper. She stared at the fire, swirling her glass of wine distractedly, a light smile hovering on her lips.

Maggie leaned around Paul and hit Jane on the leg. "And then?"

"Oh! Well, I was falling in love with him. I saw the

truth in his eyes, and I did what I had to do. I forgave him and we moved on."

"Just like that?" asked Paul. "Sounds a little too easy, Jane."

"You were there, pal! Urging me into his arms the whole time, I might add," Jane said. "No. It wasn't easy. I could tell that he was attracted to her, for however short an amount of time, and it hurt. But it was Lars. I had no choice. He won't let me down again; I have to believe that or we can't be together."

"I miss her," Paul muttered, feeling tired.

"Who do you miss?" asked Jane.

"Holly." He paused. "And Zoë…even though I'm mad at her."

"But you haven't lost anything!" cried Maggie. "Holly's Zoë. Zoë's Holly. You don't have to miss anything. You don't have to choose. You just have to forgive her for a *little* deception. Little, Paul."

"Doesn't feel little to me."

"Oh, for Chrissakes!" Maggie exclaimed. "Enough with your high ideas and hurt feelings! She made a mistake by concealing her identity because she couldn't bear to lose you. But she's a good person. You know she is. It's been killing her to deceive you because she's so afraid she'll lose you."

Paul flinched, leaning away from the fury in her voice.

"You listen to me, laddie! She misled you, yes. But why? *Why*? Because she loves you." Maggie leaned forward, gripping his hands as she slowly and carefully articulated the words again. "She. *Loves*. You."

He stared at Maggie as her simple words finally made it through the mess of hurt feelings and wounded pride and mistrust. *She loves me. She loves me.*

He felt hope—real and sure—like a promise, unfurl in his heart, and for the first time, he thought about the whole person who was Zoë Holly Flannigan, not just the two separate people he'd become accustomed to considering. Holly and Zoë were one and the same. And in one miraculous moment, he realized he could have all the things he loved about Holly and all the things he loved about Zoë in one, imperfect person. He didn't need a fairy tale; he needed Zoë, flesh and blood and mistakes and good intentions and contacts and anklets and tears and heat. He needed Zoë. He *loved* Zoë.

"Maggie," he said softly. "She loves me."

"She does." Her shoulders sagged in relief and she nodded, grinning back at him. "Our work here is done, Janie."

Both women stood up, and Paul walked them to the front door.

Maggie took Paul's hand before he opened the door for them. "As soon as she gets back, sort it out, Paul. She's the one for you. Don't let her go. Promise me?"

"I promise. I'll sort it out. I won't let her go." He squeezed her hand and leaned forward to kiss her cheek as she stepped onto the porch.

"'Night, Paul."

"Night, Janie," said Paul, giving her a hug. "Thanks for coming over."

"What're friends for?" She stepped away from him, pushing a brown curl behind one ear, and Paul remembered her own struggle to accept love only a few weeks ago. With any luck, he and Zoë would find their way as well as Lars and Jane had.

"'Night," he said, pulling the door shut behind her.

He put the glasses in the sink and took the pizza box out to the dumpster. Cleo roused herself from her cushion by the fire to follow him upstairs and he stripped and got into bed without turning the light on, appreciating the dark of his room for thinking. He laced his hands behind his head and got a good fix on Zoë's face—her full lips and dark eyes. Her black hair, bangs like fringe on her forehead and the lavender scar that ran the length of her face. And he knew in the deepest recesses of his heart he was in love with Zoë Holly Flannigan—with *all* of her.

"God, what a relief," he breathed into the darkness, still finding traces of honeysuckle clinging to his sheets, tangible proof that she'd been here with him just two nights ago.

He didn't need to make any promises to Maggie to be sure of his intentions. He couldn't lose Zoë. If she really loved him as much as he loved her, they'd find their way.

*****

"How're you feeling about everything?" asked Nils, glancing over at her before returning his eyes to the road.

They were about thirty minutes from Gardiner and with every passing mile, the butterflies in Zoë's stomach multiplied. Despite the peace she'd found in her conversation with Nils on Tuesday night, she couldn't help worrying that Paul had put everything together and wouldn't want anything to do with her.

"Nervous," she admitted with a shaky breath.

"Don't be. Put your cards on the table. He won't walk away, Zoë. I know him."

She nodded, grinding her teeth together. "But, what if—"

"He loves you. Be brave," Nils said simply, nodding at her once before rolling down his window. The ensuing white noise signaled the end of their conversation.

Zoë looked out the window at the mountains and meadows that rushed by them.

It had been a good two days, and surprisingly, the brusque and moody Nils Lindstrom had turned out to be the perfect company. For the rest of her life, she would be grateful to him for the sanctuary he offered her during the tour. She felt a searing jealousy toward Jenny Lindstrom for being able to claim him as her older brother and wished she'd had someone so strong and unexpectedly intuitive and thoughtful in her own life.

Thea had been strong and intuitive when their mother had passed away, taking weeks off from college to spend time with her grieving little sister. Zoë had curled up beside Thea every night, crying herself to sleep in the loving comfort of her big sister's arms. Yes. She'd had Thea. Once upon a time.

Being around Nils had made her think a lot of Thea. Coupled with Paul's advice to mend things with her sister, she was determined to make it happen when she got home.

She'd call Thea—or no, she'd just go over there one evening. She'd show up with calla lilies and two, no, three Snickers cupcakes from Sweet Cakes for her and Thea and Brandon. And she'd keep going back until Thea opened the door and let her inside. She wasn't going to be a stranger to her sister or nephew anymore. She would apologize for the accident every day for the rest of her life if that's what it took…but she would find a way to be a part of their lives again. No matter what.

Which left her with thoughts of Paul.

Being away for a few days had been a double-edged sword.

Alone with her thoughts made her examine her feelings thoroughly. To be far from him was such a bitter ache and she knew, without any shadow of doubt, that she was totally and completely in love with him.

That said, she had made herself a promise: if she told him the truth and he rejected her, she would walk away. After everything she put him through, she would turn, walk away, and leave him in peace. It would deplete whatever strength she had in her broken body, but she would summon it—every last bit of it—and she would respect his decision. If he didn't want her, she wouldn't beg him to reconsider or make her case or plead for second chances. She wouldn't put him through that. She would pray for him to find a woman worthy of him and she would go home and try to get over her own heartbreak and bitter regrets. It was the least she could do. Give him a clean break.

When she thought of his lips on hers, his hands on her

body and his breath in her ear, she had to steel her will. She wouldn't be weak. She wouldn't make him bear any further burden at her hands.

Nils's words gave her more hope than she had a right to. His words made her heart clench with pathetic hope and useless wishes for forever. She forced herself not to think about the future, despite her heart's achingly stupid optimism. Her future lay uncertainly in Paul's unaware hands, and until he decided her fate, it was best to hope for nothing.

As they whizzed under the Roosevelt Arch, Zoë tensed in her seat. A few minutes later, they passed the football field adjacent to the high school before turning up two more streets and pulling up in front of the Mountain View.

"Good-bye, Zoë dear!" said the ladies in the back of the van and Zoë waved at them with a small smile. She hadn't gotten to know any of them very well, keeping to herself or hanging out with Nils for most of the trip. "See you tonight at the dance, dear!"

Nils left the motor humming, while he opened the back of the van to get her small duffle bag and hand it to her.

She swallowed, looking into his bright blue eyes, afraid to release them, afraid to let go of the hope that they offered her.

Seeming to know what she needed to hear, he pushed her hair aside, leaned down and whispered in her ear, "Don't be afraid. He loves you. Trust it."

As he leaned back, catching her eyes, he opened his arms, and she fell into them gratefully, her hands flat on the broad expanse of his back. For the rest of her life, she would be thankful for this gruff, quiet man.

"Thank you, Nils," she whispered against his chest.

Then he patted her back and let her go.

CHAPTER 18

Paul had been reading in the rocking chair on his front porch for the past half hour, wondering when the van holding Zoë would pull up at the inn a few doors down.

He'd specifically left school as soon as the last bell sounded and had run home for a quick workout so that he wouldn't miss her return. He didn't plan to pick her up until six for the Harvest Dance, but he couldn't resist the opportunity to see her step out of the van and up the steps of her inn. He glanced at his watch again.

Four forty-five? It's getting late. They better be back soon.

He took another sip of coffee and looked up from his book in time to see the van turn onto Stone Street, passing his house and pulling up in front of the Mountain View Inn.

After a long moment, there she was, getting out of the passenger side of the van, sunglasses obscuring her eyes and a stubby black ponytail unable to keep black wisps from framing her face. She was wearing jeans and a black camisole top that showed the tan she'd picked up in the park. His whole body reacted to seeing her there, suddenly so close after two days apart, and he strained his neck to see her circle to the back of the van and wait for Nils.

But his eyes narrowed as Zoë stared up at Nils. They talked for a minute or two, intently, totally focused on each other, which bothered Paul...but it wasn't until Nils brushed her hair back and leaned down to whisper something in her ear that his book slid from his hands to crash onto the floor.

"*Fuuuuck*," he breathed, his fingers curling into fists as he stood up, transfixed on the scene unfolding down the street. His chest heaved with the effort of controlling his breathing and his nostrils flared with fast-onset jealousy.

His breath caught again as she practically threw herself into Nils's arms, and dread uncoiled in his stomach as Nils held her, rubbing her back. Had they formed an attachment? What next? Would they kiss?

Please God, I can't take it if I have to watch her kiss Nils Lindstrom in front of me.

Thankfully, she pulled back from Nils without kissing him, but her eyes were intense as she said something else to him. Paul couldn't see Nils's expression, but he saw his friend's hands curl into fists, just as Paul's had just done.

What the hell was she saying to him to have that effect? What had happened between them that had them acting so connected? So...*focused* on each other?

Finally, she turned and walked away, giving a small wave before she disappeared from view at the top of the inn stairs.

"No! This is *not* happening," he said out loud, jumping down the front porch steps and striding purposefully toward the Mountain View Inn in his bare feet and sweaty workout clothes. Two minutes later, he knocked on the door of the inn.

"Well, Paul Johanss—"

"I'm here to see Zoë."

"Well, I don't—"

"What room is she in?" he asked in his most no-nonsense principal voice.

"Well, she's in the Mountain Laurel Room, but I don't think—"

Paul took the stairs in front of him two at a time, pivoting around the banister. Edelweiss. Forget-Me-Not. Mountain Laurel.

He knocked on the door twice. Loudly.

"Coming!"

She turned the doorknob, and he pushed it open, stepping into her room and kicking it shut behind him.

***

Paul was here. Out of nowhere. Standing in front of her. In her bedroom. Looking furious.

"H-hi," she murmured, unable to look away from his face.

Her heart had launched into overdrive at the sight of him, her chest moving up and down dramatically with surprise and excitement. She licked her lips nervously before biting her lower lip.

"Are you with Nils?" he growled, eyes flicking to her lip before capturing her eyes with a stark, desperate intensity.

"Am I—with N-Nils? No! Absolutely not!" she said, shaking her head back and forth.

"Thank God," he breathed, reaching for her.

He pulled her into his arms, his mouth coming down on hers without warning as he groaned against her lips, his fingers kneading her hips, drinking her in with a yearning that surprised her at first. But after a moment, her whole body relaxed into him and she parted her lips, welcoming his tongue into her mouth as she stepped up on her tiptoes, her fingers lacing around the back of his neck. He lifted her up and she wrapped her legs around his waist, locking her ankles as he stumbled to the bed, sitting down on the edge, holding on to her hips as she straddled him intimately.

His fingers clutched at the edge of her camisole, and she pulled away from his lips to whip it over her head before threading her hands back into his damp hair and reclaiming his lips. He readjusted her, slamming her tightly up against him, holding her with one hand as he tugged his shirt up and over his head, then squeezed her backside, fitting her even more closely against him. Her naked breasts pressed up against the hard contours of his chest as he feathered kisses along her jawline. She tilted her neck to the side, sighing as he took her earlobe between his teeth, tugging gently at the soft skin, urging soft, breathy whimpers from the back of her throat.

"I missed you," she murmured, eyes closed and heart thumping against his chest with grateful relief. Their phone conversation must not have given her away, after all. He still didn't know who she was. She would be able to tell him in her own way, and then offer herself to him, hoping it was enough.

"I missed you more," he whispered into her ear, running his hands up and down the planes of her warm back.

She rested her cheek against his shoulder, her lips near the hollow of his neck as he nuzzled her ear.

"I'm filthy," she sighed, her fingers bending and flexing over the smooth, hot skin of his back.

"Me too. Sweaty. Sorry." He rested his chin on her head, his hands still gliding up and down her back. "I couldn't wait to see you."

She swallowed, wiggling in his lap. His hands moved like lightening to her backside and he grasped her uncompromisingly, pulling her as close to him as possible, his hardness stabbing her through the material of his shorts and her jeans, making it clear what he wanted.

"How was your trip?" he asked, resting his lips against the pulse point in her neck. She shivered, sliding her hands to his chest, and laying them side by side over the fierce pounding of his heart.

"It was, um, good," she breathed, her eyes fluttering open then closed, barely able to catch her breath, feeling dizzy with want. He was hard as a rock. She was straddling him. On her bed. She didn't want to talk about her trip. She wanted him. Her fingers curled against his skin, making him flinch from the contact of her nails on his chest.

"Good."

His breath was hot in her ear. He leaned back and she looked up, pleased to see that his eyes were dilated and heavy-lidded as he stared back at her. He still held her body flush against his, his hands clasping her to him, laced against the small of her back.

He was so beautiful; she felt tears prick the backs of her

eyes. It was almost unbearable to love him this much when the possibility of a future with him was so precarious. She didn't want to think about that right now. She wanted the distraction of his body, naked, moving against her, buried inside of her, obliterating any uncertainty for a few minutes as he forced her to meet him, stay with him, making her scream his name as wave after wave of pleasure rocked her body and made her buck and shudder against him. That's what she wanted. Now.

He searched her eyes for a long moment before his lips tilted up in a teasing smile. "I have to go."

"W-What?" She practically sobbed in disappointment.

He released her backside, moving his hands to her waist and gently pushing her away from him until her bare feet hit the floor. He stood up in front of her, steadying her, letting his gaze linger over her flushed body before meeting her eyes.

"I just wanted to say hi."

She had never seen anything as sexy as him in her life and every inch of her body was throbbing with want.

"You just wanted—"

"I'll be back for you at six."

He leaned down and picked up his shirt, throwing it over his head as he sidestepped her bewildered, statue-still form. He paused at the door and turned to face her, a wide grin making his face almost boyish.

"This is just an intermission, Zoë."

Then he opened the door and slipped out of her room, leaving her half-naked and completely frustrated.

***

Paul knew what she wanted.

Leaving her topless, with those big, brown, liquid bedroom eyes staring up at him had taken almost superhuman strength, but there was no way he was having sex with her until they'd both put their cards on the table. When he finally made love to her, he wanted to be free to tell her he loved her—both parts of her, *all* of her. And he couldn't do that while deception still hovered uncertainly between them.

When he walked back over to the inn almost an hour later, showered and shaved, he couldn't help the excitement he felt. He could finally be with Zoë without feeling any guilt about Holly. The romantic side of him that had been waiting so long to do something for the woman he loved had a surprise for Zoë Holly Flannigan tonight. Later. Later, after she'd told him who she was and he had reassured her that he wanted her in his life more than ever.

She was waiting for him on the porch swing and stood up as he approached, smoothing her hands down the skirt of her dress. He stood at the bottom of the inn steps looking up at her, all of his buoyancy turning to heat as he stared at her. She wore a royal blue strapless dress that hugged her breasts tightly before falling to her ankles, one of which wore that seductive silver anklet. What was it about a girl in a strapless dress that made a man's throat go thick and mouth go dry? Probably because most men assumed that a girl in a strapless dress wasn't wearing a bra, which meant that her breasts were exactly one piece of fabric away from being touched. And once your mind went there, it was pretty impossible to stop the direction of your thoughts.

"Hi," she said, and he was forced to look up from her chest and meet her eyes.

Her eyes.

Oh, my God.

Her eyes were *blue,* and she wore barely there, frameless glasses over them. He stared at them in awe, at their luminous, bright, clear-blue color, fringed with thick dark lashes.

"I, um, I took out my, um, contacts. Just for tonight," she said in a soft voice, and he could hear the worry in it.

"Blue eyes," he murmured, held hostage by their unexpected beauty in her pale, dark-haired, dark-lashed face. Knowing she was blue-eyed and actually seeing them in person for the first time were two very different things.

"Yeah." She swallowed and gave him a worried smile. "I have blue eyes."

"You hid them," he said softly, remembering Maggie's words.

She shrugged. "After the accident, I—I guess I didn't want to look like myself anymore, or something. My face looked different from the injuries, so I, um, I dyed my hair and got brown contacts."

"What color's your hair?" he asked because he felt he should, even though he knew the answer.

"Blonde. Sort of a honey blonde, but it used to get really light in summer."

"Black suits you too," he said gently, meaning it.

"You're beautiful."

Her lips parted in surprise and pleasure, finally tilting up in confidence, and she took a deep, ragged breath. "I didn't know if you'd be...you know, I don't know, mad or something."

"Mad?"

"That I hid my eyes."

Damn, he wouldn't have thought it was possible for her to be more beautiful, but she was. Smiling lightly in relief, she was stunning. She was the most beautiful thing he had ever seen. He nodded slowly, reaching a hand out to her and lacing his fingers through hers as she walked down the steps between them.

"I guess people have reasons for hiding things."

Her eyes widened just a touch, and he heard her breath catch as she leaned toward him.

"I guess so," she breathed in such a low, intense whisper, he could barely make out the words.

"Any more secrets?" he asked, raising his eyebrows at her, bringing her hand to his lips and brushing them back and forth against the warm, pale skin.

"Um...Well, I—I don't—" She swallowed, and he looked up to see her eyes turn from pleased to stricken.

"How was the park?" he asked lightly, pulling on her hand until she stood on the bottom step. He didn't want to force her to tell him the truth until she was ready, even though he was anxious to get it over with.

She grimaced briefly, staring up at him. And she may have been about to tell him the truth about herself, but she made the critical error of biting on her shiny, glossy lower lip. His eyes darted to it and he pulled her flush against him, leaning down to kiss her. He would never tire of holding her in his arms. He couldn't imagine a day when he wouldn't want to kiss her. He wished she would just tell him her secret so they were both free of it, but he could feel her holding back.

"Ready to go?" he asked against her lips.

"Yeah, I mean, but I should tell you—"

"You want to go get a sweater or something?"

"A sweater?" she glanced down at her exposed chest, where goose bumps had raised after the brief contact of their lips.

"N-No. I'm not cold."

"Great. Then let's go."

"I have something I should tell you…"

Her voice trailed off, her bright blue eyes held his and he saw the agony in them.

He shrugged, giving her an encouraging smile.

Man, she had a million tells when she was withholding something. It comforted him to know it made her so *un*comfortable. It meant that it wasn't commonplace. It meant that Maggie was right: it troubled her deeply that she had deceived him and probably wouldn't be a pattern in her dealings with him. It also meant it was out of character, and Paul's experience dictated that behaving out of character generally meant that strong feelings were involved. He squeezed her hand to reassure her.

"Maybe tell me later?" he suggested gently, offering her

a reprieve, pressing his lips to hers one more time. This time he deepened the kiss, slipping his tongue past her lips and winding one strong arm around her body, pulling her up against him.

This is Holly. This is Zoë. This is my woman. And I love her.

When he drew back, he almost wondered if he'd said the words out loud because she stared at him with such wonder in her eyes, he knew they'd never get past the bottom step of her inn if he didn't stop kissing her.

He tugged on her hand and started walking back toward his house.

"We'll take my car, okay?"

***

There was something different about that kiss.

No, not just different. New.

She clasped his hand tighter as he talked about the dance, and she only half listened, having already heard the details from Nils. She couldn't stop thinking about the kiss he'd just given her. It was so tender, so possessive…it's not that it felt more emotional than other kisses they'd shared. But more open. As though some barrier that had kept him from her had been eliminated. Was it his feelings for Holly dying? Was that it?

Because that kiss was about all or nothing. No. There was no "nothing" about it. That kiss was about "all." About being all in. About being in love. That's it, she thought, and her hand may have trembled in his as the realization became truth. Love. It was all about love.

But he couldn't love her yet! Not like this. She needed

more time. She needed to tell him—

"You're quiet," he said, breaking into the urgency of her thoughts as he led them down his driveway, opening the passenger side of his black Jeep.

She stepped into the SUV and buckled her seatbelt.

He circled around and sat down next to her, putting his key in the ignition then turning to her before starting the car.

He was wearing a light blue dress shirt tucked into khaki pants, and he wore the preppy New England look like he was born to it. He had the shirt sleeves rolled up to reveal his tan, muscular arms, dusted with freckles and curly blond hairs that were soft under her fingers when she reached out to touch him.

"Paul…"

"You okay?"

She looked up at him, searching his eyes with hers. *Do you love me? Will you still love me when I tell you the truth? Is there anything I can do to ensure you will? Because I can't bear to lose you.*

She took a deep breath and gave him a small smile before looking away. "I just missed you. That's all. I'm glad to be with you again."

"Zoë," he started, his voice serious, "before, you said you wanted to tell me something. If there's something on your mind, I mean—we can talk."

She turned to look at him, remembering the reality between them. Tonight might be all she had with him. If he pushed her away after she told him who she really was, she would turn and walk away. She had promised herself. She wouldn't put him through any more if he rejected her once he knew the truth. But she couldn't give up whatever time they had left together.

"No," she said, deliberately lightening her voice. "I'm just happy to see you. Well, and…I leave on Saturday morning. It makes me sad. But I'm not going to let it ruin tonight."

"Saturday morning isn't the end of us," he said softly, reaching for her hand.

"No?" she asked, her heart beating faster.

"No way. This is just the beginning."

"It is?"

"Definitely."

She clenched her teeth together, tears springing up in the backs of her eyes. Could she do this? Could she enjoy tonight knowing she had to tell him the truth before they said good night? He squeezed her hand, but she couldn't look at him. If she did, she'd start to cry. The answer was no. She'd finally come to the end of the line; she had no strength left to carry on the charade.

"Paul—" she started.

"Zoë—" he said.

"You first," she said, staring down at the hand on her lap.

"I have a surprise for you. I was going to save it until after the dance, but I'd like to give it to you now if that's okay."

"Sure," she murmured, taking a deep, uneven breath.

He dropped her hand and started the car.

***

When she'd mentioned leaving on Saturday, something inside of him had changed, snapped, hit a wall.

Theoretically, he knew she'd be leaving at some point, of course, but he hadn't spent a lot of time dwelling on it, at first because he didn't feel right pursuing her, and then because he couldn't imagine his life without her. Because he knew: even if she had to go back to Connecticut, they were far from over.

But hearing her say the words "I'm leaving" suddenly made the reality less theoretical and more actual, and Paul found he couldn't stand to waste another moment of their time together with half-truths hovering between them. It was time for them both to come clean, and if she couldn't bring herself to initiate the conversation, he would.

He'd meant to save this surprise for the end of their night together, but from the moment he'd picked her up, her eyes—her beautiful baby blues—had been unbearably sad and conflicted. If they didn't talk, it would be a miserable evening filled with fake levity and inner turmoil, grinding out the hours until she confessed. He wanted to get it over with. He wanted her to feel the same freedom to love him that he felt to love her, and he'd figured out the perfect way earlier today.

So, he'd surprise her now, not later. Hell, they'd waited long enough to be together.

He drove in silence down the two or three blocks to his school pulling up in the fire lane, in front of the double doors.

"School?" she asked.

"Yeah," he said, smiling at her with every bit of love in his heart. "Do you trust me?"

Her face flushed and she bowed her head. He knew that the word "trust" had hit a nerve.

He reached over and cupped her cheeks, forcing her to meet his eyes, briefly surprised by bright blue where brown used to be.

"Zoë, love. Just trust me," he murmured, leaning forward to press a light kiss to her lips before drawing back and opening his door. He walked around the car to help her out, taking her hand and leading her to the front door.

***

His words seared her soul. He asked for her trust when she hadn't been able to offer him honesty. It just about flattened her.

At the same time, she couldn't deny that underneath all of her fear and regret, curiosity was also making a play for her attention. What were they doing at his school? Wasn't the plan dinner and the dance and then—unknown to him—her choking out her confession that she was really Holly? What was going on?

He unlocked the door and pulled her inside, lacing his fingers through hers, the dim red glow from the emergency lights making the school hallways a shaded rose color that felt strangely warm and intimate in such a cold and public place. Her flip-flops smacked lightly on the shiny tiles as he pulled her in the direction of the art studio where she'd pilfered supplies on Sunday.

"Zoë, I have a confession."

He had a confession?

"I can really seem like a jerk about some things," he continued. "Shallow. About looks and status. It's a remnant of my fairly screwed-up childhood to be initially impressed with beauty or power, but I swear to God, it's not really who I am. It's just a shitty leftover bit of my upbringing. The truth is, I care about who people are, not what they look like or what they do."

She was following his words, one by one, unable to process where he was going or the big picture of what he was saying.

"Okay," she whispered beside him, and he squeezed her hand tighter.

"If it ever turned out that I made someone I loved feel less than spectacular, less than wonderful, less than *amazing*, I'd hate myself for it, even if it was inadvertent."

"Paul, *you're* the most amazing per—"

"No." He stopped in front of the art studio door and took her other hand. "You are."

His eyes sparkled in the dim light, bright and shiny with emotion, as she held them.

"I'm not," she insisted. The words were soft and thready, a sob waiting in the back of her throat. She couldn't bear to look him in the eyes. She looked away.

"Zoë."

He squeezed her hands, demanding her eyes again, and they prickled and watered behind her glasses until one tear fell from the well of her eyes, coursing by her nose to rest on her lip. He reached up to brush it away with his thumb.

"*You* are the most amazing person, Zoë. The bravest. The kindest. The sexiest, most tempting girl I've ever met in my entire life."

Her face crumpled and her head fell forward, shaking back and forth in misery.

"I'm not. You don't know," she sobbed.

"I know, Zoë. I know who you are, Zoë Holly Flannigan," he said.

Her head snapped up, blue eyes wide and watery and shocked.

"Y-You know?"

"I know I will never love anyone as much as I love you," he said softly. He flicked his eyes to the art studio door and when she followed them, she saw a neatly handwritten sign taped over the existing teacher's name, reading "Miss Flannigan."

When she looked up at him, he grinned at her.

"Oh…also, I need an art teacher. I was sort of hoping you'd stay."

CHAPTER 19

It was too much.

It was too much to have everything her heart desired presented to her so hopefully, so lovingly, as though she deserved such immense, selfless sweetness in her broken life.

Her face fell and her chin hit her chest. Her shoulders rolled forward as all of her fears and sadness and worry engulfed her, chased by bewilderment and—finally, unbelievably—relief. Sobs wracked her body as she clutched her arms around her chest, which heaved from the effort of crying.

It was too much goodness for her to process at once.

She wasn't supposed to win.

She wasn't supposed to have good things in her life.

She wasn't supposed to have this sort of love.

She wasn't supposed to be happy. Not like this. Not like fairy tale-style happy. She didn't deserve it. No matter what he said, she didn't deserve it.

And yet…here it was.

He pulled her into his arms, offering her sanctuary and solace, offering her his compassion and understanding and love. She pressed her cheek against his chest, trying to convince herself that this was real, that his beating heart belonged to her.

"Aw, sweetheart. Don't cry. Please don't cry, Zoë. It's

going to be okay now."

"Y-you knew?" she asked, realizing he'd just called her by "Holly's" nickname and the sweetness of it made her sob harder.

"Not all along. I figured it out on the phone. Tuesday morning."

His hands rubbed her back, slowly up and down, as her sobs subsided to those deep, intense ragged breaths that follow an epic cry.

"Can we sit down?" she asked, the shakiness of her legs a result of her feelings, not her injuries.

"Sure."

He slid down the painted cement block wall behind him, settling on the floor, holding a hand up to her. She took it and sat down beside him.

"Too far away," he said, pulling her between his legs and wrapping his arms around her.

"You don't hate me?" she asked softly, laying her tired head back against his shoulder, and trying to get her mind around the full scope of the massive shift between them.

"I just told you that I love you, woman. Weren't you listening to my speech?"

A laugh bubbled up inside of her as she leaned back, comfortable against him, in the bliss of his arms.

He knew. He knew who she was. And he still loved her. Still wanted her.

"Oh, man. I always loved that giggle. From the beginning."

"You're not angry with me?"

"I was." His voice grew dark for a moment. "I was pretty angry on Tuesday."

"What happened? How did you—"

"How did I get from there to here?" He sighed. "Maggie, partly. I lit into her on Tuesday morning, but she explained a lot to me. How you felt unlovable after your accident, which kills me since you're the most…" His voice broke and he squeezed her tighter, kissing the top of her head, before resting his chin on her black hair. "She and Jane helped me see that you're you, whether you're Holly or Zoë. They helped me see how much courage it took for you to come out here."

"But I lied to you."

"You did." He paused. "Don't do it again."

"I won't. Not ever." Then she added, turning to look at him, "Can you really trust me?"

He searched her eyes before offering her a reassuring smile. "I want to."

"I promise I'll never lie to you again. Not about anything. I'm so sorry I hurt you."

"I'm not hurting anymore, Zoë."

His face was so bare, so open and vulnerable and stunningly beautiful, her breath caught.

"You know. You know who I am," she whispered with wonder. Tears flooded her eyes again as she gazed at him in the ethereal pink glow of the empty high school hallway. "You have no idea where I was when you found me. You gave me hope that life still had something good in the wings for me. You gave me my life back."

She rotated in his arms, kneeling between his legs, reaching up to touch his cheeks, tentatively at first, with tenderness and awe.

"My God, what a relief," she whispered, cradling his face in her hands.

She leaned forward and he bowed his head as she tilted hers. Their lips fit together perfectly, soft and flush, waiting, then ready. He slid his hands down her back to her hips, kneading his fingers into the soft flesh, before moving them around to rest them flat on her thighs.

She broke off their kiss and drew back from him, capturing his eyes. His hand was resting over the ragged bunches of scar tissue on her right thigh.

"Is this okay?" he whispered, his fingers continuing their gentle exploration of her broken flesh through the fabric of her dress.

Zoë swallowed against the painful lump in her throat as big tears ran down her cheeks, but she didn't look away and he didn't move his hand. The old question haunted her...*What if I repulse him when he sees? How can anyone love this fractured, imperfect body?*

As though he could read her mind, his lips turned up tenderly and he whispered. "I love you, Zoë Holly Flannigan. I love all of you."

Her heart exploded with love for him and she couldn't speak. The tears rushed from her eyes as she covered his hand with hers, lacing her fingers through his as he flattened his hand along the ravaged skin of her injured leg. She leaned forward to kiss him again, pressing her open mouth to his, their tongues finding one another urgently. She wrapped her arms around his neck, her fingernails scraping lightly against the short, prickly hairs there, until she felt him shiver in her arms.

His hands returned to her hips, and he pulled his legs together, shifting her onto his lap as the skirt of her dress bunched up around her waist. He pulled her up against him until her chest was flush with his, until she felt his hardness pushing through his pants. His hand slid up her leg slowly, tracing the warm, soft skin of her thighs until it dipped inward, finding no barrier between his hand and her mound of soft curls.

He tore his mouth away from hers like he'd been electrocuted. "You're not wearing—!"

She touched her lips, smiling at him, holding his eyes. She panted softly as she shook her head back and forth slowly.

His eyes were wide and wild, his hand resting over her most intimate place.

"Zoë," he groaned through a strangled breath.

"I want you," she gasped, arching forward. Her blue eyes held his, her chest heaving with the force of her breathing. "I know we have a lot to talk about. But…"

His eyes burned for her. He flicked his glance to her lips, then back to her eyes, his fingers still stroking her gently.

"I want you to make love to me," she whispered.

He searched her eyes, and for one, brief moment she wondered if he'd push her away, if he'd insist they should wait, or tell her they needed to sort things out first.

"My place or yours?" he asked in a low, taut voice, sliding his hand back down her thigh and holding her waist to help her stand up.

"Yours," she answered, her insides hot and liquid. "Now."

He stood up beside her, kissed her lips then pulled her back down the hallway, back out the double doors, back into his car, driving back to his driveway with alarming speed, without dropping her hand except when they got into the car.

When they pulled in front of his house, he cut the engine, but neither of them made a move to leave the car. His thumb rubbed the pad of her palm softly in silence and his other hand lingered on the steering wheel, staring straight ahead in the sudden silence of the car.

Finally he turned to her and her heart clenched in gratitude, in wonder, in disbelief...in belief, in spite of everything. He belonged to her. His eyes said so.

"Are you sure?" he asked softly.

"Paul. I am—" She reached out to cup his cheek with her palm and smiled back at him, her voice soft and certain. "—*madly* in love with you. I've never been so sure of anything in my life."

He twisted his head just enough for his lips to graze her hand, his smoldering eyes holding hers.

"We still have a lot to talk about," he whispered.

"We will. Later. Right now, I just need to *be* with you."

As he drew back, his eyes narrowed briefly and he

shook his head, love making his face soft and reverent. His words were trance-like, soft and rhetorical. "How did this happen? How did I finally get the girl?"

"You're all turned around." She grinned tenderly, stroking his cheek with the backs of her fingers, her body throwing off heat with the force of her want, with the strength of her love, with the certainty that he was all she would ever need. "The girl finally got you."

***

An hour later, she lay beside him on her side, facing him, her arm under a pillow and her face illuminated by the moonlight that flooded his room from the window over his shoulder. His body mirrored hers, one of his legs thrown over hers, his arm resting on her naked hip and his face close enough to feel her breath on his skin, to stop talking and kiss her whenever he felt like it.

She was telling him about the group of older ladies who had accompanied her and the Lindstroms to the park, and he smiled distractedly at her, barely able to concentrate on what she was saying. She had a tiny, flat, dark mole on her face, on her left cheek, and he stared at it, marveling at it, wanting to own it, desperate to kiss it every morning when he woke up and every night before he went to sleep. He never wanted to get into bed again without seeing that little mole last of all things in the world before he fell asleep. He felt a profound yearning for her, wild and real—a longing to own her, to possess her, even to hate her a little if that tiny brown speck was ever further from him than it was right this second.

"You're not even listening to me," she said, and he took

a deep breath, gazing into her eyes.

"I am," he whispered. "I can't believe you're here. I can't believe we just…"

"We did." She smiled and leaned forward a fraction of an inch to touch her red, swollen lips to his.

"Don't leave on Saturday," he whispered against her shoulder.

Don't leave ever, whispered his heart.

"I have to," she murmured.

He maneuvered her onto her back and braced his weight on his elbow beside her, hovering over her.

"Don't."

"I have to. I have a surgery scheduled in a few weeks." She swallowed, rolling her head to the side, hiding her scar.

"What?" he asked, softly tilting her head back up so he could see her eyes. His brows knotted together in worry as he stared at her.

"My face," she whispered, her eyes filling with tears, and he couldn't bear it.

"When?"

She sniffled once as a tear spilled from her right eye, catching in the lavender crevasse of her scar before sliding into her hairline.

"C-Columbus Day weekend," she murmured.

Columbus Day weekend. The weekend he was supposed to go and visit her. *Oh, my God. No wonder.*

"That's why," he said, feeling terrible that his insistence on seeing her had forced her into this situation. "That's why you didn't want me to come. Why you had to come here instead."

"Only partly," she said, reaching up to cup his cheek, her cool fingers a relief on his hot skin. "I had to come to tell you the truth. No matter what."

"I'm sorry, Zoë. God, no wonder you were so upset on the phone…"

She nodded, giving him a small smile. "I felt so bad. Making you stop talking, hanging up on you."

"No. No, I was an…an ass to force your hand. I just wanted to see you. So badly."

"I'm glad everything happened the way it did. It got us here."

He leaned down and kissed her, and she rolled under him, arching her body into his.

And then there were no more words needed.

***

The tremors in her body were subsiding, but she shivered lightly in his arms, the aftershocks of their lovemaking raising goose bumps along the soft flesh of her belly and hip. His arm under her breast held her back tightly up against his chest and his lips rested on the back of her neck, his panting slowly changing to breathing, though still fast and ragged against her damp, heavenly skin.

"Happy," he murmured between breaths, his arm relaxing, then tensing, then relaxing again as the last shudders eased him into an exhausted, sated contentment. His eyes were so heavy, he closed them, burrowing into her neck. "Zoë, I'm coming to Connecticut. In October. I want to be there for you."

She turned in his arms to face him and he opened his eyes to find her face stricken and hopeful at once. "Oh, you don't have to—I mean, I don't expect—"

He leaned forward, resting his lips against hers, more to stop her words than to kiss her. He moved his lips softly, brushing against her lips, licking them then brushing them again. When he drew back, he could make out her eyes in the moonlight, blue pools of worry, of hope, of uncertainty.

"I love you, Zoë. *I love you.* They're not just words I said to get you in bed."

"I know that. But, you also didn't sign up for—"

"Yeah, I did. The second I said: 'I love you,' I signed up for all of it. All of it. In fact, it's mine. It's mine now. It belongs to me." He saw the muscles in her jaw clench and release, and he released her hip to brush her hair away from her face slowly, holding her eyes. "This is true love. Do you think this happens every day?"

She sniffled and grinned at him. *The Princess Bride.*

He nodded and kissed her nose.

"So, I'll be there when you go under and I'll be there when you wake up, okay?"

"Okay," she said. She tried to smile, but her lips didn't quite turn up. "I don't deserve you."

"Shush. I don't deserve you," he murmured.

But the quiet sweetness of his declaration was interrupted by her stomach, which groaned and growled loudly between them. Her eyes flew open and she burst into an embarrassed chuckle.

"Do you have a small child in there?"

"Well…after tonight…"

"You said you were on the pill!"

"I am! I'm just kidding!" she said, raising her eyebrows and biting her lower lip in teasing.

"Quit that."

"Why?"

"It drives me crazy."

"Maybe I want you crazy."

"You want round three?" he asked, jerking her body against his, evidence of his readiness obvious. "And here I was thinking you wanted dinner."

She leaned back from him, grinning, eyes sparkling. "Can't I have both? Food first, you for dessert?"

"You can have whatever you want."

"Dinner would be good. Then I want to come back here and stay right here until the second I have to fly home." She traced the outline of his lips thoughtfully, leaning forward to press a kiss against them.

"Speaking of you going home…" Paul started.

"You'll come see me in October. In three weeks."

"I will. But, I can't stay past the weekend. And I…I mean, I meant it at school tonight—when I offered you the job. Will you, I mean, would you consider—"

"Yes," she said, taking a deep breath and releasing is slowly. He could see her making the decision before his eyes. "Yes, I'll take the job. I'll come back."

"You'll come back," he whispered.

She smiled at him and nodded.

He clasped her to him, pulling her against his body and

356

threading his hands through her hair, closing his eyes and kissing her neck.

"Will you live here? With me?" he asked, barely daring to hope.

"You want me to move in with you?"

"It will kill me if you living in this town doesn't include you sleeping in my bed every night."

"I wouldn't want to be responsible for your death. I like you too much," she said, and then more quietly. "I *love* you too much."

"When can you come back?"

"Well, I have the surgery and then a follow-up appointment three weeks later, and…" Her voice trailed off and she looked away from him, thoughtful for a few seconds before finding his eyes again. "I have to work out things with Thea before I leave for good. I know this will sound weird, perhaps especially to you, in light of your history with Jenny Lindstrom…but Nils said I reminded him of her—of Jenny—and hanging out with him made me realize how much I miss being someone's little sister. I need to make things right with *my* sister before I move here. I don't know how long that will take. But, let's say this…if she and I haven't worked things out by Thanksgiving, I'll come either way. I'll be here by Thanksgiving at the latest."

"Thanksgiving." He couldn't help the heaviness in his voice. It seemed like a million years away.

"But possibly as soon as Halloween," she added. "I have a follow-up three weeks after my surgery, and after that, I'm done." He winced and she shook her head. "I know it

357

sounds bad, but it's the last one. I'm sort of excited."

"Well, I'm going to be a wreck."

She kissed him lightly. "Don't be a wreck."

"So then what?"

"Well, I rent my apartment from Sandy, so I don't have to break a lease. I'll resign from my job with Stan when I get home and work the two weeks until the surgery finishing up projects for him. I don't want to leave him in the lurch. He was kind to me, you know, when I was so lost."

"It must have hurt to give up teaching."

"You have no idea."

"You'll teach again. In just a few months."

She smiled and nodded at him. "Remember what I said before? At the school? You gave me hope. You gave me my life back. You keep doing it. Making things better. Making *me* better. How do you do that?"

"You *let* me. Maggie used to say...." He adopted a crisp Scottish accent. "Ye have all this bonnie romantic energy. I hate to see it go to waste." He smiled at her, running his hand lightly up and down the warm, soft skin of her back.

"It's not going to waste anymore."

"Thanks to you."

She narrowed her eyes, staring into his. Finally she blurted out, in an amazed whisper, "Why do you love me?"

He reached up and caressed her cheek, tracing the line of the scar gently, holding her eyes.

"Sweetheart, I've been waiting for you all my life." The dueling images of Alice and Gia, of Princess Buttercup and Miss Temptation stood side by side in his mind until they merged like chalk on a sidewalk during a rainstorm and all that was left was Zoë. She was everything he had ever looked for. "You're brave and beautiful and noble. Hot and mysterious and vulnerable. Strong, but you still let me help you, love you. You're funny and light…serious and dark. Adventurous and courageous, but still searching and uncertain and…you're complicated and sad sometimes but then you smile or giggle and it's like life can't get any more perfect. You're full of contradictions, and the thing is? The thing that scares me to death? I don't know if I would have recognized you if we hadn't happened the way we did. I wouldn't have seen Miss Temptation. I would have been blinded by Buttercup. I wouldn't have realized that what I actually wanted—*needed*—was both. Does that make any sense?"

She nodded at him wordlessly.

"What I needed…" he finished, feeling the relief of knowing his search was over and Zoë belonged to him as surely as he belonged to her. "…was *you*."

She pushed him onto his back, lying across his body, holding his face between her hands and lowering her lips to his. "Dinner later."

CHAPTER 20

They barely made it to the kitchen.

"Hey!" said Zoë, peeking in his refrigerator, his light blue button-down shirt rolled up to her elbows, and hanging down just above her knees. "We never had dessert on Monday night. Do you still have everything I brought over?"

He came up behind her, wearing flannel pants and a smile. He put his arms around her, burrowing his face in her hair. "Yes."

"Want me to make you something?" Her stomach grumbled again. Loudly.

"For God sakes, yes, before that small child summons legions."

She smiled, turning back to the fridge, taking out the eggs, dark chocolate and butter.

"Hey," he said, as he hefted himself onto the counter opposite her. "The tattoos on your shoulders. I got to study them, um, during round two."

She glanced up at him through lowered lashes, amazed by his beauty as he hopped onto the kitchen counter, his gorgeous, bare chest on full display. The space between her thighs ached, but she wanted him again. *God, he made her hot.*

"And?"

"What do they mean?"

She swallowed, holding an egg suspended in midair. "The accident. One when it happened because we survived. The other in honor of Brandon, my little lamb."

He jumped down off the counter and took the egg from her, placing it on the counter beside her and pulling her into his arms. "You're going to make it right with Thea, sweetheart. I know it."

She took a ragged breath then nodded at him. "I will. And fast. I won't come back until I make peace with her, and I can't stay away from you for long."

He dropped his lips to hers, kissing her longingly, rubbing her back through the cotton of his shirt.

"Let me make cookies," she murmured as he kissed her throat, then released her regretfully, resuming his perch on the counter.

"Nils has a tattoo," she said softly, then added, "I think something terrible may have happened to him." She looked up. "Do you have a mixing bowl?"

Paul's eyes were concerned as he pulled one down from a high shelf, handing it to her. "What do you mean?"

"What happened to him ten years ago?"

Paul shrugged, thinking a moment before answering. "Beats me. He would've been…eighteen. That's years before I got here."

Zoë measured flour and sugar from canisters on Paul's counter and found her baking soda sitting on top of the microwave.

"Something happened," she sighed.

She cracked the eggs into the bowl and added butter

melted from the microwave, careful to separate the two with the flour and sugar mountain in the middle so the eggs wouldn't scramble. She handed him the three bars of dark chocolate. "Break these up into chunks, okay?"

She stood across from him, against the kitchen sink, stirring the cookie dough as he broke the bars into uneven pieces.

"What makes you so sure?"

"He has two small crosses tattooed over his heart, along with the year. When did his mother pass away?"

"Umm, just a few years ago."

"Then it's not about her." She paused then looked up at him. "You asked about my tattoos. You know, I wasn't the sort of girl to get a tattoo before the accident. But it changed me, and marking my body was a way to keep it close. Terrible things can become so much a part of you, it feels almost wrong not to *wear* them. And somehow—at least for me—by wearing them, you acknowledge them as a part of you forever, and there's a peace that comes from that."

Paul nodded, pouring handfuls of chocolate chunks into the bowl as she stirred to blend them into the batter.

"Here's where I'm going with this…Nils has a tattoo over his heart of two small crosses and a date. It means something to him. Something big. Something important. And I think whatever it is, it keeps him from being free." She shrugged. "I just wondered if you knew anything."

"I don't," he said. "But it's interesting what you said about him not being free, because he's loved Maggie forever, but they've had an awfully hard time finding their way."

Zoë nodded. "I know. And I think that tattoo has answers."

The kitchen was quiet for a bit before Paul broke the silence. "Hey, um, I want to be sensitive here and I care about Nils, but…should it bother me that you saw his naked chest?"

Zoë rolled her eyes at him, holding the bowl against her chest as she mixed the ingredients. "I'm not even dignifying that with an answer. Cookie sheet?"

"So, it *shouldn't* bother me?"

She put the bowl on the counter and stepped into him, looking up at his face. "You see me?"

"I see you."

"I *only* see you, Paul. That's how it is. That's how it's been since I met you. That's how it's gonna be."

He put his hands on her waist and lifted her onto the counter so they were eye to eye. He braced his hands on the counter on either side of her, hanging his head, staring at his shirt covering the upper part of her thighs.

"Paul," she whispered, without touching him. If she touched him, she'd have to have him. Right there on his kitchen counter. "There's only you for me."

He looked up, his face taut and intense, reflecting the full measure of his love for her.

"Then can you *please* finish these cookies? Fast?"

She grinned at him and he backed up, reaching down to open a cabinet and hand her a cookie sheet.

***

Thirty minutes later, they sat on the sofa in front of the

fireplace in his back parlor, eating cookies and drinking cold milk with Cleo curled up on Zoë's lap.

"These are good," he said, biting into a third cookie, intending to eat his fill before carrying her back up to his bed. He needed his energy for rounds four, five and six. And maybe seven. And hell, while they were at it, maybe eight too.

"It's the dark chocolate," she said, grinning at him, a fleck of chocolate hanging on the edge of her lip. "My mom swore by it."

He leaned forward to kiss the crumb, then sat back, grabbing another cookie.

"She was a good cook? Your mom?"

Zoë nodded. "She and my aunt owned a restaurant."

"So, that was true."

She raised her eyes to him, looking worried. "Paul, you have to know…almost everything was true. You just got some information out of the order it actually happened."

"Was anything *not* true?"

She seemed to consider his question for a moment before he saw her lips tilt up in a little grin.

"What?" he asked.

"Well, really and truly, *almost* everything was true. Just out of order. I was a teacher before the accident. I had a great relationship with my sister and nephew before the accident. There was really only one bold-faced lie that I can think of."

"Which was?"

She blushed. "I *never* wanted to be pen pals."

He stared at her for a second before laughter, deep and pure, bubbled up from his chest, and he pulled her to him, disrupting poor Cleo, who leaped to the floor just in time before being squished between them. He held Zoë on his lap, in his arms, enchanted by her, beguiled by her, totally in love with her. How in the world was he going to make it two months without her?

"What's wrong?" she asked, as his laughter subsided.

"I'm going to miss you a lot."

"You'll come see me in October. And hey—if Thea and I can work things out? I could be back by November first."

"Will you come home with me for Christmas?" Paul asked.

"To your family? In Maine?" She bit her lip in thought. "You know, come to think of it, you weren't one hundred percent honest with me either. I should probably be a little mad about that. You sure glossed over your relationship with them."

"Yeah," he exhaled. "It's not good. I don't love going back."

"Well. Maybe just for this year, we could both stay here together. For our first Christmas we could just stay home."

He looked into her blue eyes and just like that he knew: wherever she was, that would be home. And in an instant, his house wasn't his anymore...it was *their* home, *their* bedroom, *their* kitchen, *their* dog. Everything he had was hers too. Just like that: Zoë Holly Flannigan was Paul's true home.

Whether or not he would ever work things out with his

family was ambiguous; who he wanted to be with for the rest of his life was not. He would have to figure out how to best go about making that happen. But not now. Not right now. Right now he was too happy thinking about his future to be distracted with heartache from his past.

She ran her fingers through his hair, pushing it off his forehead, and he couldn't bear it anymore. He had to have her. He stood up, scooping her into his arms and heading for the stairs.

"Round four?" she asked, burrowing into his shoulder and sighing contently.

"Round four," he confirmed, continuing up the stairs of their home to their bed, where he would memorize every inch of her body so that he could dream about her until she was home for good.

***

Because her flight left early on Saturday morning, she only had Friday while Paul was at school to say her goodbyes to Maggie, Jane, Lars and Nils. As Zoë walked to the Prairie Dawn, she saw Gardiner through a new lens: she looked at her surroundings and assessed them as her future home.

To finally let go of that fear and be free to love him was so incredible, it made everything look, feel, appear new. Blissfully, beautifully new. Almost as though she'd been given a new chance at life, Paul's heart—his love for her— paving a new path, a whole new direction for her.

She hugged herself against the chill of the morning air, happiness bubbling up inside of her and telling her for the first time in two years that she was going to be all right. Life was going to be all right again. She had found love, and she was ready to open her arms to it, welcome it into her life and protect it with every bit of strength in her small body.

Having her future ripped away so shockingly would always be a touchstone in her life—a corner of intense wreckage and change—but without the accident, she never would have found the love of her life. She would spend the rest of her days in awe of the strange way that life can take away and give back at once, in unexpected, even bewildering, ways.

She swung open the door of the Prairie Dawn and found Maggie behind the bar.

"Well," said Maggie, lips tilting up in a surprised, yet somehow knowing, smile. She snapped her laptop closed and put her hands on her hips. "Look what the cat dragged in. I've been wonderin' which way it had gone. But, now, oh, look at you, Zoë! It's all been managed, hasn't it?"

Zoë scrambled toward Maggie just in time to wrap her arms around her new friend as she made her way out from behind the bar.

The women hugged each other and giggled and cried a little and when Maggie finally released Zoë to make her a cappuccino, she demanded to know the details of the big reveal.

"He offered me a job," said Zoë, grinning from ear to ear as she sat down on one of the stools. "And a place to stay."

Maggie nodded, pressing down on the steamer. "Of course he did. Doesn't want you out of his sight. So, you're stayin'?"

"Well, no. I mean, I'm not staying right now, but I'm definitely coming back. By Thanksgiving at the latest."

A momentary worry passed over Maggie's face and Zoë knew it was a remnant of their distrust. She was anxious to reassure her friend, to win back her trust.

"I have one more surgery on my face two weeks from now. And then another three weeks to recover. And I need to try to make things right with my sister before I move here. I'm coming back, Maggie. Nothing—" Her voice broke a little with the intensity of her feelings. "*Nothing* could keep me away. Not for long anyway."

Maggie slid a cappuccino to Zoë, and when she looked down, Maggie had shaped a heart in the foam. Zoë looked up at her with a smile, then glanced over at the windows, where Graham stood, staring outside, distractedly wiping the same spot over and over again. Huh. She hadn't noticed him there. He hadn't come over yet with his usual smarmy charm and innuendo.

"How was the dance?"

"The dance? Oh, the dance! We never made it."

Zoë gave Maggie an inquiring look and Maggie giggled, looking happier than happy. Huh. Interesting, that.

"So all is well?"

"All is *very* well," confirmed Maggie.

"Though not with everyone, perhaps." Zoë took another quick glance at Graham, who stared out the window, his hand making the same, slow circular pattern with a rag, a bottle of cleaner in his other hand, limp by his side. "What's up with Graham?"

Maggie looked over at her cousin and shrugged. "He's been like that all mornin'."

"Was *he* at the dance last night?"

Maggie nodded, still looking at Graham when the door swung open and Julie Sørensen walked into the café, standing on the welcome mat uncertainly as she scanned the room. Zoë watched as Graham's whole body shifted toward the door, his hand holding the rag falling limply to his side. Julie must have seen him—Zoë could have sworn they stared at each other for a tight moment—but she huffed softly, turned away from him, and headed quickly to the bar.

"Good morning, Maggie," she said in a clipped, polite voice.

"Heya, Julie. Coffees for your uncle and cousins?"

"Yes, ma'am," she answered.

"I know their orders. But I don't know yours."

"I don't want anything," she said, looking down.

Suddenly, seemingly from nowhere, Graham was sitting on the stool next to Zoë, on her other side. He nudged her gently.

"How's the cutest lass in all o' Gardiner?" he asked, pushing his too-long, red bangs off his forehead, and giving Zoë a flirtatious smile.

"Umm…" She darted a puzzled glance at Julie, who might have flinched. "…fine?"

Graham trailed a finger down Zoë's bare arm. "We never got that drink while you were here visitin'."

He wasn't looking at her as he spoke. He kept shifting

his gaze to Julie, who remained statue-still, but for the tight flexing of her jaw.

"You are *quite* the Casanova," Zoë replied, shaking her head at his teasing ways, and she could have sworn she heard Julie snort softly beside her.

Graham must have noticed too because he narrowed his eyes, withdrew his finger, stood and turned on his heel, pushing aside the curtain to the back room as he stalked away and jerking it shut behind him.

Maggie smiled brightly at Julie as she turned back around, missing all of the drama, and offering the young woman a tray with three paper cups of coffee. "All set. House account."

"Th-thanks," mumbled Julie, taking the tray and heading for the door.

"Mags," said Zoë, watching Julie go. "I'll be right back. Going to go say a quick goodbye to the Lindstroms."

"Oh, sure! Leavin' me for greener pastures!"

"No way! I'll be right back! Keep my coffee warm!"

She rushed out the door and caught up with Julie quickly.

"Hey, Julie! May I walk with you?"

Julie turned around and Zoë could see it on her face. Yep. Something had happened between Julie and Graham, no doubt about it.

"Zoë, right? *The prettiest lass in Gardiner*?" Her face was sour, but Zoë thought she probably didn't mean any personal offense.

"I don't know about that."

The younger woman walked at a clip, her kitten-heeled shoes clapping angrily on the asphalt of the sidewalk. She suddenly stopped short, turning to Zoë. "You're older than me...so, maybe can you tell me this: Why are guys such jerks?"

"Well..."

"Because some of them are really, *really* jerky."

Zoë reached out and touched Julie's arm. "Some aren't."

Julie's brows furrowed, her lips tightening. "Some *are*."

"In my experience," she started, setting a more leisurely pace that Julie, mercifully, followed, "the jerky ones are complicated. They're trying to hide something, overcome something..." she shook her head, searching for the right words, "...or sometimes they're just afraid."

"Afraid of what?"

Zoë shrugged, trying not to grin. "A really pretty girl who makes him feel things he doesn't want to feel, for starters."

Julie took a deep breath and sighed.

"And some?" Zoë amended. "They're just purely jerky. It happens."

"How do you know which is which?"

"You have to get to know him. You have to let him get to know you. You have to be honest. That's most important of all. Believe me, I know. You'll figure out quickly if he matters. I promise."

Julie reached for the door of Lindstrom & Sons and gave Zoë a small smile.

"Thanks, Zoë."

"Anytime," said Zoë, and followed her inside to say her goodbyes to Lars, Nils and Carl.

***

That night, she lay with her ear resting on Paul's heart, listening to the steady rhythm of beats as he ran his palm up and down her spine.

She'd been waiting for him in their bed when he got home from school, lying naked on her side, glasses off, blue eyes sparkling with mischief. It hadn't taken him more than ten seconds to strip and join her there. That had been two hours ago, and the sun was just starting to set now, the golden light intense in his bedroom, bathing their bodies in a warm glow.

Being with Paul, feeling her body intimately fused to his, him moving inside of her, his lips on her skin, on the most intimate parts of her body, was the most exquisite completeness she had ever known. She wanted the gift of his heart to always be visceral to her. She promised herself never to take him—or their unconventional love story—for granted.

She thought about Jane and Lars, Maggie and Nils, even Julie and Graham. She hated that she had to miss even a few weeks of their love stories unfolding. She couldn't wait to come home for good.

"Lots of drama in this little town," she mused lightly, tracing the words *I love you* on his chest with her fingertip.

"I love you too," he said softly, pulling her fingertips to his lips for a brief kiss then resting them lightly on his chest again.

She sighed contently, pressing her lips to the solid warmth of his chest before settling her cheek back down comfortably.

"What kind of drama?"

She leaned up on his chest, her blue eyes catching his. "Oh, you're a sucker for the gossip, aren't you? I didn't know that."

"All guys are suckers for the gossip. We just act like we're above it."

"Something happened between Graham Campbell and Julie Sørensen at the dance last night."

"What do you mean?" His tone was terse, and his eyes narrowed.

"Graham's just a kid, Paul. You could help reform him, you know. I bet you have heaps of experience with difficult kids."

"He's got a foul mouth on him, and Julie's a nice girl. I'm telling Nils and Lars that he's going after their cous—"

"You will not!" said Zoë, leaning up and catching his eyes. She pointed a finger in his face. "What I tell you here…in *our* bed? It's between us. You and me. You don't go running off to—What?"

He was staring at her, his face so focused—so shattered and raw and full of love, she felt the air rush out of her lungs, leaving her breathless, leaving her amazed.

He put his arms under her shoulders and pulled her up against him, searching her eyes fiercely. It took Zoë a second to realize they were glistening with emotion.

"What is it?"

"You said *our* bed."

"Mmm," she said, understanding, her heart overflowing with love for him, all other thoughts dispersing like dust in the wind. "Is that okay?"

"It's a dream," he whispered. His throat bobbed as he swallowed, and she knew there was a lump in his throat. She could almost see it.

She cupped his cheeks in her hands, desperate to reassure him, to let him know the dream was real. "No, love. It's not just a dream anymore."

"Promise me you'll come back," he whispered, and she saw the worry in his searing gaze.

"You see me?" she asked.

"I see you," he answered.

"I *only* see you. I love you. I love you forever," she said, her hands trembling lightly. "Wherever you are is my home, and I'll always come home."

CHAPTER 21

Four Weeks Later

"You look like a wreck," Zoë said, searching his eyes.

Paul shifted lightly in the chair beside her bed in the hospital room that would be Zoë's home away from home for the next two days.

"I told you I would be." He took a deep breath, playing with the thin plastic bracelet on her wrist before lacing his fingers through hers. "And you know how I feel about lying."

"Don't you want me to be beautiful?" she teased.

"Impossible to make improvements on perfection."

She chuckled, brushing the tape on the back of her hand that held the IV line in place. He knew it was bothering her. She kept touching it.

"Can I get someone to help with that? Make it more comfortable?" He wanted to be useful to her. He didn't like how helpless he felt sitting beside her bed waiting for her to be wheeled into surgery. But there was nowhere on earth he'd rather be than with her. That was certain.

"It's okay," she said. "I'm glad you got here yesterday, and we had a day together before this."

"Me too," he said. "Have I told you my favorite thing about your apartment, sweetheart?"

"Nope."

"All those half-packed moving boxes."

"That's your *favorite*?"

"Okay," he said, feeling his expression softening, thinking of her bed. "My second favorite."

He hadn't seen much of Mystic since arriving in Hartford yesterday morning. They'd spent almost every minute of the last twenty-four hours christening her apartment: her bed, her couch, her kitchen counter, the bean bag in the corner of her room, and the shower stall in her bathroom. Twice.

He took a deep breath, his body remembering how good it felt to be with her—every single time—and goose bumps raised up on his arms. Nothing like a few weeks apart to make them ravenous for each other. He barely remembered her driving them back from the airport, only that he couldn't stop looking at her, couldn't stop reaching over to touch her, and that it took every ounce of willpower not to make her stop the car and pull her onto his lap.

He looked up as a nurse entered the room.

"Zoë, I'm going to check on your vitals. We're going to be wheeling you into the OR in about twenty minutes. Dr. Chester will administer the anesthesia, but Dr. Drew will be there the whole time too. Do you have any questions for the doctor before they get started? I'm happy to let him know—"

"No, thanks," said Zoë, with a warm smile. "Dr. Drew and I are on the same page. Just anxious to get it over with. It's my last one."

"I heard that. Congratulations. You're going to be even more beautiful."

Even more beautiful. As if that was possible. He wasn't kidding before. In his eyes, the Zoë he met on his front porch cradling a shivering Cleo would always be the most beautiful girl in the world. No matter what.

Paul squeezed her hand then released it so the nurse could take her pulse and check her blood pressure. He stood up and walked to the windows, looking outside at the manicured green lawn and tidy bricked patio where several people drank coffee on benches set artfully under vibrant autumn trees.

Loving her from so far away was a constant ache. Being away from her was proving more emotionally and physically challenging than he could have imagined. Despite calls, emails and texts, he was frustrated. He didn't want her in Connecticut. He wanted her in Montana, in his life, in their home, in their bed. And it seemed like Thanksgiving was her best bet for moving at this point, rather than Halloween, as he'd hoped.

From what he gathered, her attempts to connect with her sister had not gone very well. Thea wasn't answering Zoë's texts, emails or phone calls and the two times Zoë had camped out on her sister's doorstep, her sister hadn't answered the door. He clenched his jaw in frustration and anger. He understood Thea's position but there was nothing Zoë could do to reverse the past. Rejecting her efforts to apologize and reconnect after two long years seemed like plain meanness to Paul. And the longer Thea held out, the longer Paul would have to live without Zoë.

He thought about going to see Thea while Zoë was in surgery, trying to reason with her, ask for her forgiveness on Zoë's behalf. But two things stopped him: one, he didn't want to leave the hospital until he knew Zoë was okay, and two, it simply wasn't his battle to fight, as much as it hurt him to see her struggle for forgiveness. He had to let her sort it out herself, which sort of pissed off his inner Westley, who wanted to swoop in and save the day.

The nurse gave Zoë a gentle pat on the arm before looping her stethoscope around her neck. "You need anything else, hon? I'll be back in a few minutes, okay?"

Paul turned around to see Zoë take a deep breath and nod, reaching for Paul. His chair scraped against the floor as he sat back down and scooted closer, taking her hand. He had something to say to her and with only a little time left before her surgery, he guessed now was the moment. He brought her hand to his lips and rested them against her soft, warm, pale skin. When he looked up, he knew his eyes were probably glistening.

"Zoë—" he started, his heart in his throat.

"Zo! How'ya doing?" asked Sandy, appearing in the doorway of Zoë's hospital room.

He bit his cheek. What he needed to say would have to wait.

Zoë's aunt smiled warmly at Paul. He'd barely said more than hello to her since arriving, but he got the feeling she approved of him. "How're you doing, handsome? You look a little worried. He hasn't been through as many of these things as us, huh, Zo?"

Zoë smiled up at Paul before looking back to her aunt. "You didn't have to come, Sand."

"And miss lucky number four? Are you kidding?" She pushed Zoë's black bangs off her forehead and leaned down to kiss her niece. "You doing okay? Really?"

Zoë nodded, squeezing Paul's hand.

"I think you're good for her," said Sandy, smiling at Paul.

"She's good for me," he answered. "Too good."

"I like him, Zo. I like him so much."

Paul smiled back at Sandy, grateful for her in Zoë's life, and—in that moment—grateful for her in his life too.

Sandy shifted her weight, flicking her eyes from Zoë to Paul nervously. "Uh, Zoë. There's uh, there's someone here to see you. Someone who came with me."

"Rob?"

"Uh, no."

Paul looked up to see a blonde, blue-eyed woman standing in the doorway, her arms crossed over her chest.

"Me," she said, staring at Zoë.

Zoë dropped his hand. She covered her mouth, and when he looked down, tears were pouring out of her eyes. And then he knew. This was Thea.

"Hey handsome," said Sandy, gesturing for Paul to follow her. "Buy me a cup of coffee, huh?"

***

Paul's eyes told her he wouldn't leave her unless she wanted him to.

"I-It's okay," Zoë managed through sobs, pushing her tears away with the back of her hand. "Th-this is my sister. Th-thea. Thea, th-this is P-Paul."

She watched as her boyfriend crossed to her sister and offered her his hand. "Good to meet you, Thea. Really glad you came."

"Thanks," said Thea, and Zoë could tell she was a little impressed.

Paul came back to her side and leaned down, kissing her lips softly. "I'll be back in a little bit?"

She nodded, mouthing *Thank you* to him as he followed Sandy out the door.

Thea. After two long years, she was alone in a room with her sister, whom, coincidentally, she hadn't seen since surgery that saved her life. Sandy claimed she'd come to the hospital to check on her for days after, but Zoë didn't remember seeing her. And once Zoë had made it through the woods and was lucid, Thea never came back again.

Zoë patted her bedside, but Thea pulled a stool over from the corner of the room and perched on it, about a foot from Zoë's bed, out of reach. Zoë folded her hands over her belly. *Don't expect too much. She's here. She's here. It's more than you could have hoped.*

"You nervous?"

About my surgery? No.

To see you? Yes.

"No," said Zoë. "I'm okay."

Thea looked at her little sister, shifting on the stool.

"I'm still mad at you, Zo."

Zoë nodded, tears burning her eyes. She looked down at her hands.

"But I still love you too."

Zoë felt her face crumple into creases as her eyes filled with tears that coursed down her face as she shook her head back and forth. She didn't realize how much she needed to hear those words, how much she had missed them. But the agony in Thea's voice hurt her heart too.

Thea inhaled a ragged breath before continuing. "I know you've been trying to reach out to us. I'm getting there, okay? It's just hard."

Zoë peeked up through watery eyes to see her sister's face similarly wet with tears. She remembered all the nights Thea had held her in her arms after their mother died, how much she had needed her sister and how much she'd been there for Zoë. She reached out her hand, belatedly realizing Thea probably wouldn't take it.

Thea bit her bottom lip, shaking her head back and forth as tears trailed down her face, leaving red blotches. Then, suddenly, she lurched off the stool to sit on the bed beside Zoë, carefully taking her sister's hand.

"I'm so…I'm so sorry, Thea," she sobbed softly.

"I know you didn't mean to hurt him."

"I will be sorry every day of my life."

"He's doing okay," said Thea, caressing Zoë's cheek with her free hand before leaning down to kiss her little sister's cheek. "He's a really amazing little kid."

"I miss him every day. Both of you."

Thea looked away, and Zoë knew she wanted to change

the subject away from Brandon.

"I like your boyfriend," Thea said, sniffling again. "He doesn't look like an asshole."

Zoë squeezed her sister's hand, smiling through her tears. "He's not. He's the best."

"You really moving to Montana?"

Zoë took a deep, shaky breath and nodded. "Yep. Sandy told you?"

Thea nodded. "It's good, Zo. Make a life for yourself. Mama would've been proud."

"Will you…will you two come and see me?"

Thea swiped at her tears with the back of her hand and smiled at Zoë. "We'll see. Okay? A day at a time."

Zoë nodded. Seeing Thea was more than she'd hoped for. Hearing the words I love you and holding hands? Her heart was full. They would find their way now. It might take a while, but they'd figure out how to be a family again.

Thea let go of her hand and stood up.

"Good luck today, little sister," she said. "Let's grab a slice before you fly away, okay? Next week or something?"

Zoë swallowed, nodding at her sister. "I'd love it."

Thea headed for the door.

"Thea!" Zoë's voice broke. Her sister turned around. "I love you, too."

"I know," said her sister, offering Zoë a small smile before walking out the door.

***

"Give 'em another minute," said Sandy, flicking her nervous glance down the corridor. "We'll see Thea when she comes out. I'll walk her to the car, and you spend the last few minutes with Zoë before they take her."

"You have more experience with this," he sighed. "I'm worried. I—"

"Aw, don't be," said Sandy, giving him a warm smile. "It's just plastic surgery. No major organs. No major arteries. Nothing to worry about. Zoë's a champ."

"You're pretty amazing too," he said. "How'd you get Thea here?"

"Told her Zoë was moving away." Sandy shrugged. "You should've seen those girls when my sister died. Never saw two sisters hang onto each other so tightly—not even me and Carly. That accident with Brandon was a terrible thing, but it was even more terrible because they abandoned each other. And now Zoë's leaving with you. Time goes too fast, you know? You can't put off things for tomorrow if there's time to do them today."

"That's good advice." He paused. "You know, Sandy, if Zoë had a mom or dad, I'd talk to them about this, but she has you, and you're everything to her, so I'll talk to you instead: Is it okay with you if I ask her to marry me?"

Sandy's mouth dropped open and she gasped before her lips turned up into the biggest smile Paul had ever seen. "I knew it!"

"What did you know, Sandy?" asked Thea, approaching them from Zoë's room.

"I knew that Paul was good for Zoë."

"Better be," said Thea, looking him up and down with a hard look. "Take care of her, huh?"

"I aim to," he said, grinning at Sandy, before standing up. "Excuse me, ladies."

He knocked lightly on her door before entering. She raised her arms to him, and he rushed to her, sitting next to her on the bed, wrapping his arms around her as she sobbed against his shoulder.

"Sh-she said she l-loved me," said Zoë between sobs.

"Of course she does, sweetheart. How could she not love you?"

"You th-think I'm a better person than I am."

"Nope. You're an amazing person who's made mistakes. That doesn't make you any less amazing. It makes you human."

She took a deep, noisy breath through her nose and leaned back.

"I look awful."

"I've never seen you look more beautiful than right this minute."

She searched his eyes before taking a deep breath and giving him a blotchy smile. "What did I do before I had you in my life?"

She reached out and ran her fingers through his hair, and he bent his head closer to her, his heart hammering the hell out of his chest. *Now or never, Paul.*

"I don't know. But if I get my way, you'll never know another day without me."

He leaned his head up, meeting her blue eyes that still surprised him sometimes, as they did now.

He reached into the back pocket of his jeans and pulled

out a tiny white velvet pouch, held together with a braided white, satin drawstring. He held it in his open palm so she could see it.

"I have something I need to ask you," he said softly.

Her eyes widened and she gasped. For the second time in an hour, she dropped his hand and covered her mouth.

He knelt down on the floor beside her bed, pulling the hand away from her mouth and kissing the palm gently before lacing his fingers through hers.

"Holly Morgan, Princess Buttercup, Miss Temptation…Zoë Flannigan, I love all the facets of you. I love your light and your dark, your happy and your sad, your giggles and your tears. I love your eyes whether they're brown or blue, and I love your hair whether it's like sunshine or night. I love your heart and the way it spoke to mine. I love the way you listen and the way you tease and the way you feel in my arms. I love you whether you're a teacher or a web developer or an artist. But what I'd really like for you to be is…my wife."

He released her hand to loosen the draw string then shook the little velvet bag until a platinum band holding a simple, perfect diamond plopped into his hand.

He held up the ring with one hand, and took her hand with the other, smiling into her glistening eyes.

"Zoë Holly Flannigan, will you marry me?"

"Yes!" she exclaimed, and she started crying and laughing at the same time, nodding her head, and holding out her trembling left hand.

He'd been pretty sure she would say yes, but it was a

relief to hear the words. How he managed to work the ring onto her fourth finger without dropping it, he didn't know. But when he looked back up into her eyes, it didn't matter. He leaned forward, kissing her tenderly, reverently, kissing his fiancée, his future wife, and if they were so blessed, the mother of his future children.

She leaned back from him and smiled, then lowered her glance to the ring, admiring it. "If I'd been really clever, I'd have answered 'As you wish.' like the fairy tale."

He cupped her face in his hands and kissed her again.

"We don't need to be *like* the fairy tale," he whispered. "We *are* the fairy tale."

She kissed him back, her tongue slipping between his lips and finding his, deepening the kiss. He shifted on the bed, pulling her closer to him, making him almost forget that she was about to go into surgery until they heard an awkward "Ah-hem" behind them.

"Dr. Drew!" said Zoë, resting her forehead on Paul's before looking over his shoulder with a blinding smile. "I'm getting married!"

***

Zoë had to stay in recovery for an extra hour before going back to her room, just to make sure that she came out of the anesthesia without any issues, but she had designated Paul as the person who could keep her company there.

He braced himself when they came to get him. He was relieved that the surgery went well, but nervous to see her bandages. It would hurt him to see her hurting.

To his relief, she was lying comfortably on her back

when he got there, eyes open, bandages white and fresh around her face. He sat down in the chair beside her bed, taking her hand and bringing her wrist to his lips. He held it there for a long time, her strong pulse beating against the sensitive skin of his lips. She was okay. She was going to be okay. He was so relieved, he almost felt like crying.

"I had the strangest dream while I was under," she murmured, her other hand falling softly on his bowed head. "I dreamed you proposed to me."

He looked up with tears in his eyes, smiling tenderly at her bandaged face. This was the face he would hold in his hands and kiss at their wedding. The face that would shudder with pleasure when they made love and smile at their children. The face he wanted to see first thing every morning and last thing every night. The face that was Zoë Holly Flannigan, the woman who belonged to him, who owned his heart, who was his home.

"You weren't dreaming," he said, taking her hand and gently holding it up. He pulled the surgical tape off the ring, winding it once, twice, until it was free. The overhead lights caught the diamond and cast a rainbow of sparkles around the simple white walls of her recovery room. "And I hate to break it to you, sweetheart, but you said yes."

"Thank God," she whispered, smiling at him. "When can we go home?"

"Soon, love," he answered, smiling back at her with all the love in his heart. "Soon."

***

Once upon a time, there was a boy named Paul Johansson.

Paul had big dreams about falling in love.
He just didn't have the best luck.
Until he met Holl—er, um, Zoë.
And they lived
        Happily
                Ever
                    After.

THE END

CHAPTER 1

May Day

Maggie Campbell was drunk.

She was good and drunk and having a damn good time, but a frustratingly difficult time keeping her balance. The revelers from the annual Gardiner May Day celebration had somehow ended up at the Blue Moon Raccoon Saloon when the rain started pelting them from every direction. Everyone who'd been listening to the band on the high school football field had run for cover and a sizable crowd had amassed at the local suds purveyor. After a few hours at the bar, Maggie and her friend Paul Johansson were definitely the worse for wear.

"Maggie, give us another toast!" demanded Maurice Evans, beer held high over his head, shaking in his unstable grip to shower him lightly with sloshes.

Likely owing to the fact that drunken Maggie had a strong, cheerful brogue and a cache of ribald toasts bestowed upon her young ears by her often-drunken Scottish father, she'd become a crowd favorite and they unplugged the jukebox every thirty minutes or so to request another celebratory cheers. Of course, this meant that twice an hour Maggie chugged a beer, the effects of which were affecting her aforementioned balance.

Maggie put her hand on her friend Paul's shoulder, bracing on the foot rung of the bar stool, and held up her own full beer with her other hand. The crowd grew still as all eyes turned to look at the petite redhead balancing precariously on a bar stool.

"May there always be work for your hands to do.

May your purse always hold a coin or two."

She turned toward the door and then grinned back at the crowd.

"May the sun always shine upon your window pane…"

They chuckled with approval as she added,

"May a rainbow be certain to follow each rain.

May the hand of a friend always be near to you and

May God fill your heart with gladness to cheer you."

She beamed at the crowd, licking her lips as her beer teetered in her wobbly grasp and added with flair, "*Alba gu brath*!"

The crowd roared in approval, clinking their glasses together and chugging down their beers, none the wiser that they were all drinking to Scotland's long life. The jukebox was plugged in again and the raucous fiddles of Mumford & Sons thundered over the cheering of the crowd.

That's precisely the time the room started to spin.

Even Paul didn't notice as Maggie started to lose her balance, swaying as she finished her beer and started to lower the hand that held the glass. Maggie closed her eyes, feeling the swirls starting, knowing she was likely going to fall and letting her muscles go to jelly to lessen the impact. She certainly didn't have enough strength to stop herself.

She heard the screech of the stool's wooden legs as it skittered a short way across the floor and heard the hard clunk of her empty pint glass hitting the wooden bar. She looked down, as though in slow motion, to see Paul's horrified eyes, his arm flailing upward to grab her before she fell backward.

And then suddenly, a hard, warm wall slammed into her back and strong arms encircled her. She let her head fall back until it rested on the flannel shelf of a shoulder, and she heard his voice, soft and urgent in her ear, "I've got you, Maggie May."

His breath on her skin made her eyes flutter closed and she leaned back into him. When her feet hit the floor, he released her, reaching for the bar in front of her and holding on to it, protecting her from the jostling crowd by trapping her between his chest and the bar as she caught her breath.

"You okay?"

His lips were so close to her ear she trembled lightly. Every time he took a breath his chest pushed into her back and she was having trouble concentrating on anything else.

"Mags?"

The concern in his voice deserved an answer, so she took a deep, ragged breath and turned around, looking up to find familiar light blue eyes searching hers with worry.

Nils Lindstrom.

Over six feet tall and built like a lumberjack, Nils

towered over her. He wore a plaid flannel shirt over a white T-shirt, both tucked into standard Levi's that were a touch too tight in the front, showing a bulge along the inseam of his right thigh.

Her tongue darted out to wet her lips and her shoulders slumped with the wave of longing that crashed over her. Nils Lindstrom was one of her circle of friends, but—unbeknownst to him—he'd also pretty much owned her heart for the past four years.

He hooked a finger under her chin and drew her eyes up. "You going to be sick?"

She stared up at him, wishing for the thousandth time that he could see her as more than a friend. Of course he would have been somewhere in the bar watching her make a fool of herself standing on bar stools and yelling toasts in Gaelic. She reached up to wipe her lips with the back of her hand, feeling her already-flaming cheeks heat up like a pagan bonfire. She was drunk, she almost face planted into the bar floor, and he was making sure she wasn't going to vomit all over him. Oh, for the love of—Could she never, ever catch a break with this man?

"I'm fine," she said tightly, her accent more pronounced in her ears than usual. She turned her neck to her left to detach his finger.

Her friend Paul grinned at her sheepishly over Nils's arm. "Sorry I didn't catch you in time, Mags."

Maggie grinned at her drinking buddy. "No harm done."

"*Could've* been harm done." Nils's voice was thick with

censure. When Maggie looked up at him, he was eyeing Paul with annoyance.

Paul Johansson was the best friend of Nils's younger brother, Lars.

"Wasn't Paul's fault if I chose to get up on a bar stool and act like a drunkard." She gestured to the bartender for another beer.

"Another, Maggie?"

"Lots of anothers," she answered, annoyed her words sounded so jumbled. Not that she minded, really, but she wondered how long Nils planned to keep her imprisoned between his arms. Must have been the beer that prompted her to ask him. "So, how long are ye' trappin' me here, Nils? Keen to babysit me t'night, are ye?"

His blue eyes captured hers, searching and intense, narrowing at her tone. "A *thank-you* wouldn't be remiss, Maggie May."

Maggie couldn't explain why his words got her back up, but they did. She didn't want to thank him for saving her. She wanted him to see her as a woman, as more than just a friend. She wanted him to kiss her. She wanted him to take her back to his place or over to hers and tear her clothes off. Preferably with his teeth.

"Thaaanks," she said slowly, licking her lips in a way she hoped was seductive, but they were so dry she re-licked them a few more times before catching herself. From the gaping look on his face, she was pretty sure she'd somehow managed to look more like a lizard than a *femme fatale*.

Nils stared at her lips for a moment then flicked his

eyes to hers. His nostrils flared lightly and his jaw pulsed once, twice, before he dropped his arms and turned to Paul. "Do a better job looking out for her."

Then he turned on his heel without another word, parting the crowd as he headed out of the bar.

ALSO AVAILABLE
from Katy Regnery

a modern fairytale
(A collection)

The Vixen and the Vet
Never Let You Go
Ginger's Heart
Dark Sexy Knight
Don't Speak
Shear Heaven
At First Sight

THE BLUEBERRY LANE SERIES

THE ENGLISH BROTHERS
(Blueberry Lane Books #1–7)

Breaking Up with Barrett
Falling for Fitz
Anyone but Alex
Seduced by Stratton
Wild about Weston
Kiss Me Kate
Marrying Mr. English

THE WINSLOW BROTHERS
(Blueberry Lane Books #8–11)

Bidding on Brooks
Proposing to Preston
Crazy about Cameron
Campaigning for Christopher

THE ROUSSEAUS
(Blueberry Lane Books #12–14)

Jonquils for Jax
Marry Me Mad
J.C. and the Bijoux Jolis

THE STORY SISTERS
(Blueberry Lane Books #15–17)

The Bohemian and the Businessman
The Director and Don Juan
Countdown to Midnight

THE SUMMERHAVEN SERIES

Fighting Irish
Smiling Irish
Loving Irish
Catching Irish

THE ARRANGED DUO

Arrange Me
Arrange Us

ODDS ARE GOOD SERIES

Single in Sitka
Nome-o Seeks Juliet
A Fairbanks Affair
My Valdez Valentine

STAND-ALONE BOOKS:

After We Break
(a stand-alone second-chance romance)

Braveheart
(a stand-alone suspenseful romance)

Frosted
(a stand-alone romance novella for mature readers)

Unloved, a love story
(a stand-alone suspenseful romance)

**Under the sweet-romance pen name
Katy Paige**

THE LINDSTROMS

Proxy Bride
Missy's Wish
Sweet Hearts